# BAND OF EA

Frank Barnard turned to writing fiction after a career in journalism, public relations and advertising. His debut novel, *Blue Man Falling*, which focussed on the RAF in the Battle of France, was hugely acclaimed. He lives near Rye, Sussex.

Praise for Frank Barnard:

'This is a fast moving story of wartime derring-do, full of high-minded heroes and lovely villainesses and plenty of dicing with death. It is an adventurous yarn and a good read, certainly, but also a timely reminder of the great sacrifices made by the real-life prototypes, more than a half a century ago, in defence of our freedom'

Julian Fellowes, bestselling author of *Snobs* and Oscar winning script writer of *Gosford Park*

'Truly authentic. A jolly good read' *Sunday Express*

'Barnard subtely deflates the rhetoric of derring-do with never a jarring hint that his tenderly drawn pilots are not wholly rooted in their time. A fine balance of freshness and authenticity'

*Telegraph*

'Admirable. A compelling and engrossing novel'

*Newbury Weekly News*

'A triumph. This is boys' own adventure stuff, Biggles on speed – an excellent read' *York Evening Press*

*Also by Frank Barnard and published by Headline*

Blue Man Falling

# BAND OF EAGLES

FRANK BARNARD

headline
review

First published in 2007 by HEADLINE REVIEW
An imprint of HEADLINE BOOK PUBLISHING

First published in paperback in 2007 by HEADLINE REVIEW
An imprint of HEADLINE PUBLISHING GROUP

3



Cataloguing in Publication Data is available from the British Library

ISBN 978 0 7553 2558 0

Typeset in Galliard by Palimpsest Book Production Limited,
Grangemouth, Stirlingshire.

Printed and bound in Great Britain by
Mackays of Chatham plc, Chatham, Kent

Headline's policy is to use papers that are natural, renewable and recyclable products and made from wood grown in sustainable forests. The logging and manufacturing processes are expected to conform to the environmental regulations of the country of origin.

HEADLINE PUBLISHING GROUP
A division of Hachette Livre UK Ltd
338 Euston Road
London NW1 3BH

www.reviewbooks.co.uk
www.hodderheadline.com

To Jack and Jess, Amy and Jay,
for whose futures such men fought

'A band of eagles fears no foe'

Comte Anatole de Perignac
1767–1821

# AUTHOR'S NOTE

*Band of Eagles* is a work of fiction. The squadron depicted did not exist and neither did its personnel, whether in the air or on the ground. However, some of the actions described are based on actual events and *Band of Eagles* is dedicated to the men and women of many nationalities, including the people of Malta itself, who endured the longest siege in British history and saved one of the most strategically important Allied strongholds of the Second World War.

# Part one

## June 1941

'A funny kind of paradise'

# One

Two hours before dawn Kit Curtis was shaken awake. The able seaman's hand was rough on his shoulder. The stubby fingers dug into his flesh and, still drowsy, he flinched, expecting a stab of pain from the transverse fracture at the neck of his humerus. But there was none. It had healed perfectly more than half a year ago. Still, he groaned. 'God, what's the time? I've only just gone to sleep.'

The man remained by his bunk, swaying with the motion of the ship, as though he expected him to close his eyes again and fall back on the pillow. Kit fumbled for his service-issue Longines on the shelf by the bunk. The watch showed three a.m; only three hours since he had clattered down the companionway from the wardroom where the commander of the carrier and his officers had done their best to give the RAF men a decent send-off.

The pilots had been polite but reflective, conscious of what the morning held. They had gone easy on the drink, aware that they needed pin-sharp reflexes when the moment came to take off from HMS *Revenger*'s short and unstable flight deck; aware too that ringed by naval types, with their clipped delivery and starched white collars, the reputation of their service was under scrutiny. Their courage was not in question. Their demeanour was.

The able seaman was still moving to the rise and fall of the ship as it drove through a heavy Mediterranean swell. He was looking at Kit doubtfully, waiting for him to make a move. Kit suppressed his irritation. 'Right. I'm with you now.'

The man relaxed. 'Aye aye, sir.'

'Breakfast?' said Kit.

'Oh-four hundred hours.'

'Right you are. Thanks.'

'Aye aye, sir.' The man stiffened, gave a vestigial salute, and stepped deftly out of the cabin, closing the heavy steel door behind him. The dull boom of metal on metal was lost in a clangour of close-to and far-off bangings, creakings and gratings, of shocks and vibrations running through every corner of the carrier's hull as her four-shaft steam turbines thrust her eastwards at twenty knots towards the fly-off point.

On a hook near the small washbasin Kit's tunic appeared to defy gravity, one moment hanging out from the wall and the next, as *Revenger* rolled to port, flattened back slantwise before describing a neat arc as the bow dug into a trough. Finally, as the carrier heaved to starboard, the tunic hung away from the wall once more and the process began again, regular and unvarying, while from below and all around came the ceaseless din of the living ship. It was like a performance by a thousand mad percussionists and, secure on its hook, the swinging tunic seemed to move coyly to the rhythm.

Kit had grown used to, if not fond of, his little cabin. As a flight commander he rated one to himself. Others were not so lucky, assigned to hammocks. At Greenock, on the Clyde, he had been among the first of the squadron to board, in time to see the eighteen Hurricanes arrive at the quayside on their Queen Mary transporters. He had watched them swung on board, mostly tired old Mark 1s straight out of service, but with a brace of new machines fresh from the Hawker factory at Kingston. They still required much work; the fitting of long-range fuel tanks and muzzled air-intakes to cut down the dust and sand sucked into the Merlin engines.

So it was true. They were bound for the tropics. The rumour was the Western Desert. It sounded good, looking down from the deck of the *Revenger*, as curtains of rain raced across the grey expanses of the Greenock docks. One of the Fleet Air Arm pilots, bearded, with a buccaneering air, had joined him, leaning on the rail, staring out towards the distant town.

'Hello, Air Force. Ready for your cruise with the Grey Funnel Line?'

Kit had laughed. 'Until the last bit. I've never flown off a carrier before.'

'Nothing to it, old chap.'

'You fly Fulmars?'

'Yes. You know 'em?'

'I know its cousin. Saw the Battles in action in France.'

'Ah.' A pause. 'Not the right kite for that particular job.'

'No.' Kit remembered flights of sluggish twin-seat Battles dropping down to strafe Panzer columns near Rheims when the Phoney War turned real in the spring of 1940; how only a few survivors had struggled back to base, most blown from the sky by the yellow-nosed boys, the Messerschmitt 109s, handy, fast and lethal.

'Different kettle of fish, the good old Fulmar. Ideal for ship-board work,' said the Fleet Air Arm man. 'You know, solid, always get you home.'

'That's one thing I don't have to worry about,' said Kit. 'Landing back on this thing.'

'Don't be so sure, old boy. If your engine turns ropy it's better than ditching in the drink. Believe me, I've done it.'

'I thought you said the good old Fulmar always got you home,' said Kit.

'Almost always,' said the Fleet Air Arm man.

Easing himself out of his bunk Kit reflected that, for an airman, he had had a good deal to do with the sea: picked up by a destroyer after brolly-hopping over St Nazaire during the chaos of retreat in June 1940, and recently brushing the Channel waves at zero feet attacking Jerry convoys, deadly yet depressing work, costing the squadron many good pilots for little profit. Like Frazer Cole who, when his engine failed a mile or two off Margate, had tried to ditch instead of baling out, put a wing in and gone down with his machine; mixed-up Frazer with his brain in a muddle over that girl at the Blue Diamond Club and his veins running with too much alcohol from the night before. The loss was met with scant sympathy by the rest of the squadron. 'He should have jumped when he had the chance. Getting blotto over some bit of fluff. Wasn't thinking straight, the silly clot.' And Kit was aware that Frazer Cole's fate meant very little to him, apart from the futility of it. It was difficult to remember his sense of shock when someone failed to return when, more than a year before, he and his comrades had lifted off the grass airfields of Lorraine to meet the Luftwaffe fleets after so many months of waiting.

Kit washed, shaved and brushed his teeth. As he returned the various bits and pieces to his canvas toilet bag he wondered if he would use them again. The thought was gone in a moment. Cool reason suggested that the little matter of dying, and soon, was unavoidable; that it was not a question of if but when. Oddly comforting: one anxiety less, so why dwell on it? After what he had seen, the experiences he had endured, that was the rational way. But a deeper, inner voice told him this was so much nonsense. He could not be killed. The others, yes. Him, no. The irony was that he knew the others felt the same.

He packed the last, most portable of his belongings and went down to the hangar where the Hurricanes were stowed. They were still lashed down, quivering from the vibrations of the carrier under way, as though eager to escape from the darkness, to return to their element, the air. Soon they would be raised to the flight deck. He climbed up onto the wing of his machine. It smelled of newness. He had pulled rank to get it and christened it already. The name *Epicurus* stood out in white letters on the nose.

In the cockpit it seemed that every available space was already packed with stuff he would need when he landed at his new, unknown posting. It reminded him of the camping punt he and his father had taken up-river from Pangbourne to Oxford in '34, just the two of them, Farve's idea, one last adventure, the interior of the craft growing more chaotic by the mile until they had given up roughing it and booked into hotels. Fresh from Marlborough, Kit had been distracted and impatient, poised between child and man. Farve had done his best to conceal his hurt at his son's eagerness to take his place at Trinity, aware that the golden days had gone. Poor old, dear old Farve. Now Kit thrust the final bundles into any remaining space, taking care to make sure they did not interfere with the controls. Even the ammunition boxes in the wings were put to use, empty of three thousand .303 Browning machine-gun rounds. They would be flying unarmed . . .

The pilots had the canteen to themselves. No starched white tablecloths and silver service here. No pink gins. The comforts and hospitality of the wardroom seemed an age away, not hours. The faces of the kitchen hands were set and stony. They seemed uninterested in their guests in paler blue, dishing up breakfast with cursory grunts and raw red hands.

'Whatever happened to Jolly Jack Tar?' said Micky Thomas.

Kit eased onto the bench beside him, his egg and bacon sliding on the greasy white plate. 'Touch jumpy probably. We're only fifty miles north of Algiers.'

'You'd think they'd get used to it,' said the pink-faced flying officer.

'Do you get used to it?' said Kit.

He admired the cool fatalism of the carrier's crew, steaming south from Greenock through the Irish Sea, then heading west, deep into the Atlantic to fox the U-boats, before changing course again, south-east, to Gibraltar and the gateway to the Med. In this enterprise *Revenger* was not alone. Around her, other vessels had driven through the big seas: another carrier, HMS *Beowulf*, laden with more Hurricanes; a County class heavy cruiser, HMS *Coningsby*, fresh from duty in the North Sea, protecting Russian convoys; and half a dozen destroyers, warlike, fast and reassuring. A brief stop in Gibraltar, with its bright lights and disturbing air of normality, then the convoy had sailed due east, back into the Atlantic, watched by German agents on the Rock, before turning, once more on an easterly course, and slipping through the strait at night. Routine work, perhaps, but the seamen could be forgiven for a touch of resentment about the handful of pilots and planes that had brought them to this most hazardous point on the chart, within reach of enemy attack.

Further down the table Peter Howard said: 'I wouldn't be a matelot for a night with Mae West.'

'Don't mention Mae Wests, for God's sake,' said Micky Thomas. 'The sooner I'm back on *terra firma* the happier I'll be.'

'You won't be so chirpy when those little yellow buggers come to get you,' said Howard.

'They haven't got me yet. Quite the reverse, old boy. I've done in two of the sods.'

'Ah,' said Howard. 'That may well be. But I understand that

where we're going we'll be outnumbered ten to one. You can knock down dozens of the bastards but there'll always be more to take their place.'

Pilots at the other tables had fallen silent, listening. Kit saw anxious faces, apprehension in their eyes. 'That's nothing new,' he cut in. 'Suits me fine. Personally I can't wait to get back to some proper fighting. It's what I signed up for.'

'You don't mean you volunteered for this trip?' said Micky Thomas.

'Certainly,' said Kit. 'Didn't you?'

'Did I hell. My CO hated my guts and kicked me out. "There are doers and deadbeats," he said, "and you're in the latter category." Just because I wrote off a couple of kites. You'd have thought they were his personal property.'

'A couple of kites?' said Kit.

'Yes,' said Thomas. 'Mine and his. Bit of a misunderstanding practising head-on attacks at Hornchurch. We both took to our 'chutes and got out okay. Never understood what all the fuss was about. No ruddy sense of humour, that was his trouble. Couldn't see the funny side at all.'

'Still,' said Howard, 'you might say he had the last laugh.'

'I'm not laughing,' said Micky Thomas.

'Jesus,' said the American, Buddy Hoyt. 'Why don't you guys put a sock in it?'

'I say, Yank,' said Thomas, 'not getting the wind up, are we?'

Kit noticed that Hoyt's breakfast lay untouched. The man was a different kind of American from Ossie Wolf, withdrawn to the point of sullenness, inclined to loaf in his hammock reading comic books. He had missed out on the big show, arriving fresh from training in Canada when what they called the Battle of Britain was over. Once operational, something had happened on a sortie near Calais, guarding a convoy. His flying ability had been questioned.

That was the official line. It was a short step from that to being judged suitable for a posting, preferably overseas. All Kit knew for certain was that Hoyt was untested in one-to-one combat.

They got the call for the final briefing and clattered out of the dining room without the usual gusts of banter. Kit found himself close to Buddy Hoyt.

'Are you all right, Hoyt?' he said.

'Yeah. Why?'

'You're in my flight. Blue Section. Is there something I need to know?'

'Like what?'

'If I knew the answer to that I wouldn't ask. I saw you talking to the padre in the wardroom last night. It seemed like a long conversation.'

'It was between him and me.' Hoyt quickened his pace, not looking at Kit, his jaw working.

'Of course,' said Kit. He came up level with the American, then turned and held up his hand. 'Hang on a minute, man.' Hoyt halted, head down, frowning. Further along the corridor Micky Thomas and Peter Howard glanced back questioningly. 'I need to know I can rely on you, Hoyt,' said Kit. 'This fly-off is likely to be a dicey show. Even dicier when we get to wherever it is we're going.' The American said nothing. 'If you don't feel you can go through with it I'd rather know now.'

'You saying I'm yellow?'

'Well, are you?'

Hoyt reddened. 'You can count on me, boss.'

'Really?'

'Sure. As long as I don't miss what Pop's got to say at the briefing.'

Kit stood back and let Hoyt push past. The man was hunched, hands in pockets, eyes fixed on the floor. He had looked that way the night before when the padre had touched his shoulder and moved away, leaving him alone near the bar with a warm whisky in his hand.

There was a big chart on the wall of the operations room, with a white ribbon secured by pins, stretching from a point three hundred nautical miles due east of the Gibraltar Straits, *Revenger*'s present position, to two small brown-green outlines in the blue sea south of Sicily. They could have been smudges but they were printed: Malta, oblong like the carcass of a chicken, and above it Gozo, the head. No ribbon led further east or south. Those who had wagered Woodbines on North Africa, India, Burma, Hong Kong groaned. 'Damn,' said Peter Howard. 'I was hoping for Singapore. My brother's with the artillery there.' The chart bore other marks, Axis territory: Cagliari in Sardinia; the island of Pantelleria poised in the centre of the Sicilian Channel, not far from the Tunisian coast; and closest of all to Malta, Catania, the main enemy airbase on the eastern flank of Sicily. Two large hatched areas covered the sea on the western approaches.

Pop Penrose shuffled his papers. This was the squadron leader's first fly-off. A previous attempt, four months ago, under another's command, had not gone well: an airlock discovered in the new-fangled long-range fuel tanks, gremlins in the armaments, missing spares. Little of this had been the fault of Penrose's counterpart but he had been forced to abort the operation; a brave but humiliating decision. Penrose was determined that his fly-off would not end in failure. So, still he shuffled his papers, even now checking that he had covered every eventuality, while at his shoulder the daunting Paxton, commander of *Revenger*, breathed heavily and glared out at the RAF men from beneath fierce eyebrows.

In the lull Kit studied Buddy Hoyt. The man was sitting slightly apart from the others, chewing his fingernails. His eyes seemed to bulge as he gazed into the middle distance. He looked very slightly mad. Not like the other American Kit knew so well, also very slightly mad but in a different way. The last time he had seen Ossie Wolf had been that night in the Blue Diamond Club off Regent Street when Frazer Cole had been working his way through a bottle of Scotch with the hostess, Rita, and Buster Brown, burned and despondent, had disclosed that the medicos had told him he would never fly again. Wolf had woven his way between the tables, with two sergeant pilots, insouciant as ever, with lots to catch up on and much to say, most of it profane. If he had not encountered Wolf that night, Kit reflected, he might not be here now.

Penrose was ready. He took up a wooden pointer and rapped the chart. 'Malta,' he said. 'Yes, it's Malta.' He gave a faint, wry smile. 'I'm well aware that some of you chaps have been craving real action, after the excitements of 1940. Well, you're going to the right place. It's a fighter pilot's paradise. But before I tell you how we're going to get there, safely and in one piece, Captain Paxton has something to say.'

Paxton stood up and cleared his throat with a noise more like a growl. 'The senior service hopes you have enjoyed your voyage. This is not the first time we have played host to the gentlemen in light blue. On the last occasion things did not go well. As a result we returned to Gib with the full complement of men and machines we embarked with. The Royal Navy does not care to risk its vessels needlessly in enemy waters. Squadron Leader Penrose assures me that this time we will not have a repeat of that fiasco, that the aeroplanes are ready and so are their pilots. You certainly look ready to me. Good luck and good hunting.' And with that he left the briefing room.

After a moment of startled silence Penrose said: 'He's right, of course. It was a logistical cock-up of the first order, absolutely at odds with our normal standards. Nobody can explain quite why it happened but it did. That's why it's vital you fellows get it right today, to remove any shadow of doubt that we know our jobs. Make no mistake, we dented our credibility in the eyes of the Navy. This is our chance to restore their faith and our reputation.' He aimed the pointer at Kit. 'Curtis, you're the brainbox. Tell us what you know about Malta.'

Kit flushed, instantly transported back to C House at Marlborough; a new-bug put on the spot by a mischievous master. 'I seem to recall that St Paul was shipwrecked there in AD 60,' he said, 'on his way to Rome. Melita, it was known as then. And, of course, there were the Knights of St John . . .'

'Not bad,' said Penrose. 'Better than the ignoramus who thought it was off the coast of Spain.' He smiled grimly. 'The Jerries probably wish it was. As it is, Malta is probably one of the most important strategic pieces of land we've got. It means our aircraft and submarines can hammer the Axis lines of supply bound for North Africa. It also means we can keep open our routes to Egypt and the Suez Canal. So, suddenly this very small rock in a very big sea assumes critical importance.'

He turned to practicalities. They would take off from *Revenger* at thirty-second intervals, circle and formate into three flights of six. He would lead A Flight, Kit B, Peter Howard C. The carrier would be steaming at twenty knots into a 40 m.p.h. headwind from due south so lifting off should be simple. Here, the pilots laughed. They would then climb to 10,000 feet, adopt a heading of 095 degrees, hugging the coast of Algeria and Tunisia, before skirting the Bay of Tunis to Cap Bon. A change of course here, to 169 degrees, taking them clear of Pantelleria. Twenty-seven minutes later a slight correction, to 160 degrees, would point them straight at their destination, Takali airfield, in the centre of the Maltese plain. The trip would take three and a half hours, cruising at a constant airspeed of 165 m.p.h. to conserve fuel. On landing they would have covered 700 miles of open sea.

Penrose paused for emphasis. 'Piece of cake. Questions?'

'How do we communicate, Pop?' said Micky Thomas.

'You don't. Total R/T silence until we raise Control in Malta. It's possible you may pick up instructions on the last leg, ordering a new course. Ignore them. It'll be the Jerries trying to dupe us into landing in Sicily.'

'Any tips for getting unstuck?' Buddy Hoyt was still gnawing his fingers.

'Open your throttle smoothly and quickly, hold her on the brakes until she begins to kick and you feel the tail start to come up. Then give it all you've got. Remember, you've got less than seven hundred feet of flight deck to play with – oh, yes, and keep your canopy locked open in case you go for a dip.'

'What about bogeys?' Buddy Hoyt again.

'We may not be attacked *en route*. They hardly need to risk bouncing us over the sea. But don't worry. They'll be keen enough to give us a warm welcome at Takali. Plenty of 109s hiding in the circuit and Ju 87s and 88s eager to drop their loads on your heads. As I said, real action. Talking of which,' he added, 'you know all about our friends the Luftwaffe. You may not be so familiar with the Regia Aeronautica. I strongly advise you to discount any yarns you may have heard about the Italians being a pushover. Generally they're good pilots and determined fighters. Too many of our chaps have found that out to their cost.'

'Your chart,' said Peter Howard. 'It's clear enough but what are those hatched areas?'

'Minefields,' said Penrose. 'So if you must ditch, don't ditch there because no one will come to get you.' He held up a handful of flight cards. 'You'll find all the gen you need here. I recommend you memorise the information. It has been known for clots to drop their cards in the cockpit once in the air. Okay. Good luck. Take-off in fifty minutes. Flight commanders to me.'

As the others filed out Penrose handed Kit and Peter Howard small-scale replicas of the wall-chart. 'Superimpose your flight-track on these. Belt and braces, I know, but I don't want any foul-ups. And one more thing: as flight leaders you've got it easy. All you've got to do is maintain constant airspeed and height, absolute consistency and uniformity. Nice little test of your flying skills. But keep an eye open for the chaps on the flanks. If your leading's erratic they'll guzzle juice maintaining station and you know what that might mean. Very well. Again, good luck.' Then: 'Kit, a word.' Penrose was frowning, searching for words. 'This Yank,' he said. 'Seems a pretty rum cove to me. You know, distant, can't get through to the fellow. What do you make of him? I don't want any bad apples on this little party.'

'I tackled him just now. He says I can count on him.'

'Do you believe him?'

'I have to, don't I? What's the alternative? Lose a pilot and a plane?'

'We may do that anyway,' said Penrose. 'The man seems in a complete funk. Can't look you in the eye, doesn't trust himself to speak. I've seen it before. Unmistakable.'

'Perhaps,' said Kit. 'Perhaps not. I think we have to give him the benefit of the doubt. It's too late to do anything now.'

'Grab a word with the padre,' said Penrose. 'I saw the Yank bending his ear last night. He might be able to shed a little light. After all, isn't that his business?'

Kit smiled ruefully. 'I'll try but I don't hold out much hope. It's a question of confidentiality.'

'Oh, between a man and his soul, you mean,' said Penrose. 'Well, to hell with that. I've got seventeen other souls to worry about, including you and me, and I'm buggered if I'm going to allow ourselves to be put at risk by a jittery bloody colonial. For God's sake, why did the man sign on in the first place?'

'I think he might be asking himself that very question,' said Kit. He cursed inwardly. Damn it, he hardly had time to quiz the padre about a single, disaffected pilot. But he found him soon enough, in the chapel. Peter Howard was kneeling in prayer and several others too: Max Astley-Cobb, Bruce Cooper, Cliff McDill, men from his flight. They got up awkwardly and shuffled out, passing close to Kit but saying nothing. He did not look at them but walked briskly between the bolted-down pews. The padre watched him approach. He was frowning slightly, wanting Kit to be aware that he had intruded on a private moment. Kit had no time for niceties. 'I want a word about Pilot Officer Hoyt.'

'Oh, yes?'

'We're concerned about him.'

'He's a very disturbed young man.'

'In what way disturbed?'

The padre sighed impatiently. 'I understand your position, Flight Lieutenant, but you must understand mine. This is strictly a matter between Hoyt and his God.'

'No,' said Kit. 'It's a matter between Hoyt, God and the Royal Air Force. I need to know this man will perform as we expect him to. Lives may depend on it. The lives of the men who were here a moment ago.'

'The mind of Pilot Officer Hoyt is troubled,' said the padre, 'but that's not unusual these days. He finds himself in extreme circumstances, as we all do. Some can accept it more readily than others. That is my role, to support those who are seeking strength.' He smiled, as though this settled the matter. 'A man may put himself forward for the very best of motives, Curtis, or even the worst – bravado, say, or the urge to play the hero. I don't know which in Hoyt's case. It could be both. But sooner or later we are all confronted by reality and we are forced to overcome our fears and weaknesses in our different ways. Most do and no doubt it will prove so with Pilot Officer Hoyt.' He smiled again and added: 'It might be said, you know, that this isn't actually his war.'

'That's rubbish,' said Kit hotly. 'It was his war the moment he signed on the dotted line.' Then, confused by his sharpness, he muttered an apology. But the padre shook his head, still smiling, infuriatingly forgiving, and instantly Kit felt another surge of anger.

'I understand your reaction,' said the padre, 'but I suppose you're aware that by volunteering he stands to lose his American citizenship? Washington doesn't like its huddled masses swearing allegiance to the King.'

'I suspect he's worried about losing more than his damned passport,' said Kit.

'I'm sorry,' said the padre, 'but only Hoyt can know what's in his heart.' He touched Kit's arm. 'Do you want a moment to restore yourself, a minute or two of contemplation, perhaps a blessing?'

'No time,' said Kit. 'And, anyway, I've contemplated this fly-off quite long enough.'

'I'll pray for you,' said the padre. 'I'll pray for all of you. I'll pray for Hoyt.'

'Perhaps you'll pray that he does his duty,' said Kit.

The eighteen Hurricanes had been raised from the main hangar to the flight deck on the clanking aft-lift. Nearly five hundred feet long, the hangar, without its flock of fighters, had the appearance of an empty cathedral. On deck a rising force eight drove spindrift into the faces of the pilots as they climbed into their cockpits. They could taste salt on their lips.

Kit had carried out his usual pre-flight check, pacing slowly round his fresh Hurricane, scrutinising the control surfaces, testing the movement of rudder and elevators, trying each cowling button with a screwdriver to make sure it was fully home and secure. Only when he had completed this ritual did he sign off the ground-crew's inspection form. Now he settled himself onto the parachute that formed the base of his seat and, helped by a corporal rigger, strapped himself in like a baby in a pushchair.

This was a leisurely affair, Kit thought. In France he had perfected a routine for scrambles that had had him in the air in ninety seconds: parachute on the port wing so he could loop himself into it on the run, flying helmet on the cockpit gunsight already plugged into the oxygen and R/T sockets and little Les Gray, nimble and deft-fingered, snapping shut the belly-buckle of the Sutton harness. But this was a measured business as the corporal bent into the cockpit and pulled the webbing straps of the harness tight over Kit's shoulders and thighs.

Somewhere a Merlin engine had fired up and the force of the air thrown back by the propeller blew the airman's forage cap from his head. The uncropped black hair on his crown twisted in wild tangles. He grinned at Kit and gave him a questioning thumbs-up. Kit nodded, adjusting the chin-strap of his leather helmet, and the corporal jumped down from the wing, joining the men connecting the starter trolley.

The carrier was pitching and rolling, heading into wind at twenty-four knots. On the starboard flank of the group of fighters, Kit glanced to his right and found himself looking down at the sea. Beneath him he could feel the Hurricane's hydraulic shock absorbers cushioning the movement. Then, as *Revenger* heaved to port, the glimpse of water was replaced by steel-grey sky and the aircraft trembled again. Spray was drifting back from the bow, covering the windscreen with a haze of moisture. Kit opened the fuel control cock, primed the engine and flicked on the magneto switches. He glanced down at the corporal trying to keep his balance on deck. A thumbs-up exchange, and then he pressed the electric starter-button below and to the left of the main instrument panel.

The Merlin coughed, churned and caught, the individual blades of the propeller vanishing in a silver disc that caught the first rays of a pale rising sun. Blue-black smoke poured from the three grey exhausts on each side of the angled nose. In the half-light of dawn, flames mingled with the thinning smoke as he throttled back. Between the tilted fuselages he could make out the half-dozen machines of Pop Penrose's flight waddling towards the centre-line of the deck in threes, their rudders moving from side to side. He checked his instruments and drew breath sharply. The needle of the radiator temperature gauge had swung past the usual sixty degrees and was climbing. Everything else showed normal but he knew this would not last. Already steam was beginning to rise from beneath the engine cowlings. He shut the Merlin down and the propeller slowed and froze.

The corporal was quickly on the wing again. He gestured for Kit to leave the cockpit. The first machines of Penrose's flight had reached the start point on the runway, directed by Navy wandsmen. They scurried about the flight deck signalling with their batons like frenetic magicians, marshalling the bellowing fighters. The Hurricanes took off singly and at first their speed down the runway seemed alarmingly slow. The pilots had been warned that, even under full throttle, they would be moving at only 40 m.p.h. when they reached the end of the runway. It sounded little enough but add to that the twenty-four knots that *Revenger* was making through the water and a forty-knot windspeed and they knew they should be safely airborne when the deck fell away.

As Kit watched, each machine was, for a breathless moment, lost below the bow but then reappeared in a climbing turn to port, making height and ready to formate. Kit was overcome with frustration but hid it with a show of outward calm. Ground-crew had already removed the engine cowlings and he watched them intently as they began their inspection. They found something soon enough.

'Well?' Kit shouted. 'What is it, man?'

'Coolant cap's been left off, sir,' yelled the corporal. 'Dry as a ruddy bone. Needs to cool down a bit. But we'll have her topped up in a jiffy.'

On the starboard side of *Revenger* rose the island, the towering structure that contained the vessel's principal control rooms, and Kit imagined Captain Paxton glowering down from the bridge, witnessing yet another RAF foul-up.

Close by a familiar voice said: 'I suggest you shift yourself, old boy, unless you want your head taken off by a prop.' It was Tim Ross, the Fleet Air Arm man, bending under the wing-tip of a Hurricane that was on the point of moving forward. In the cockpit Buddy Hoyt stared down impassively, looking like any other pilot, a small figure, leaning forward slightly, his goggles on his forehead, his oxygen mask obscuring the lower part of his face. Ross pulled Kit aside. 'What's the problem?'

'Bad show, I'm afraid,' said Kit. 'Coolant's boiled away. Unforgivable.'

'We've seen worse,' said Ross. He signalled for Kit to follow him. Two airmen ran past them, heading for one of the companionways that led down to the hangar where the glycol was stored. 'Someone's bloody for it,' Kit heard one say.

'Won't take your fellows long to sort, will it?' said Ross.

'Don't know. Just hope I haven't cooked the lump.'

'Well, you shut her down quickly enough.'

By now most of Kit's flight was in the air. Unless the ground-crew got him going soon, Micky Thomas would take over as leader and set course for Malta. Only sensible, Kit told himself. Stooging about waiting for a lame duck was no way to use precious fuel, even with long-range tanks.

Buddy Hoyt was the last to go. They paused at the base of the island and turned to watch his Hurricane taxi forward to take its place on the threshold of the runway. The engine revs mounted and the tailwheel started to bounce, then rise. At a signal from the wandsman the American released his brakes and rolled forward. But slowly, too slowly, surely?

'Christ,' said Ross. 'He's in coarse pitch.'

'Impossible,' said Kit, but instantly he knew it was not. The low engine note was enough to tell him so. It was as though his blood had frozen in his veins. Unless the blades of Hoyt's propeller were set to fine pitch, a small angle of attack, he could not achieve maximum revs. Trying to take off in coarse pitch, used for cruising once in the air, was like setting off in a car in second gear: low power, no lift. It was a classic blunder. Even Bader had done it.

'He's in coarse pitch all right,' shouted Ross, as the Hurricane approached the end of the runway. The tone of its Merlin was unvarying: there was no suggestion of it braking or veering from its course. 'And he's not going to make it.'

Launched into clear air the fighter tilted abruptly forwards at a steep angle, showing its pale blue undersides, the tailplane almost vertical. Then it fell out of sight. Men ran to the rails but Kit did not care to look. He knew that the bow of *Revenger* would have sliced the Hurricane in two, that the huge screws at the stern would have sucked in and spat out whatever wreckage remained. The carrier did not pause in its progress. There was no point.

'Poor bugger,' said Ross. 'What a hell of a time to make that mistake.'

Kit wanted to say: 'That was no mistake. The bastard decided he wanted no further part in this thing.' But he said nothing. Any comment would only make things worse in the eyes of the Navy. And for a moment he hoped his instinct might be wrong. But then he heard Hoyt's voice again, that nasal, expressionless drawl telling him what he had wanted to hear: 'You can count on me, boss.' He hadn't been convinced, not convinced at all. The voice had been lifeless, resigned. He imagined the man had made his decision even then.

Astern, the lop-sided outline of the other carrier, HMS *Beowulf*, was digging deep into the big seas, more Hurricanes rising from her deck like dragonflies emerging from a pond in summer. Overhead the flights were assembling, some in the traditional six-strong V-formations, wing to wing and nose-to-tail; delightful to look at, wonderful to attack. But others, more battle-hardened, adopted the loose finger-four with aircraft positioned like the fingers of an outstretched hand; a tactic learned from the enemy the hard way.

In France, towards the end, Ossie Wolf had been among the first to break with convention. His tally of kills, marked by a row of small swastikas on the flanks of his Hurricane, proved that. But the lessons had been largely overlooked in the confusion of retreat. Back in Britain, in the momentary lull after the defeat, Ossie Wolf, like Kit, had found himself a supernumerary instructor to trainee pilots still learning to handle their Spitfires. Their pupils, poised to engage the Luftwaffe in the biggest battle of all, were eager to acquire what they could of the finer points of air-fighting. But from Ossie Wolf the novices had also learned to doubt the rationale of the V-formation. It had got him into trouble with senior officers, who still liked to see their squadrons in neat, tight vics: the traditional test of a pilot's skill. The American had been moved quickly to an operational squadron.

Kit had found him throwing his few belongings into the passenger seat of his hard-used M-type MG. He had grinned hugely. 'Seems they figure I'm such a pain in the ass to my superiors that I should resume being an even bigger pain in the ass to the Hun.' But there had been still more trouble ahead, Kit knew, and not all of it to do with the enemy.

Now, on *Revenger*, he was finally back in his cockpit, coolant restored, a thousand horsepower of Rolls-Royce Merlin pulsing through his body. The engine was healthy. He was ready to go. This time the needle of the radiator temperature gauge held steady on sixty degrees. He set his compass and direction indicator and lowered the flaps fifteen degrees. He was licking his lips, trying to create moisture to take into his dry mouth. The taste of salt was still strong.

Near the island Tim Ross, the Fleet Air Arm man, gave him a double thumbs-up. Kit raised his gauntleted hand. He looked down at the expectant wandsman and nodded. The man waved him forward and he opened the throttle and taxied slowly towards the centre-line. He held her on the brakes, the Hurricane shuddering under the force of the thrust. For an instant he felt very alone, the last to take off into an empty sky, watched by *Revenger*'s thousand-strong crew. He did not think about Buddy Hoyt. The wandsman was signalling urgently.

With his left hand Kit eased the throttle lever forward against the brakes. He could feel the tail starting to lift, just as Pop had said it would. Peak revs now and maximum boost. Right hand grasping the control column, he freed the brakes and she started to move, rumbling down the runway no faster it seemed than a man on a bicycle. The controls felt dead and sluggish, hardly biting against the rush of air. He held her straight, with the slightest touch of right rudder to counter *Revenger* rolling to starboard, and waited until at last she began to lighten and lift. They passed over the end of the runway in a rush, and below was the open sea. He felt the tug of gravity and downdraught as he pushed the stick forward to gain flying speed.

Suddenly the controls firmed up. He was flying, moving ahead over rolling, white-capped waves. They were grey, the troughs streaked with foam. Welcome to the sunny Med, he thought. Then he pulled up into a climbing turn and passed the carrier to port. For a moment he considered waggling his wings but dismissed it as a line-shoot. He turned on course, starting his climb to 10,000 feet. He knew that Micky Thomas and the others were somewhere ahead. But they would be following orders, cruising at 165 m.p.h. He was doing nearly twice that. He would catch them soon enough and nothing would be lost. Except that something had been lost already: a man named Hoyt, defeated before the battle had even begun.

He caught up with the flight off Cap Bon. He approached them cautiously, wary of appearing too suddenly in their mirrors. The sun was well above the horizon and their eyes would be strained behind their smoked-glass goggles. He had been soaked with sweat on take-off; a touch of nerves, perhaps, but also the cumbersome Sidcot overalls he had struggled into on the flight-deck. The others, in lighter flying gear, had laughed. 'It's shirt and shorts where we're going, Kit, not that ruddy siren suit.' Now, even at 10,000 feet, he was glad of it. On this speck of an island there might be milk-warm seas and temperatures of a hundred-plus but at 25,000 feet, the height at which they were likely to mount their attacks, it could be sixty degrees below. Despite the

Sidcot's bulk he reckoned it was a good investment. And then there was fire . . .

They had been so casual in France, flying lightly clad. Too many had paid the price. Like Buster, in shirt-sleeves that day in June 1940 when, along with the rest of the flight, he had chased Messerschmitt 110s striking targets of opportunity as Allied troops embarked from Le Havre. A French anti-aircraft crew, confused by the kaleidoscope of aircraft wheeling above them, had caught him in the sights of their 25mm Hotchkiss. Friend or foe, the bullets had had the same effect and the flames were just as impersonal. It was a different man who had struck the water close to the British frigate, enfolded in the silk canopy of his parachute.

Kit throttled back, watching the needle of his airspeed indicator unwind to 170 m.p.h. From behind and slightly below the Hurricanes were four dark crosses silhouetted against the rosy eastern sky. Spread out abreast as he had ordered, they still did not appear to know he was there. He would take Micky Thomas aside when they landed. The man needed to get his finger out or he would be dead before he got his knees brown. It was not what he expected of a flight commander, even a temporary one. But still, the formation made a brave sight, moving as one on the currents of air rising from a warming sea. As he eased forward to take up position the temptation to break radio silence was strong. The bulletless Brownings might not be a threat but collision was.

The strengthening rays of light began to pick out the matt camouflage of the fighters, cloud-shaped patterns of dark green and stone on top, sky-blue beneath. The roundels on their flanks, red, white and blue, with a final circle of lemon-yellow, stood out like targets. Ten thousand feet below, the waters of the Mediterranean were starting to turn from grey to a shimmering aquamarine. This was more like it.

And now Micky Thomas showed he was aware of Kit's approach. No sudden snatch at the controls, no suggestion of surprise. He simply moved smoothly aside for him to assume the leader's slot. At least the man could fly, was cool in the air. Perhaps he had seen him all along, Kit speculated. Maybe he wouldn't need that little chat after all.

At the head of the formation he felt a wash of optimism and enjoyment. It was thrilling to be flying again, at the controls of a brand-new machine; controls that had become fluid and easy to the touch, the throttle a little sticky but already bedding in. He was enveloped in the fighter's power as it quivered and shook from its passage through the air and the drumming of its engine. Like him, he thought fancifully, it was eager to get at the enemy, man against man, machine against machine, the kind of battle Sydney Camm had designed it for, not tedious but deadly escort duty shepherding British bombers to targets in northern France, or protecting convoys of crawling merchantmen, or shooting up Hun supply ships making their own run down the Channel.

Brown-green Cap Bon, furthermost point of the Maouin Peninsula to the east of the Bay of Tunis, was fringed with breaking waves. It slipped by to starboard as they banked onto a new course and began the penultimate leg of their flight: a seventy-mile stretch to be covered in less than thirty minutes. Pantelleria lay to the north-east, a distant outline partially obscured by sea mist. They scanned the sky for signs of Messerschmitts rising to meet them from the underground hangars tunnelled into the island's volcanic rock but it seemed they had passed the danger point undetected. They did not care to consider how they would fare against attack, unarmed and heavily laden.

By now they had been in the air for nearly two and a half hours, over halfway. From time to time they glanced across at each other, grinning, circling thumb and forefinger or jabbing a thumbs-up, alert to the beat of their engines, constantly checking their instruments for the first sign of a problem, conscious that their lives depended on the health of the single Merlin that held each machine, apparently motionless, high above the featureless expanse of sea.

Then, as they changed direction for the last time, moving onto a heading of 160 degrees, a course that would take them straight to Takali airfield, a voice crackled in their earphones. After three hours of R/T silence the effect was startling. 'Hello, Hurricane Leader. Steer zero-two-zero for base. Vector zero-two-zero for forty-five minutes for base. Respond, please.'

Instantly four pairs of eyes focused on Kit. He shook his head slowly and gave an emphatic thumbs-down. Micky Thomas began to laugh, seen but unheard in the confines of his cockpit: the ruse had been so clumsily done. Did the Luftwaffe really think they would fall for it and land tamely in Sicily? But Kit wasn't laughing. It was no joke to learn that the Jerries knew they were there. It seemed certain that a hot reception would be waiting for them at Takali.

Ten minutes out, Malta began to show on the horizon. What had Pop Penrose said? 'A very small rock in a very big sea.' Eighteen miles long and nine wide it was marginally smaller than the Isle of Wight. Only its location made it a crucible of war, disputed by Phoenicians, Romans, Arabs, French and English.

To the Maltese a siege was nothing new. Four hundred and fifty years earlier the Knights of St John had almost been overwhelmed by the forces of Suleiman the Magnificent, Sultan of the Ottoman Empire. But forty thousand Turks had been unable to dislodge ten thousand defenders, helped by the Maltese people. Now, as the outline of the island became clearer, Kit felt he was once more a protagonist in history, as he had been in France, no longer a mute witness to great events, kicking his heels on that damned lecture tour while his comrades fought the Battle of Britain. Here, Heaven sent, was another siege, the island's garrison again outnumbered. He liked the odds. They offered him a chance to make his mark.

At this he caught himself. He remembered – it seemed a long time ago – that day at Revigncourt in late '39, the day that he and Ossie Wolf, ostensibly testing their machines, had somehow strayed across the border into Germany and strafed a Hun airfield. He heard the CO's voice again: 'Self-indulgent, irresponsible, stupid. Imbeciles without a brain between them, who could have cost me two Hurricanes. Fools who seem to think they're fighting a private war. I don't want schoolboys out here, Kit. I want men.' Brewster had been right, of course. Kit despised himself for forgetting that. There was no room in this enterprise for glory-seekers. Victory would come by working together. Not that Wolf had been a glory-seeker. He had been driven by other motives.

Kit felt better about himself. He had confronted a weakness. Yet had he? Still, he knew, the vanity persisted. That idiotic name on the nose of his machine: *Epicurus.* He would have it painted out when he landed. He forced himself to think about the others: Micky Thomas, Max Astley-Cobb, the New Zealander McDill, young Cooper. No doubt they and all the others simply hoped they would give a good account of themselves, do their best, not let anybody down, be up to the job in hand. That was all he should hope for too. He wondered what they could expect from the Maltese. Would they also give a good account of themselves or would it be like France, where the Germans were not the only enemy as society collapsed in the face of invasion?

The flight was within sight of the south-western coast of Malta now, losing height over the scrub-covered cliffs of Dingli, falling sheer to a rocky shoreline. Gradually details of the landscape emerged: stone-walled fields of dun earth, dust-grey lanes, stark square buildings scattered here and there like children's bricks, a jumble of dwellings clustered round a tiny harbour. Suddenly another voice sounded over the R/T, a good strong English voice, comfortingly casual: 'Shuttle Red One, Shuttle Red One.'

Kit tried to conceal his relief. 'Hello, Control, Shuttle Red One. Receiving you loud and clear. Over.'

'Welcome to Malta, Shuttle Red One. Nicely done. But you're not out of the wood yet. We've put up some cover but keep your eyes peeled for little jobs in the circuit at Takali. Good luck.'

Little jobs, the yellow-nosed boys, those little yellow buggers Peter Howard had talked about so carelessly in the dining room of *Revenger*; the stub-winged Messerschmitt 109s with machine-guns and cannon on the prowl for five oil-stained Hurricanes with nothing more in their ammunition boxes than shaving gear and tropical-issue clothing.

They were down to five hundred feet now, passing low over Mdina, the ancient buildings and narrow, shady streets of the hilltop city honey-coloured in bright sunshine. At its centre the Baroque façade of the cathedral fronted onto a broad *piazza*. A few small figures paused and stared up as the Hurricanes roared overhead. Kit hoped they looked suitably inspiring.

The southerly force eight they had experienced at sea had eased, no more than a strong breeze coming from the south-west, and they traversed the island, banking over the Grand Harbour at Valletta preparing to land into wind. The harbour's angular fortifications of mellow limestone, remnants of other wars, jutted into the calm blue waters. In the creeks many vessels were being unloaded. Beyond the harbour mouth an oil tanker was burning fiercely, low in the water, surrounded by a flotilla of small rescue craft.

Kit had slid back his canopy and already the air was more than warm. There was a pungency about it, scents of vegetation and other things, of hard-baked earth and beasts and man, mingling with the smell of the encircling sea. Overall hung an almost tangible blanket of humidity and, as the Hurricanes dipped still lower, their windscreens misted up and moisture flicked back in the slipstream. Once more Kit was running with perspiration as the grass runway of Takali appeared ahead. The Sidcot suit was stiff with sweat and hampered his movements.

He led the flight round the airfield in a perfect curved approach, in line astern, for a stream landing; down to 140 m.p.h. now, the oddly tepid wind gusting round his open cockpit, mixture rich and easing the throttle lever back, 100 m.p.h. on the airspeed indicator and falling, flaps down.

He heard a curious pulsing noise, tonka, tonka, tonka. Oh, Christ, not the engine, not now, surely? His eyes flicked over the instruments: oil, coolant, fuel, twin green lights confirming his wheels were down. All perfect. Speed spot on: 90 m.p.h. And still the tonka, tonka, tonka. To his right he saw smoke rising from a sand-bagged anti-aircraft machine-gun post and then he understood. The barrel of the Bofors was jerking with the recoil of the 40mm rounds. He looked in his mirror and saw the other machines strung out behind him. Something flashed above him from the left, so close that he was caught in the downdraught of its passing; then a second, even closer. He heard the clatter of machine-guns and the deeper note of cannon. The Hurricane rocked violently but he caught it quickly and put it down, rumbling over the grass and raising clouds of fine dust.

On the far side of the airfield pillars of black smoke were rising into the air. A stick of bombs descended, a neat formation, almost graceful, one stacked above the other, but faster now, howling towards the ground two hundred yards away. The blast lifted the

Hurricane's port wing and thrust the rudder hard against the starboard elevator. With its nose raised and pivoting on one wheel it seemed the machine would cartwheel. Thrown against the side of the cockpit Kit thrust the control column forward and kicked at the left rudder pedal. The rudder responded – he felt the wheels thump back onto the ground and the fighter roll forward again, still under power.

Two men were running towards him, bent low as more bombs came down close to a scatter of bell tents near the perimeter. He had undone the fastening of his oxygen mask, which hung loose on his chest. Already he had taken dust into his mouth, the particles crunching between his teeth. Something was flashing bright on the other side of the airfield, silver, like a mirror, blinding. For a second it caught him in the eyes and from behind closed lids dark blobs swam across a reddish haze. He was taxiing slowly now and the men ducked underneath his wings and scrambled up beside him, their boots scraping on the aluminium skin of the wings. Their faces, under steel helmets painted with stone-wall camouflage, were tanned dark brown, their teeth showing white as they shouted instructions. They were pointing towards the source of the dazzling light.

He nodded and opened the throttle a little, and they settled themselves on the leading edge of each wing, continuing to shout and point, as they bounced across the rough surface. More airmen were running past, heading for the rest of the flight touching down behind him. The bombing had ceased, but after a momentary lull a section of four grey-blue Me 109s with mustard snouts and black propellers came in fast and low, bright orange flame spitting from their 20mm cannon. A Hurricane passed him to the right, throttling up and gathering speed, preparing to take off cross-wind, anxious not to be caught on the ground. Then it lurched, struck by cannon-shells, and the tail came down, but still it was moving fast. The pilot had sunk forward, head bobbing with the motion, hanging on his straps.

Ahead, close to a few stunted pines, a ring of large stones, half a dozen deep, surrounded the crew of a tripod-mounted Savage-Lewis machine-gun, its muzzle pointed skyward. They were busy with their work and saw the Hurricane only when it was almost on them. It hit the sangar at perhaps 70 m.p.h. and spread-eagled itself on the stones, the nose forced upwards, the wings pulled forwards from the roots, its back broken. For a moment it was obscured by a pall of drifting dust. Then, as it thinned, people could be seen moving. The crew of the machine-gun began to stagger away through the scrub before pausing, suddenly aware of the unconscious pilot.

Kit knew from the letters on the fuselage that it was Micky Thomas. It seemed he might have a chance. Then, with a dull whoomph, the noise made when a match is tossed onto a Guy Fawkes bonfire primed with petrol, it was engulfed in a ball of flame. The spindly pine trees ignited and a ring of fire crackled through the undergrowth. The machine-gunners wavered, their arms held in front of their faces against the heat, but saw it was no use, turned away and stumbled on. What had Micky Thomas said at breakfast? 'They haven't got me yet.' Asking for it, of course. Poor devil, he had not lasted long in fighter pilot's paradise. Again, Kit felt ashamed: fancying the odds, seeing a chance to make his mark. What callow rot. He had not confronted death, this kind of death, since France.

He had grown soft, talking to the factory girls, his arm in a sling, their fingers touching the wings on his tunic, looking at him in that certain way. Frazer Cole had died, but that had been avoidable and down to the man himself. This was different. Micky Thomas hadn't had a choice. He'd gone down under Jerry fire, killed in the worst possible way. Kit knew he wanted to get even, to get one back for Thomas. No, more than one. It had nothing to do with making his mark. A sense of outrage was growing within him that he had known before but almost forgotten; forgotten when he was no longer sagging with fatigue and funk, scared witless by yet another near-miss, shaking with nerves and not letting it show, and going up again and again because under it all burned the knowledge that the Hun believed they owned the sky. Owned everything, even thought. Now he simply hoped, with quiet resolve, that like the rest he would prove to be up to the job that had to be – must be – done.

He saw that the source of blinding light was a blast pen of concrete-filled unpainted fuel cans. As he rolled towards it, and his position changed, the bare metal caught and lost the sun, seeming to flash chaotic semaphore across the airfield. He was very close now and the airmen on the wings jumped down from their perches and signalled for him to cut his engine. More men were gathered by the fuselage. They leaned into their task and the Hurricane began to turn on its axis. Kit snapped loose the Sutton harness, pulled off his helmet and hung it on the gunsight in his usual fashion, oxygen and R/T leads still connected. The heat was unlike anything he had known before. He felt he could swim in it. His eyes were blurred with sweat.

As he stepped out of the cockpit the sleeve of his Sidcot flying suit snagged on the frame of the canopy. Off-balance he fell heavily onto the wing, slid downwards and landed on his hands and knees in the dirt. The airmen, moving the Hurricane backwards towards the blast pen, laughed and he turned on them angrily: 'Cut that out and get on with your work. And someone help me out of this damned Sidcot.'

The men were quiet now, staring at him coldly as the fighter continued to roll.

'I'll give you a hand, sir,' said a stocky fellow, older than the rest. 'You'll melt to a grease-spot in that chuffing gear.'

'And who exactly are you?' Kit's tone was clipped, impatient. The man wore khaki shorts and a dirty singlet. His boots were scuffed, his socks round his ankles. On his helmet, tipped over one bloodshot eye, the single word CHUFFY had been painted in an inexpert hand.

'Corporal Chalmers, sir.'

'How am I meant to tell?'

'You'll soon get used to the way of things, sir.' A jerk of the head at the struggling ground-crew. 'They're good lads, sir. Treated right.'

'I don't need lessons on how to deal with the men,' said Kit. 'Make sure they pull their fingers out and get that aircraft safely stowed.'

'Yes, sir,' said Chalmers. His scalp tightened at the reproof. Then he looked up. From the north-east there came a sonorous droning, building in intensity. Very soon it was possible to make out a loose formation of twenty Junkers Ju 88s approaching Takali at about 17,000 feet. One by one they began to dive, levelling out at 5,000 feet and releasing their bombs. It was all very unhurried and efficient, as though the crews were unconcerned about the prospect of real opposition. A handful of Hurricanes rose slowly into the sky over the southern perimeter in a shaky V but too late, far too late. Kit did not give much for their chances, either to engage the enemy or, if they did, to survive.

Bombs were falling close now. Kit, free of his Sidcot, ran to the Hurricane and pushed at a wing. Beside him three airmen, naked to the waist, grunted with effort, cursing. 'Bloody Jerries, bloody fucking Jerries.'

'Don't waste your breath,' said Kit.

'While I've got it,' said the airman, 'I'll use it how I please.'

A bomb landed fifty yards away. The blast threw Kit to the

ground. He felt blood running down his face and there was a dull, heavy throbbing in his ears as though he was deep under water. Two men were lying close by. One was cut in half, the other screaming. The rest were sprinting for a concrete shelter. Kit rose to his feet, dazed and unsure of his footing. He stumbled across to the screaming airman; the man who had said he would use his breath as he pleased. As Kit crouched down he gave an odd, gurgling groan, his hands grasping Kit's shirt-front, his head craning upwards, trembling. He still looked angry, but frightened too. 'Is it bad?' he said. 'Is it bad?' Then the fingers relaxed and his eyes glazed. Kit saw that both his legs were missing.

Close to the eastern perimeter a Hurricane was diving vertically into the ground. A string of bombs advanced across the airfield towards him. He stood up and stared about him.

Someone seized his arm. It was the stocky corporal. 'For Christ's sake,' yelled Chalmers, 'don't stand there admiring the bloody scenery. These blokes are past help.' Kit walked steadily towards the shelter. He was damned if he was going to run. Behind him he felt another big explosion. Again he was thrown down by the blast. His Hurricane, half in and half out of the blast pen, began to burn.

He stepped into the shelter, blinking against the sudden gloom like a man entering a cinema. No usherette's torch here. He trod on someone's hand. 'Bloody hell, watch where you're putting your boots, can't you?' The accent was broad: Yorkshire, perhaps. He wondered at the discipline, or want of it. Something was wrong here. The place was a shambles, manned by a rabble. It seemed this so-called island fortress was being bombed to oblivion with no defence to offer. How long before it fell? Yet Chalmers had risked his life to bring him in. Initiative there, and guts. Confusing.

He pushed his way through the shadowy forms. The acrid smell of cordite was drifting in from outside, mingling with the sour tang of sweating bodies and damp concrete walls redolent of urine. The air was thick with moisture and the buzz of mosquitoes. Further back a low voice was saying: 'Ken and Harry have bought it.'

Then Kit felt himself pulled down. Someone said: 'Welcome to paradise, Curtis.' It was Pop Penrose. Beside him, grinning, was Ossie Wolf . . .

Flies had already settled on the bodies of the two dead airmen. The ambulance crew waved them away as they rolled the corpses onto stretchers, but they settled again almost immediately. A few hundred yards away gouts of flame and smoke rose from two petrol bowsers. The noses of four Hurricanes pointed to the sky, their fuselages, from the cockpit back, destroyed.

'My flight,' said Penrose. 'I hope the chaps found cover.'

'Sorry, Pop,' said Kit. 'Can't hear a word. My ears.'

'Doesn't look too brilliant, does it?' said Penrose, raising his voice and speaking slowly, as though addressing an aged relative. 'Of eighteen aircraft we've already lost seven for sure. And God knows how Peter Howard fared. Haven't seen him since we landed. He put down first. Maybe they got them safely into pens.' He paused. 'What on earth happened to Hoyt?'

'Accident on take-off,' said Kit. 'And Micky Thomas got the chop trying to get up again.' He glanced at Ossie Wolf walking beside them. His service cap was tipped over his eyes, a cigarette in the corner of his mouth. His hands were sunk in the pockets of his khaki shorts. His legs were brown and thin, flying boots making them appear thinner still. The boots scuffed up the dirt. He noticed Kit watching him. 'So you made it, huh?'

'Thanks for the recommendation,' said Kit. 'Malta looks delightful.'

'It's a barrel of laughs,' said Ossie. 'You'll see.'

They had reached the remains of Kit's Hurricane, resting under a mantle of foam. Corporal Chalmers was poking about in the wreckage. 'Hey, Chuffy,' Ossie called out. 'Anything salvageable?'

'The engine's not too bad,' said Chalmers. 'Do for parts.'

Kit looked into the cockpit. Very little was left. His carefully stored kit was blackened embers. He thought: I have nothing to fight with. Where do I go from here?

Penrose seemed to read his thoughts. 'Don't worry, old boy. We'll soon have you operational again. And I've got a spare shaving brush you can borrow.'

Ossie Wolf was standing by the nose of the machine, canted upwards like the rest. He was pointing at the painted word *Epicurus*, untouched by fire. 'Always the wise guy, huh? Got to be one up on mugs like me who go for Mickey Mouse.'

'Epicurus?' said Penrose. 'The Greek chappie? Some sort of philosopher?'

'Some sort,' said Kit.

'You know the guy?' said Ossie.

'Hardly,' said Kit. 'He lived from 341 to 270 BC.'

'Jesus,' said Ossie. 'The sonofabitch was going backwards. No wonder he was hung up on the meaning of life.'

Penrose put the inevitable question.

Kit steeled himself. 'I remembered a quotation I learned at school, that's all.'

'Pray tell, brother,' said Ossie, winking at Penrose.

'"Skilful pilots gain their reputation from storms and tempests,"' said Kit, reluctantly, in a purposely dull voice. 'At the time it seemed appropriate. Now I've changed my mind.'

'Reputation?' persisted Ossie Wolf. 'That figures. What did I call you in France? Sir Lancelot riding round the goddamned clouds looking for the Holy Grail.'

'You didn't say goddamned, as I recall,' said Kit.

'That's right. I didn't.'

A buckboard squealed to a halt near the shelter where the men were gathered. They began to queue for bully beef and mugs of tea. Kit looked at his watch. It was ten a.m. He felt as if a lifetime had passed. Someone clapped him on the shoulder. 'Still with us, Kit?'

'Hello, Max,' said Kit. 'Yes, just about. How are the others?'

'They're okay. You saw old Micky get it I take it.' Astley-Cobb's uniform was thick with dirt and his hair matted with blood from a deep wound to his left temple. 'I say, what happened to Hoyt?'

'Accident on take-off.' That simple phrase again, no doubt to be repeated in a letter to Hoyt's family.

'Bad show. Dicey business, fly-offs.'

'How about your kites?'

'Safe, by a wing and a prayer. God knows how. The stuff was falling all round us. Looks as though we're in for a jolly time.' Astley-Cobb inspected his surroundings. 'Christ, Kit, what a dump.' They both laughed. 'So,' said Astley-Cobb, 'what next?'

'Tea, I suggest, at Fortnum's over the way and then we'll get ourselves sorted.'

They joined the queue at the buckboard. Ossie Wolf was a few places ahead. He came back to join them. 'How you doing?'

'Not too shabby,' said Astley-Cobb.

'Uh-oh,' said Ossie. 'Another master of British understatement.'

At the head of the queue Corporal Chalmers was stowing his food and drink in his upturned helmet. Ossie called across to him: 'Hey, Chuffy, you did good back there.'

With a shock Kit realised he had not spoken to the man who might have saved his life. He walked over to him. 'That was a damned good show, Corporal,' he said. He extended his hand.

After a momentary hesitation, Chalmers took it. His grasp was firm, his fingers cracked and work-worn. 'You do these things.' He shrugged, his mouth full of bully beef. 'Can't afford to lose pilots, can we, sir?' He jerked his head towards Ossie. 'So you know our Yank?'

'That's right.'

'Battle of Britain?'

'Battle of France.'

'He's the business, he is.'

'Really?'

'Pity the poor chuffing Jerry who gets in his sights. He really gives them what-for.' The corporal took a sip of tea and made to move away. 'We'll soon find you another Hurry, sir, no fear. Sorry about the welcoming committee. The Jerries, I mean,' he added, with a crooked smile.

'How often does it happen?' said Kit.

'Oh, two or three times a day. Keeps you on your toes.'

Takali had not fallen silent in the wake of the raid. Already, working parties were filling in craters, rebuilding blast pens, clearing wrecked aeroplanes and vehicles. Fitters, riggers and armourers were preparing undamaged Hurricanes for action. 'They appear to be getting their fingers out,' a small voice seemed to murmur in Kit's ear. Even though his hearing was dulled, every word rang clear. The bellow of aero-engines being run-up began to roll across the stone-walled fields shimmering in the heat. In a lane that ran alongside the airfield a boy carrying a sack of grass and driving a herd of goats stopped and shielded his eyes. He waved. Kit waved back. 'Yeah,' said Ossie, 'the sound of those goddamned Merlins beats any brass hat's bullshit.'

A mile from the airfield, surrounded by a tangle of olive, fig and carob trees, lay the Castello Grima, its grey stone walls ten feet thick to thwart the Turkish invaders who had never come. Square as a box, each corner was topped with a round turret from which defenders could fire at the enemy through narrow vertical slits. A bell-tower of later date rose from the inner courtyard, topped by a ball and cross. It made a picturesque sight, even through the dust-caked windows of the battered civilian bus that had collected the *Revenger* contingent from Takali. It had been a lively journey, bouncing along primitive roads at 30 m.p.h. when ten would have been too much. 'These goddamned Malties,' Ossie Wolf had grunted. 'They like to show us fighter boys what they can do.' He was not a happy man, assigned to show the new arrivals their quarters by a squadron leader who appeared to have some vague authority.

The driver applied the brakes, to little effect, and left his seat while the bus was still moving. It hit the verge, ran along it for a yard or two before the nearside front tyre dropped into a drainage gully and brought the vehicle to a dead stop. The pilots, who had half risen, fell against each other. 'There's another life gone,' said Astley-Cobb, fingering the dressing on his temple.

The driver, short and running to fat, tossed their belongings from the door of the bus, sweat dripping from the end of his nose. As the last bag sailed through the air he took a kerchief from the pocket of his black waistcoat and wiped his face. Then, spitting into the palms of his hands and rubbing them together vigorously, he threw himself back into the driver's seat. 'Goodbye, boys,' he shouted. '*Sahha! Ix-Oxorti t-Tajba!*' The rear wheels spun as he stamped on the accelerator, and when it seemed the tyres must burst, the bus shot away.

'He wishes you all kinds of luck,' said Ossie.

As the dust cleared Kit studied the castle. 'Well, we should be safe enough here.'

'Are you kidding?' said Ossie. 'If a five-hundred pounder hits this place you'll be buried as sure as King Tut.'

'Don't be so chuffing pessimistic,' said Astley-Cobb, as Pop Penrose led the way through the castellated gateway and along the short path to the entrance. On a carved stone panel over the narrow door two lions supported a wind-worn heraldic shield.

'Lyon's cornerhouse,' said the Kiwi Cliff McDill, but nobody laughed.

The inner courtyard was dank and alive with flying insects, the high walls shutting out any sunlight. A wooden balcony gave access to the first-floor rooms, stone chambers with tiny windows or no windows at all. Scorpions moved in cracks in the mortar and clouds of tiny flies settled on the lips and eyes. If this was officers' quarters, they wondered, what were conditions like for the sergeant pilots? 'Under canvas,' said Ossie Wolf, 'along with the other poor suckers who don't rate a roof over their heads.'

It was three men to a room. Kit found himself sharing with Peter Howard and Penrose. He stretched out on the metal bed. A gecko, grey-black with splayed toes, peered down at him from a corner of the ceiling. The others had heard a rumour about a mess, with food and drink. It sounded unlikely but they had gone to look. He thought back to Hawkinge. It seemed wonderfully attractive now: an efficient and smart fighter station, with a good CO; well-ordered hangars and admin buildings, busy with ground-staff proud of their work; a decent, generously stocked mess; London not too far away; the coast of Kent, of course, brisk walks and sea air after a pleasant drive through unchanged country lanes. And, best of all, the Mark II Spitfires with their perfect balance of power and weight, instantly responsive to the slightest touch on the controls. The Channel sweeps had not been to his taste but that seemed small cause for discontent when measured against where he found himself now, bombed into a hole in the ground on a minute sweltering rock surrounded by hostile forces with only clapped-out Hurricanes at his disposal; except they weren't, apparently, at his disposal because for the moment, Penrose had admitted, there were at least three pilots to every available plane. A funny kind of paradise . . .

Ossie appeared at the doorway. He held two bottles of Farson's pale ale in his hands. 'Local stuff, kinda warm. But it goes down okay.'

'Thanks,' said Kit.

'I guess you reckon that's about all you can thank me for,' said Ossie.

'I was thinking about Spitfires,' said Kit. 'Spitfires and walking by the sea.'

'You've come to the right place for sea. We got tons of the stuff.' Ossie tipped his bottle back and beer ran from the corner of his mouth. He wiped it away with the back of his hand and belched gently. 'We need Spits here. The Hurry's a poor match for the 109. Even the goddamned Eyeties can run rings round us. I keep trying to tell anyone who'll listen. So far, nobody has.'

'You seem to do all right with a Hurry,' said Kit.

Ossie grinned. 'I got my guns synchronised on a hundred and fifty yards, like I always wanted to in France. Get in real close, a two-second burst, and it's *adios, amigo*.' He was nodding with satisfaction. 'I offered to give a little talk to the other guys. You know, pass on tips. The stuffed shirts wouldn't have it. Could have saved some skins.' He offered a pack of Player's to Kit, who shook his head. The American put a match to his cigarette and inhaled deeply. 'A lot of joes out here screwed up in some way. Not so handy in the air, not jelling it on the ground. The square-peg formula. Next thing they know the CO's slapped 'em on overseas posting. Mostly they're beaten before they start.'

He sniffed. 'Still, you got a point. It's not just down to the Hurry, I guess. Like you say, I do okay. But, then, I should. It's the other fellers who need an edge, to buy 'em time to learn. Like arming us with Spits. With them we could lam the bastards good. Christ knows, the odds are stacked against us as it is.' He looked at Kit reflectively. 'Say, when I'm not flying I practise deflection shooting with a bunch of hillbillies over Mosta way, potting rabbits. How about coming along? The gang would be tickled.'

'Thanks,' said Kit. 'It might be all I shoot at for a while if Pop's predictions are correct.'

'I guess things don't look too promising right now,' said Ossie, 'but I'm telling you, this is the place to be. The boys in Sicily know their stuff. And that goes for the Eyeties too.' He punched Kit playfully on the shoulder. 'Jesus, man, it can't be beat.'

'I know,' said Kit. 'It's a barrel of laughs.'

He remembered Ossie's phone call a week or so after that night in the Blue Diamond Club. 'Hey, I got news for you. You say you're missing out on the action? I got it for you in spades.' He had been talking fast, something about desert warfare, front-line duties head-to-head with Kesselring's flying circus. He had made it sound like a young pilot's dream.

'This is rather sudden,' Kit had said. 'You didn't mention it in town.'

A hesitation. 'Kind of came up,' Ossie had said vaguely, then talking fast again: 'Could be anywhere, of course. But the grapevine says North Africa. The thing is . . .'

'Yes?' said Kit.

'One of the guys doesn't want to go. Just married. Guess you can understand. But he's got to find someone to take his place. I thought of you.'

'How long have I got to think it over?'

'Not long. We're shipping out soon. I'll get you some more gen. Help you make up your mind.'

'All right. I'll give it some thought.'

'Say,' Ossie Wolf had said, 'how's that sad-sack kid you had in tow at that stinking club?'

'Bought it next day. Glycol leak mid-Channel. Could have brolly-hopped. Didn't. Don't know why.'

'Can't say that's a big surprise,' Ossie had said. 'He'd really taken a load on. Those goddamned joints. I'm glad I popped the Greek.'

'Popped the Greek?'

'The pimp who ran the place. After you'd gone, the boys and me, we raised a little hell. The Greek said something out of line. We put him straight.'

'Would this have any connection with your holiday abroad?'

A long pause and then a laugh. 'It didn't help. But so what? Action's action. That's what you said you wanted. Here's your chance. Call me. But don't drag your feet. Hey,' he added, 'that's rough about the kid. He sure was hung up on that chick.' He cleared his throat. 'She was the Greek's chick by the way. I guess he never knew that.'

'No,' Kit had said. 'I guess he never did.'

Within a week Kit had volunteered for overseas duty. His commanding officer had been surprised, and disappointed. 'This is important work, Curtis, and you're good at it. We can't afford to lose chaps like you.'

'I missed the big show, sir,' Kit had said. 'I gained a lot of experience in France. I think I can put it to better use.'

'I'll be the judge of that,' the CO had said, his jaw working. 'I'm not here to satisfy the whims of pilots who want to make a name for themselves.'

'It's not that, sir.'

'Are you sure?'

Kit had thought it wiser to remain silent.

'All right,' the CO had said. 'I'll put the wheels in motion. But I think you're being a bloody young fool. You could end up anywhere, you know. From what I've heard, some of the postings make this place seem like Shangri-La.'

They had been in no hurry to let him go. Ossie and the others had been flown out months before Kit found himself leaning on the rail of HMS *Revenger* at Greenock, talking to the Fleet Air Arm man about his summer cruise with the Grey Funnel Line.

Peter Howard came in. 'Hey, where on earth did you get those beers? Pop and I drew a complete blank.'

'Young Giorgio's got a stash. I'll fetch a couple,' said Ossie. He pushed himself off the wall and went down to the courtyard.

'Useful chap to know,' said Howard. 'Who's young Giorgio, by the way?'

'Search me,' said Kit.

Ossie was back in minutes. He handed Howard a bottle. 'Thanks,' said Howard. 'Who's this Giorgio?'

'Oh, he's just a kid who helps out, a batman, kinda.'

Kit said: 'Pop tells me you only lost one kite from your flight.'

'Yes,' said Howard. 'And not on the ground either. They were safely in pens when the Jerries arrived, and the chaps were already under cover. But Johnny Grimshaw went missing on the last leg. Haven't a clue what happened. Just disappeared – fuel, lost touch and got bounced, duff engine, God knows. Haven't heard anything. Maybe he'll be picked up.'

'I doubt it,' said Ossie. 'Things don't run so smooth out here, leastaways not yet. Well,' he said, taking Kit's empty bottle, 'I'm heading back to the base.'

'Tonight the beers are on us,' said Kit. 'Which is your room?'

'Oh, I'm not shacked up here,' said Ossie. 'I got another

place.' They heard him bounding down the stairs from the balcony, the bottles clinking with each step.

'I didn't realise you knew that chap,' said Howard.

'I wouldn't say that,' said Kit.

Later that afternoon, in the neglected garden of the *castello*, with its remnants of an English-style herbaceous border and battered statuary, Kit found a shady marble bench and unfolded the letter he had received from his father a few days before he had reported to Greenock. He had put off writing a reply. He did not know why. Too much to say, or not enough?

From close by, almost at his feet, came the chirrup of grasshoppers and, from the other side of the island, the dull thud of bombs and rhythmic thump-thump of anti-aircraft fire. In the sky, unseen, obscured by the brittle branches of the trees, aircraft dived and turned and climbed and spun to a chatter of machine-gun and cannon fire. Soon it would be his turn.

The thought provoked the usual throb in the pit of his stomach, as though the chemistry of his body had changed in some way. Quite uncontrollable. There was an ache in his arms and legs, a gathering of phlegm at the base of his throat. He felt slightly sick and breathless. It was always the same, faced with going up again. Not fear but unease, apprehension, something to be fought down, unhelpful, certainly not to be admitted. On his lecture tour he had tried to replicate the sensation by recalling moments when he had been almost touched by death or had simply waited on the ground; waited for the readiness phone to ring, the call that would send them stumbling towards their fighters, panting, tongues thick, lips dry. But it had not been possible. His instincts could not be tricked. Now, though, they knew, yes, they knew that soon he would be joined in battle once again, in an unknown and blank blue sky, with no cover and many enemies. Still he fought them down, his instincts; unhelpful and certainly not to be admitted. He read his father's words again:

My dear Kit,

What times! My thoughts are with you wherever you may be. How like you to seek this scrap, as if you had not already done your bit. Your commanding officer was kind enough to telephone the other day. Very guarded but I understand you are bound for warmer climes. He was generous in his praise. I can hear you saying, 'Oh, Farve . . .' but really I was immensely proud. This war is a dreadful business, tragic, but it must be fought and won, and the manner in which you and your comrades are taking on the enemy gives us all much hope. Is it too high-flown (no pun intended) to say that the Air Force has been this country's beacon in the darkest times? Who would have imagined, when we flew those little model aeroplanes together on the Downs, all those years ago, that you would yourself be taking to the air a decade later, with a much more serious purpose? However, I can sense your impatience, drumming your fingers in that way you have when your devoted father goes on more than somewhat! And I have news, great news.

The woman in whose house you were billeted before your squadron left France has made her way to England with her son. She telephoned from Plymouth and, of course, I was only too delighted to welcome her here, which I know was your wish if they should ever manage to escape. Madame Garencières (she insists I call her Juliette but I cannot get used to it) is charming and her son Louis delightful. He reminds me very much of you at that age. He is frustrated, to a comical extent, by being too young to enlist. His late father was a tank commander, I understand, so there is military blood there.

For your mother the present arrangement is not ideal (extra mouths, another woman in the house, a small boy at large in the gardens, etc.) and she is looking for alternative accommodation for them nearer London. Madame G talks of working for the wireless, broadcasting to France or somesuch. She strikes me as someone with much spirit.

As for our old friends the Maierscheldts, I fear the worst. We can obtain no news from official channels, other than that the factory at Nancy reports them missing, presumably deported. What bestial people the Nazis are. But we can derive some comfort from knowing that their daughter is safe, though here lies another mystery for although Hannah is certainly in England she has made no effort to contact us. It seems most odd but I can only imagine that she understands how it is with us and does not wish to presume. That would be like her, would it not?

For myself, neither worse nor better. The ticker continues to tick, if not as reliably as before. It keeps me from the business, which I regret, but Tomkinson is a steady pair of hands and shows great enterprise in not the easiest of circumstances. It may be that our products lack the quality and variety of pre-war years but at least there is a ready market for the cup that cheers and perhaps in our small way we are also doing our bit. Anyway, God be with you, Christopher, my dear Kit, and may He protect you always,

Your ever affectionate,

Farve

Kit refolded the letter and returned it to his shirt pocket. He was not thinking of the family business, the difficulties of importing tea. He was back in the cool *salon* of the *maison du maître* of Juliette Garencières, with the garden that ran down to the river at Boulay-sur-Sarthe where, a year ago, he and his comrades had, for a few weeks, snatched hours of troubled sleep in a barn across the courtyard before patrolling the skies above the ports of Brittany, helping to protect the remnants of the British Expeditionary Force as they took to the sea, thrown back by the forces of the Reich.

Juliette Garencières had stood before him, small, her face upturned, listening quietly as she heard the squadron was on the move again. He knew, but could not tell her, that it was to be its final toehold in France on the cliffs above St Nazaire. He had come to say goodbye but it had been a beginning also, a time to express what they had felt but left unsaid.

She had seemed fragile in his arms. He had felt an emotion he had never known: tenderness but also strong desire. 'This is not the end,' he had said. 'If you can, go to England. I will find you there.' He remembered glancing back at the big house overlooking the valley, seeing the woman with her son, still waving by the great front door, and understanding how it might be for a man to say goodbye to his family.

There was a sudden crashing in the tangled vegetation close by. A narrow path led between a lofty cactus sprouting pale yellow flowers and a twisted carob tree. Kit's arm brushed a carob branch and a cloud of brown butterflies rose into the air. Next to it a thicket of fig trees bore shiny green fruit, clustered with colonies of small pink snails. The heat was fierce now and the air heavy with the smell of wild fennel. Beyond the figs was a small clear space where a number of paths had once met but now only the single path remained.

Something was screaming, a devilish wail, then another, and another, like mourners at an eastern wake. A dozen feral cats were grouped around an object that lay in the centre of the clearing, moving slowly and with difficulty. It was a small lizard with mottled green and horny skin and cone-shaped eyes. The creature had puffed itself up and sat with jaws open, attempting – Kit supposed – to appear larger than it was. The impassive, howling cats, small-headed with elegant necks and long, tapering legs, were seated in a circle like bronze statuettes from an Egyptian tomb. First one would pounce forward and toss the lizard into the air, then another would bury its claws in the writhing body. One leg had already been pulled away. Kit's skin crawled with the horror of it: the cat-tribe's cold enjoyment of a game that could have only one end, the contortions of a victim without hope. Should he intervene? Perhaps the lizard was needed for food, once it had provided a little amusement. What did they say? Let nature take its—

A young boy, burly and dark, strode into the space. His voice was hoarse and rasping, like a smoker's. He had a man's cloth cap, its peak torn, pushed onto the back of his head, and black hair fell over his forehead. He kicked out at the cats, which scattered. He picked up the stricken lizard and held it out to Kit, grinning and talking rapidly in Maltese. One word stood out: *kamaleont*.

'Chameleon,' said Kit. 'Yes, I understand.' He did not want to take the reptile. The boy shrugged and laughed, then threw it into the undergrowth. He wiped his hands on his torn plaid shirt and saluted; an RAF salute, hand vertical against his ear. Kit returned the courtesy. 'You must be Giorgio,' he said.

'*Iva*,' said the boy. 'You have heard of me?'

'The American,' said Kit. 'He told us you were a useful man.'

The boy flushed. 'Thank you,' he said. He looked like a child again.

* * *

On the first floor of the *castello* Penrose and Howard were still unpacking their gear. When Kit stepped into the chamber they groaned. 'Good God,' said Howard. 'Talk about cramped. This place is like the Chateau d'If.'

'Edmond Dantes was locked up for fourteen years,' said Kit. 'I doubt if we're in for that long a stretch.'

'You're on readiness at six a.m,' said Penrose. 'These are the chaps I've chosen to plug the gaps. Arrange them how you will.' He tied up the neck of his empty kit-bag and pushed it under the metal bed. 'Might as well get stuck in without delay. Heaven knows, the fellows here deserve some fresh support. Rustle up your flight and go and check the kites for yourselves. I've already given them a once-over. They're a bit of a dog's dinner, I'm afraid, but they're all we've got. I've a spot of admin to deal with. I'll be down again by the time you've got yourselves sorted out.'

'What about transport?' said Kit.

'All arranged. Parked out front.'

Kit found Astley-Cobb first. 'We're in business, Max.'

'Good show. Who's on board?'

'McDill and Cooper obviously, and a couple of new boys, Duncan Reid and Ray Rimmer, shifted over from Peter Howard's mob.'

'I flew with Rimmer at Biggin. Good type. Reid, don't know.'

'We'll find out soon enough.'

The growl of engines was building from the north. Outside, the brilliance of the light was almost painful. It took time for their eyes to adjust. For moments they could hear but not see. A formation of Ju 88s was gradually emerging from a slight haze and anti-aircraft fire began to track them, to little effect, as they prepared to dive. It looked like Takali again. Four Hurricanes, in finger-four, were climbing towards the bombers but above them, at 15,000 feet, a *Staffel* of Messerschmitt 109s was circling, providing cover. A single 109 dropped down out of the sun to tempt the defenders into combat and divert them from the Ju 88s. The nearest Hurricane saw it too late. It dragged itself into a desperate vertical turn but cannon fire pierced its tailplane and it flopped away, control lines severed, helpless. Another burst of cannon fire. The starboard wing sheered off and as the machine barrel-rolled wildly the small figure of the pilot was thrown clear. His parachute opened and he came down slowly about four miles away.

Kit's eyes were clear now. To him the Messerschmitts, still circling above, had the look of the feral cats watching the contortions of their victim, complacent in their power, enjoying a game that they imagined could have only one end. He did not care to watch.

Instead he found the transport Penrose had arranged. Six shabby civilian bicycles leaned against the gateway. 'Bags the one with the bell,' said Astley-Cobb. 'We might encounter that ruddy bus again.' But then he clasped his hands on top of his head, his mouth open. 'Christ,' he said. 'Just look at that.' He pointed upwards.

The singleton 109's moment of triumph had been short. Now it was spinning to earth trailing black smoke and glycol. A British fighter was diving away. Something about the attitude of the aircraft, the smoothness with which it was being flown, the decisive way it had engaged the enemy, closing fast, firing a quick burst and getting out still quicker, suggested to Kit that he probably knew the pilot. 'Get in close, a two-second burst and it's *adios, amigo*.' The circling *Staffel* had been surprised. The predators had learned there could be more than one end to the game. That nothing was for certain.

Two more 109s half rolled and dropped down to avenge their

decoy. Their quarry had levelled out now, at no more than fifty feet, throttle open, contrails streaming from its wing-tips. It bucketed upwards into a half-loop, through 180 degrees, and rolled off the top placing it at the same altitude as the first of the Messerschmitts approaching at more than 350 m.p.h. . . .

# Two

For Ossie Wolf the first one had been easy. Showboating in front of his *kameraden* the Me 109 had followed Drongo down as the Hurricane's wing came off. The pilot had circled the Australian as his 'chute came open and for a long moment it looked as if he was going to open fire. Or maybe he was thinking how impressed his *Staffelkapitan* must be to see him knock these Tommies out of the sky like duck rising from the marshes of Nordeney. Whatever was on his mind, it was his last rational thought.

Ossie could not believe his luck: an experienced pilot sacrificing his height like that to gloat, giving him eight hundred precious feet. He had come down out of the sun, kicked his rudder to the left to get the Messerschmitt at right angles and given him a four-second burst with full deflection as the German came through his sights. Red tracer from the eight .303 Brownings ran along the fuselage, hitting the fuel tank directly behind the pilot's seat. A jet of red-orange flame shot up and the 109 spun out of sight.

Ossie pushed the stick forward and dived almost vertically. He knew the *Staffelkapitan* wouldn't let it rest at that. The goddamned Jerries had gotten used to treating the skies of Malta like their own private amphitheatre. So one of their gladiators had somehow gone down: they would send another two. It was their method, and method, they believed, would bring them victory.

The twin 109s were diving on him line astern, their wings flexing with the speed, as he rolled off the top of the loop and faced them. It placed him slightly above the leader who tried to pull up, opening fire too soon, his cannon shells whining into thin air below the Hurricane's tail. For an instant the German seemed to hang in the air, like a snapshot, colours brilliant against the flat terrain of muted browns, greys and greens a thousand feet below, its nose matt yellow with a crimson spinner and on its stubby wings big black crosses edged with white. Beneath the flat-topped canopy of darkened Plexiglass the pilot looked up, knowing he had lost. Ossie thumbed his gun-button, one, two seconds, and the 109 blew up as the bullets pierced its oil and fuel tanks. It fell slowly, glowing brightly, like an ember from a Roman candle.

Ossie half rolled and dived away, the second 109 on his tail but unable to fix the Hurricane in its sights as it jinked and slipped, twisted and turned, never still for a moment, never offering more than an end-on view of its tapering fuselage and narrow wings, always floating out of range. Now its port wing was lifting, its speed constant, still clear of the 109's gunsight, pulling into a vertical turn. Its tailplane was tantalisingly close. The 109 loosed off a burst but the cannon-shells flew wide. The turn was becoming extreme. The pilot of the 109 had to crane his head to the right to keep the Hurricane in view. His machine was shuddering with the G force. Full right rudder now and finally the Hurricane presented itself, wings perpendicular, but turning towards him, turning inside him, opening fire.

The storm of bullets took the 109's tail off. It went into a flat spin. Ossie watched the canopy push up and the pilot pull himself upright on his seat. He dragged off his helmet with its R/T and oxygen leads and pitched over the side of the cockpit head first. He waited for a sensible time, making sure he was clear of his burning aircraft, before deploying his 'chute. It had been coolly done. And Ossie liked to see it. Another pro out of action.

The bombers were turning away from their target, on a course for Sicily. The 109s broke their circle, re-forming line-abreast and heading north as well, but three of them would not be going home to *bratwurst* and *pilsener*.

The runways at Takali were pitted with fresh craters. Control told Ossie to land at the Safi airstrip not far from Marsaxlokk Bay. He called up the others, Cavanagh and Twigg, but got no response. Control had found the same. Ossie had not seen them since they closed with the 109s. But it was always like that, a crazy confusion of trying to kill and not be killed, and then the sky clear and silent, your heartbeat slowing, your body sticky with sweat and, finally, time to think, not just react. Maybe the guys were already down. And it looked like Drongo Palmer had got away with it again.

Ossie was coming in over the harbour of Marsaxlokk, ringed by pastel-coloured houses. The fishing fleet of *luzzu* boats, daubed in bright greens, blues and yellows, nodded to a gentle swell, seeming to float in the air on a transparent sapphire sea. The Hurricane kicked and snatched, caught by waves of rising heat. Ahead, he saw the sand-coloured strip of Safi. He eased the throttle and his airspeed steadied on 160 m.p.h. He slid back the canopy and the airstream washed round him, cool, refreshing. Wheels down now, then flaps. He turned in on a gentle, curved approach, airspeed down to 90 m.p.h. Nose up a little, tailwheel sinking back. He floated over the boundary, the Hurricane's attitude perfect. Very close now, the propeller raising dust. He checked the setting of the Vokes filter: okay. He held her off and held her off, then right back on the stick, and he was down and taxiing towards a blast pen where men were beckoning him forward, cloths across their noses and mouths against the dust, giving them the look of road-agents about to rob a stage. He ran the engine out, switched it off and applied the brakes.

An airman jumped onto the wing, tugging down his bandit's mask. He knew who Ossie was but Ossie didn't care. He wasn't into that. And, anyway, on an island this small it was easy to get a reputation, good or bad. 'We saw 'em come down, sir. All three of the buggers. The Jerry who took to his 'chute landed near Siggiewi.'

'What about my guys?'

'Haven't heard. One got out all right.'

'Yeah, I saw. Where do you get a drink around here?'

Within the hour came news that the Takali runways had been patched. In minutes Ossie had taken off again. When he landed the sun was low in the sky. It was good to see it go, to feel the temperature drop, still hot but bearable. In the blue shadows mosquitoes gathered, dancing in clouds. Night sounds were starting up in the tinder-dry undergrowth beyond the airfield perimeter. Drongo Palmer was stretched out in a deckchair by the Dispersal tent, reading a week-old copy of the *Daily Mirror*. He looked up as Ossie walked over in his flying kit, then resumed his study of the Jane cartoon.

'You prize jerk,' said Ossie, 'getting bounced like that.'

'Still,' said Palmer, 'you settled his hash. I had a grandstand view.'

'From the cheap seats,' said Ossie. 'What about the others?'

'They're okay,' said Palmer. 'Roy Cavanagh landed back here with his R/T up the spout. They tried to warn him off with a flare but the silly sod came steaming in anyway, and got away with it. Twiggy's stuck at Luqa with a buggered elevator. He's claimed a probable, by the way, one of the Ju 88s.'

'Gee whiz,' said Ossie. 'You don't mean someone's trying to help me win this goddamned war?' He turned his head. His neck was stiff with stress. He groaned but not because of his neck. Threlfall was wobbling towards them on his bicycle, his clipboard tucked under one arm. 'For crying out loud, it's Wingless.'

The intelligence officer eased himself off the saddle and leaned the bicycle against a tent pole, rubbing his backside. 'More far-fetched yarns of derring-do, I understand,' he said. He always tried a little joke, to ease the situation.

'Far-fetched, my ass,' said Ossie. 'Three destroyed, no question. One brolly-hopped. I watched the others burn myself.'

There was a fierce satisfaction in his voice that made Threlfall uneasy. He studied the American's face as he drawled details of the combat. At debrief pilots would often laugh too loudly, still tingling with adrenaline, or try to hide hands that shook with nerves. Or stand apart, withdrawn, reluctant to relive the battle, to contemplate the deaths of friends and even enemies while they, for the moment, remained alive. But Wolf appeared unmoved, indifferent to his experiences, his voice a monotone as he described the choreography of battle in the air. Threlfall wondered if, to him and men like him, those he killed meant no more than another small swastika on the nose of his machine. And yet on the ground he was relaxed enough, even popular – but in a way that officers shouldn't be: on easy first-name terms with other ranks and apt to spend his time with roistering types who liked to thumb their noses at authority, all of them good in the air, of course, but always discussing how different the world would be, once this war was fought and won.

Maybe it was Malta, Threlfall reflected, where many of the

usual standards had fallen away in the struggle to survive. He could see that aspects of this were good, distinctions of rank less clear-cut, each man relying on the other. But it was not the service he was used to. He supposed it was more his problem than that of men like Ossie Wolf. Perhaps they were the future, he the past. They knew, had always understood, that the purpose of an air force was to destroy. They were comfortable with that. He only knew that he was not. And there were others, too, among the pilots, who hid their trembling hands in the pockets of their flying suits, or suppressed a twitching eye, or sat quietly with their beer, preoccupied, unreachable. He was grateful that he did not have to fly but simply recorded the deeds of others in the thin, cold atmosphere where they did the killing.

Later Ossie Wolf walked back to the army tent he shared with the sergeant pilots, Palmer and Twigg. At first it had been suggested that he join the other officers at Castello Grima. Then he had been told to. Finally it had been made an order. He had even been shown the quarters he had been allocated. But still he didn't go there. Instead he returned to the small tent with the sides that rolled up or down, depending on the time of day or night, within the perimeter of the airfield. He said it was better there, that he could reach the blast pen where his Hurricane was housed in four minutes flat, be in the air in another two; that anyway there was no goddamned masonry to crush him, and as long as he flew his ass off and did everything that was asked of him, what the heck did it matter where he hung out?

Drongo Palmer had found a bar in Attard that sold him crates of Blue Label beer for half-a-crown. Now he bent down, took out a bottle and threw it to Ossie. It was growing dark, the sky blue-black above and blood-red where it met the horizon. A thin new moon was rising from behind the ramparts of Mdina, barely a mile away, and stars were showing. The countryside drowsed, the earth cooling.

Somewhere dogs yelped at each other across the small fields. The rumble of an engine sounded down the lane, then the squeal of brakes. A door slammed. Brian Twigg came into the tent out of the half-light. He was carrying his parachute and his cropped fair hair stood up straight on the crown of his head. His face was encrusted with dirt and dust. 'Put the tea on, Mother,' he said.

Drongo Palmer tossed him a Blue Label. 'Good day at the office, dear?'

'I've just heard something pretty extraordinary,' said Twigg. 'Our oppos at Luqa reckon Hitler's invaded Russia. I asked old Threlfall about it when I gave him my report. He said it was news to him, but maybe he wasn't letting on.'

'Invaded Russia?' said Palmer. 'Hasn't Adolf got some sort of Pact with the Bolshies?'

'Hey, Twiggy,' said Ossie Wolf. 'Surely you're not suggesting *mein Führer* might have broken his word?'

Twigg shrugged. 'Just telling you what I was told. Somebody knows one of the clowns down the hole in Valletta. And Control's where they'd get to know about it first. Be good if it was true, though, wouldn't it?'

'Would it?' said Palmer.

'Certainly,' said Twigg. 'War on two fronts. The Jerries would have to switch a lot of their heavy metal to the east. Might even get a little peace around here, just us and the Eyeties.' He snapped his fingers at Palmer. 'Bung us a smoke, Drongo, there's a good bloke.' He caught the packet of Woodbines, knocked one out, lit it and threw the pack back to the Australian. 'Saw you get bounced by that 109. Didn't think you'd get out of that one.'

'Wingless told us you got a bit bloody peppered yourself,' said Palmer, defensively.

'Ah, that I did, my boy,' said Twigg. 'But I gave as good as I got. A nice fat juicy Ju 88.' He pulled out a wooden draughts-board from underneath his bed. 'Come on, Drongo. Maybe you'll have better luck at chess.' He lit a candle and instantly the air was alive with a thousand insects.

Ossie helped himself to another beer from the crate. He was thinking about Spain. It was always the same, when somebody mentioned those trigger words: Bolshies, Commies, Reds. It took him back to that other place of heat and death, where multitudes of aircraft had come out of a clear sky, dropped their bombs and strafed the cities, towns and villages, virtually unopposed, and corpses rotted beneath an implacable sun.

He remembered the Lenin Barracks in Barcelona in '36 when everyone, it seemed, wore rough, working-class clothes and he had signed on for the militia. There had been hope then and a sense of unity, despite the chaos, and foreigners like him had been hailed with joy; joy that the struggle of the proletariat against the Fascists and the forces of the Right was drawing in fighters from other lands.

At first it had seemed he might fly for the Republicans. 'Ah, a pilot, wonderful.' But instead he had found himself carrying a rusty rifle in the hill-top trenches of Huesca, and then the whole damned movement had imploded, defeated on the battlefield and collapsing from within. He had been lucky to get across the border to Perpignan. Too many volunteers had ended their brief war against a wall, shot by former comrades. But he had gotten himself another chance, in England, where he found folk who were prepared to check him out and take him on and give him a nice new airplane to fly. They knew about his time in Spain, all right, and he'd quickly proved he was good in the air so he was soon assigned to fighters. The Battle of France had been his opportunity to even some scores but finally that campaign had also ended in a sorry mess. But not disaster, like in Spain. France had bought the British time, and when the Luftwaffe had darkened the sky in July 1940 he had been there, ready to fight again, and send some more of the Fascist sons-of-bitches to an early grave.

Drongo Palmer was losing at chess, mostly because he didn't understand the rules. His king was three moves from being pinned down but he hadn't seen it yet. He glared at the board, cracking his fingers. He knew he was in trouble but didn't know why. Ossie regarded him wryly. He was in danger of being fond of the guy. They had endured a lot together in 12 Group, flying Hurricanes from a desolate, featureless airfield north of Norwich, swept by North Sea gales. They shared a dislike of Bader's Big Wing theories. Both had been in trouble, at different times and in different flights, during that bright, dangerous summer of 1940, for breaking formation, dropping down on targets of opportunity instead of sticking with the wing leader's strategy of patiently assembling sixty fighters for a bigger show entirely. Ossie reckoned Drongo had done it because, as with chess, he hadn't really grasped the rules. He himself had had no such excuse. His instinct was that the only rules to be obeyed were his own. He knew there was a broader picture but, hell, there were always plenty of other guys ready to toe the line. And too often he had been the first to spot bandits, singing out a warning and forced to wait for Phelps, the flight commander, to get his brain in gear, like when he'd seen a *Staffel* of Messerschmitt 110s climbing up behind them over the Thames estuary and Phelps had told him they were Blenheims.

'They're not, you know,' Ossie had shouted, biting his tongue because he wanted to add, 'you dumb sonofabitch.' Finally Phelps had recognised the 110s for what they were, but minutes had been lost and two men died who might otherwise have survived.

After that he had played by Ossie rules, convinced that if he chose to attack a Hun, any Hun in any circumstances, the bastard would burn. And that was his purpose, that was why he was here, what he was meant to do. Wasn't it? He reckoned his score spoke for itself: twelve confirmed, three probables. Enough said, surely?

Even so, his tactics had gone down badly with the others. 'Not done, old boy, peeling off like that, leaving the flight unprotected. What would happen if we all did it?' He had found himself cold-shouldered. He reckoned few things were more icy than a pissed-off Limey who thought you were letting the side down. He felt bad about it, no question, but sore as well. He had tried sticking to the game-plan and guys had bought it. Now he followed the maxim he had always believed in: do it to him before he does it to you. He gave up trying to convince the others he knew his stuff, reminding them he had led a flight in France to good effect. 'That was a different kind of show,' was all they said.

Finally he had gone to the CO. 'I'd like to request a transfer, sir. To 11 Group.'

'Reason?'

'I think I'd be better suited there.'

'Reason?'

'It's the front-line, more like France, with no time for this Big Wing stuff.'

'"Stuff", you call it? So you think you know better than Air Vice-Marshal Leigh-Mallory?'

'I'm not saying there isn't a place for it. Sure, up here we can round up sixty or seventy airplanes before we make our move. The Hun aren't on our doorstep. But the guys in the south-east don't have that luxury. Try Big Wing tactics down there and they'd be sitting ducks. They've only got minutes to react and that's my style, where I'm best. I'm strictly a small-squadron man.'

'Request denied.'

'Mind telling me why, sir?' Ossie had said.

'You're a decent pilot, Wolf,' the CO had told him. 'In case you hadn't noticed, they're in short supply.' He had tilted his head back, regarding the American through narrowed eyes. 'Perhaps there's a different way of doing things where you come from, and no doubt in France you grew accustomed to a certain . . . what shall we say? Spontaneity? It was a question of learning the ropes, fending for yourselves because, let's face it, towards the end there was precious little control. Well, now we're following a plan we believe will work. That plan depends on firm control, on each of us playing his part, and while you're here that's exactly what you'll do.' His tone softened a little. 'I don't want to lose you, Wolf, you're a useful chap to have around. But unless you keep your nose clean I'll have no hesitation in posting you out of here, but not to Air Vice-Marshal Park's group. You'll find yourself back training sprogs in bonny Scotland.'

In fact it didn't matter. By October the Luftwaffe had seemed shaken by the price it had been forced to pay: 130 bombers and fighters destroyed, more than five hundred men, in the dying days of September alone. Raids continued but without the usual intensity and scale. It seemed significant. Fighter Command sensed a turning point. It was time to consider other priorities.

Three weeks later the squadron moved to Anglesey, to an airfield just as hostile, scoured by wind, rain and sand, distant mountains capped with patchy snow, no trees, the nearest village fifteen miles away, the work monotonous: convoy patrols, flying in pairs fifty miles out to sea, protecting shipping for ninety minutes, waiting for the engine to miss a beat, looking for bad signs on the instruments. Often Ossie would find himself teamed with Drongo Palmer. Two of a kind, it was said. He remembered them slicing through mist, visibility down to two hundred yards, low enough for their propellers to draw up spray from the wave crests, holding their course and emerging from a grey curtain to see the convoys spread before them. It was dangerous enough, God knows, and took a lot of nerve. But, still, it wasn't like being in a fighting unit.

Stood down, the pilots played rugby on frozen pitches or raced each other on blistered feet round the lake of Llyn Alaw or took a bus to Holyhead, where Ossie and Drongo usually headed for the warmth of the Empire cinema; a comfortable seat in the one-and-nines and a chance to catch Hollywood's latest swashbuckler – *The Sea Hawk*, *The Mark of Zorro*, *The Santa Fe Trail.* They usually had Dick Little along, to take his mind off the new wife he'd left behind in Finchley. They would finish the night in one of the smoky pubs down by the docks before tumbling onto the last bus back. The young sergeant pilot had been married five months. In the bus he would tell them how beautiful his young wife was. In the morning they would find him clutching his pillow.

They did not see the Luftwaffe. The enemy they fought was less tangible but all around them: high winds blowing in from the Irish Sea, dense cloud, sheets of rain and sleet, snow and sand. Sand in eyes and mouths and ears, penetrating engines, drying oil, lifting paint, jamming controls. If for any reason their single engines failed, pilots died far out to sea. Nothing to be done. A few final words, futile instructions trying to guide the man down, and then an explosion of foam, white circles radiating outwards, diminishing, finally lost in the broken water. Keith Phelps had gone that way; Phelps who had mistaken Me 110s for Blenheims. Even the CO himself, leading by example, whose Merlin failed at 4,000 feet. He baled out, landed close to a corvette but was lost among the waves.

'The plan depends on each of us playing his part.' The CO's

part had turned out to be small: a tidy desk, a reputation as a decent type, fair with the men, a so-so pilot, two probables only, no confirmeds. The new man had been in place within a week.

Ossie continued to play his part but it was hardly a matter of choice. All he could do was fly where he was ordered to fly, but among the other officers the ice began to thaw. It seemed the American could be counted on at last. Rough round the edges, of course. Not really one of the chaps, more at ease with the NCOs. That was the trouble with battlefield commissions. These days you never knew who would turn up in the mess.

Ossie was aware they thought like this. After France, where prejudices had fallen away as they fought to survive, the ranks had closed again: the old values, the traditional ways of doing things had been restored, particularly in squadrons with a touch of starch in their collars, even in the face of waste and death. How did it go? Gentlemen and players, yeah, that was it. But the poor mugs didn't see they were fighting for a world that had gone for good, even if they won.

Ossie had watched the new CO with care. The moment had to be right. As yet he didn't know the guy. Nobody did. He had a reputation as a martinet. They'd seen no signs. He seemed okay. Soon, very soon, Ossie would walk back into that office and get himself a move to Keith Park's outfit. It was cock-eyed, sticking a flier with twelve kills in his bank account in this crummy backwater. He reckoned the new man would see sense. After all, hadn't he kept his goddamned nose clean like the dead CO had told him? What could possibly stand in his way?

A few days later he had decided to take some leave. It had piled up, unused. Drongo Palmer and Dick Little were keen to come along. They hitched a lift on a de Havilland Dominie that had flown in on communication duty. It dropped them at Northolt and they ordered a taxi to London. The driver was reluctant because of the Blitz but money made him brave. Dick Little was edgy and confused. His wife was not in Finchley but in Bristol with her parents. He would travel down by rail the next day, on the first train out of Paddington. 'Don't mope, mate,' said Drongo Palmer. 'That means you can spend the night on the town with us, getting pissed as parrots. And I know just the place.'

Ossie looked at Drongo now. He had lost interest in chess. He was lying sideways on his bed, eyes closed, but not asleep because he wasn't snoring. Maybe he was going over how he'd got out of that burning Hurricane, how maybe next time he wouldn't. Or maybe thinking how they had come to find themselves in yet another God-forsaken hole. Suddenly he opened his eyes, stretched and yawned. 'The bloody Blue Diamond. If we hadn't wound up there that night we wouldn't be here now.' He had said it before but this time it was like he had read Ossie's mind.

When the taxi had dropped them off at Tenison Court, where it ran off east from Regent Street, a raid had been developing over the London docks. The driver flinched at each whistle of falling bombs and every distant explosion. The sky was crimson with fire, and the jangle of fire engine and ambulance bells carried on the air. The man's hand was shaking when he took their money but he still licked his fingers and counted the notes.

A police constable in a steel helmet ran across the road. 'Oi, you. What the bloody hell do you think you're doing? Counting out the money for your funeral? Park this vehicle and get under cover now.' He saw the three pilots and touched his helmet. 'Sorry, gents, but I suggest you make your way to the Piccadilly underground line.'

'That's okay, Constable,' said Ossie. 'We've made our own arrangements.'

The policeman saw the flight lieutenant's rings on his sleeve. His manner changed. Old soldier, Ossie thought. 'That's up to you, sir,' the policeman said. 'You're safer down the tube.'

'You're probably right,' said Ossie, 'but don't fret none. We're used to taking a risk or two.'

They walked on down the narrow street. Bombers were passing overhead, their engines thrumming. The stark white beams of searchlights swooped across the sky, sometimes fixing on a whale-like outline, then losing it again. A storm of anti-aircraft fire rose into the air but it was impossible to tell if the shells had hit their target, if they had a target. More likely the gun-crews were loosing off in hope and anger. Shards of shrapnel were landing in the road, still hot, melting the tar.

Even surrounded by the tumult of the raid they could hear the racket from the Blue Diamond Club, fifty yards away. They clattered down the basement steps. The door swung back an inch or two, secured by a chain. The doorman saw their uniforms, undid the chain and let them in for six shillings each. After the blackout the rush of heat, light and noise was startling. The place heaved with a crush of bodies, people screaming at each other to be heard. There was shrill laughter, the sound of an occasional breaking glass. Cigarette smoke hung in the air like fog. On a small stage a band thumped out 'Oh, Johnny, Oh, Johnny' and drunks sang along with the woman crooner, whose voice was cracking.

A blonde and a redhead came over to them as they reached the bar.

'More fighter boys, Phyllis,' the redhead said. 'We are being honoured tonight.'

'Well,' said Phyllis, 'aren't you going to buy a girl a drink?'

'Sure,' said Ossie, 'as long as it's soda.'

'Wise guy,' said Phyllis. Her face was painted on her head like a doll's, her small mouth widened with lipstick. 'Hey, are you a Yank?'

'Are you?' said Ossie.

'Do I sound like one?' The girl was pleased.

They cleared some space for themselves at the bar and ordered whisky. The bottle, when it arrived, was labelled Fine Old Scotch. Ossie noticed that the wire seal on the metal cap was missing. It came with five glasses: three large, two small. The women were quick to take the small ones, turning them between their slender fingers. Ossie flipped off the cap with his thumb and poured them both a slug. They sat looking at it. The redhead was biting her scarlet lip. 'Go ahead,' said Ossie. 'What are you waiting for?'

'You,' said Phyllis. 'It's not polite to start on your own.'

'Whatever you're doing,' said the redhead, and laughed a thin, forced laugh. She was glancing from face to face. Ossie guessed she was working out whom she disliked least, who looked softest. Her eyes rested on Dick Little, who was hanging back, saying nothing, looking vulnerable, wanting to be in Bristol.

Ossie poured a little liquid from the bottle. The colour was right, pale gold, but the liquor burned his mouth, like the moonshine he had drunk as a kid in St Louis speakeasies. He pushed the bottle back. 'Bartender,' he said, 'get me the real stuff.'

The barman rested his hands on the bar, not touching the bottle. 'You opened that. You pay for it. Rule of the house. Four pounds.'

'If we drank this stinking hooch we'd never fly again. Get me the real stuff.'

A fat man in a tuxedo, smoking a cigar, came across. He nodded at the women and they started to get down from their stools and move away. He sniffed the bottle. 'Nothing wrong with that. What's the problem?'

'Who are you?' said Ossie.

'We don't want any trouble,' said the fat man. 'Why spoil everybody's fun?'

'Who *are* you?'

'Nicco Demakis,' said the fat man. 'I own this club.' He allowed a trickle of cigar smoke to drift in Ossie's direction, his cheeks distended, pale and waxy.

'We don't want trouble either,' said Ossie. 'We just want whisky we can drink without losing our goddamned eyesight or going crazy.'

'You damned pilots,' said Demakis. 'You think you're God's gift.' He was smiling but his eyes were expressionless.

'That's right, Nicco,' said Ossie. 'We're crackerjack.' He turned away. 'Like I say, we'll take some real stuff, Bell's, Glenlivet, VAT 69, as long as it's in a sealed bottle. We'll get ourselves a table and you can bring it over. Clean glasses, mind.'

They started to force their way through the crowd. People were trying to dance, rubbing up against each other, laughing. There were plenty of uniforms and women in cheap dresses.

Drongo was shouting over Ossie's shoulder: 'You sure trod on that whacker's corns.'

'The crooked sonofabitch,' said Ossie. 'We ought to work this place over.'

Then he saw the table in the corner. Three Air Force uniforms and a Latin-looking girl, very cute, in a low-cut green dress. One of the uniforms was standing up, holding out a hand like it was welcoming guests to a country-house weekend. It was Kit Curtis and next to him, not standing but holding a cigarette in a holder with a twisted hand, was Buster Brown, the eyes the same and the set of the head, but the flesh of his face distorted and his hair burned away on the left side of his skull. The cute girl in green was stroking the cheek of a very young pilot officer who gazed at her blearily, struggling to keep his eyes in focus. He had a bottle on the table in front of him labelled Fine Old Scotch. It was almost empty.

'Hello,' said Kit Curtis.

'Hello,' said Ossie, falling into the English way, not asking why they were there. 'Last time I heard you were on the Hallelujah Trail.'

'Something like that.'

Ossie nodded at the almost empty bottle. 'I'd get the kid off that rot-gut. Guys have been paralysed drinking fake whisky. I've fixed for us to get some good stuff.'

'We're celebrating,' said the pilot officer. 'Celebrating my engagement. Meet Rita, the woman I'm going to marry.' He leaned over and kissed the girl in green on the neck.

'This is Frazer Cole,' said Kit. Then, lowering his tone: 'He wanted us to meet his fiancée at his club. We didn't realise it was this kind of club.'

'Or this kind of fiancée,' said Buster Brown.

'Hey, Buster,' said Ossie, staring him straight in the eye. 'You look like hell.'

'Thanks, old boy,' said Buster. 'At least I've got an excuse.'

'The quacks have told Buster he won't fly again,' said Kit. 'We popped up to town to help him drown his sorrows.'

'What do those medico bastards know?' said Ossie.

'They're not all bastards,' said Buster Brown. 'Although you think they are when they dip you in a saline bath.'

'Meet the woman I'm going to marry,' said Frazer Cole.

'You told us already,' said Ossie. He jerked a thumb at his companions.

'Drongo Palmer, Dick Little.'

'Drongo?' said Buster.

'A dumb animal that flies,' said Ossie. He picked up the bottle with its crooked label and stood it on the floor.

The pilot officer frowned, then shrugged and grinned. He kissed the neck of the girl in green again.

The band had picked up 'Love Is The Sweetest Thing', tuneful and tender. The girl started to hum along. She made quite a picture, the pilot officer's head snuggled into her long neck, the upper part of her breasts quivering as she moved. Ossie had always liked that. She was honey-coloured, her face long with prominent cheeks, her teeth strong and white; the face of a flamenco *danzante*.

'So you're the blushing bride-to-be,' he said.

'That's what they tell me,' said the girl.

'Bollocks to that,' muttered Drongo Palmer in Ossie's ear. 'She hasn't blushed since she was six.'

'Planning a long engagement?' said Ossie.

'I wouldn't say we're actually engaged,' said the girl. 'That was his idea.' Frazer Cole had closed his eyes. 'He's very sweet, but you know what they say. Never fall for a fighter boy.'

'Is that what they say?'

'That's what Nicco says. If we fell for fighter boys then where would we be?'

'Yeah, where would you be? What if they fall for you?'

'They're so young. They don't know what it's all about.'

'I guess you know what it's all about, all right,' said Ossie. 'Maybe you'd better tell him when he comes round.' He turned away, but he didn't want to. He wanted to continue taking her in, storing away the details of her, so she could play a part in some future dream, when he needed a dream like that.

On the dance-floor couples were shuffling slowly round, holding each other close. In the dim light they looked like real lovers. A bottle of Johnnie Walker arrived, its metal cap sealed. It looked all right but Ossie unscrewed the cap and took a swig straight from the bottle before handing the barman a five-pound note. 'Brother, what a racket.'

'This place was Cole's idea,' said Kit Curtis. 'Can't say I care for it overmuch. Some rum coves knocking about—' He broke off as Ossie laughed. 'What's funny?'

'Not a thing,' Ossie said. 'So tell me, how was it acting the hero?'

He knew that Kit had been despatched on some kind of propaganda stunt, talks to boost morale in factories, after he had busted an arm in a rough-house in the mess, playing indoor rugby with the student pilots. And so, grounded, he had missed out on the main event.

'It made me realise we're not the only ones doing our bit,' said Kit. He described the works canteens, the rows of upturned faces as he mumbled his way through his notes, the bigwigs pumping his hand, hoping some of the glory would rub off, spreads laid out in panelled boardrooms, where company directors munched their way through fish-paste sandwiches and talked of biffing the Hun, while on the factory floor the workers went back to their machines.

'But you're operational now,' said Ossie.

'Convoy protection,' said Kit. 'Cover for Blenheims. The usual stuff these days. And you?'

'Ditto, in the ass-end of nowhere. I'm angling for a posting closer to the action but so far no dice.'

'Even if you pull it off you'll probably find it's not the kind of action you're after,' said Kit. 'Sounds as though we're both in the same boat.'

'To hell with boats,' said Ossie.

Frazer Cole was moving slowly round the dance-floor with Rita. He was very tall and occasionally, as he stooped to whisper in the girl's ear, he lost his balance and swayed dangerously. The girl steadied him and they moved on, lost in the swirl of people. The song was almost finished.

Watching them, Ossie reckoned that fate might bring Frazer Cole any number of things but it wasn't likely to be love's story. They were coming off the dance-floor now, the pilot officer releasing his hold on the girl reluctantly. He tried to take her hand but she slipped it free and fanned it in front of her face, cooling herself, pursing her lips. She was glowing with sweat. A trickle ran down from her temple and was lost between her breasts. Ossie saw she was looking across the dance-floor to the bar. Demakis was there, lighting a fresh cigar, talking to the barman and another man, bigger, broader, with a flattened nose.

The girl wriggled down between Ossie and Buster Brown. Frazer Cole stood uncertainly in front of them. 'Budge up, can't you? Give a chap a bit of space.'

'Can't be bothered to move old boy,' said Buster. 'Besides, I want to get to know the future Mrs Cole.'

The girl laughed. She gave no sign of revulsion at being so close to this ruin of a man. Either she had good instincts, Ossie thought, or she didn't give a damn. 'He wants me to meet his people,' she was saying. 'They own a hotel in Hove. Very genteel. Can you imagine?'

'I can imagine you in quite a lot of situations,' Buster said, and she laughed again. Ossie felt her warmth against him. She knew he was there and was leaning on him a little. He felt a stiffening. He understood all about her, and so did Buster, unlike Frazer Cole, the two-bit mug, who didn't understand a thing. He'd also understood the glance she'd shot at Demakis, the fat Greek. It didn't matter. He'd settle for whatever she was prepared to give, later, after the others had gone.

'Why don't you put the poor sucker out of his misery?' he said.

She turned and looked at him, her eyebrows raised. 'Misery?

I'm sure I don't know what you mean.' She gave him the official line but her eyes told him something else. He noticed she affected a refined English accent that slipped a little, phoney but kind of touching.

'Sure you do,' he said. 'It doesn't matter. Have a drink. A proper drink.'

Across the table Frazer Cole had the face of a kid who'd lost his candy. 'She comes from Camden Town,' he was telling Drongo Palmer. 'Have you ever been to Camden Town?'

'That reminds me,' said Buster. 'Damndest thing. I was telling Kit. Something I saw in Hampstead. Or someone.'

'Hampstead?' said Ossie.

Kit had overheard. 'I think we may have solved a mystery. At least, partly.'

'The quacks booked me in to the New End Hospital,' said Buster, 'just off the Heath. Thyroid specialists. You know, throat stuff. Seemed I might have singed some glands that control the larynx. If I had it could have affected my vocal cords. Not good for a new-bug controller. Anyway, I hadn't. So after they'd given me a clean bill of health I strolled up to the Holly Bush for a jar. That was when I saw her.'

'The mystery her?' said Ossie.

'Absolutely,' said Buster. 'Coming out of a block of flats in Holly Hill.'

'Hannah,' said Kit. 'Hannah Maierscheldt.'

'The vanishing lady,' said Ossie. 'How did she look?'

'I'd say England agreed with her.'

'You're sure it was her?'

'Well,' Buster hesitated, 'pretty sure. Except . . .'

'Except?'

'I don't recall her being quite such a cracker.'

'Did she see you?' said Ossie.

'She noticed me,' said Buster Brown, 'but she didn't recognise me, which is hardly surprising.'

Ossie turned to Kit. 'This is screwy. She's like a sister to you, right?'

'I suppose you could say that.'

'You've known her since you were kids, your families were real close, then she escapes from France but her mom and dad don't make it, so she's alone. And still she doesn't get in touch? C'mon.'

'Well,' said Kit, 'perhaps she's not quite ready yet.'

'Ready for what?'

'Pretty traumatic, you know, what's she's been through. I think I understand.'

'Really?'

'No. Let's change the subject.'

On the other side of the table Frazer Cole was reaching for the Johnnie Walker. Ossie moved the bottle out of reach. 'Easy, kid. Any more and they'll be pouring you into the cockpit.'

'Perfectly *compos mentis*, thanks,' said Cole, speaking very carefully. 'Ten minutes with the old oxygen mask before take-off and I'll be as right as rain.'

'Yeah,' said Ossie. 'We all know the morning-after routine. But you've taken a real load on.'

The redhead had come over. She was talking to Dick Little, murmuring softly, rubbing his thigh. 'You seem a nice boy, darling. Why don't you buy a girl a drink? I'd love a liqueur. Why don't you treat me to a liqueur? I'd be ever so grateful.'

Little looked at her dully. 'Leave me alone. I'm married.'

'Well, fuck you, darling,' said the redhead, and went back to the bar. She was talking to Demakis and the man with the flattened nose. They stared across at the pilots, listening, nodding.

Ossie watched them out of the corner of his eye. His heart-rate had increased a little. He recognised it for what it meant.

He knew the signs, after a hundred bars, clubs and drinking dens from the Mississippi levees in St Louis to the little alleys off the Ramblas in Barcelona, from the dark corners of the Pigalle to this crummy joint in Tenison Court.

Kit Curtis had stood up, unaware. 'Well,' he said wryly, 'it's been a delightful evening.'

The girl Rita allowed herself to be embraced by Frazer Cole. He was acting very serious, trying to be dignified, wanting to leave her with a good impression. 'Well goodbye, dear. We really must get down to Hove. My parents are dying to meet you.' The 'dear' made him sound middle-aged.

'Yes, all right,' said Rita, like a nurse addressing a patient, soothing and detached; just another case to be dealt with.

Kit shook Ossie's hand again. Ossie was amused by the formality. 'Well, cheerio,' said Kit.

'So long, pard.'

'Yes, absolutely.'

Buster Brown was going too. 'Good luck, you infernal Yank.' He gave Ossie a nudge with his folded-in fist. 'Incidentally, if you've got designs on the future Mrs Cole I think she may be spoken for. I'd be careful there.'

'You don't mean the crazy kid?'

'You know what I mean. An overgrown schoolboy is one thing, business as usual, but a bolshie little bugger from Missouri who knows what's what is another.' He looked at Demakis, who was making his way round the tables, jovial, leaning into conversations, waving his big cigar to emphasise a point, its ruby-red glow tracing patterns against the shadows. 'These types are not to be crossed. Be a pity to lose a decent pilot over a cheap tart.'

'I don't reckon she's so cheap,' said Ossie.

'Whatever the price, you can't afford it, old boy,' said Buster.

'You might end up like me, a bloody penguin. Got wings, can't fly.' His mouth tightened into a crooked grin. 'You can certainly pick 'em.'

'How'd you figure that?'

'The mademoiselle you were so hung up on in France.'

'Bébé Dubretskov.'

'That's her. The little countess who killed herself. Funny that.'

'Funny? How?'

'She never struck me as the kind to do something like that. Not a quitter. Always an eye for the main chance. But I don't need to tell you that.'

'No,' said Ossie. 'She was quite a gal.'

'Certainly gave you the run-around,' said Buster. 'And a lot of others too. But I'll tell you something else that's funny. That girl I saw in Holly Hill, I'd have said she was Dubretskov, if I hadn't known she's dead.'

'So you're on hanging on for a bit,' said the girl in the green dress.

'That's right,' said Ossie. 'I'm hanging on. For a bit.'

'You'd better buy me a liqueur.'

'Bull,' said Ossie.

'I can't stay here, then.' She moved, and the stuff of her dress rustled.

Ossie caught the drift of her perfume, not cloying but subtle and light, a reminder of many things: lemon groves, maybe, under a hot sun, or the tang of breaking surf. Ossie's mouth was dry from looking at her. He signalled to the barman.

'That's half-a-crown,' the man said, placing the fluted glass of pink liquid in front of the girl. Ossie reached across and tasted it.

'Uh-huh,' he said. 'You won't get a headache from drinking that.'

The girl laughed. Then her face went serious. 'You know you're wasting your time,' she said.

'Oh, sure,' said Ossie. 'You're already engaged.'

'You know what I mean.'

'People keep on telling me I know what they mean. Why don't you tell me what you mean?'

'I don't have to.' She touched his arm. 'Look, I know you think you're different from the others. Maybe you are. But I've got no time for you or anybody else.'

'Only the fat boy, huh?'

'What's the point in this? Nicco doesn't like me getting too involved. Nasty things happen. I don't want that to happen to you.'

'You're breaking my heart,' said Ossie.

The Greek was quite close now. She cracked a bright, false smile. 'What do you fly?' she said.

'Classified.'

'Fighters, I bet. You don't look like a bomber boy to me.'

'What do they look like, then?'

'Sensible,' she said.

'You ought to get out of this lousy joint,' he said.

'For what? Cut my hair and work in a factory fourteen hours a day? Or join up and live in a hut for five bob a week? No, thanks.'

He knew it was hopeless but he couldn't let go. He wanted to play it to the end. Nicco Demakis helped him. He slid in beside the girl and ran his arm round her waist. 'This is mine,' the gesture said. 'You've been suckered, just like that scrawny kid.'

'I don't like what you're doing here,' said Ossie.

The Greek took a long drag on his cigar. 'You're very particular for a fellow who looks as though he knows the ropes.'

'Maybe that's why I'm particular.'

'This is a club like any other. We give the punters what they want.'

'Correction,' said Ossie. 'You give them stuff that looks like what they want.'

'Haven't you heard? Things are getting scarce. You have to get the product where you can.'

'And sell it how you can.' Ossie glanced at the girl, then back at the Greek. 'Your cigar's gone out.'

Drongo Palmer put a heavy hand on Ossie's shoulder. 'I reckon it's time to shove off, mate.' Dick Little was already moving towards the door.

'So soon?' said the Greek. He relit his cigar, smacking his lips, watching the flame of the match burn down and touch his skin, before flicking it into an ashtray. 'So easy to get your fingers burned,' he said. 'Anyway, fighter boy, you can't leave yet. You've got a bill to settle first.'

'I'm paid up, brother,' Ossie said.

'Four pounds,' said Demakis. 'Four pounds for the whisky you opened and didn't drink.' The flat-nosed man was standing next to him, clasping and unclasping his hands.

That old maxim came into Ossie's head, the one he had lived by for a long time now. 'Do it to him before he does it to you.'

He leaned forward and pushed the palm of his hand against the end of the Greek's cigar. It flattened against the man's face, embers dropping down the front of his dinner jacket. He spat it out, roaring, and began to rise. Ossie hit him over the head with the half-empty Johnnie Walker bottle. Demakis fell back, blood running down his face, rolled sideways and disappeared under the table.

The flat-nosed man reached in to seize Ossie by the collar of his tunic. Ossie's head was under his chin. He raised it sharply and heard the man's teeth snap together. He reeled back, holding his jaw, and Ossie kicked him between the legs.

The girl was screaming, the palms of her hands flat over her ears. Tables and chairs crashed down as people struggled to get clear, some sprawling in a mess of broken glass. Ossie saw the redhead staggering towards the bar, a deep gash on her leg, not making a sound, dumb with shock.

On the stage the woman singer ran into the drummer, and hi-hats, bass drums, snares and cymbals went down with a brassy crash that rang through the club like a musical finale.

Behind the bar the barman had picked up a telephone and was dialling a number, his hand shaking. Ossie stepped over the flat-nosed man, who was squirming on the floor. He went behind the bar. The barman shrank away, the telephone still in his hand. A tinny voice was sounding at the other end.

Ossie took the phone and listened for a moment. 'All right, all right,' a voice was saying. 'We'll get there straight away.' The girl in the green dress was bending down, looking under the table at the Greek. She was trembling, crying.

Drongo Palmer had the doorman pinned against the wall by his neck, his feet barely touching the floor. He released him and the man fell forward, coughing. Clutching his throat, he unchained the door and swung it open, stepping back to let them pass out into the street.

Ossie felt good. Drongo Palmer was laughing. Dick Little was shaking his head. 'For Christ's sake, haven't you silly bastards had your fill of fighting?'

'He called you a silly bastard, sir,' said Drongo.

'I show you guys a good time,' said Ossie, 'and that's the thanks I get.'

The air-raid was over. The stench of cordite and burning buildings carried on an easterly breeze. Ambulance and fire bells could still be heard but the bombers had gone and the guns were silent. The heels of their shoes made a clatter as they walked away, not towards Regent Street but down Tenison Court in the direction of Kingly Street. Ossie was careful not to hurry.

'There's a place in Soho I heard about . . .' Drongo Palmer tailed off. A squad of policemen had burst round the corner of Kingly Street. The airmen halted. 'Strewth,' said Drongo. 'How did those buggers get here so fast?' But the policemen ran straight past them. The door of the Blue Diamond was kicked back and they could hear shouts and screams from inside.

'Looks like we got out just in time,' said Ossie. Then, behind them, a vehicle drew up and studded boots scraped on the pavement. 'Stay where you are,' a voice bellowed. 'Nobody leaves the area.' They turned and saw three red-capped military policemen coming down the road, walking abreast, smiling, enjoying the job they were about to do.

'Does this mean I'm going to miss my train?' said Dick Little.

Four weeks later Sergeant Pilot Dick Little missed another train from Paddington, the midday service to Plymouth. This time he was very happy about it. But still it seemed incredible. Ossie Wolf had made a phone call, talked to someone he knew who was ready to take his place on the overseas roster. It meant Little could stay on with the squadron. Soon his wife had taken a room in a boarding-house in Holyhead so they saw each other quite often, when he wasn't on patrol fifty miles out, over the Irish Sea.

The Plymouth train was slow, rumbling through towns with names that meant nothing to Ossie Wolf and Drongo Palmer: Slough, Reading, Newbury, Hungerford. And as the hours passed, the West Country stops, Dawlish, Newton Abbot, where they crossed the valley of the Dart, and Totnes, waking memories in some of the others of long holidays, the sound of gulls and barking dogs, the lap of waves and distant laughter, the building of castles in the sand, castles that had seemed strong and likely to survive until the sea swept in and they were washed away. All this passed Wolf and Palmer by, the only pilots of the six in the compartment who knew each other. At Paddington there had been the usual brief introductions but names had quickly been forgotten, except for the light-haired sergeant in the corner reading *Lilliput*. 'I'm Brian Twigg.' He had grinned. 'You might as well call me Twiggy. Everybody does.' After that the rest said little. Mostly they dozed or rubbed away the condensation on the window and watched the countryside from their window. Ossie guessed they were saying goodbye.

Kit Curtis wasn't with them. He hadn't made this trip. His squadron had been in no hurry for him to leave. He was going later, on a carrier, lucky sonofabitch. That was something Ossie liked the sound of, a fly-off with no time to practise, a tough test of flying skill, no question. Instead, he and the rest were shipping out of Plymouth next morning, on board a Granny, a bumbling Short Sunderland flying-boat, bound for Malta, some crummy little patch of earth at the far end of the Med, its only value its location, perfectly positioned to harry Hun supply lines between Italy and North Africa. Except the garrison wasn't doing much harrying at the moment but simply hanging on, being bombed to buggery by all accounts, likely to be invaded at any moment, which meant they could all end up in the bag.

Suddenly Anglesey didn't seem so bad – Dick Little, for example, enjoying home comforts with his moon-eyed bride when he wasn't flying. But maybe that was as it should be. The kid hadn't even thrown a punch in the Blue Diamond, Ossie reflected, so it was only fair that he had managed to pull it off, to get Kit Curtis to take his place, to give him some more time for that bony little wife of his because, like all of them, nobody knew how much time they might have left. But trying to make sure that Little was in the clear had been only part of that rugged grilling by the new squadron leader back at base, after the cops in London had let them go.

'Do you deny you struck this fellow Demakis first, an unprovoked attack?'

'I struck him first, sir, no question, but I'd say it was provoked.'

'Explain.'

'These guys are selling hooch to pilots like us when the country needs us most. Some of the stuff is lethal.'

'It's not your job to sort them out. The police can take care of that. You saw them raid the club that night. They had the matter well in hand. The place had been under surveillance for weeks. They even had their own man in there, behind the bar.'

'Uh-huh. Okay. We couldn't work out how they got there so quick.'

'You went to that club looking for trouble, Wolf, and when the opportunity presented itself you took the law into your own hands. That's the truth of it, isn't it?'

'Something like, I guess.'

'You've brought disrepute to the service, Wolf. Only your flying record has saved you from a court-martial and demotion. You've been guilty of behaviour totally at odds with what we expect of an officer, a thoroughly bad example to the men who serve under you. I'm posting all three of you overseas with immediate effect. The squadron is better off without ill-disciplined louts. Anything to say?'

'Yes, sir. Sergeant Little played no part in any of it.'

'He was there. I understand he made no attempt to detach himself from what went on. He was with you when you were arrested.'

'That's correct, sir, but he wasn't involved in any way. In fact, he'd just expressed the opinion that Sergeant Palmer and I were silly bastards who ought to have had our fill of fighting.'

'In that, of course, he was bang on. Tell him to report to me. If what you say is true I might be prepared to let him stay on, but only if he can find someone to replace him.'

'Thank you, sir.'

'You're a damned fool, Wolf, and a troublemaker. I hope you've learned from this. Keep your fighting instinct for the Luftwaffe. Don't waste it on petty spivs or anyone else who happens to annoy you, out of the line of duty. However, I suppose I should tell you that this Demakis character is facing a twelve-month prison sentence and his club has been placed out of bounds to officers and men, effectively putting it out of business.'

'That's good news, sir.'

'The pity of it is, Wolf, that it would have happened anyway. Meanwhile your stupid irresponsibility has cost me experienced pilots I can ill afford to lose. Your record will follow you, wherever you end up, have no doubt of that. Now get weaving. You're operational while you're here and you're on patrol in forty minutes. You've got a lot of ground to make up. I suggest you start the process now.'

The Plymouth train was crossing the Ivybridge viaduct, the wheels of the carriages sounding hollow against the space below, with the rising hills of Dartmoor to the north. The sky was streaked pink, promising good weather for the following day. The fragrance of heather and bracken drifted in through the open window, mixed with the smell of grey-black smoke billowing back from the locomotive. A glowing smut landed on Ossie's tunic, just below his pilot's wings; he brushed it to the floor and ground it under his shoe. He worked at the fragments until they were no more than powder. There was a bitter taste in his mouth that he reckoned must come from burning coal.

A fifteen-hundredweight Bedford truck was waiting for them at the Plymouth terminus. It took them to a cheap hotel. After a meal they made their way through the Barbican's labyrinth of lanes and alleys to the Dolphin Inn. But no one felt much like drinking and they turned in early, sleeping badly.

They were woken at dawn for breakfast. The same truck delivered them to Cattewater Harbour where the two great hangars of the Mount Batten seaplane base rose up beyond the shoreline and half a dozen Sunderlands tugged at their moorings, big and ponderous, like tethered circus beasts waiting for their act to be announced. A tender took the men out to their aircraft, slapping through the chop, the spray fresh and cold on their faces, coating their service caps with a fine mist of salt. The dull green interior of the seaplane's hull was stark and functional, stripped down to essentials, its portholes blacked out, rudimentary canvas seats bolted to the floor. On the forward upper deck they could see the crew: two pilots, flight engineer, wireless operator, navigator; five men who would take them to that distant touch-down in Kalafrana Bay.

The Australian first pilot clambered down to greet them. 'You blokes may think you've got a boring flight ahead. Personally I like to keep it that way. But if you're looking for excitement there are a couple of spots to watch out for. Near Brest, about ninety minutes out, we're within range of free-hunt Me 109s so we'll follow a course due west, as far out from the peninsula as we can, and we'll also be flying low, under the Jerries' radar cover. The second dodgy area comes three hours later, heading south across the Bay of Biscay. There we're up against long-range Ju 88s operating from Bordeaux. All being well, however, we'll arrive in Gib about ten hours from now. Make yourselves comfortable and enjoy your trip. The stewardess will be round after take-off to take your order for cocktails.'

No 109s were seen, no Ju 88s, no stewardess. But, like the others, Ossie Wolf was unable to relax. He did not like the thought of someone else at the controls, his fate resting in another man's hands. The seaplane crew seemed capable enough but he knew this fat old Granny was dead-meat if a keen-eyed bogey spotted them. Unless he was in the cockpit, in which case he reckoned they might have a chance.

After nine hours in the air, off the Portuguese coast, the navigator reported their position: due west of Cape St Vincent, world's end to the ancients, Europe's most south-westerly point, its cliffs as grey as the Atlantic pounding the jumbled rocks. The Sunderland turned south-east maintaining cruising speed at 140 m.p.h., the note of its four Pegasus engines constant and reassuring.

Not long after take-off the pilots had given up trying to be heard above the thunder of the air-cooled radials but that was not the only reason for their silence. Now, as the outline of Gibraltar sharpened through the windscreen of the flight-deck, they began to talk and joke and laugh even though the stopover was a short one and soon they would be heading east, towards the enemy.

The Sunderland banked round, losing height west of the Rock, its hull skimming the surface of a calmer sea. It eased down, starting to part the waves and finally settled, rising and falling, the water slamming against its nose as it surged towards its mooring buoy. The pilots gathered by the forward hatch. It was odd to see the shimmering lights of Gibraltar and, beyond it, Algeciras and the frontier of Spain; a surprise to realise how quickly, back in Britain, blackout had become a way of life.

No hotel room this time, a few drinks only at the Bristol, a saunter round the shops and bazaars, ears still ringing from the engine roar, buying nothing, unable to understand the cries of the street vendors, seeing only white teeth against brown faces, the heat extreme, their uniforms sticking to their backs, each casual beer inducing another rush of sweat; and women passing, eyes shining, heads turned, looking back over bare shoulders as they were lost to sight in the throng. And the sky blue-black, pierced with a million points of light. Then moving back to the assembly point, down by the quay. Voices in the darkness, the tender bumping against the harbour wall, water slopping over slippery steps, a clumsy sprawl into the gunwales, no one bothering to laugh; the burble of the in-board engine as the bow of the tender swung round and moved towards the silent Sunderland, passing over the dark and unseen waters of the harbour.

Tumbling, again unsteady, through the narrow forward hatch below the cockpit, windscreen glinting yards above, nostrils taking in the meld of fuel and metal, salt deposit and sour evidence of men. The cough, splutter, roar of engines firing up, one by one, the bare-boned carcass of the great machine shuddering under power as the mooring rope was loosed, splashed down, was coiled back inside the hull. Pushing through the darkness now, white bow-wave spreading from its nose, turning into wind and gathering speed, bouncing, bouncing, lifting, finally free, and climbing, banking onto an easterly course with a thousand miles to cover, flying through the night, bound for Malta, landing at first light, before the raiders of the Luftwaffe and the Regia Aeronautica launched their attacks and, for the defenders, another day began.

The interior of the Sunderland was dimly lit. The faces of the pilots had a bilious hue, the feeble yellow light reflecting on the matt-green paintwork. For eight hours they had moved with the pitch and roll of the aircraft, the vibration from the engines pulsing through their bodies like a constant electrical charge.

They had passed through storms, buffeted by turbulence, engine revolutions rising, falling as the throttles were adjusted to maintain speed and altitude, throwing them against each other, or the metal formers of the fuselage, as the seaplane dropped three hundred feet, flattening out at last, pressing their chins against their chests. In a lull the navigator worked his way back from the flight-deck, stepping between them, heading for the lavatory in the stern.

'Where are we, mate?' said Drongo Palmer.

'Due south of Cagliari,' said the navigator. 'Sardinia. Mostly Eyeties there. Don't reckon they'll come out to play. It's Pantelleria you want to get in a fret about. Coming up in about ninety minutes. Those flaming 109s.'

'We like flaming 109s,' said Drongo.

The navigator grinned. 'Another three hours, fellers, and we'll be there.' He had picked up Drongo's accent. 'Where you from?'

'Melbourne,' said Drongo. 'You?'

'Brisbane. Ever been there?'

'Me and my old man were there in 'thirty-one. Saw Bradman get his two hundred and twenty-six against the South Africans at the Gabba.'

'Would you reckon it? I was there myself. The Don gave it a fair old do that day.' The navigator paused. It was clear his thoughts, like Palmer's, had switched to another time, another place, where a game that had seemed important had been played out to time-honoured rules, understood, respected. Compared with this bigger game, where rules were scant, more often flouted, a contest between twenty-two men in white appeared trivial, without meaning, a childish pastime. He nodded briefly, his full-stop to the conversation, and moved away, holding out his arms, balancing himself like a tight-rope walker, wanting a piss not a trip down bloody Memory Lane.

Pantelleria fell away to port. No bandits. A panorama of many blues, shading subtly into greens, and greys where land thrust through the sea. No sign of man at all, as though millennia had been wiped away. The Sunderland turned onto the final dog-leg course to Malta. Within an hour the island began to unfold beneath them, glimpsed between low streaks of cloud, already breaking up: in the hinterland small farms, terraced fields, dust-white lanes; a sprawl of buildings clustered round a church, pretending to be a town; and Valletta, silent and exposed, gathered on its promontory, graceful-looking, pierced by parks and squares, cut across by steep and narrow streets of ancient shuttered houses, tier on tier, looking out over waving palms towards Grand Harbour where shipping lay at anchor or was berthed alongside in the creeks.

The wind was from the south. The Sunderland passed low above the city, and landed smoothly south of Delimara Point. It taxied in and took up its mooring in the sheltered waters of the encircling Kalafrana Bay. Its engines, after eleven hours, were finally shut down. But as their thunder died away the moan and wail of sirens rose and, far to the north, but not so far, the tump-tump-tump of guns began.

'The bloody Blue Diamond. If we hadn't wound up there that night we wouldn't be here now.' Sure enough Drongo Palmer, stretched out on his bed and yawning in the small tent with the sides that rolled up or down, was ploughing the same damned furrow. It wasn't the first time and Ossie knew it wouldn't be the last. Drongo usually dragged it up when he'd got the twitch and his nerves were raw, like now, when he'd been so close to Death he could smell his breath. But Ossie didn't waste time brooding. So he'd punched the Greek's lights out that night in Tenison Court. So what? The creep had been about to make his move. He'd beaten him to it, like he'd beaten guys in the air by thumbing his gun-button hundredths of a second before they did. End of story. He didn't regret a thing. And, hell, maybe in Malta they were living rough and grub was short and what little they got was crummy; maybe they were outnumbered ten or even twenty to one and when you heard the bogeys were coming in from the north you had to struggle to gain height south of the island, out of their reach, before you turned back in again to hit the bastards, thanks to the poor old Hurry's lousy rate of climb. All of this was how it was, but countered by the happy fact that there were no more Big Wings crawling across the sky, with stiff-necked characters just waiting for you to step out of line, ready to have your guts if you didn't hold formation; no more tripping over yourself trying to match your speed to Blenheims crawling their way to targets on the Pas de Calais flat-lands, trying to protect the poor sods' hides when they turned for home, shot full of holes; no more waiting for the Merlin to miss a beat, way out to sea, where the convoy crews could only watch as you went to the bottom, thanks to a failed component worth a dollar.

Though it wasn't strictly true about Big Wings. There were Big Wings, all right, but they bore the black crosses of the Reich and the picky little black and white insignia of the Regia Aeronautica, said to be a symbol of authority from ancient Rome, a bundle of rods with projecting axe-blades known as *fasces*; an easy gag for those who wrote off the Eyeties as a shit air force, a judgement that had proved a little hasty . . .

For some of the guys arriving on the island, Ossie knew, it had seemed a kind of purgatory, a place in which they found themselves because, somehow, some way, someone had concluded they hadn't cut the mustard. They came to it with a dangerous sense of having failed, usually a question mark about how good they were as pilots. And so, deep inside themselves, they doubted their ability to survive – and they were right: two weeks was average. Others found it difficult to adjust to the looseness of living under siege, the falling away of differences in rank and class, the need for officers to work shoulder-to-shoulder with the men, constructing blast pens, clearing runways, manning machine-gun posts; they found it hard to accept the crudeness of everyday existence where everything was in short supply, except dust, disease and ever-present danger.

But to Ossie, and some others, Malta seemed a promised land, a dream where scrambles happened many times a day, a handful of machines, no more, only flying thanks to spares retrieved from wrecks, throttles wide and bucking along the cratered runways, often quickly on their own, rising to meet the Ju 88s advancing in mass sweeps with fighter escorts stacked above; where every skill you'd ever learned came into play, juggling with position, hiding in the sun, choosing your prey and diving down, one to one, focussed on this single target, aware of other threats but ignoring them for now, no distractions, waiting, waiting, careful not to rush it, screwing up one eye behind your goggles, judging the angle of deflection, always more than you might think and loosing, finally, the Brownings and seeing the enemy, swallowed in smoke and flame, roll onto its back and fall away, diving vertically into the sea, leaving a neat white circle against the green. But not hanging around to admire your work. That way you'd make a neat white circle of your own. Instead pulling back on the stick, throttle through the gate, scrabbling for height, knowing even fifty feet could make the difference, head screwing right and left, up and down, eyes straining for another bogey so you could do it all again. Single combat, every instinct and reaction down to you, no orders crackling in the earphones of your helmet. Knocking down the sons-of-bitches and claiming back the sky; a sky they had no right to, like the sky of England where they'd found themselves kicked back across the Channel, wondering why the numbers hadn't worked, how just a handful had beaten back the air force of the most heavily armed nation in the world.

This was how it was, for Ossie and men like him, but gradually they had found they were not alone, that with every passing week and month there grew a unity, a common purpose, in the air and on the ground. Pilots who doubted their ability to survive, but somehow did, came to realise they were better than they knew. Others grew to understand that deeds spoke for them, not how many rings were on their sleeves or codes of behaviour that now seemed laughable, belonging to another place and time. They came to find, whatever their nationality, and there were many, that somehow they had become the same, understanding the role they had to play, sharing hardship, working together to endure, seeing the island as an aerodrome of pink and ochre rock, a long, long way from home, hard to supply but tougher to defeat, resolved to resist and fight back, despite the odds. 'We won the Battle of Britain. We're going to win this too.'

And when they paraded for grey-haired men with scrambled-egg peaks who walked up and down their lines and looked from face to face, each one shared the same expression and the grey-haired men quickly sensed that there was no need for stirring phrases or even praise, just support to keep them supplied and in the air. But in the air with what?

A few days before, outside Dispersal, Ossie had cornered a squadron leader, his tunic bare of wings. 'What me and the boys would like to know is when in hell we're going to get some Spitfires.'

The man had looked at his watch, irritated at being detained. He was on his way to Lascaris Control in Valletta with some statistics for the Air Officer Commanding. 'I really can't be badgered like this. There's a time and a place. And, anyway, as the AOC points out, it isn't the aeroplane, it's the man.'

Ossie's face had changed colour but that was the only sign of how close the squadron leader had come to being late for his appointment. He mentioned the incident now.

Brian Twigg snorted. 'It's like it was in France. Whitehall reckons we're going down so why take decent aircraft with us?'

'Maybe,' said Ossie. 'Except this Russian deal, if it's on the level, means Kesselring's going to be after every goddamned airplane he can rustle up. And that includes the bastards across the water. No more sunbathing for those suckers. They'll be up to their asses in snow before you can say Hermann Goering. The Hun thinks he's got us pinned down good, that the Eyeties can keep it that way, that Rommel can depend on getting what he needs. Well, we know different.' He took a cigarette from Drongo Palmer's pack of Woodbines. 'This is our chance to hit the Axis hard. If the big cheeses have got any sense they'll realise that and ship out Spits right away.'

'You've answered your own question,' said Twigg. 'They won't do a bloody thing.'

Drongo Palmer sat up, rubbing his face, as though it was morning. 'Well, I reckon we can handle anything the bloody Eyeties care to throw our way, Spits or no Spits. A bloke told me three Cants dumped their bomb-loads into the sea near Delimara Point a couple of days ago. Got in a panic when they spotted our boys. The locals were happy as pigs in mud. They rustled up everything that could float in Marsaxlokk and picked up more dead fish than they could catch in a month.'

'Radio Rome's been claiming they've bombed the marshalling yards at Kalafrana,' said Twigg, 'when everybody knows the only railtracks on the whole bloody island are those piddling little lines in the dockyard, where they move plant about. It's comic-opera stuff. If the Jerries do move out it'll be a turkey shoot.'

'You guys shouldn't be so cocky,' said Ossie. 'Remember that Macchi 200 me and Cavanagh came across? We chased that sonofabitch damned near to Sicily and he threw us every trick in the book. Ventilated Roy's tailplane good and almost got a bead on me. Then, when we ran low on gas and turned back for base, he turned with us and gave us one final blast. There are guys in the Regia who know their business, no question, and in their hands those damned Macchis are more than a match for the Hurry. If you reckon otherwise you'll wind up dead.'

'All the more reason to give us Spits,' said Palmer. Listening to the American his bravado had drained away. With the rest he liked to hear the latest yarns of Italian funk, scoff at their irresolution, feel that they were weak and not a serious threat. When a man like Ossie Wolf suggested otherwise, it stopped him short.

'Give us Spits?' said Twigg. 'Fat chance. We've had our reinforcements. All those ruddy museum pieces that flew in today. Quite good enough for the likes of us. Still, at least we won't have to play musical chairs, running round a bunch of kites fit for the scrapheap, trying to land a seat and finding every time there's one more missing.'

'You know who to blame for that,' said Ossie, nodding at Palmer.

'No one's going to nail me out of the sun again,' said Palmer. 'I reckon you learn by experience.'

'You've had the goddamned experience,' said Ossie. 'When are you going to learn?'

It was almost dark. Some miles away aero-engines fired up. 'That'll be the boys at Luqa,' said Twigg. 'Marylands and Blenheims. I saw them bombing up for a night attack. Jerry troop convoy heading for Tripoli.'

They had not lit a lamp. Occasionally their faces were illumined by a reddish glow as they drew on their cigarettes. They listened as the bellow of the distant engines rose to a crescendo. They could imagine the crews hunched at the controls, staring down the flare-path, the machines tugging against their brakes, heavy with a 2,000-pound bomb-load. The pilots would be thinking about those damned stone Maltese walls criss-crossing the fields beyond the base, thinking about dragging this weight of ordnance into the air before the runway ended, thinking about those times when Kenny or Les or poor old Bob hadn't made it, ploughing ahead, tyres barely leaving the ground, knowing what was to come, vaporised as the bombs detonated, lighting the sky with a sudden glow that quickly died, the explosion heard in Sicily.

Outside the tent someone was moving clumsily. There was a clatter, as though something metal, largish, had been dropped; then a mild and muttered curse; a click-click-clicking, familiar but at first unplaceable. Of course, a bike. A beam of light as a torch came on, flicked towards the tent, went out again. A figure pushed its way inside, tall and stooping, stumbling over the crate of beer.

'Don't get up, chaps,' said Kit Curtis.

'Who's getting up?' said Palmer.

'Cavanagh said I'd find you here.'

'Well, you've found us. So who the bloody hell are you?'

Kit Curtis was peering about him, trying to locate the hostile voice. He said coldly: 'You should know you're addressing an officer.'

'How the fuck are we meant to know that?' Palmer was enjoying himself, anonymous in the darkness. Kit lit the torch and held it upwards, illuminating his face, then turned it on the occupants of the tent. Drongo Palmer was glaring at him. 'Strewth, it's our old mucker from the bottle club.'

Kit ignored him. He looked straight at Ossie. 'My fellows are on readiness at six a.m. Been down checking the kites. Thought I'd pop in and pick up some tips.' His eyes were adjusting to the light, or lack of it.

Ossie thrust out his lower lip and nodded. He handed Kit a Blue Label. 'Straight from the bottle, feller. We don't run to glasses.'

Kit took it but did not drink from it immediately. 'We saw your little set-to this afternoon. Cavanagh filled me in. You got three, I understand. Good show.'

'Yeah,' said Palmer. 'Absolutely wizard.'

'This is the jerk who had to bale,' said Ossie. 'Ignore him.'

The fair-haired pilot hadn't spoken yet. Now he said: 'You'd think he'd pipe down, writing off a kite like that. I'm Brian Twigg.'

'Good to meet you, Sergeant,' said Kit, automatically, his tone formal, cool.

'You too,' said Twigg, adding, after a fractional pause, 'sir.' Ossie caught him shooting Palmer a meaningful glance.

'Twigg got a Ju 88, confirmed,' said Ossie. He did not want the Englishman to underestimate these men, or they to underestimate him. 'That makes it four, huh, Twiggs?'

'Impressive,' said Kit Curtis. His voice was languid, seemingly indifferent, perfect to raise the hackles of any good Republican.

Ossie remembered how long it had taken him, in France, to get behind that shield. He needed to show the others that there was more to this man than a drawl and a condescending manner. He turned to the matter of combat, Malta-style. 'I guess you don't need no lessons from me about what formations to fly,' he said. 'We do the same as the Hun. Finger-fours. No vics. Even take off line-abreast. That way no one kicks up any crap to get into your engine. Once you're in the air you'll find Control in Lascaris are really on the ball. Those guys are good and getting better all the time. They'll take you to the big jobs right on the nose, with all the gen you need – what's showing on their radar, position, altitude, total package. They're our aces-in-the-hole, all right.'

'There's going to be another ace down that particular hole,' said Kit. 'Buster Brown's a qualified controller now. They've posted him here.'

'Whose idea was that?'

'Who do you think?'

'The old firm, huh?' said Ossie. 'Boy, if only we'd had this set-up in France instead of those damned *poilus* crouched in ditches with field telephones.'

'You'd got me to the big jobs,' said Kit. 'Right on the nose.'

'That's right. I had. So when you hit the bombers, well, then it's down to you. But try to stay in pairs, give each other cover. Doesn't often work, you know how it is up there, but worth a go.' He was talking to Kit as an equal. That was rare. The others knew it and thought that maybe, after all, this wasn't your average high-and-mighty toff. 'It's like as always,' Ossie was saying. 'Take the formations from the rear. Get in fast and get out faster. By that time you'll find you're mixing it with the little jobs, 109s and Macchis, and, brother, that's when the fun really begins.'

'Or not,' said Drongo Palmer. He grinned ruefully. He was ready to make peace.

'Happens to us all,' said Kit. 'I baled out in France, crashed twice. Wrote off three machines. All the CO said was "I can always replace aeroplanes but I can't replace pilots." He was right, dead right. All you can do is brush yourself down, put it out of your mind and press on.'

Somewhere above them, at high altitude, came the thrum of slow-revving engines. To Kit the sound meant nothing, might as well have been the Blenheims and Marylands from Luqa, safely in the air and making height. But Drongo Palmer said: 'Bloody Cants on another phoney raid. Pretty soon they'll be heading for home with their bomb-bays empty, getting their ruddy stories straight. What'll it be this time, Twiggy?'

'Who knows?' said Twigg. 'I've got no imagination. They'll come up with something good. Like I was saying, comic-opera stuff.'

'The hell with comic,' said Ossie Wolf. 'Those are real bombs. They jettisoned a load on Marsa just last week. One incendiary landed on a bus. Twenty-one killed, mostly women and kids. As dead as if they'd been the goddamned target.'

'They are,' said Kit Curtis. 'It's all part of the same rotten business. Like Spain, Poland, France, England. There's no reason why the Hun should treat this tiny island any differently. They'll do their best to flatten it into submission.'

'Too right, mate,' said Palmer. 'They say it's only a matter of time. The whackers reckon they've trapped two hundred and fifty thousand prisoners on this island.'

'Seems I've heard something like that before,' said Ossie.

A stick of bombs came down, out of a velvet sky. They listened to the rising shriek. They were landing close, one, two, three, marching across the terrain, making the ground tremble. Another stick, rushing earthwards, whistling through the air, shrill at first, then deepening, a fearful roar, unstoppable and malignant, ending with a succession of massive blasts, closer still, shockwaves fanning out across the farmland, ripping through crops and vegetation, flattening trees and tumbling walls, bursting into buildings shuttered against the night, leaving man and beast sprawled dead, a distance from the point of detonation, without a mark to show how they had died, except for beads of fresh blood, vivid scarlet, running down from their ears and nostrils. Another stick, this time inside the perimeter of the airfield. A searchlight that had been ranging the sky went out. A Bofors 40mm ceased to fire. Somewhere men were screaming. Another stick descended, a rushing noise, shocking, like an express train bursting from a tunnel, but the explosions further over, missing the runways, striking something that began to burn a mile or so away.

The mellow engine-notes of the Cants began to diminish. They were turning, light of bombs, eager to be back in Catania, sharing *caffè normale* in the mess, speculating on what they might have hit, aware only of passing slowly over blackness punctuated, here and there, by gouts of flame from unknown sources.

Kit Curtis was standing outside the tent. He had hold of the bicycle, one hand on the saddle, the other on the handlebars. He was inclining his head, moving it from side to side, as though trying to listen beyond the noise of motors and emergency bells and countless voices coming across the airfield to them on a silky waft of warm air. His face, in the light of distant conflagrations, seemed to freeze. 'My God,' he said, almost to himself, 'that last load. It must have come down close to the *castello*.'

The third of a string of four five-hundred pounders, dropped by a Cant Z1007 trimotor now making its way safely back to base across the Malta Channel, had struck the eastern wing of the Castello Grima. The masonry, huge limestone blocks, had been shattered into fragments or, further from the core of the explosion, had been thrown down by the blast and lay, spread out or heaped, a formless jumble, like nursery bricks abandoned by a careless child, lit by the roseate glow of crackling timber – beams and floorboards, rafters, doors, good and ancient furniture; close by, the fragments of a painting, the features of a haughty Maltese aristocrat melting into oblivion; a twisted chandelier; a shattered chamber-pot; papers flicking in the gusts of heat and flying away as luminous embers. And bodies, some indicated by a single bare foot protruding from the rubble, others entirely visible, spread-eagled and eviscerated.

Kit found the rough location of his room. The remains of a blackened kit-bag smouldered at his feet. The stencilled name said 'Sqdn Ldr J. K. Penrose'. 'Good God,' he said. 'Poor old Pop.'

Something moved in front of him. A few dislodged stones tumbled down the slopes of a mound of debris and rattled about his feet. There was a crest to the slope and beyond it, out of sight, came a faint sound, so faint that he wondered whether he had heard it at all: a shifting of some kind and a moan, little more than the sound of a single, escaping breath. He stumbled up the slope, spreading his feet to keep his balance, occasionally falling forward and digging his fingers deep into the yielding, slipping scree to keep his balance.

Behind him Ossie Wolf was using his footholds, panting with the effort, supporting him with two hands beneath his buttocks, pushing him upwards towards the top of the mound. When he reached it the crest crumbled beneath him and for a moment it seemed he would tumble headlong into the dark hollow that lay below. Instead he allowed himself to slide back down a few feet, jamming his elbows into the loose stones so that his head and shoulders protruded above the rim. He closed his eyes and opened them, once, twice, three times to make sense of the object that lay below. It was a formless mass, bruised and bloody, spread across the bottom of the crater like a dark pool. And yet in the centre of the mass a single blue eye stared up, conscious and apparently aware.

Ossie pulled himself up, alongside Kit. 'Jesus Christ. Who is it?'

Kit shook his head. 'I don't know. Penrose, I suppose. And he's still alive.'

'How?' said Ossie. 'It's like there's nothing there.'

'We must do something,' said Kit.

'Like what?' said Ossie.

Kit knew, but he could not imagine the act. Anyway, he did not have a pistol. And if he'd had one, did he really believe he could pull the trigger, watched by that single, staring eye? Yet even as he struggled to compose his thoughts the eye underwent a change, no longer focussed but blurring, as though a veil had been drawn across it, consciousness fading until, finally, it was overcome by a stillness that had grown from within. Kit wondered what it might have seen in those final moments, what images might have been passed to the ruined brain as it struggled to comprehend. He felt grateful that he did not have to descend into the recesses of the crater and hated himself for it, slowly letting go his hold and slipping back down the mound, overcome with a heightened sense of being alive and whole and hating himself for that as well because somehow the sensation seemed born from seeing someone die. He pushed himself round, ready to get to his feet.

A figure was standing over him. 'It's Peter Howard,' said Pop Penrose. 'Most of us were talking shop in the garden. The medics are on their way.'

Ossie had slid down too. 'No point,' he said. 'He's a goner.'

'Oh,' said Penrose. He appeared drained of emotion. 'Well, that's for the best, thank God. Unbelievable what the human frame can stand.'

'Who else got it?' said Ossie. 'Do we know?'

'A chap named Cavanagh,' said Penrose.

'Shoot,' said Ossie. 'Is that for sure?'

'Positive, I'm afraid. Plus a few more we haven't dug out yet. Damned rotten luck. A hundred yards more and the Eyeties would have missed us altogether.'

Ossie moved away and kicked at the dirt with the toe of his flying boot. He looked like a surly kid, frowning, eyes screwed up, jaw set.

In the flickering light and dark someone was crunching across the stone-strewn ground towards them. There was a murmur of voices, hoarse and low. Penrose hurried towards the advancing medics.

Kit was left alone. He could not erase from his mind the image of that staring, conscious eye. It seemed to have no possible connection with Peter Howard, sturdy and dependable, with his tales of dry-fly fishing the chalk waters of the Test, his dreams and schemes for the little family farm near Stockbridge. Now, an end to dreams like that. It had finished here, in a hole in the ground thousands of miles from home.

Someone pushed past him, a medical orderly, brisk and efficient, knowing what to do, mounting the mound of rubble and passing out of sight over the rim. There was a smaller figure close by, the boy Giorgio, his face blackened with smoke. He saw Kit and moved towards him, giving him a grave salute that Kit returned reluctantly, feeling the pantomime was out of place. He was disturbed that this child should see what there was to be seen in the *castello*. 'Go home,' he said. 'There's nothing you can do.'

'My job is here,' said the boy. 'Already I have helped many people.'

'Let him be,' said a second medic, waiting at the foot of the mound. 'He's a right little ferret, that one. Wriggles into spaces us fat bastards can't manage.'

The boy looked proud. Kit stared at him, undecided. Then he gave in, recalling the matter of the chameleon, the way the horror of it had not touched the child, how he had seized the mangled body and tossed it out of sight, then laughed and kicked out at the feral cats; he had acted in a brutal, casual way, understanding that this was how things were. Beside him now, Kit felt he was the child, squeamish and shaken by what he had seen, ashamed that he had been unwilling to descend into the crater to ease Peter Howard's final moments.

By dawn they knew they had lost four men: Howard, Roy Cavanagh and two members of a Beaufighter crew who had shared a room. The pilots were called to parade outside the *castello* with its breached fortifications, thrown down and burning as though at last the Turks had come. New quarters had been identified in Mdina. They should be safe from bombs there, Penrose said. Mdina was a holy city. The Pope, it was believed, would not allow the Axis to attack it. Laughter ran down the ranks but some allowed themselves to hope that it might be true.

A bus had been arranged to transport them to the hill-top refuge. Kit had no belongings to throw on board with the others. Everything had gone, even that damned Sidcot suit. All his snaps: Juliette seated in some studio in Le Mans, unsmiling and composed, her hands clasped on her lap and, beside her, Louis, also solemn, his smaller hand resting on her shoulder; Farve and Mother on the terrace at Linch Down with Ben the Airedale at their feet and Agnes Hobbes poised by the trolley laid for tea; the crumpled print of him, Hannah Maierscheldt, Ossie Wolf and the little Russian who had killed herself, the women resembling each other so closely they might have been sisters, the picture taken for them by the friendly *flic* as they walked in the Tuileries before the invasion. And letters, some from Juliette that had somehow reached him from France, carried by the escaped, trite and disclosing nothing in case they were intercepted, trusting him to understand what she had left unsaid; a number from Farve, anxious and sentimental, not helping, not helping at all, just one more concern, although at least the latest had told of Juliette's escape. He wondered if she and the boy had found accommodation. He imagined what it might be, near to London so she could find work. England seemed a very long way off. He hoped he would remember to reply to Farve. He also wondered briefly whether he might be granted time.

The driver of the bus was gunning the throttle. '*Ghaggel, ghaggel!*' Blue fumes rose from beneath the bonnet. Kit pulled himself on board. The boy Giorgio was leaning against the driver's seat, his small arm stretched behind the man's hunched back. The boy grinned, excited at the brief trip. Whatever he had experienced in the ruined *castello* appeared forgotten. 'Go, go,' he shouted at the driver. 'All are here now.'

Not all, thought Kit. The driver thrust the gear-lever into first and dropped the clutch. Lurching against Penrose, standing next to him, Kit saw Ossie Wolf, seated further down the bus. They nodded.

Penrose noticed. 'I understand you know that fellow rather well.'

'We flew together in France.'

'Odd type. He's coming with us now, under some duress. Didn't like it at all. Kicked up a hell of a fuss. He's been living under canvas, you know, with a couple of sergeant pilots.'

'Yes, I know,' said Kit.

'No doubt the chap's earned his commission but if he's happier with his own kind, why bother?'

'There's rather more to it than that,' said Kit.

'Really?' said Penrose. 'What exactly?'

'You'd better ask him,' said Kit.

'I did,' said Penrose. 'Got nowhere. The fellow clammed up.' He rubbed dirt from the window. They were starting the climb towards the old city, seven hundred feet above the plain. The twin bell-towers of the cathedral were outlined against the sky. 'Anyway,' said Penrose, 'it's Mdina for him now, with the rest of us. No exceptions. So he'll just have to learn how to hold his knife and fork properly.'

'If the Hun have their way,' said Kit, 'we can polish our table manners to our heart's content but soon we may find there's nothing on our plates.'

'Just a figure of speech,' said Penrose, stiffly. 'You know what I mean.'

'I'm not entirely sure I do,' said Kit. 'We're all going to have to adjust on this benighted island. The old ways don't apply. Wolf knows that and he's proved his point. He may have rough edges but he's one of the best we've got. The chaps can learn from him, not the other way round. By all means make him one of the crowd, but don't box him in. It won't work.'

'That remains to be seen,' said Penrose. 'At short acquaintance things seem to have grown pretty lax round here.'

'I thought that,' said Kit. He heard again the voice of Corporal Chalmers, after he had jumped down from his Hurricane. Had it really been only yesterday? 'You'll soon get used to the way of things, sir. They're good lads, treated right.' He recalled his reaction: that the place was a shambles, manned by a rabble. And yet Chalmers and his men had shown initiative and courage, dragging him to safety in the shelter. And in the air the enemy had suffered, paying a high price in men and machines for a few casualties on the ground. 'Yes, I thought that,' said Kit again. 'And from what I've seen there's certainly an element of muddling through. After all, it's the English way. But I suppose you're right. Things do need tightening up.'

'So I can count on your support?'

'Of course. But it's a different game out here. I suggest we try to learn from chaps like Wolf, who know the ropes, before we start trying to set the world to rights.'

They were closer to Mdina now, passing between dun-coloured fields with sparse green crops and tangles of cactus rearing up beside the road, taller than a man. At last the bus dragged itself round the last few twists and turns, corners that wound back upon themselves, steep and cambered, and passed through the Howard Gardens. The flower-beds, formal in the Victorian style, showed neglect, shadows of what they had once been. Among the dead and dying shrubs and plants prowled thin, marauding cats. A few elaborate benches, iron and wood, lay broken. Beyond the gardens a monumental gateway, rich with carved embellishments, faced them across a bridged-over moat.

Ossie Wolf had pushed his way between the seats, bending low to see through the windscreen. 'Gee whiz,' he said to Kit, 'you're going to feel at home. It's goddamned Camelot.'

'I hear you've got a seat at the Round Table,' said Kit.

The bus plunged through the narrow entrance, flanked by lions rampant clasping shields in their stony paws, the bellow of its engine bouncing back from the city ramparts. It made a tight right turn, almost scraping the walls of an ancient chapel, and juddered to a halt in a broad open *piazza* paved with flagstones, worn shiny. Birdsong echoed round the enclosed space. A honey-coloured *palazzo* lay on the northern aspect, flat-topped and two-storey, almost Georgian in design, tall windows closed with shutters thrown back. '*Hemm hi Sinjuri*,' shouted the driver. 'We are arrived.' He heaved at the handbrake, supported it with a piece of notched wood and, with the boy, began to unload the baggage and carry it into the *palazzo*.

The pilots gathered by the bus. 'I say,' said Max Astley-Cobb, 'this is more like it. And with a grandstand view of Takali too. We'll be able to see all the fun.'

'For God's sake, Max, put a sock in it,' said Kit. 'Think about why we're here.' He moved towards the *palazzo* and almost stumbled into Ossie Wolf.

'So you've been talking to this guy Penrose, huh?' said Ossie. 'The cock-eyed bastard wants me where he can see me. All cheps together.'

'Maybe he's got a point,' said Kit.

'Has he hell. I can be in the air in six minutes.'

'Maybe so. But what about the new fellows? They haven't got a clue about what they're up against. Could be the brass hats think you can play a bigger role, getting the poor devils up to scratch, if only you'd stop treating it as your own private war.'

'Oh brother,' said Ossie. 'Seems I've heard that before someplace.'

'You can't argue against discipline,' said Kit. 'It's the basis of the whole damned service. Face it, man, things are pretty chaotic round here. Remember what happened in France when things went the same way.'

'Malta's not France,' said Ossie. 'They may be bombing the bejesus out of us but they can't dent morale and that goes for the Malties too.'

'Things are going to change,' said Kit, 'and you might as well accept it. It's a question of balance. Aggression in the air has got to be supported by efficiency on the ground. From what I've seen, the Hurrys we've got are barely operational. The spirit's there, all right, but it takes organisation, too. And types like Penrose can help to pull things round.'

'Organise all you like,' said Ossie. 'What we really need is Spits. And unless we get 'em the goddammned Jerries are going to be marching up the beaches of this stinking island. Then you'll get some organisation. Those bastards will organise you right out of goddamned existence.'

'From what I've heard,' said Kit, 'Spits will be a long time coming.'

'Then we're dead.'

'A touch gloomy,' said Kit, 'when there is another possibility.'

'Oh, yeah? What?'

'If the rumour about the Russian Front turns out to be true, we'll be facing the Regia Aeronautica, not the Luftwaffe. At least the Hurricane has a better chance against a Macchi 200 than an Me 109. It might be just the breather we need.'

'You know,' said Ossie, after a long pause, 'maybe you're not the dumb mug you're cracked up to be.'

# Part two

## July–October 1941

## ‘A merciful glance’

# Three

It was ninety degrees and rising, even in the shade of the sideless Dispersal tent, even at ten in the morning. From habit the pilots watched the sky, sitting in rickety chairs and trying not to move too much under the protection of the canvas, which was thick but still not thick enough to obscure the burning light. Sweat ran from their scalps into their eyes and on down their naked torsos, flowing more freely at the slightest shift in their position. The sun stood alone in a sky that was otherwise curiously empty, as it had been for days. Yet still the pilots watched, their eyes as red from fruitless scanning as they were from sweat.

From over by the blast pens where the Hurricanes were came the constant chatter of petrol motors charging the external accumulators used to start the Merlin engines. It was not a deafening noise but constant and irritating, loud enough to stifle conversation. Though conversation was far from lively, because for every hour in the air five were spent waiting on the ground.

'For Christ's sake, can't somebody get that ruddy engineer officer to turn those motors off?'

'You tell him.'

'I'm stuck to my seat. I think I've melted.'

A long pause, listening to the clattering motors. 'It's insufferable. Those dratted chore-horses are driving me mad.'

'You'll be madder still if they turn them off and you can't get your kite started.'

'Who needs to get it started? The only things flying today are these dratted mozzies. Look at the sods. They're eating me alive.'

'Someone get the Flit. Corporal, fetch the Flit.'

'Yes, sir.'

'Ignore him, Corporal. Flit only works in an enclosed space.'

'Yes, sir.'

'Since when did you come to know so much about Flit?'

'Everybody knows it only works in an enclosed space.'

'Well, I didn't.'

'Well, you do now.' Another pause. 'Those bloody chore-horses. They're driving me round the bend. Someone should have a word with that damned engineer officer.'

They had not seen a German aircraft for ten days now. It seemed that, for once, the grapevine was accurate. Certainly Hitler had launched his attack on Russia. That much at least had passed down to the pilots. And in Control in Valletta it was also known that Operation Barbarossa had opened with massed attacks on airfields in western Russia. It was even rumoured that, within a single week, four thousand Soviet aircraft had been destroyed. The quieter Malta skies suggested that the Luftwaffe's Sicily-based *Geschwader*, still tanned from the Mediterranean sun, had played their part, helping to decimate close-packed formations of unescorted Ilyushin, Tupelov and Sukhoi bombers attempting to strike the invaders in daylight on suicidally steady courses and at constant altitude; easier meat than the pilots of the RAF who knew the Luftwaffe's ways – often, had learned from them.

Once, three days ago, a brace of rotary-engined Macchi 200s had come in low over the Takali field, stubby and handy-looking, making a fine show, their pilots clearly visible in their open cockpits, sweeping empty ground with their 12.4mm Breda machine-guns before climbing away, one throwing in a victory roll, suggesting more bravado than the will to kill.

Four Hurricanes had set off in pursuit but it was a token scramble, one even turning back with falling oil pressure and crashing beyond the perimeter when the engine seized; a rogue machine that all who flew it had hated, left wing low in any dive and always apt to yaw to the left if the pilot was tardy on the rudder. This time Max Astley-Cobb had been at the controls, stepping out of the battered remains with a broken nose, his only comment, as it burst into flames, 'If the bugger hadn't burned I'd have set fire to it myself.'

Less than a month earlier, in time for Ossie Wolf to make his mark but not for Kit Curtis and the rest of the *Revenger* contingent, the squadron had been scrambled four or five times a day, the voice of Control crackling in the earphones of the pilots of a handful of oil-stained machines bouncing down Takali's dust-white runway, rudders swaying, countering the Hurricane's tendency to swing. 'Eighty plus bandits approaching from the north. Climb to angels one-five.' Eight against eighty.

And there they were, Ju87 Stukas, Ju88s and Messerschmitt 109s, flying in their usual stepped formation, their impassive crews watching the Hurricanes struggle for height, not altering course or deviating from their flight plan, despite the flak from red-hot-barrelled anti-aircraft guns bursting all around them. The British fighters on full throttle now, at maximum rate of climb, black smoke pouring back from glowing exhausts, white needles of airspeed indicators quivering on the 140 m.p.h. mark. Then going in among the bombers, closing fast from positions that simply had to do, no time for something better, like more height maybe or using the deceitful brilliance of the sun, anything that might give you a better chance, but going in, Merlin screaming, fuselage shuddering, wings flexing from the engine's power but also from the G force of the dive and recoil of the Brownings; the controls getting stiff, approaching 380 m.p.h. now, plunging through streams of tracer as the gunners of the Ju 88s hose the air from front and rear locations in the Junkers cockpit and from the deadly ventral gondola in the aircraft's grey-painted belly. And now the yellow-snouted 109s plummeting down, a few at a time at first while the rest circle and wait, the sky criss-crossed with vapour trails left by desperate individual battles to destroy or simply to survive.

Puffs of smoke and then a jet of flame as a fighter rolls onto its back and falls away, a tiny figure detaching itself from the inferno, turning and tumbling, brought up short at last by the streaming canopy of a parachute that finally fills and spreads, delicate and vulnerable like a drifting dandelion seed.

A Ju 88 going down, dropping away in a graceful curve, white smoke gouting from an engine; more 'chutes, one, two, no more, and then the bomb-load detonates and fragments of the bomber spiral lazily down towards the surface of the island, mottled brown, 15,000 feet below. The Stuka *Staffel* over Takali now, others diverting to Halfa and Luqa, further south, each loosing 4,000 pounds of bombs from beneath their wings, the note of their twelve-cylinder Jumos rising as they bank away, lighter and more responsive without their load, and setting course for Sicily.

And then the sky suddenly empty and Control calling up from deep below the bastions of Valletta, in the war rooms of Lascaris, where the plotters have heard the cries of battle: 'Pancake, chaps. Good show.' Though not all the chaps receive the order to land, some gliding down on 'chutes and very quick to tell pugnacious locals they are RAF, others burning on the ground, in the twisted framework of their machines, or in the sea, struggling free from the harness of the smothering, spreading parachute, for the moment still afloat but growing very cold, looking for a rescue boat, not knowing if their position has been reported. Others never seen again, their final moments unrecorded, their fate a blank, just static on the R/T when the flight commander does his checks. The rest coming in to land, another trip survived, using throttle and rudder to weave a rumbling course between fresh bomb craters, juddering to a halt beside the blast pens, running her out, switching off and finally applying brakes. And easing out of the sweat-soaked seat and jumping down from the wing and grinning, taking in the perforated rudder, the star-crazed windscreen struck a glancing blow by a cannon shell, lucky that, and watching smiles break across brown faces with the news that, yes, I got a Ju 88, just blew up in front of me, and hit a 109 as well but didn't see what happened after that.

All this before the lull, before the Germans had gone away. Accounts that met with mixed emotions from those who had arrived too late. To miss a show like that, everything a fighter pilot dreams of, on a good day when his confidence is high and he knows he cannot die. But on a bad day, flying a battered Hurry, limping through the air with eyes glued to the tell-tale gauges, the yarns provoking a spike of fear, aware that even against a well-flown Macchi chances of survival were marginal, let alone a returning pack of 109s fresh from kills on the Russian Front.

If the respite gave the introspective too much time to think, at least order began to be reimposed. It was even rumoured a new CO was on his way from England. Neglected machines were serviced and, where found wanting, withdrawn from operations until repairs had been completed. No short-cuts, no bodging and proper records kept; Form 700s keeping track of an aeroplane's service history, daily inspections signed off by the fitters and riggers as well as the pilot whose life was in their hands; grass-green ground-crew weeded out and given training or assigned to other duties; all of them disciplines that had been eroded by the intensity of constant battle, carried out in tropical heat by men pummelled by raid after raid, reduced by fatigue, disease and meagre diet, yet who somehow, through it all, had kept the Hurricanes and Blenheims, Beaufighters and Marylands airborne and striking the enemy with force and to good effect.

Green pilots were also taken on one side, some fresh from Operational Training, short of flying hours and untested in combat, now gifted time to polish their skills; time that might buy them a few more months in action until they finally learned their trade or, inevitably, died. And finally the sergeant pilots and other NCOs had more than canvas above their heads, shifted into a neglected building, said to have been a pottery before the war, little more than a mile from the airfield and nicely obscure from the air, quickly transformed from dereliction to a tidy billet by a blitz of bull.

The move meant Ossie Wolf breathed easier in the officers-only *palazzo* contained within the echoing walls, the cool and narrow streets of the medieval city the Holy Father had told the Germans they must not bomb. And yet he remained reticent and aloof, unable or unwilling to involve himself in the clouds of nonsense generated by the others, schoolboy humour laced with milder forms of smut, or line-shoot sessions, each pilot trying to top the other with tall tales of prowess in the air, tongue placed firmly in cheek in case the other fellows really thought you reckoned yourself a decent pilot: accidents avoided by a whisker, accidents not avoided, recounted in ghoulish detail, watching the circle of youthful faces for signs of distaste. Ossie failed to see the joke. 'I don't figure these guys. Are they serious or what?' And although he would unbend a little after a whisky or two, then he became morose and confrontational. As with Vey Geary and Max Astley-Cobb, who amused themselves by conversing in fifth-form slang.

'Can't say I'm much impressed with the rest of the new-bugs, Geary.'

'No, a vey girlie bunch.'

'Frightful wets and weeds. Don't know what the service is coming to.'

'First sign of trouble and they'll be off blubbing to Matron.'

'And good eggs like us will have to bear the brunt.'

'What exactly is a brunt, Astley-Cobb?'

'Haven't a clue, Geary, but we've got to bear it. Absolute swizz.'

'Perhaps we could pass the brunt to the junior ticks, when they get back from Matron's office.'

'*Cave*, Astley-Cobb. Here comes that swankpot Wolf. He looks vey cheesed.'

'Who the hell are you calling a swankpot?'

'All Americans are swankpots, Wolf. We learned that in General Knowledge.'

'I guess you fellers think you're very funny.'

'Yes, vey. I say, Wolf, hang on a mo. There's something we want to ask you.'

'What now?'

'Would you like a brunt?'

But occasionally the mood took a more serious turn, after someone was badly smashed or the Italians in Catania dropped a message to say that the popular man who had gone missing was dead and had been buried with military honours. They could be disarming that way, a considerate enemy, and after the twin Macchi 200s put on their low-level show with that theatrical victory roll, the talk in what had been the *salon* of the commandeered *palazzo* and was now the bar, turned to the Regia Aeronautica and what such gestures might mean. Was their heart not in this war or were they still imbued with some archaic code?

'Surely it suggests a certain fundamental decency,' said Kit Curtis. 'They're bound to fight because their country compels them to but on the evidence it seems they're attempting to do it in an honourable way. Give me one instance when an Italian has machine-gunned a chap who's done a brolly-hop or strafed someone in a dinghy. The Hun have no such scruples.'

Ossie felt himself on firmer ground. 'You mean the Regia are like your goddamned knights of old in tin-can suits, not hating the sonofabitch on the other side but respecting him as an equal, man to man? And may the best man win?'

'Who knows?' said Kit. 'What about those Christmas cards they dropped? "To the gentlemen of the Royal Air Force from the gentlemen of the Regia Aeronautica".'

'Bull,' said Ossie. 'It's just a ruse. They figure that when we get them in our sights maybe we'll think what decent guys they are and hesitate. They're looking for an edge, like all of us. An edge to get us first or an edge that means they'll save their hides.' He threw back a shot of Johnnie Walker. 'Let's face it, the Eyeties are bright enough to know they had a choice. Fall in with Il Duce or do the other thing. They opted for the fat Fascist phoney and now they find they've got to face the consequences. Maybe it doesn't seem like such a good idea, after all, but they've got to follow it through. Their business is to send us down, no question. And your corpse is just as stiff whether it's a Macchi or a Messerschmitt that gets you, even if the pilot does it with a goddamned sigh.'

Astley-Cobb leaned forward, the smoke from his cigarette curling up towards the lofty ceiling where, in a shaky fresco by an obscure Maltese, God held out his hand to Christ ascending. 'My view is they sometimes act the way they do because they lack the guts to carry things through to their logical conclusion. It's like children fronting up to each other but not really wanting to get hurt. "I won't hit you if you don't hit me." As a nation the Eyeties are weak. Everyone knows they're weak. Look at what they said about their navy. "Nothing can catch our cruisers and destroyers." In my book that just about sums it up.'

'Remind me not to read your book,' said Ossie. 'Write off the Regia as a bunch of jerks with a yellow streak and you'll find yourself in big trouble. They're pragmatists, sure, not like the square-heads, who'll stick to orders even when flames are licking round their asses. But they sure know how to handle an airplane. Any flying circus would be proud to have them on the bill. And that goddamned Macchi has got the drop on the Hurry, no question. At least, the Hurrys we've got saddled with.'

'All I know,' said Astley-Cobb, 'is when you see one of those mottled Eyetie jobs it's a different thing from spotting a yellow-nose.'

'We're straying from the point,' said Kit. 'The question was whether the Italians retain a vestige of chivalry in the way they're conducting the war. Wolf's view is unquestionably no. To him these little acts of humanity are simply devices to put us off our balance.'

'And you?' said Astley-Cobb.

'I'd like to think otherwise.'

'That figures,' said Ossie. He smiled but it was the hard, thin smile of a man who has suddenly perceived a weakness that can be worked on; the smile of a boxer spotting a swelling eye, the smile of a gladiator seeing a *retiarius* drop his net, and begin to stagger from loss of blood, moving in for the final thrust. 'Talking of mottled Eyetie jobs,' he said, 'I've got me a peach of an idea.'

Next morning the American called in at Stores. He came out, wearing the same hard, thin smile, carrying paint pots and brushes, and strolled across to his machine. 'Hey, Chuffy, roll her out of that goddamned pen so I can get me some room. And rustle up a couple of guys to give me a hand here. We're going to pretty her up some.'

Corporal Chalmers nudged an LAC. 'Now what's he chuffing up to?'

Thirty minutes later Pop Penrose came past on a bicycle. And squealed to a halt. 'What the blazes is going on?'

'Hey,' said Ossie stepping back, pointing at the Hurricane with the dripping brush loose in his hand. 'What do you reckon to our handiwork?'

An airman was daubing splotches of dark green paint on the leading edge of the starboard wing. The background, barely dry, was sand-tan, the shade used on Army tanks. Another man was working on the nose. Wolf was decorating the port wing on his own.

Penrose understood immediately. 'Good grief, man, you'll look like a damned Eyetie.'

'Only from a distance,' said Ossie. 'Even if it gives me a fraction of a second closing, confuses them for just a moment, I reckon we can narrow the odds between the Macchi and the Hurry.'

'Don't know if I should permit it,' said Penrose, doubtfully. 'I'm not sure it accords with the rules of war.'

'Ain't it the truth?' said Ossie.

The news spread quickly. At Dispersal, Astley-Cobb took Kit aside. 'I suppose you've heard the latest about your Yankee chum?'

'Now what?'

'He's decked his kite out Italian-style.'

'Good God,' said Kit. 'Is that allowed?'

'Just the nose and wings,' said Astley-Cobb. 'Not the whole shebang.'

'Nose and wings is bad enough,' said Kit.

'You think so?' said Astley-Cobb. 'Wolf excuses it on the grounds that it'll even up the odds.'

'What does Penrose say?'

'Somewhat flummoxed. I think he's shoved it up the line. On the quiet I think he rather hopes Wolf will find himself thoroughly peppered by one of us. You know, in the heat of things. Just to teach the chap a lesson.'

'He could be right.'

'I don't fancy trying it,' said Astley-Cobb. 'The belligerent little bugger's far too good a shot.'

Two days later Ossie Wolf destroyed two Savoia-Marchetti SM. 79s carrying torpedoes, twenty miles east of Valletta harbour. The Savoias took no evasive action at his approach, heading for a tanker and two merchantmen carrying full cargoes of ammunition, guns and men as well as oil, inbound from Gibraltar and threatened all the way by U-boats and raids by Axis aircraft operating from Libya. The Savoias, cruising comfortably abreast, identified the Hurricane only when it had closed to within a hundred yards; too late. The pilots had no time to more than break to port and starboard in feeble banks, the gunners firing wildly at an unseen enemy that was already on them, lacerating the bombers' fuselages with short and lethal bursts. Within three minutes they had both plunged, burning, into the sea; no survivors.

Ossie was triumphant. 'Like I said, you got to have an edge.'

But none of the others followed his lead and soon the order came through for his machine to be restored to its standard livery, which it duly was by a grumbling Corporal Chalmers. 'About time they made their chuffing minds up. My lads have got better things to do than turn themselves into chuffing camouflage artists.' But, like many of the bombed and battered other ranks, he reckoned the pugnacious Wolf had been on to something, not party to nice distinctions debated in the bar of the *palazzo* in Mdina, of considerations of a nation's fundamental decency and even the possibility of vestiges of chivalry persisting in the way in which the Regia Aeronautica was conducting its campaign. Chalmers took the old-fashioned view: he who kills the most emerges top, like the prickly little Yank always said. End of chuffing argument, surely?

Kit did not mention the episode in the letter he had begun to his father. He tried generally to maintain a reassuring tone, concerned that the old man should not grow too anxious, but wanting him nonetheless to understand something of the reality of their situation. Too easy to settle for the commonplace, trotted out like schoolboys quizzed about their day at school – 'Fine, all fine' – as many of the pilots did in letters home, bored with explaining to those who could never understand, so giving the impression that Malta was a picnic. But there were certain boundaries and he knew that Wolf's quest for an unfair advantage would go down badly. He could hear his father now, pacing the study, his letter grasped in a shaking hand. 'Not playing the game. Not playing the game at all. It makes us as bad as them.' And so he left it out, continuing to write in his careful hand, the notepad resting on a bamboo table in Dispersal:

> We have been going up quite regularly, Farve, but a lot of it's unproductive. Mostly the fun starts when it gets dark. There's talk of painting some of the Hurricanes black and doing a spot of night-fighting. As one of the chaps said: 'Sounds like a good frolic.' Sometimes I wonder if I'm back at Marlborough! It's mostly Italians we come across now. For the time being the Hun have other fish to fry. But at least it's given the squadron a chance to get things sorted out. It all seemed a bit chaotic

at first but the powers-that-be seem to be on to it. A new squadron leader's on his way and it's rumoured it's Douglas Brewster, our old CO from France. If so, what luck. Bags of energy and initiative and jolly handy in the air, if only they allow him to fly, that is. More a question of stopping him, I'd say! Anyway, if the grapevine's right he'll soon lick this place into shape. And any time now we can expect another familiar face, Buster Brown, the fellow who got rather badly burned over Le Havre in June '40.

Actually I'm afraid that poor old Buster's face is somewhat changed but through it all he's been his usual stoic self. Now he's trained up as a controller and has wangled a posting here. And, of course, there's Ossie Wolf, the bolshie little American type who, as you know, got me involved out here originally. Naturally he's revelling in the set-up (thinks it a fighter pilot's paradise, no less) and has proved himself quite an ace. So, quite the old firm, as they say!

Accommodation's not too bad. They've shifted us into an old *palazzo*, very grand, but not everything is rosy, even with the Luftwaffe busy elsewhere. Apart from the terrific heat, very muggy and hanging over everything like a blanket, the food is pretty awful. They do their best to provide us with a decent diet but there are only so many ways you can serve up bully beef, and as for the local vegetables, well, on the face of it they're all right but I won't tell you what the locals spread on their fields. Suffice to say you're lucky if you don't go down with a bout of what they call the Malta Dog, a particularly nasty form of dysentery, bad enough to get you grounded. I've been lucky but they tell me it's just a matter of time.

Sandfly fever's another bane of our lives, as well as the

ever-present mosquitoes. And dust gets into everything. You find yourself grinding your teeth on the stuff, rubbing it from your eyes, your hair full of it. It also has a nasty habit of finding its way into engines, despite the so-called tropicalisation of our machines, Vokes filters and the like. You have to watch your instruments like a hawk, particularly on take-off, because there are rows of jolly little stone walls just waiting for a chap who has to hit the deck in an emergency. The word for such eventualities is 'spitchered' which I'm told derives from the Maltese 'spicca', which means 'no further use', but it's come to be applied to pretty well anything that malfunctions or is destroyed (lots of both out here)! But at least it makes a change from the usual tedious expletives!

Sorry not to write before, dear Farve, but the past few weeks have been more than hectic. However, you and Mother mustn't worry about me. The experience I've gained, particularly in France, will stand me in very good stead, and in some ways the situation here is not dissimilar, an isolated small-scale force facing some rather daunting odds. In that case we also had the French to contend with and were badly let down. But we're all very conscious of what the chaps achieved in the summer of 1940, showing what the British can do when left to their own devices, so everyone is convinced we will prevail.

On a more personal note I was delighted to hear that Madame Garencières and her son not only escaped from France but have made themselves known to you. You are right. She is a fine person with great spirit. Anything you can do to help them establish themselves near wherever she chooses to find employment would, I know, be hugely appreciated.

As for the 'mystery' about Hannah Maierscheldt's whereabouts, I believe I may have a clue, although it still doesn't explain why she hasn't been in touch with you since her arrival in England. It seems most odd but perhaps, as you say, she doesn't wish to presume. Or possibly she's been affected by the loss of her parents and would find the sight of old family friends too distressing. Who knows? What I do know, however, thanks to pure chance – Buster Brown the witness but I won't go into details now – is that she's apparently got a flat in Hampstead, Holly Hill, just round the corner from the Holly Bush public house. Buster said she looked absolutely fine, although she didn't notice him. In fact blooming, so I don't think we need to be worried about her, although it's still a puzzlement why she's kept herself to herself. No doubt it will become clear in due course and

Kit did not complete the sentence. The jangle of the Dispersal telephone cut the air. The duty corporal snatched it up. 'Flight scramble!' Ossie Wolf was instantly on his feet, then Vey Geary and Astley-Cobb.

Kit knocked over the little bamboo writing-table as he threw back his canvas chair. His pad and pen skittered across the dirt. 'Corporal, rescue that stuff. Hang on to it until I get back.' He was running hard towards his Hurricane, adrenaline coursing through his veins, breathless, panting, swiftly in his cockpit now, running through the old routine but forcing himself to think about each step, not complacent, wholly focussed, knowing that a single error could bring disaster, just as surely as any foe.

The sun's heat was being thrown back by the Hurricane's broad wings, exposed metal searing to a careless touch. He knew a great impatience to be in the air, anxious to feel the cooling rush but compelling himself to take his time, methodical and thorough. How did Augustus have it? '*Festina lente.*' Make haste slowly. Yes, don't curse the LAC for fumbling with the harness. Treat him with easy calm, pretend it's just another sortie. Probably nothing up there, like the last time, a flap for nothing. Fuel cock to main tanks on, throttle a half-inch open, propeller control fully forward, radiator shutter open. Ignition on. Press the buttons on the starter and booster coil. The Merlin begins to turn but reluctant, coughing. Twenty seconds and still she hasn't taken. Release the button. Wait another thirty seconds, like it says in *Pilot's Notes*, each second an eternity.

The others are moving away, leaving him behind. He is enveloped in a choking fog of dust. He pulls down his goggles and holds his oxygen mask tight against his mouth. He is wet with sweat. Thirty seconds.

Again he stabs the starter button, the Merlin churning, churning, and then it bursts alive, the airframe pulsing with its power. Slowly open up. One thousand revs, watching the oil and radiator temperature needles rise. More checks: rudder, elevator, propeller control, flaps, then finally moving towards the runway, the others already in the air, circling, waiting but not for long. Opening the throttle now, slowly, slowly, using the rudder to counteract the swing.

Moving faster, bumping, bouncing, tyres briefly kissing the ground, wheels spinning. Lifting, engine strong, God, what a wonderful sound. Undercarriage up, wheels thumping home. But not a moment to relax, not for an instant. Undercarriage selector lever into neutral. Nose-heavy like it always is at this crucial point, so retrim quickly. How's the speed? 140 m.p.h. on the airspeed indicator, top left on the dull-black instrument flying panel. The optimum speed to take the kite up to 16,000 feet. Ready to join the waiting trio already turning south to make some height. Ready, finally, to fight . . .

Ossie Wolf was flight leader. No problem for Kit. By any standards the man was an old Malta hand, someone to watch, to learn from, in these huge and seemingly empty skies, empty even of clouds, with nowhere to wait unseen, planning your attack, unless you used the sun, and nowhere to hide if hard-pressed, struggling to survive. This was another chance for the freshly arrived – 'us new ticks', as Geary had it – to study the art of survival. Wolf was like a ghillie, sharp-eyed and alert to every hint of prey, leading his guns forward, gathering them for the kill, men who could shoot but in this new environment did not know how to stalk.

'Red Leader airborne, Control. Over,' Ossie Wolf called into the R/T.

'Roger, Red Leader. Four big jobs at angels-twenty, thirty miles north. Over.'

'Only four,' said Ossie. 'Gee, you're spoiling us. Out.'

The Hurricanes were spread in finger-four formation, wingtips twenty feet apart, moving not quite as one through the thinning air, governed by the amount of throttle applied, a fractionally heavier touch on the control column, the personal quirks of the individual plane. Kit looked to his left but Ossie Wolf was staring straight ahead, his eyes invisible behind his tinted goggles, though, from the inclination of his head, Kit could see they were fixed on the far horizon where a milky haze hung over Malta's sister islands, tiny Comino, little more than a rock, and Gozo, larger but still half the size of Malta and, from the air, similarly arid and austere. Gozo, where legend held that Ulysses spent seven years in Calypso's thrall, offered the gift of immortality, until Jove ordered the sea-nymph to release him from her spell. The gift of immortality. That would come in useful now as Ossie Wolf led them in wide figure-of-eights at 22,000 feet. They were thirty miles out to sea, due north of St Paul's Bay, and then they saw them, 2,000 feet below, a quartet of green-brown mottled Cant Z100s, cruising at little more than 250 m.p.h., unescorted, their five-man crews lulled by the steady bellow of the triple air-cooled Piaggio engines, believing this far out they must be safe, thoughts already turning to what diversions they might find in the shadowy alleys of Benghazi.

Ossie took the Hurricanes into a steep climbing turn to the left, building on their height advantage. 'Going down,' he said, his voice laconic, and half rolled onto his back, then dived on the Cants, approaching them in a shallow dive, head-on at 360 m.p.h. He opened fire at less than two hundred yards. The leading Cant shuddered, pieces of fuselage flying off, then reared up, turned over and flicked into a spin.

Kit was second down. One of the Italians had turned and dived away. Kit pulled into a wrenching vertical turn and came in from the Cant's port beam, kicking the rudder and skidding to his left, levelling his wings. Vivid scarlet tracer from the dorsal gun-turret was whipping past him to the right. He thumbed the gun-button, a long burst, and saw his bullets track a course from cockpit along the tapering fuselage to the tail. The barrel of the dorsal machine-gun tilted upwards, not firing any more. Kit dived beneath the bomber's belly, centralised the control column then pulled back hard, the Hurricane shaking with the stress. At the top of the loop he rolled out and stall-turned back towards the Cant, which was losing height and trailing engine smoke and glycol. The pilot in the shattered cockpit saw him coming. The aircraft rolled from side to side, the wing-tips rising, falling, waggling his wings, defeated, helpless.

Kit's thumb moved on the gun-button. Finish it, finish it now. Yes, now. But no, too late. The Cant was already half a mile behind him, wallowing and dropping towards the sea. He pulled round into another vertical turn. This time, this time. And saw a Hurricane climb smoothly up, below and behind the Cant and rake it with a quick, efficient burst and break away. A man jumped from the bomber, then another, their parachutes opening cleanly. They floated down, hands gripping their harnesses, chins sunk on their chests, gazing at the approaching sea. The surface was scoured with flecks of white. There was no comfort there. Better perhaps to have gone with the others, sprawled in the bloody ruin of their fine machine.

'Red Two, you got a problem?' On the R/T Ossie's voice was casual still, only mildly curious.

'Missed my chance,' said Kit. 'Little rusty, I'm afraid.'

'You did okay,' said Ossie. 'You hit him good. The sonofabitch just needed a *coup de grâce*.' He pronounced it 'coop de grass' but Kit could not smile. He imagined the American standing over a stricken man, implacable, a pistol in his hand. He would do it, in that circumstance. He was capable. His finger would not hesitate on the trigger. He would direct the bullet into the back of the head and turn away, thinking only that that was one less enemy to deal with. He wielded death without emotion, Kit knew, because he was convinced that he was right and they were wrong. He had seen what the Fascists did in Spain, in France, in England, and now they were in Malta, following the same bloody path. He would go on until none were left, if that was what it took, because they had followed willingly where they should not. And in his mind Italy was not exempt. They might lack the fervour of the Reich but they had cheered for Mussolini when he postured on his balcony and told them: 'The function of a citizen and a soldier are inseparable. Believe, obey, fight!' So Ossie would pursue it to the end because he believed that victory could only be achieved by matching the doctrine of hatred instilled by false leaders with hatred just as calculated, just as cold, even if a wounded pilot asked for mercy.

They turned for home, the sea passing slowly beneath them. 'Hello, Control,' said Ossie. 'Red Leader here. Bogeys out of business. Over.'

After a moment: 'Good show, Red Leader. Watch out for half a dozen little jobs in the vicinity of St Paul's Bay, angels twenty thousand. Over.'

'Okay, Control,' said Ossie. 'Hear you loud and clear. Out.' He took the flight to 25,000 feet.

Vey Geary was in good spirits. He had downed one of the Cants, his first confirmed victory since a Heinkel 111 over the Isle of Dogs. His R/T switch had been left on and he was singing a ditty that had been going round the squadron, striking a chord with men compelled to go up in machines they could no longer trust. His voice was a pleasant tenor, melodious and tuneful.

*'If ever an Eyetie should get on your tail*
*this is a vey good foil.*
*Be cool, be calm, be very sedate,*
*don't let your British blood boil.*
*With a hell of a crash go right through the gate,*
*and you'll cover the bastard in oil.'*

Ossie let him get to the end of the verse. Then: 'Button it, Red Four.'

Control came on again: 'Good to know you chaps are having fun. You should see the bogeys very soon, five thousand feet below you. Over.'

Ossie was the first to glimpse them, six Macchi 200s flying an immaculate curving course, ten miles out from St Paul's Bay and making for Grand Harbour. They were down-sun in tight formation and had not picked up the Hurricanes bearing down on them.

'Okay, Control,' said Ossie, 'we see 'em. On the button. Thanks. Out.'

If the Italians anticipated an attack it was not from seaward. Ossie led the way down, rolling onto his back in a quick wing-over and coming at the Macchis upside down, firing his Brownings in short bursts as the nose of his machine fell into a vertical dive and they passed through his gunsight. A flash of flame erupted from beneath the cockpit of the nearest Italian. The canopy flew off. The man stood up on his seat, fighting against the slipstream tearing at his flying suit, ready to jump, but the fuel tank exploded and he vanished in a ball of fire.

A second Macchi dived away to sea level, swooping up and down, the control lines to its elevators clearly hit, giving its pilot a roller-coaster ride. But not for long. Abruptly it dipped at high speed and hit the sea, bouncing high, momentarily intact, before cartwheeling into a thousand fragments.

The impact caught Kit's eye as he pulled out of his own violent dive, the G force squeezing him into his seat. Momentarily distracted, he heaved back on the stick, almost blacking out. He had lost sight of his own target, a Macchi spinning violently, apparently out of control but with no obvious sign of damage. As his vision cleared another machine flashed across in front of him, left to right, vortices curling from its wing-tips. For an instant, details of the Italian fighter seemed imprinted on his brain, suspended in time like a flashlight photograph: blunt-nosed and, up front, the big Fiat radial engine with its distinctive ribbed cowl, the cockpit set well back behind the wings, the outline of a figure craning forward at the controls, the broad white band encircling the tapering fuselage in front of the small-looking tailplane, the big white cross on the wildly yawing rudder with, at its centre, the elaborate coat of arms of the House of Savoy. They had missed collision by yards.

The closeness of the encounter robbed Kit of breath. He was gasping into his oxygen mask, his throat so dry he could barely swallow. 'Christ almighty,' he said out loud. His hands were shaking on the controls as a wave of shock ran through him. 'Christ almighty,' he said to no one, 'that was bloody close.'

He heard shouting in his earphones: 'Red Three, for Christ's sake break. The sonofabitch is on your tail.'

Then Astley-Cobb, laughing weakly: 'Crikey, Red Leader, he nearly had me there.'

And Ossie Wolf: 'Crikey, hell. Keep your goddamned eyes skinned, Max. The show ain't over yet.'

Not always one-sided then, Kit reflected, when you bounced the Regia. He was down to 16,000 feet and somewhere off Qawra Point. He could not see the others and called them up but now all he heard was the crackle of static, as though the R/T was dead. He felt exposed and vulnerable, at low altitude and apparently alone, although the voices of the others had given the illusion that they were close.

He dropped the Hurricane's nose and dived to pick up speed, pushing firmly against the resistance of the throttle lever, his spirits rising with the revs: 2,850 r.p.m., driving him aloft. He checked the needle on the altimeter winding smoothly clockwise and then, at 21,000 feet, eased the throttle back, dropping the revs to cruising speed, the ASI showing 160 m.p.h., never on a steady course, always twitching, jinking, head swivelling and eyes wide, straining to pick up any far-off threat that, in seconds, might close on him and bring him down. And then, nine hundred feet below, passing over what he thought must be Mellieha Bay, heading out to sea, he saw the outline of a Macchi, also climbing and, from its constantly changing attitude, vigilant, alert.

The rays of the sun were coming into Kit's cockpit over his right shoulder, catching the glass of the instruments, dazzlingly bright. He screwed his eyes closed and turned his head deliberately to the side, trying to restore his focus, ready to concentrate on his attack, but when he looked back down the Macchi wasn't there. He banked urgently to left and right, throttling up, making height, always making height, and then he saw the Italian rolling off the top of a loop, only five hundred feet below. For a moment the Macchi seemed to hang motionless and Kit plunged down, his arms shaking from the vibration of the control column, squinting through the reflector gunsight, thumb ready on the gun-button.

But the Italian had already rolled to port and fallen away. Kit followed him down, two hundred yards astern. He opened fire, short hopeful bursts, but his quarry floated clear and free, darting lightly about the sky, not out of range but never within the illuminated circle of Kit's sights, one manoeuvre leading to the next, flick rolls, spins, high-speed stalls, dropping inverted like a stone, skidding through the air in aileron turns that drove blood from the brain but did not affect the Italian's grip on the leaping, bucking machine that, in his hands, seemed joyously alive, like a wild horse barely broken, full of vigour and striving to have its head yet always bending to his will. Kit felt he must know this man. Such pilots were rare. He wondered if he had seen him perform at Hendon, in one of those pre-war displays of aerobatic skill when nothing more than national pride had been at stake.

The fighters traced an elaborate course across the Marfa Ridge, then back and north along the South Comino Channel, twisting and turning as one, never more than yards apart, Kit's Brownings barking vainly. He watched his bullets flying wide, frustrated by his elusive target, yet somehow not wanting to bring the combat to an end, reluctant to destroy such rare ability. Because, of course, it was he who would make the kill, the pursuer from the first.

And then, with a surge of apprehension, he realised the Italian had not made a single aggressive move, had simply anticipated his with consummate ease.

Perhaps that was what it was, a deadly game, a crack pilot amusing himself with an unmatchable display, waiting until Kit tired or his ammunition ran out before turning and shooting him to pieces. Even as Kit thought this the Macchi's wing-tip slipped momentarily within the circle of his gunsight. At last he'd got him, had proved himself as good. And this was how it had to end. He felt a twinge of regret. But this was no time for fine distinctions. He jabbed the gun-button.

Nothing, only the hiss of compressed air through the breech-block, like a gasp. Ammunition gone. And Kit knew he was a dead man, unarmed, out-flown and far from home, halfway to Sicily now, so far had the duel taken them. The tables turned, he was the hunted, not the hunter.

His options flashed through his mind, none of them appealing. Turn for home and hope he could outwit the man who had proved himself incomparably the better pilot? How long before he went down, like the others, burning perhaps or baling out, injured, unable to give his position over the useless damned R/T and being swallowed in the sea? Or jump now, at least intact and mind alert, better able to take his chances? Was that an option, to abandon an undamaged and perfectly functioning aircraft, without a final attempt to fight or at least evade, even if the Brownings didn't work? Or ram the swine and take them both to kingdom come?

Except the Italian was not a swine, rather the victor in a trial of skill and guile, a fair-square fight that Kit had lost, in which he had been prepared to kill and now must be prepared to die. These potential actions passed through his brain in the space of a single breath, even while the Macchi continued to evade his guns, not knowing they were silenced.

And as he kept up the charade, chasing without the means to kill, Kit realised there was another option, if he planned his move with care. Perhaps he could simply outrun him with the Hurry's marginally higher speed, somehow stay outside the range of the Macchi's guns, even if he hated the idea of running.

He slowed, allowing the Macchi to get away. The distance between them lengthened, in an instant, to half a mile. He imagined the Italian glancing in his mirror and seeing nothing, or maybe just the distant outline of his Hurricane, turning away and diving now, throttle wide. The Italian too had options, fewer, though, actually only two: to chase or not to chase. Perhaps he would assume the Englishman was low on fuel or had been ordered to break off the engagement. Easy, then, to let him go. Or would he somehow sense the truth, interpreting correctly the sudden cessation of machine-gun fire when at last it seemed he had drifted within the Englishman's sights?

Now Kit looked in his mirror and saw the Macchi pulling out of a climbing turn, banking through 180 degrees, fast, levelling out and coming after him. He knew. The clever bugger knew. Something seemed to throb deep in his stomach, like a cube of ice. For God's sake, get a grip. He had the advantage, didn't he?

Then he checked his airspeed, saw with a shock that it registered barely 280 m.p.h. Something must be running hot. These bloody kites. But he had given it one hell of a hammering. And, yes, it was the oil all right, the pressure only about thirty pounds, not the usual seventy; but the needle constant, the engine saveable if he flew with care, went easy on the revs and nursed her home. Not possible, of course, with a triumphant Eyetie on your tail and getting close now, very close. Might as well end this the way it had begun.

He was resigned now, calm. He went into a shallow dive, raised the Hurricane's nose forty-five degrees, opened the throttle and half rolled onto his back. It was a slow manoeuvre and he hung for a moment on his straps as he pressed forward on the stick and bottomed out of the loop but facing in the direction he had come and right way up. The Macchi shot past him to port, surprised but instantly clawing into a vertical turn. The man was incredibly quick; exceptional. Better to fall to someone who really knew his stuff.

He began to throw the Hurricane around the sky but the engine note was roughening and she would not respond as before. And he did not need the mirror to know that the Italian was firmly holding station on his tail, anticipating his every move. He wanted it to be over. Why wait? He did not care for cat-and-mouse.

He thought about the feral cats at the Castello Grima, toying with the *kamaleonte*. He thought about his unfinished note to Farve. He thought about Juliette. He pulled back on the throttle lever and pushed the canopy fully open. Above the oil-and-petrol smell of baking engine he caught the whiff of sea, rising on the humid air. He thrust up his goggles and unclipped his oxygen mask. He could feel the warmth of the sun on his face, even at this height, even at 16,000 feet. A beautiful day for flying, the Merlin burbling, unstressed at last, ready to take him home, except he wasn't going home. Where was that bloody Eyetie? Eyetie. What a rotten word . . .

The Italian was no longer hovering in his slipstream. He had pulled alongside, slowly, looking across the twenty yards that separated the two machines. His goggles, too, were on his forehead, his oxygen mask hanging loose and swinging with the fluctuations of the Macchi. He was a small man, wiry; reminded Kit of Tazio Nuvolari, the Flying Mantuan he'd seen wrestle the D-type Auto-Union to a Grand Prix win at Donington in '38. Kit was confounded, looking across the space between them, face set and grim; questioning, expectant.

The Italian was nodding now and grinning, waving a leather-gloved hand, held upright, fingers bent, moving at the wrist; a racing driver's wave acknowledging the chequered flag. There was a roar of gunfire. The Macchi shook with recoil. The Italian was showing what he could have done but did not care to. Then the Macchi's nose reared up and the fighter rolled and plunged away to the brown-grey Sicilian shore where waves were breaking on the rocks.

'So,' said Threlfall, 'a share of the Cant that Wolf polished off?'

'That's right,' said Kit.

'Nothing more?'

'Nothing claimed.'

Threlfall studied the pilot's face. Curtis was reticent at the best of times but now he seemed to be holding something back. 'You had a spot of bother,' he said.

'Yes. The damned R/T, and then I lost oil pressure.'

'Dodgy,' said Threlfall, wanting the man to open up.

'Yes.'

'I understand you only just got down. Minutes to spare before she seized.'

'That's right.'

'Close shave.'

'Quite close.'

'Am I right,' said Threlfall, 'or is there something you're not telling me?'

Kit Curtis did not reply. He picked at his fingernails, abstracted, staring across the airfield to the blast pen where the ground-crew were working on his Hurricane.

'Is there?' said Threlfall.

'What?'

'Something I should know?' The intelligence officer cleared

his throat. 'Look,' he said, 'it seems to me you've had some sort of shaking up. I'd like to get to the bottom of it. It's quite possible, you know, that it could be something significant, although it may not seem so to you.'

'I understand you've got your job to do,' said Kit.

'Glad to hear it,' said Threlfall. 'It sometimes seems to me that all you chaps think I've got to do is keep the score. It's more than that, much more. Small incidents that may seem trivial help to build the bigger picture.' He dug into the pocket of his sweat-stained shirt, knocked out some cigarettes from a packet of Craven A, offered one to Kit, who shook his head, and lit one for himself. 'Let's see, you got back more than thirty minutes after the others landed. I'm very curious to know what took so long. It wasn't just the gremlins in your Merlin, was it?'

'No,' said Kit resignedly. 'There was something. The trouble is . . .'

'What?' said Threlfall.

'The trouble is, it doesn't seem believable. The chaps would have a field day.'

'Surely you don't care what they think, Curtis, do you?'

'No. Well, yes, I suppose I do but, still, you're right, I shouldn't.'

'Well, then?' Threlfall said.

Kit described the encounter with the Macchi, the baldest facts, no mention of the fear that had gripped him, hearing the hiss of air that told him the magazines were empty and he was about to die; or of his hands shaking on the control column, aware that all his skill and knowledge had come to nothing faced with a better pilot. It sounded matter-of-fact the way he told it, an inconclusive spat between two fighters, until he acknowledged flatly that the man had got him cold and chose to spare him.

Threlfall had been a little bored by Kit's emotionless, clipped account, but at this sat up. 'You mean he deliberately let you get away?'

'That's right.'

'Hmm,' said Threlfall. 'This is what I mean, do you see? Small incidents that build a bigger picture.'

'Such as?'

'Come, man,' said Threlfall. 'What does this incident suggest to you?'

'I don't know,' said Kit. 'Humanity, perhaps, camaraderie, respect for the other fellow, who's given a good account of himself.'

'Ah, yes, I see,' said Threlfall. He stood up. 'Well,' he said, screwing the top back on his pen, 'it's not for me to debate the point. No doubt that can be left to Squadron Leader Penrose.'

'What is there to discuss?' said Kit.

'Oh, I'd say he's going to have a view,' said Threlfall. 'But you know me, old boy. Just a humble hack. No opinions of my own. Simply record what I've been told and pass it on.'

'As long as it's through the proper channels,' said Kit. Threlfall, like many small men entrusted with a confidence, was prone to disclosing it, to prove how much he was trusted.

Kit walked across to check his Hurricane. Chalmers was leaning into the engine bay, back arched, blue-knotted veins standing out on the calves of his bare legs. 'What's the verdict, Corporal?'

Chalmers straightened up, his face shining with sweat and grease. 'Stress fracture in one of the oil lines, sir. You only had a couple of chuffing gallons left.'

'Reckon you can get it fixed?'

'Don't you worry, sir,' said Chalmers. 'No other damage that we can see. We'll have you back in the chuffing air in no time.'

'Good show,' said Kit. Walking away he began to laugh. 'Good chuffing show,' he murmured to himself.

Suddenly he felt wonderfully alive, joyful almost, his senses vibrant, gulping in the muggy air, taking it deep into his lungs, heart pounding, firm and steady, muscles taut and tingling with sudden energy, eyes eagerly scanning the shimmering landscape, so beautiful, even here; picking up the pace now, striding, tiny sand lizards darting away to right and left, dust rising in ochre puffs; hurrying fast towards the Dispersal tent where the other chaps were gathered. Hurrying away from what might have been – the darkness; hurrying towards the light, where he could hear the distant strains of music, played by a familiar figure in flying gear, leaning back against a tent pole.

It was Ossie Wolf, on Dispersal readiness with three others, his parachute already in the cockpit of his machine close by, set to go again, but for the moment blowing and sucking on a battered Hohner harmonica, some kind of blues, American, bizarre in this desolate place, or maybe not because the blues were born out of desolation and hard times. Wolf paused and knocked out the rusty instrument against his brown left hand, saliva dripping into the dust. 'Hey, pard, we thought maybe you were swimming home.'

'If you're going to stay out late, Curtis,' said Astley-Cobb, 'at least you could warn us. You know we worry so.'

'Now the flight lieutenant's back does it mean I can bugger off back to my billet?' said Brian Twigg. He made a show of gathering up his kit and preparing to leave.

'Sorry, Sergeant,' said Kit. 'My kite's u/s for the moment.'

'Trying to dodge Games, Twigg?' said Vey Geary. 'Where's your house spirit?'

The duty corporal hurried across. 'Your stuff, sir. Good to see you back.'

Kit took the pen and the half-finished letter to his father. 'Thank you, Corporal. Any chance of a cuppa before I shove off?' He nodded at Ossie's harmonica. 'Where on earth did you get that thing?'

'Won it off Twiggy,' said Ossie Wolf. 'He bet me you'd got the chop.'

'I got this sixth sense,' said Twigg, awkwardly.

'Sense didn't come into it, you jerk,' said Ossie. 'I told you it would take more than a bunch of grape-stompers to knock Lancelot off his horse.' He breathed a few chords on the harmonica. 'Say, did you see the way that sonofabitch Cant went through the old wing-waggling routine? Like, oh, no, you got me flat-footed so I give up. I mean, who's kidding who? These Eyeties crease me.'

'Sorry for those chaps who baled out, though,' said Astley-Cobb. 'Looked distinctly chilly down there. How long do you reckon they'd last?'

'Too long,' said Kit. He took the mug of tea from the duty corporal and cradled it in his hands. Even in the stifling heat its warmth was comforting and welcome.

Ossie Wolf breathed into the harmonica, trying a few experimental chords. Astley-Cobb was chewing his lip. He seemed on edge. 'Christ almighty, you Yankee bugger, stop slobbering over that ruddy mouth-organ in that disgusting way. Either play the thing or chuck it.'

'Mouth-organ hell,' said Ossie. 'You're talking about the Mississippi saxophone.' He played a riff or two and he was good – good enough to summon up a vision of westering Americans, poor people on long, straight roads, coming from nowhere and travelling to infinity. His song was called 'Dust Bowl Blues' and after each verse, sung in his dry, strong voice, he echoed the plain, spare tune on the Hohner. The pilots listened quietly, their faces as expressionless as Ossie's was alive, his eyes shut, his teeth a slash of white as he sang, nodding to the beat, fierce-looking as though it was a tribal chant. He blew a final, savage reprise and there was a long silence. Then he slipped the harmonica into the pocket of his flying suit. 'Could have been written for this God-forsaken hole, but it wasn't. Feller name of Guthrie, kinda homespun, but he's got some right ideas.'

'Left, you mean,' said Astley-Cobb. 'Isn't Guthrie a bloody Bolshie?'

'Well, brother,' said Ossie Wolf, 'you know enough to be ignorant. He's just a guy who believes in people, believes in people nobody else believes in. But I'll tell you what he's got painted on his guitar. "This machine kills Fascists." That's good enough for me.' He rubbed his chin. 'Hell, maybe I should stick that on my Hurry.'

'Hardly,' Kit said quickly. 'Otherwise the chaps might think you're a wise guy, trying to be one-up on us mugs who go for Mickey Mouse.'

Ossie opened his mouth but before he could speak the Dispersal phone rang, harsh and discordant after the music of the blues, and the flight was scrambled. Ossie fumbled in the breast pocket of his flying suit as he ran, and threw the harmonica to Kit. 'See if you can get a tune out of that, you cock-eyed Limey.'

'Isn't it meant to catch a bullet?' shouted Kit. He moved outside the tent to watch them go.

The sun was at its highest now, and quitting even the partial shade of the tent was like wading into liquid, the atmosphere glutinous and clinging with no hint of the slightest breeze. The crimson wind-sock hung straight down, limp, over by the runway. The four Hurricanes were line-abreast, propellers gleaming, throwing up great clouds of drifting dust and then, as they drew away from the turbulence created by the fighters, the clouds began to slow, hanging in the still air and changing shape, curling and building, like djinns from a tale of the Arabian nights. The Hurricanes were accelerating now, moving as one, bounding down the runway and lifting, wheels retracting. Kit sensed the thump as the hydraulic rams folded the undercarriages smoothly away to their in-flight position between the centre-section spars. He always liked that moment when the plane was free of drag, lively, as though it had shaken itself and come alive.

'You going up again today, sir?' said the duty corporal.

'Only if someone finds me another kite,' said Kit. 'For the moment I'm on mess readiness. Can you rustle up some transport?'

Kit made the artillery orderly on the sand-coloured M20 BSA drop him at the main Mdina gate. He winced at the thought of the 250cc side-valve blaring down the pinched-in streets and alleys where balconies nearly touched; the 'silent city', as the locals had it, which seemed to slumber out of time. He walked slowly across the bridge over the dry moat and through the gateway, past the courtyard façade, in the French style, of another *palazzo*, its stonework mellow gold, built two hundred years ago, he knew, by Grand Master de Vilhena whose bellicose coat of arms adorned the gate he had just come through.

Around the corner, in the mess, Penrose was speaking on the phone. He waved at Kit to sit down in one of the cracked-leather armchairs. He held up a glass of Scotch and raised his eyebrows.

'I'm still on readiness,' said Kit.

Penrose held his hand over the mouthpiece. 'Relax. No more flying for you today.' He snapped his fingers at an orderly.

The man brought Kit a Scotch, and brackish water in a small white jug. He added a little and sipped the whisky slowly, feeling mellow, quite euphoric still, taking measured breaths, sitting low in the armchair, studying the brightly coloured frescoes.

Penrose finished his conversation. He plumped himself down, puffing out his cheeks, right foot resting easily on left knee, and staring at the ceiling too. 'Not a patch on the Sistine Chapel.'

'Oh?' said Kit. 'Have you been there?'

'No. But I bet they're not a patch.' He signalled to the orderly for another Scotch. 'So,' he said, 'Threlfall tells me you've had quite a day.'

'No more than any of the other chaps,' said Kit.

'Unusual, then,' said Penrose. 'This Eyetie fellow . . .'

'Ah, yes,' said Kit.

'Why do you think he did it?'

'You mean didn't do it, I suppose.'

'Extraordinary behaviour,' said Penrose. He paused while the orderly placed a fresh Scotch on the side-table.

'You sound quite peeved that he didn't send me down a flamer,' said Kit.

Penrose gave a short, mirthless laugh. 'Don't be ridiculous, old man. But you've got to admit it's rum.'

'Yes,' said Kit.

'Threlfall suggested you put it down to some sort of chivalric instinct, knights of the sky and all that stuff.'

'Did he?' said Kit. 'I really wouldn't know.'

Penrose shook his head. 'Good grief, this bloody man's at war yet he allows an enemy pilot to live to fight another day. Clearly the chap's not yellow but it seems to me he hasn't got the guts to kill. He's playing at war. One gent to another. Cheery wave be buggered. He was a damned fool and if he was in my squadron I'd have him shot. Anyone who thinks this is just a game should go down to Imtarfa Hospital and take a look at some of the women and children who've been bombed to blazes by this joker's chums.'

'You don't mean me, I hope,' said Kit.

Penrose reddened. 'No, of course not. I know you did your best up there. But Threlfall's been ordered to keep this under wraps and I expect you to do the same. I don't want there to be any doubt about why we're here. The little gestures the Eyeties throw up from time to time, they just muddy the water. Good God, one of the pongo infantry officers even had the brass nerve to tell me he found it hard to see them as enemies. I soon gave him short shrift, I can tell you. Our job is to go in bloody hard and shoot the buggers down. They're Fascists, that's all we need to know.' He smiled placatingly, still pink round the ears. 'But of course I don't need to tell you any of this. If you hadn't run out of ammo you'd have done for him. As it is, you had a lucky escape, thanks to your little chum being a misguided, romantic fool. But, then, what do you expect of the Italians? These Latin races, they lack the belly for a fight.'

'Unlike the Hun?' said Kit.

'The Hun's a good fighting man,' said Penrose, 'whatever else you might say.' He seemed pleased with the way he had clarified the situation for young Curtis, had shown him what Threlfall called the bigger picture, and sought to bring the conversation to a positive conclusion. 'You see, it's weakness that you saw today. And it raises a question: how deep does that weakness go? If the Regia lacks commitment as a fighting force then our task could prove much easier.' He smiled with satisfaction. 'Valletta shall hear of this.'

'They've probably heard already,' said Kit. 'Threlfall's hugger-mugger with a gang of those intelligence types lurking down the hole in Lascaris.'

Half an hour later word came through that only three Hurricanes had returned from the scramble. Vey Geary's machine had been seen to dive vertically into the sea off Zonqor Point during a hectic dogfight with four Macchis returning from a strafing raid on Halfar. Despite the fierceness of the engagement it appeared the Italians had finally made off, apparently unscathed. When he heard the news, Penrose went quiet, avoiding Kit's eye, and walked out on to the terrace of the *palazzo* where he stared down at the Takali base, spread out on the plain before him, watching for the survivors of the flight to touch down.

Kit left him to his thoughts and did not ask when he planned to contact Valletta, to explain his theories about the bigger picture.

# Four

Ossie Wolf did not care for dreams. He always felt uneasy that his mind could wander free through stuff over which he had no control. He liked to claim he did not dream because he saw it as a weakness, and even believed it when he said it because whatever night visions came to him always vanished when he woke, only leaving him with a lingering sense of having been away somewhere, someplace in the past where bad things happened, or aroused and with a hard on he could do nothing about, apart from the obvious solution and that again he saw as a weakness. But no remembered details, thus easy to dismiss. But then, as July wore into August, a dream began to come to him, not every night, but when it did the same, and when he woke each detail was so fixed and clear that it took him moments to realise where he was, in the room at the *palazzo* in Mdina, the quarters he shared with Kit Curtis and Max Astley-Cobb, and not trapped in this other place.

It was not an elaborate vision but, simple though it was, it seemed to stretch in time so Ossie felt it occupied many hours, took perhaps all night, although what little occurred could really have taken only minutes.

Each time he found himself walking slowly along a domed

tunnel, quite dark, the walls bricked and glistening with moisture that he felt compelled to touch as he passed. His trailing fingers left marks in the slime and when he snatched them back they were stained green and smelled of decay. The tunnel seemed to slope down and then rise and curve away to the right. Now he was treading on unseen objects, not animate but cracking and crumbling under his feet, like honeycombed stone or bone. And then as he climbed, the tunnel filled with light, gradually at first, but growing in intensity as he stumbled forward, luminous and blinding, and he felt himself on a threshold, not a drop but a point beyond which he could not go. With his arm across his eyes to shield them from the brilliance, he found himself fixed to the spot, frozen with a kind of rising apprehension at something unseen that might be approaching. He heard himself asking, like a kid scared of the dark, afraid to look under the bed: 'Is someone there? Is someone there?' But still he could not move although he sensed shapes coming closer, crowding in, blocking out the light. And although they were almost on him now, still he could not move . . .

He caught Kit and Astley-Cobb studying him the first few times but they didn't say a thing. That was the way it was. Guys were left to their own devices, each man handling in his own way whatever was thrown at him. No point in chewing the fat about what they already knew and understood. That didn't help any, unless it was the start of some kind of more serious crack-up and then usually nobody could say a damned thing to help, even the doc, and all you could do was hope the guy came out the other side. Which, after a time, when they'd disappeared into themselves or behaved kind of screwy for a while, or been given a leave, they usually did. If not, and this was rare, they found themselves shipped home, not talked about again, tucked away in obscurity, where they'd be less of an embarrassment to the

Service. A pity because they'd probably done good things, fought well, endured tough situations without complaint, but they were no longer any use in the role for which they'd trained, the fighter pilot's role, in which a man was required to battle with his nerves just as surely as with any more tangible foe.

Ossie knew he wasn't in that situation. He'd had a lousy nightmare, that was all. Just a little fatigued, he guessed. It didn't make any kind of sense so why waste time brooding about it? And, anyway, by the time he'd shaved he'd stopped thinking about that goddamned tunnel and the feeling that something was coming towards him out of that dazzling light. Or made himself, because if he allowed himself to turn his thoughts that way he found the details remained just as real to him as the tanned face looking back at him in the small, cracked mirror.

But then one morning he snapped awake, rigid on his bed, feeling darkness folding round him, his brain alive, his body as though pinioned, shouting as he sensed shapes leaning in towards him, closer than ever now and almost touching. 'Jesus,' he said, as the horror fell away, 'Jesus Christ.'

And because he had spoken first, Kit Curtis murmured: 'Rotten dream?'

'Impossible,' said Astley-Cobb, easing out of his bed. 'Yanks never dream. He told us that.' He collected his toilet gear and set off down the corridor to the wash-room, whistling.

'Look who's talking,' retorted Ossie, loud enough for Astley-Cobb to hear. 'Jesus, that schmuck's been hollering for weeks, keeping us all awake.'

Kit yawned. 'We all do it. Living like this, it takes us in different ways. Nobody's immune.'

'The hell with that,' said Ossie. Standing there, in the morning light with everything normal, he knew he could beat this thing, push away the crazy phantoms that came from nowhere and told him nothing, fight back like he always did, needing no one, stronger, harder, impervious to this kind of psycho crap, sissy stuff that just got in the way. So, no more hollering out, no more waking, shaking, thanks to some nameless dread that was down to goddamned imagination and didn't mean beans.

The trouble was, he had told himself this before.

But then a twist. The Italians seemed less inclined to come across by day. Instead they bombed by night, Fiat BR20s, Savoia-Marchetti SM.79s and Cants, often single, flying high and intending to unload on Grand Harbour or the airfields.

Hurricanes went up, threading between the towering beams of searchlights that rose to 2,000 feet and scoured the moonless sky above the island; night fighters flown by volunteers, advised on height and vector by Control, watching for the hump-backed profile of a raider caught in overlapping circles of brilliant light. They waited for Control to call off the guns, circling until the salvos ceased, yellow-red exhaust flames streaming back along the noses of their machines, then moved in swiftly from line astern, gunsights on, gun-buttons set, sharks beneath a whale, floating, patient and unseen, ready for the perfect moment, and then the tracer flashed through the darkness, little streaks of light, like crimson crayon marks on coal-black paper, and puffs of ghost-white smoke from an engine or fire erupted from a wing-root where the fuel tanks were, and a bomber, Fiat, Savoia or Cant, went droning down, its shape now indistinct, a fireball, falling from the sky, lighting up the ground for a moment as it struck.

So this was the twist, that Ossie flew by night, the first of the pilots to step forward, and found that when he slept by day he did not find himself in that goddamned tunnel with the stained-green walls and stone or bone crunching underfoot and, on the threshold, knowing that something was out there, in the searing light, and always coming closer. He forgot that he had ever been concerned and found he got by with little need for sleep at all. He flew occasionally with the other guys in the usual way, by day, whenever he could find a machine although, while he was night-hawking, command of his flight had passed to Kit Curtis, learning fast and building a decent score despite the Regia seeming less inclined to show itself in daylight hours.

In the mornings, when he had been stood down, he liked to watch them go, from the terrace of the *palazzo*, eyes still raw and smarting from stalking shadows at 20,000 feet; Curtis, Twigg, Astley-Cobb and Rimmer, with whom Astley-Cobb had flown at Biggin Hill, stocky and pugnacious, some said in the American's mould. No mention now of Geary, whose body had not been recovered from the sea off Zonqor Point; Vey Geary, part of the schoolboy act abandoned by Astley-Cobb, who flew with fresh determination but did not laugh as much.

Gradually, though, a change in Ossie Wolf became apparent. Already thin on meagre rations, like the rest with no spare flesh, he grew gaunt, with dark circles underneath his eyes, which now protruded, his cheeks drawn in, blue veins showing at his temples. Penrose took him to one side as he stumped up the stairs to his room in the *palazzo*, returned from night patrol. 'I hear from Spy you got another BR20.'

'Boy, did I! The bastard went up like an aerial shell on the Fourth of July.'

'I think you've earned a break. I suppose you know you look like something the cat's dragged in?'

'Who gives a damn?'

'The MO for one. He thinks you're asking too much of yourself. Sooner or later it'll come to a head.'

'You mean a crack-up?'

'Something like that.'

'Quit worrying. I'm having me—'

'A barrel of laughs. Yes, I know how it is with you. I'm serious, Wolf. You're driving yourself too hard. I don't want to lose a pilot because your reactions are all to cock or because you're not as tough as you like to think.'

'Okay. Fine. That it?'

'Get your head down. That's an order. You're stood down until you hear from me. We've got plenty of chaps keen to take a crack at our Eyetie fly-by-nights.'

'Well, maybe I will hit the hay at that.'

Ossie climbed the broad staircase with its elaborate iron balustrades, going up two steps at a time to show Penrose just how bushed he was. The first time he had seen the *palazzo* he had thought it showy and high-falutin', like the stage-set for a vaudeville show, but he liked it now. He liked it for its coolness and space. Despite its gaudy decoration it was somehow restful to the eye and echoed with the past in a way he had never experienced in St Louis, Missouri.

He stripped naked and stretched out on his bed. He looked along his dead-white body, the belly sunken, the hipbones sticking out, the legs tanned yellow-brown, as though he'd been standing up to his thighs in mud, bony as an Egyptian mummy's. He thought if he stepped on some scales he'd be lucky to make 120 pounds. Egyptian mummy. He remembered the time Miss Appleton had taken a bunch of seventh-graders on a trip to the St Louis art museum on Forest Park, sniggering and fooling around, and how they'd wound up by this case with a dead man in it, from thousands of years BC, they said, laid out just as he was now, but bone showing through little tears in the skin, yellowish-brown like his, and Miss Appleton saying, real severe, how they should have respect because it was a privilege to see this guy who was the most popular object in the collection, and him and Billie Ellermann laughing like hell and scaring the crap out of the girls by saying the stiff was going to rise up and take a bow. And it was like he was back in that gallery looking into the case with the dead Egyptian guy in it, but he was alone, and then he found himself walking away, walking slowly, along a domed tunnel, the walls bricked and glistening with moisture and he trailed his fingers in the slime and smelled the decay and now he was treading on unseen objects, hearing them crack and crumble, and stumbling up a gradual slope towards a brilliant light and he began to raise his arm to shield his eyes . . .

He felt a hand on his shoulder and tried to cry out, but his mouth was dry and his tongue seemed swollen, lying back in his throat, so he could only utter rough sounds, low and hoarse, meaningless croaks. The hand shook him more urgently. He opened his eyes.

Giorgio, the boy, was leaning over him, frowning, puzzled, but smiling nervously. 'We go,' said the kid.

'Huh?' said Ossie.

'It is Saturday,' said the kid. 'You don't fly. We go. We go now. They are waiting at Targa Gap.'

Ossie Wolf pulled on his clothes, feeling nauseous. Maybe it was the lack of food or maybe it was the crummy dream about that goddamned tunnel, coming back pin-sharp just when he'd thought he'd got it licked. Maybe it was all these things and more. Maybe Penrose was right; the MO too. Stuff builds up. Maybe he had been pushing too hard. Pushing too hard for years. What had Penrose said? 'You're not as tough as you like to think.'

Giorgio was by the door, beckoning him urgently with a small brown hand. The palm was white.

'Yeah, yeah,' said Ossie. 'Give a guy a break. Any sign of Squadron Leader Penrose?'

The boy made a swooping motion with his hand. 'He flies.'

'Okay,' said Ossie.

They went down the broad staircase and out into the open space in front of the *palazzo*. The sun was fierce, and as he passed out of the shade of the building Ossie raised his arm to shield his eyes.

They took one of the pool bicycles to travel the rough dirt road to Tal-Bistra, two or more miles away, swooping down the steep incline from the ramparts of Mdina, the rush of air welcome but still hot, and then, harder going now, skirting the edge of Mosta, the great dome of its church made indistinct by the heat waves rising from the plain, the image shimmering and moving like a mirage, yet tangible and weirdly grand for its surroundings, encircled by a straggle of simple white-block buildings.

The boy had taken off his waistcoat and folded it as a cushion, perching on the handlebars, his feet dangling at either side of the front wheel. His man's cloth cap with the torn peak was pulled low over his eyes. The seam at the back was also torn and his hair spilled down his narrow neck, shiny like black silk. Ossie Wolf felt a warmth towards the kid, watching his small head move with each thrust he gave to the pedals; a gritty little guy with spirit, unafraid and self-reliant like all the other Malties he had come across.

They met up with the others near the catacombs of Tal-Bistra, dug out of the soft rock of the Targa Gap by early Christians. The hunters had no interest in the past. Their minds were set on killing *fniek*. The hounds were eager too, six long-snouted *kelb tal-fenek*, dogs of the rabbit, amber-eyed with rust-coloured coats, short-haired to suit the Maltese climate, able to search out prey for eight hours at a stretch, covering miles of rough limestone terrain. They struggled at their leashes, surging forward, yelping as the boy jumped down, pulling on his waistcoat.

Ossie threw the bicycle against a wild-thyme bush. The situation seemed unreal. For a moment his senses swam, like they did when he'd taken a drink too many. The four men came towards him, leather cartridge belts across their chests, cloth-capped and wearing waistcoats like Giorgio's, despite the pulsating heat. They cradled shotguns in their arms, the barrels broken, angled down. They looked like guys he'd known on the Aragon front in '36, dug in on the high sierra under the Republican militia's scarlet flags, which cracked and flapped in the sirocco blowing from the south.

The shortest of the four had a second shotgun slung on his left shoulder. He shrugged it off and held it out. '*Bongu*, Ossie, *bongu. Kif inti*?'

Ossie took the weapon, balancing it in both hands: a twelve-gauge Italian Bernadelli, single-barrelled, single-shot with fancy scroll engraving. They'd given him the best. 'How you doing, Joseph?' he said. He shook the short man's hand, which had the feel of a well-worn leather glove, hard and shiny. Joseph Farinacci did not look like his son, except in style of dress. Giorgio looked on grinning, impatient for the fun to start.

The thin one with the broken nose, Salvator Boero, offered him a wineskin, the bristles brown and cream, the pelt of one of the goats once seen everywhere but less so now, killed for meat, not kept for milk and breeding. Ossie missed his mouth with the jet of wine and the hunters laughed, even Bonnici, the sullen one, who never talked but spat and listened to the others.

They moved out across the limestone outcrops, line-abreast, battle-formation Maltese-style, boots scraping on the rock, guns loaded but with safety catches on, hounds loose now, rushing from place to place, picking up the rabbit scents, frantically sounding off.

Farinacci chuckled at their excitement. 'Plenty *fniek* about today. I feel it.'

'Uh-huh,' said Ossie. The red wine, its sour tang still on his lips, was slopping around his empty stomach like the wine in the goatskin bag that bounced on Salvator Boero's back.

'You killing plenty Germans?' said Farinacci.

'Italians now.'

'You killing plenty?'

'Some, yeah.'

Farinacci grunted. 'You kill a man. How does that feel?'

'You kill a rabbit,' Ossie said. 'How does that feel?'

'Nothing.'

'A man the same.'

'The same with a man?' Farinacci's eyebrows went up. 'It is a big thing, to kill a man.'

'Your first rabbit, when you were a kid like Giorgio, that was a big thing, I bet.'

'Yes. That is true. You become accustomed.'

'The same with a man. You become accustomed.'

The hounds were calling now, a wailing cry, not quite a bark. 'The *kurriera*,' Farinacci said. 'We are on them now.' A dozen rabbits, the usual browns and greys, long-limbed and fast, burst from a tangled clump of white-flowered boar thistle. They were a long way off, perhaps a hundred yards, and racing to the left, towards fresh cover. Ossie fired before the others had their gun-butts to their shoulders. A fat tan buck somersaulted into a narrow gully. A volley of shots rang out across the steppe. As the men reloaded, the hounds delivered five dead *fniek* to the feet of Joseph Farinacci and a sixth still living that he finished with a blow. 'Lord,' he said to Ossie, 'but that was a miracle of a shot.' He held up the fat buck. 'A big old fellow. He will feed us well.'

Farinacci noticed that the American did not say modestly, as would an Englishman, that it had been a lucky shot. Clearly the man knew luck was not involved.

Ossie knew it too. He had seen the fleeing buck as though in slowed-down time, adjusting the elevation of the Bernadelli's barrel and tracking a yard or so ahead of it, squeezing the trigger gently to avoid the slightest snatch. Deflection, pure but not so simple . . .

They hunted until the sun was high, more *fniek* and other creatures that strayed across their path: a heron, struck by shot in a puff of grey-white feathers, spinning to earth with big wings spread like a falling angel, a hedgehog, a peregrine falcon, hunting too but falling to another predator, sparrows, lizards. The oldest of the party, Daniel Falzon, whose eyes were bad for hunting, brought down a feral bitch with bulging teats raising a litter of hours-old young, still blind, in the hollow of a wall, Giorgio wanting to save a couple but beaten by the hounds too fast.

The men were happy. They laid out their haul and Ossie snapped them with Farinacci's worn Box Brownie, the hunters offering their best sides to the camera, big and proud, gun-butts resting on hips, standing over the line of fur and feather corpses.

Then Farinacci came over and took the camera, pushing Ossie into the centre of the little group, Salvator Boero tall enough to loop an arm round his neck and Giorgio squatting grinning at his feet, Bonnici and Falzon leaning in, rugged hunters, grim and beady-eyed. As the shutter clicked the tough guys dropped their pose.

There was a distant cry. On the other side of the wall, where Daniel Falzon had shot the bitch, ran a narrow track that seemed to mark the limit of the limestone steppe. Beyond it, behind another wall, ranks of stunted vines protruded from the reddish earth. And between the vines, her small feet scuffing up the soil, a young woman was making her way towards them, moving slowly, leaning against the weight of a bamboo basket swinging from her left hand. She stopped and placed it on the ground, rubbed her hands together, then cupped them against her forehead, shadowing her eyes, stooping slightly, peering round.

Giorgio shouted: 'Claudia! Claudia! *Hawn, hawn!*' She straightened up and waved and Giorgio ran to meet her, vaulting over the first wall, which, along its length, had tumbled down, and scrambling over the second, intact and well maintained. He took up the basket and led the way back, talking and laughing, making much use of his hands as he described the hunt.

Closer to, as they stepped over poles laid across a gap in the good wall, a little further along, where it was easier to manage the basket, Ossie could see the woman was a girl, about fifteen, with a proud head and hair like Giorgio's, curling and shining black.

'*Bongu*,' she said, looking from face to face.

'*Bongu*, Claudia,' said Salvator Boero, quickly. He was looking at her in a certain way but she ignored him.

'My daughter,' said Joseph Farinacci to Ossie.

'Yeah,' said Ossie. 'I can see.'

Farinacci looked pleased that the American had perceived a resemblance, but he was wrong. The girl was so like Giorgio that Ossie knew she must be his sister.

There was food in the bamboo basket. They laid it out on the rocks: *hobz*, loaves of crusty Maltese bread that the men cut with their hunting knives into thick rounds. They dipped them into olive oil, then rubbed them with the pulp of ripe tomatoes and topped them with capers, olives, garlic. There were *pastizzi*, tartlets of ricotta cheese and egg or meat and anchovies, *kwarezimal*, a cake of honey, nuts and cinnamon, made without butter, eggs or milk, suitable for Lent but eaten any time, date-filled pastries, treacle rings and almond macaroons. And fruit: plums and oranges, peaches, grapes and melons.

For a long time no one spoke. The only noise was that of

eating. The girl had sat down a little to one side, her arms clasped round her knees, her long skirt gathered modestly at her ankles, glancing occasionally at the dead birds and animals, then back at the men, with a hint of amusement in her dark eyes and the faintest smile curving her lips.

'You people eat well,' said Ossie to Farinacci. For a moment he looked confused and Ossie realised the spread had been arranged for him.

Farinacci did not respond directly. 'Claudia,' he said. 'Fruit for our American brother.'

The girl rose easily to her feet, graceful, like a dancer. Salvator Boero watched her, frowning, his head tipped back, big mouth open, gulping down a stream of wine from the brown-cream-bristled goatskin. She gathered up some fruit and brought it across to Ossie in a small reed bowl, kneeling quickly in front of him and offering it, her thick hair veiling her face and tumbled round her shoulders. Behind her the barren landscape stretched away, eastern-looking, like one of those coloured pictures from the family Bible the Old Man kept in his study back home. She seemed eastern too, dark and submissive, offering fruit, looking up a little shyly, but again her lips curving in that faint, faint smile. He took a fig and broke off some grapes. '*Grazzi.*'

'*M'hemmx imn'hiex*,' she said. 'You're welcome.'

He held out a grape but she shook her head and moved back, then rose to her feet. He stared up at her. She was outlined against the sun. He raised his arm to shield his eyes.

He was back in his room in the *palazzo*. He had cycled back to Mdina alone. Giorgio had set off across the vineyard with the others, his sister carrying the empty bamboo basket. As Joseph Farinacci had stepped across the poles that lay across the gap in the well-maintained wall and entered the red-earthed field with the vines, Ossie had said: 'Short-cut, huh? You must know the owner.'

Farinacci had laughed. 'I do. I am. Our farm is in the valley, one mile to the east.'

Now Ossie was alone and once more naked. He had regained his room unseen. His face and limbs burned from the sun. He wanted to sleep but when he closed his eyes he began to think about the guy in the case in Forest Park with his bones showing through his parchment skin and he became the guy and he was walking, walking slowly, aware of a noise like cracking bone but he could not tell if it was underfoot or his own bone giving way and he was trailing skeletal fingers in slime and going up a gradual slope towards the brightness and there was someone, something in the brightness. At first he thought, with a leap of his heart, that it was Claudia Farinacci, but it wasn't her and it wasn't just a single figure: there were more, shuffling and moving, coming forward, silhouetted against the streaming light . . .

He was awake and cold with sweat yet burning from inside and this was more than a crummy nightmare that wouldn't let him go: this was something new, like his stomach was being gripped by an unseen hand; gripped hard and then released, then gripped again but even harder, the pain extreme as though claws were digging in. His guts seemed liquid, making the slopping, gulping sound of lousy plumbing in a run-down motel. He knew he could not risk a fart but made it to the john and emptied his insides, shaking and overcome by the stench. He finished, panting. Maybe that was it. He cleaned himself, then showered. At last he sensed the corruption being washed away. He'd gotten rid of it all right. Must have, whatever the cause. Goddamned wine or fruit or almost anything; maybe those grapes and figs, beautiful but tainted, offered him by Giorgio's kid sister. Bitten at last by the Malta Dog, or Claudia Farinacci.

He felt weak and shaky but still he reckoned he could beat this thing by pushing it aside, denying it and acting normal. The bed looked good but that was part of crying quits, so he forced himself to drag on his clothes and go down the broad staircase, running his hand along the banister but not supporting himself because that was what his body wanted him to do.

Penrose and some others had clattered in through the entrance hall, their uniforms stained with sweat and oil from flying. 'Get your head down?' Penrose asked.

'Sure.'

'That's the ticket,' said Penrose.

'Any trade?' said Ossie.

Penrose shook his head. Two flights had patrolled for forty minutes, big figure-of-eights at 20,000 feet, but had not seen a thing. The Italians spotted by Control had jettisoned their bomb-loads in the sea south of Gozo and turned back.

'Perhaps I'll have more luck tonight,' said Kit Curtis, as the group broke up.

'Tonight?' said Ossie.

'I'm taking over your kite.'

'Says who?'

'Pop.'

'Uh-huh,' said Ossie. 'You flown at night before?'

'Not here, but I understand it's straightforward enough. You chaps seem to have got it pretty well sorted, what with flare-paths and Control on the ball co-ordinating things with the search-light and artillery types.'

'I'll come down to the field,' said Ossie, 'and show you round my kite. She's got her ways.'

'That's very decent,' said Kit Curtis, unaware of the man's vague motive.

'Who you flying with?' said Ossie.

'Your chum,' said Kit. 'Sergeant Palmer.'

When it was dusk they went down to Takali on bicycles, riding side by side, the tyres hissing as they swept over the dirt, scrabbling for grip on the corners. To ease the jolting Ossie tried to raise himself from the saddle, standing on the pedals. It all felt loose down there, flaccid and unpredictable. The air was sickly warm and mellow, rich with the scent of thyme, pine and ripening fruit, and the salt-sea smell drifting in from the distant shore.

The Hurricanes had been pushed out from their blast pens and stood out against the darkening sky. Drongo Palmer was sitting in the cockpit of his machine but not strapped in. He pulled himself up, stepped out and jumped down at their feet. Underneath the port wing two armourers were completing the installation of fresh ammunition boxes, securing the covers with half-turns on the Dzus fasteners.

'How you doing, pal?' said Ossie.

'Still got a touch of that ruddy sand-fly fever,' Palmer said. 'Can't seem to shake it off.'

'Seen the doc?'

'He reckons I'm fit to fly.'

'You've never been fit to fly,' said Ossie.

'You unfeeling bloody Yank,' said Palmer. 'You've never been sick in your life.'

Corporal Chalmers came across with Palmer's rigger and fitter. 'Just your moniker on the DI sheet, Sarge, and then you're set to go.'

Palmer signed the daily inspection form. 'Things are looking up,' he said. 'DI went walkabout when Jerries were ruling the bloody roost.'

'If you're feeling rocky,' Ossie said, 'why not let me take up this heap of shit?'

Palmer laughed. 'Tempting, mate, but Pop would have my guts for garters.'

The duty corporal hurried across from the Dispersal tent. 'Control's been on. Take-off in thirty minutes. Still no sign of bogeys. Orders in the air.'

'Let's run her up, blokes,' said Palmer. 'See if the ruddy prop goes round.'

'Hey, Drongo,' Ossie said, 'I was on the level, feller, if you're not hunky-dory.'

'Never knew you cared,' said Palmer, from the cockpit. Behind him the ground-crew had wheeled a trolley-accumulator into position and connected it to his aircraft, ready to start the engine. Within minutes it burst into life, the propeller throwing back a storm of dust and sand, lashing at Ossie's back as he turned away. He felt an urgent need to be where Drongo Palmer was. He knew he would be all right then, conquer this thing, come alive again back at the controls, seeing those wing-tips shake, belted in behind that tilted nose, advancing down the runway, slowly, but feeling her gather speed and begin to lighten, lifting, rising into the placid, dangerous sky, letting his thumb move over the gun-button ready to loose-off streams of tracer at the first sonofabitch who floated across his gunsight.

He walked slowly towards his Hurricane. His legs felt oddly heavy, as though encased in lead boots like deep-sea divers wore. Kit Curtis was there and Chalmers, and a couple of other characters he couldn't make out in the gloom. Jesus, it was dark. How could they expect a guy to fly in this? He stumbled round the tailplane and raised his right foot with a grunt, pushing it into the stirrup-step below the fuselage. Somehow he had forgotten he wasn't flying, or had he planned this all along? He began to heave himself onto the wing. He felt himself being pulled down, or was he falling? He heard Kit Curtis's voice: 'Nice try, old chap. Not this time. Don't worry, though. You'll be in action soon enough.'

Ossie slumped forward against the wing. 'I don't feel so hot,' he said. Wetness was running down his legs. He flattened himself against the wing's metal skin, which felt cool against his cheek, but then he began to slide, his fingers squeaking across the alloy, and finally he fell.

# Five

When the guns started up and explosions began shortly before dawn, to the north somewhere, the talk was of invasion. How else to explain the distinctive thump-thump of the twin-barrelled six-pounders guarding Grand Harbour, muffled, deep-toned and shaking the ground, that mingled with the more usual bursts of anti-aircraft and machine-gun fire, by now expected and almost routine? After all, just two months before, only six hundred miles away, south-east of the Greek mainland, Crete had been stormed by twenty thousand German troops dropped by parachute, flown in on gliders and Junkers Ju-52 transports or put ashore by invasion craft embarking from the Axis flotilla standing out to sea. In eight days Crete had fallen. So now there was one thought. Perhaps the Reich was less hard-pressed on the Eastern Front. Perhaps they had returned.

The walls of Mdina rang with the sounds of distant battle. In the wing of the *palazzo* set aside for the sick, Ossie Wolf was out of bed, his legs trembling, steadying himself against a wall. Flashes of light illuminated the plastered wall facing the small window, followed by the drumming of the barrage, renewed and furious, rolling towards the hill-town like an approaching summer storm. 'Jesus,' he said. 'The sons-of-bitches are coming in.'

'If they are,' said Leaf, the pilot officer in the bed by the door, 'I'm in the ruddy bag.' He tapped his broken arm. 'That's rotten luck. They were shipping me back to Gib next week.'

An orderly came into the room with a torch.

'What in hell's going on?' said Ossie.

'Back in bed, sir.'

'Sounds like the goddamned balloon's gone up.'

'I wouldn't know about that, sir. Come on, back in bed.'

'Get me a goddamned handgun,' said Ossie. 'That's an order. And bring my clothes.'

The torch flicked to floor then doorway, and for a moment the room went dark. Then the plaster wall started lighting up again. Ossie heard the orderly going down the stairs. He sat back on the bed and held his hands in front of him, palms upwards, fingers extended. They were shaking, like an old man's, uncontrollable. He realised his head was shaking too and beads of sweat were dropping onto his bare thighs. He clenched and unclenched his fists, forcing the feeble tendons to tense and strengthen, remembering the heaviness of a Webley .38. He wrapped his stiff fingers round an imagined butt, feeling for the trigger.

Leaf was apprehensive. 'I say, have you had weapons training, old boy? Personally I haven't got a clue.'

'I can handle myself,' said Ossie.

'And I thought my luck was in,' said Leaf. 'I prang my Hurry and walk away, and now I'm going to be caught in the *Gunfight at the OK Corral.*'

Ossie looked up at a sound. Torches again.

Penrose was standing in front of him. 'You're not making Mitchell's job any easier,' Penrose said. The orderly was peering over his shoulder.

'I gave the guy an order,' Ossie said.

'A pistol, yes, I heard. That's all we need, a trigger-happy dysentery case prowling the palace and popping off at shadows. Get back in your damned bed, man and stop making a nuisance of yourself.'

'So I sit here and wait for a goddamned Nazi paratrooper to read me a bedtime story, huh?'

'That's no invasion you're hearing,' said Penrose, 'just a bunch of Regia Nautica glory-boys trying to have a go at merchantmen unloading in Grand Harbour. It worked in Crete. Their damned explosive motor-boats got HMS *York* in Suda Bay. This time their EMBs have come unstuck. Control says they're in the process of being cut to pieces.'

They heard the growl of engines. On the plain below Mdina, where low mist glowed in the thin light of dawn, pairs of Hurricanes were lifting off from Takali, some heading for St Paul's Bay, others on a course for Valletta.

The Italian task force had reached its base point, twenty miles north of Malta, shortly before midnight. The attack had been planned for weeks. Almost immediately something had gone wrong. Of the nine nineteen-foot explosive motor-boats, each with a single pilot, lowered into the sea from the auxiliary support ship *Diana*, one malfunctioned. But still, as *Diana* turned north for her post-action meeting point, the remaining EMBs set course for Grand Harbour as planned, supported by two sixty-foot high-speed motor-torpedo boats and two smaller MTBs, *motoscafo turismo* models, one supporting the EMBs, the other carrying on-deck a brace of human torpedoes, *maiali*, pigs, to their two-man crews.

By three in the morning the group was five miles off Valletta where the twin *maiali* were unshipped. Another malfunction. Only a single electric-motored human torpedo approached St Elmo Fort, perched above the entrance to Grand Harbour, close to the breakwater viaduct, the first barrier to the harbour. Nine hundred yards off-shore the gaggle of motor-boats, capable of thirty knots, circled in the darkness, fore-sections packed with seven hundred pounds of explosive, the pilots poised to identify their targets, lock rudders, push throttles wide and pitch themselves overboard, to be picked up by their own support craft or taken prisoner, if they survived.

But the garrison was waiting. The Regia Nautica did not know that captured decoding equipment enabled the Malta defenders to monitor most enemy naval movements and that radar had quickly pinpointed *Diana* and her fleet of little ships. Soon enough the sound of motor-boat engines was heard along the coast and observers reported tell-tale wakes near St Elmo Fort. At X-Hour, four thirty a.m, the lone *maiali* glided in. When the explosion came it brought down a single span of the breakwater viaduct but also killed the *maiali*'s crew.

Now it was confirmed the harbour was under attack by an unknown force. Unknown until the searchlights plinked on and swept the waters. There, on full power, plunging through the waves towards the harbour mouth, was the handful of explosive motor-boats, the EMBs. For a moment the pilots were plainly seen, like actors caught off-guard when the curtain rises. Then, from their positions around the harbour, the gunners opened fire, the naval-type six-pounders, Bofors guns and close-range weapons of every kind churning the water to a rosy froth.

Numbers of the racing EMBs were hit, exploding, scattering themselves in fragments across the surface of the sea. Others went down holed by gunfire or scuttled by their pilots. It was over in less than fifteen minutes: eleven enemy craft destroyed. None of the crews had penetrated the harbour or even glimpsed their objectives, the elusive merchantmen berthed in the French, Dockyard and Kalkara creeks where cranes continued moving back and forth above the open holds, lifting and lowering cargoes with calm deliberation despite the roar of battle. And now the four survivors of the Regia Nautica task force, the big *motobarca armata* torpedo-boats and the *motoscafo turismo* launches, as fleet as pre-war racers, turned and powered away to rendezvous with *Diana* forty miles to the north, close to the haven of a Sicilian port. But even as the crews took comfort in the thud of bows, clouding spray and curving wakes they heard, above the bellow of their engines and approaching fast, the British fighters.

Stood-by since midnight, the Hurricanes had been scrambled at dawn, Kit and Astley-Cobb directed to Valletta, Palmer and Twigg across St Paul's Bay to a point due west of Gozo, on an intercept. In the air more information. 'Hello, Nightjar Leader. Spot of mopping up. Seaborne bogeys eight miles north of you, proceeding north.'

'Okay, Control. What's the story?'

'Seaborne assault on Grand Harbour. Unsuccessful. Action seems to be concluded so we've stood down the gunners to give you safe passage for a pass, just to make sure. Don't hang about to admire the scenery. There's always a chance of itchy trigger fingers. Over.'

'Okay, Control. Out.'

They came in over Marsa Creek at five hundred feet, heading straight down Grand Harbour with the heights of Valletta rising on their left. Crowds of people were gathered on the terraces of the Lower Baraccas, waving. To their right flashed, in quick succession, the dockyards, untouched. It was growing lighter by the minute. Around the harbour entrance bodies were floating, face down, limbs spread. In a mess of wreckage men were moving, supporting themselves on shards of wood. Close to a broken bow, upright, rising and falling like a marker buoy, the sea was burning and survivors were striking out, arms flailing, towards grey Royal Navy launches manoeuvring to pull on board the living and the dead.

Beyond the coast Kit was quick to pick up the curving wakes of the Italian craft. They had spread out, roughly line-abreast, leaping over a rising swell, in any other circumstance a stirring sight, which seemed to have no link to war. It reminded him of watching Achille Varzi on Lake Garda in '35, winning the Duke of Spoleto Cup in the 1,000-h.p. racer *Asso*. A great tradition, boats like these, but fashioned for other purposes now. On the stern of one of the bigger boats, running at forty knots, a crewman clung to a mounted machine-gun, standing astride to keep his balance as the commander powered his vessel into a sliding turn to starboard, then veered back to port, corkscrewing as the Hurricanes passed overhead. Tracer trailed into the sky but hopelessly off-target. Kit watched for a sign that might mean he did not have to do this thing, but none came. The boats had spread out wide, trailing eccentric wakes that marked their flight, erratic, desperate and, unless they hove-to, doomed.

'Nightjar Leader to Control. With the seaborne bogeys now.'

'Nightjar Leader, understood. Watch your tails. Picking up some little jobs in your vicinity, to the north and above you at seven thousand feet. Over.'

'Okay, Control, thanks. Out,' said Kit. Then: 'Okay, Max. Turning hard to port and going down.'

'Okay.'

'Going in now.'

He came in low, from the east, on the big torpedo-boat's starboard beam. The small figure of the crewman was struggling to lower the elevation of his machine-gun. He loosed a few rounds that hissed past the Hurricane's tailplane. A pretty good show, Kit thought. He gave a little kick on the rudder as he closed, so the Brownings would sweep the vessel from stem to stern as he opened fire, a four-second burst with full deflection. The noise of his guns seemed obscenely loud. The bullets worked their way along the superstructure, pieces flying off the bridge, slicing a high-mounted stubby radio mast that toppled down slowly and hung suspended by wires over the port side-deck, twisting and thrashing in the water though, by now, the vessel was quickly losing its way. One of two torpedoes secured to the deck on either side of the ruined bridge came loose and rolled into the sea. Kit wondered why they had not detonated. Perhaps they had not been armed. He saw, as he climbed away, that the crewman on the stern had gone. As he banked to starboard, very low still, levelling out and looking for another target, he heard the stutter of Astley-Cobb's guns strafing the smoking hulk that was already half a mile away. In his earphones he heard a voice: 'Nightjar Leader, mind if we join the party?'

Above him and to the right two Hurricanes were dipping down: Palmer and Twigg working their way back along the coast from their intercept point off Gozo.

'Nightjar Leader, help yourselves,' he said.

From finger-two they fell into line-astern and went in fast. Kit felt relief as he climbed away. It was not a job he cared for, like raking a regatta on the Solent. Sea and sky were one, a gentle blue.

Control came on: 'Nightjar Leader, little jobs very close, coming in from the north at angels one four.'

Kit's altimeter showed a thousand feet. He pulled back on the stick and throttled up. His head was tilted and rolling from side to side, eyes straining, seeing nothing. An aircraft rushed below him, diving, and his machine rocked in the turbulence. He heard machine-gun fire above and to the left. He pushed forward on the control column. Black smoke was rolling skywards from three points on the surface of the sea. Another machine shot past him, twenty yards away, a Macchi 200, its pilot crouched forward, firing short bursts at a target five hundred feet below, a Hurricane, turning, wheeling onto the tail of another Macchi. How many were there, for God's sake? No doubt about it, the Eyeties had bounced them good and proper And they had a good deal to avenge.

At sea level something glowing orange burst and skittered pieces over the white-capped waves. A Hurricane was screwing into a vertical turn, its wing-tip close to the sea. Drongo Palmer was shouting: 'Twiggy, you little ripper.'

Then Astley-Cobb: 'On your tail, Drongo. For Christ's sake, break.'

And suddenly another machine was burning, close to the sea, flying straight and level but losing height, its cockpit obscured with smoke and fire. Then, almost imperceptibly at first, it began to climb. It passed him five hundred yards away, almost vertical now, its engine stuttering, the flames licking back along the fuselage, consuming the wood and fabric, eating into the leading edge of the tailplane. He realised with a shock that it was a Hurricane.

'Bale out, you silly bastard,' someone yelled.

As if in answer, the burning Hurricane toppled off the vertical onto its back and a figure detached itself and fell away, arms and legs spread wide, spinning slowly, and then the canopy of the man's parachute billowed open, pristine white, slowing his descent a little before he plunged beneath the surface of the sea. If he had hit the ground that fast, Kit knew, he would have been a goner. Lucky that. And then he caught himself. Lucky? He thought of Buster Brown.

On impulse he tugged at his canopy, making sure it was locked open, needing to know that it would not slide forward if he, too, had to brolly-hop in a hurry. Brolly-hop in a Hurry. Yes, good, a neat pun that. He must store it for later, when he got back to Takali.

He flipped into a half-roll, suspended by his straps, hanging for a moment with the breakers drifting from left to right below his head, hard blue and cold-looking, prompting him to consider, for an instant, how it must be to pass from furnace-heat to shuddering frigidity in less than thirty seconds. The note of the Merlin stuttered as it always did inverted, then picked up strongly as he dived, looking for a target. He was very calm, checking oil pressure, coolant temperature, the reflector sight, the range and wingspan indicators, taking in unconsciously what his instruments told him, somehow reassured by following the routine, knowing that nothing could happen to him as long as he held his concentration and everything stayed normal and familiar in the functional space in which he had spent so many flying hours.

He pulled out of the dive six hundred feet above the sea and came up behind a Macchi that was easing away into a gentle bank to port. Its attitude seemed unhurried and complacent, as though the pilot had concluded that the engagement was over and it was time to turn for home; or maybe he was occupied with thoughts of how he had downed a British fighter and the tales he would have to tell his comrades back in Catania.

Kit closed to within four hundred yards and gave the Italian machine a two-second burst. Pieces flew off, black against milk-white smoke, whipping past as lethal as any bullet. Another burst, the Macchi part-hidden in an opaque cloud of vapour that was darkening now and spraying a thin haze of oil across the toughened glass of the Hurricane's windscreen. Yet still the Macchi slid away to port, unhurried and showing no sign of alarm, as though oblivious to the storm of bullets tracking its course. Again Kit thumbed the gun-button, keeping it depressed for longer this time, a good four seconds, wondering if the unknown man, this fellow flier, was also calm and following routine, believing nothing could happen to him as long as he maintained his concentration and everything stayed normal and familiar. Or was he dead, fallen back against the bulkhead, struck by a round that had pierced his armour-plating even as he imagined the congratulations of his comrades when he taxied in?

Something came across Kit's left shoulder, downwards, whipping through the space left by the pushed-back canopy and punctured the instrument flying panel. The altimeter, airspeed indicator and artificial horizon burst apart, showering his face, unprotected by goggles or oxygen mask, with shards of glass and metal fragments. He felt a long, deep wound open on his cheek and then an odd, flapping sensation as though the flesh was hanging loose, caught in the rush of air as the Hurricane pulled itself into an uncontrollable tight loop. He was squeezed down hard in his seat and blacked out.

When his vision returned it was blurred by G force and blood. He snatched at the control column but its feel was loose and vague, the elevators unresponsive, barely moving. He heard an odd pffft-pffft-pffft. Holes appeared in the starboard wing and his own bullets began to explode inside the ammunition boxes, blowing bigger holes in the stressed alloy skin. He had few options now and thrust at the rudder, with no real plan in mind other than evasion, snapping the Hurricane into a series of flick rolls, wild and violent, that slammed him against the cockpit sides. He was enveloped in acrid smoke and began to choke on the stench and taste of petrol, oil and glycol coolant. He felt the airspeed fading, the three-blade propeller thrashing to keep him in the air. He dropped his hand to increase the revs but the throttle lever had been shot away. Waves of heat were pulsing back from the faltering Merlin and the fuselage shook and trembled as the Hurricane prepared to stall and dive. The starboard wing lifted. He pulled the pin in his Sutton harness and the webbing straps fell away. He was standing on the seat now, his parachute hanging heavy, wrenching away the oxygen and R/T leads. His leather helmet was snatched from his head and he found himself falling clear, towards the sea, that hard-blue sea, seeing the line of the horizon seem to rise and flatten. He pulled the D-ring of his 'chute and as it opened to slow his fall he drove down deep into ranks of waves creamy with foam, which rushed and bulged, rose and fell so that for a fraction of time before he struck his feet were ankle-deep in water, then hanging clear in a dizzying trough. And then he was under and his ears were full of the glugging, swirling sound he remembered from leaping off the topmost diving-board at school, his lungs compressing as he speared on downwards, bubbles of oxygen, shimmering and silver, escaping from his mouth and rising in streams.

The canopy of his 'chute had spread across the surface of the sea and his harness pulled tight, stopping him sinking deeper. He pushed the spring-release catch, at first to no effect, his hands made feeble by the pressure of the water. Then it snapped, yielded, and he struggled clear, bursting into daylight, gasping and gulping, bringing up the bread and jam and sweetened tea he had consumed at Readiness to pass the time. The sugar taste was mixed with salt and blood.

He pushed himself back and up to bring the central ring of his Mae West clear of the water and pulled at it feebly, hearing the puff of the gas bottle as the life-jacket inflated. He knew it should have been inflated before he hit the sea. Then he would not have gone so deep. But there had been so little time, with barely eight hundred feet on the clock. Except there was no longer any clock. No Hurricane either, just a rainbow film of oil and a floating spar or two a few hundred yards away. Still, he was alive and not uncomfortable, the buoyancy of the Mae West keeping his head and shoulders clear of the passing waves. He rinsed his face and ran his fingers through his hair, feeling the sting of brine on his wound, touching the flap of skin that drooped from his right temple to his jaw.

He looked around, hoping he might see one of the fellows coming in for a low pass, waggling his wings. The sky was empty. Had he been spotted or had they been too busy with those damned Macchis? Perhaps they had missed his brolly-hop, assumed he had gone in with his kite. At last he understood the reality of his situation, a small thing in a vast expanse of sea, with only the Mae West's splash of yellow to signify that there, among the waves, was a man. The coldness was creeping into his limbs. It was early still and the sun hung, huge and shimmering, above the eastern horizon. He knew they had been bounced ten miles out from Salina Bay, due west. He turned in the water, feeling the vague warmth of the sun on the nape of his neck and his wet hair. He began to swim, short, steady strokes, encouraged by the sense of moving through the water, sticking to a plan that gave him hope. It was swim or accept the inevitable.

He pushed his way along for perhaps thirty minutes. He suspected he had not moved far from where he fell. A lively westerly breeze ruffled the surface of the sea and snatched at his head and shoulders as he bobbed along, occasional gusts strong enough to spin him round and drive him back. But he persisted, lacking other options except one he didn't care for. Instead he thought about people he knew and people who knew him; people who might soon learn that he was missing. He imagined the telegram arriving for Farve and Mother. He knew how it would go: 'Deeply regret to inform you that your son Flt Lt Christopher Miles Curtis is missing as a result of an operation on 26 July 1941 Stop Letter follows Stop Any further information received will be immediately communicated to you Stop Please accept my profound sympathy Stop Officer Commanding.' Then the letter. 'Deeply sorry . . . took off and has not returned . . . searches instituted but without results . . . chance we may hear of his safety . . . among the keenest pilots in the Squadron . . . personal effects have been collected by the Squadron Adjutant.' Nothing remarkable there. One more pilot lost, who knew how and where? In the mess little to be said, an anecdote or two, perhaps, but press on, that was the thing, press on. And at home, well, Farve would find it hard but have a sense of pride at duty done, and Mother, yes, well, Mother would be Mother.

And he and Juliette? The truth was they scarcely knew each other, just a fleeting encounter in a country gripped by war, their murmured promises no doubt soon forgotten or remembered as a poignant romantic interlude until she met another man and faced a different future. Then he shouted out, his voice tiny against the surge of the sea: 'For God's sake, get a grip. You're going to make it. You're going to be all right.' And even as he felt a heady moment of well-being he was raised on the crest of a wave and saw, half a mile away, a boat. He knew it for what it was quite soon. The wind had eased and moved round to the east.

He struck out strongly, full of purpose now, and reached the *motobarca armata* in less than an hour. The big torpedo-boat was pitching and rolling, head down and listing to port, holed along the waterline but also leaning to the weight of the radio mast still swinging from its tangled cables. A pall of greasy smoke was rising from the hulk, its dark shadow passing over the brilliant sea, and there was the smell of fuel, oil and something else. He clung to an empty depth-charge rack projecting over the transom, too weak to pull himself on board, gathering his strength, half out of the water, balancing with bare feet on one of the twin rudders, the sun much higher and hotter now, feeling his clothes begin to dry and savouring the warmth. He heard a movement on deck and looked up. The muzzle of a .32 Navy-model Beretta pistol was levelled at his head.

They studied each other for a long moment, Kit and the Regia Nautica crewman. He was pinched and nervous, his hair caked to his skull with engine oil that clung in thick lumps to his seaman's sweater. His gun hand moved and Kit stared down at the sea surging round his feet and waited for the bullet.

The man said something in Italian. Kit looked up. The crewman had moved the pistol from his right hand to his left and was reaching out, fingers trembling. His grasp was slippery with oil but firm. In a moment Kit felt the deck beneath him, hot to touch and dry. He crawled a few feet and sank against the pedestal of the Breda 20/65mm mounted machine-gun, its barrel twisted and bent, pointing towards the sky.

'*Non si muova*,' said the Italian, the Beretta again levelled at Kit's head.

'*Si, capisco*,' said Kit. For the moment he did not plan to move. '*Non parlo bene l'italiano*.'

The man pointed at Kit with the Beretta. '*Inglesi?*' It was said flatly, more a statement than a question.

'*Si, inglesi*.'

The Italian waved the pistol from side to side, indicating the smouldering boat, and jerked his head skywards. '*Inglesi*.' He made a diving motion with his left hand, a tck-tck-tck with his tongue behind his teeth, a fighter plane on a strafing run. Kit raised his eyebrows as though he had not heard or did not understand. He knew who this fellow was. The gunner who had put up a pretty good show, who had gone over the side, no doubt, when he came in to attack. Did the Italian, in turn, suspect who he might be?

The man began to speak very quickly, his face agitated, tears starting in his eyes. The Beretta was loose in his hand. Kit considered the chances of a lunge. The man was weak but for the moment he was weaker. He felt the urge to sleep but the Italian was waving him to his feet and pushing him towards the ruined bridge where five dead men were sliding around on a floor running with blood and oil and water. The Italian indicated each one in turn.

'Sottotenente Muratori, Rossi, Marsello, Sforza, Battisti.' He wanted to name the corpses, make Kit understand that they had been comrades, men he had served with, men he knew well, men he would remember, and not as they were now. Through the bullet-holes in the cabin walls, bars of light caught drifting specks of dust. A chart of the Sicilian Strait lay, specked with blood, on the navigator's table, and near the wheel, which aimlessly tugged and turned, was tucked a sepia photograph of a family group, four generations, toothless old to black-haired young, and children, many children, smiling outside a farmhouse with, behind, a long, rustic table laid for lunch. Kit felt the Beretta push into his spine but gently.

The forehatch doors of the engine room stood open and against the big 1,000-h.p. Isotta Fraschini, silent now and cold, sprawled two more men in overalls, one face down, the other sitting upright, head lolling to the motion of the boat. There had been a fire and both were charred and blackened. 'Borsellino,' said the Italian, '*e* Pietro Taparelli.' Kit could see from the man's eyes, and because he had given the dead Taparelli a first name, that there had been a special bond. From the same village, perhaps, both volunteers, received as heroes on their leaves at neighbourly gatherings much like the one in the sepia print. A sickening smell of roasted flesh rose from the open hatch and drove them back to the stern.

Kit thought about the dead men who had been named, given identities, no longer simply mutilated cadavers, anonymous and grotesque. He did not know what he felt. He expected guilt, regret, compassion. Instead he experienced a new, disturbing, dull acceptance. After all, this was the price. He had killed and he would kill again, until perhaps he himself was killed. Yes, all pilots talked of attacking machine not man but they accepted that at the brightest point of trailing fire there was a man – or men – much like themselves who questioned his actions and excused himself because he was a simple flier. It seemed to him, at that moment, a kind of hypocrisy to see the dead men, rolling in their blood on the floor of the bridge or in the grease and oil of the engine room, any differently from the many who had fallen to his guns from blue skies where clouds or rushing earth or sea obscured those final agonies. It was granted to the airman to destroy, but at a distance, his workplace a dominion of light, infinite space and towering cloud-shapes, insubstantial peaks and crags dispersing as quickly as they had formed, a landscape of nobility and constant fascination that separated those who fought there, or so they thought, from what lay below. Somehow this made it possible for them to suppress much morbid speculation about how it was for those others, who went down, although they knew, in time, that they too might find themselves at that brightest point of trailing fire, a place of no illusions or deception, the price that must be paid.

And so, he thought, it was correct to remain unmoved by the Italian seamen who had been named, the men whose lives he had extinguished; to imagine, stretched out beside them, the bodies of more than twenty others, whose wounds, contortions, faces he had never known, whose lives he had also ended. It was only fair to treat them all alike. This he told himself, gripped by a coldness of spirit, as though his senses and emotions were numb, shut-down.

A voice came to him from a long time ago, a lazy drawl: 'You shoot the hell out of a guy in the air. You knock a guy's brains out with a rifle butt in a trench. What's the goddamned difference? This isn't a game, for Christ's sake. Face it, brother, the good guys will lose unless our body-count beats theirs.' Was he now like Ossie Wolf? Was he, as the American would say, wising up? Or was he losing something that should not be lost, an awareness of what was being done and how, which held a positive meaning for the way this war was fought and for how things might be when finally it was over?

He was startled by another, not imagined, voice close to.

'*Vuole dell'acqua?*' said the Italian.

'*Acqua? Si, per piacere.*' Kit sat down again, leaning back against the pedestal of the twisted, useless machine-gun. The Italian disappeared into the bridge, the Beretta still in his right hand, and quickly came back with an earthenware jar. Kit uncorked it and gulped warm pure water. He wiped it off and handed it back. Before the Italian could drink from it too they heard the faint drone of an aero-engine. The man's eyes widened with hope. He thrust the earthenware jar into Kit's hands and hurried to the bow. Soon they made out the silhouette of a high-winged biplane, moving slowly towards them, like an ungainly bug, a seaplane of some sort with a V-shaped hull.

'*Eccolo!*' shouted the Italian. '*Un' Cant!*'

But as it drew closer it became clear that it was not a Cant but an amphibious Walrus on search-and-find from its base at Kalafrana Bay.

The man's expression changed and he walked back down the deck, listless now, his shoulders down. '*Inglesi*,' he said resignedly. He threw the Beretta pistol into the sea. '*Passerá a prenderci?*'

Kit found himself shrugging like an Italian. He did not know if the Walrus would land and pick them up. He did not know the form. He remembered it had something to do with the state of the sea and if there were bogeys about. Rescue planes were fair game now for either side.

The Walrus was circling cautiously, out of range, and Kit pulled off his Mae West and waved it above his head. He resisted the impulse to shout. The Walrus turned and moved towards them, the note of its single Bristol Pegasus pusher engine rich and reassuring. A smoke bomb curled down, marking their position, and it turned away on a course for Kalafrana.

Twenty minutes later they were in the sick bay of a Type 2 Whaleback high-speed launch from the RAF rescue fleet at Marsaxlokk, bounding towards Malta at thirty-six knots. They were not alone: a familiar figure, somewhat burned, his face a patchwork of black and red, white where his goggles had been, lay on one of the bunks.

Kit said: 'Hello, Drongo.'

Drongo Palmer slowly turned his head. He winced, the simple movement causing pain. 'Hello, mate. You're looking bloody second hand.'

'That's rich,' said Kit, 'I must say.'

'Well,' said Drongo, 'I was due for a trip back to Blighty, but it's one hell of a price to pay for a ticket.'

'I think I saw you go down.'

'Yeah, I heard Max bawling and then the kite went up. I got one bugger, though, and Twiggy got another.'

'Good show.'

'Bloody Eyeties.'

'Yes. They caught us properly on the hop.'

'The Yank will kill me for this.'

Kit reached out and touched his shoulder. 'I'd say you're doing quite well on your own. Anyway, Wolf's in no condition to kill anyone.'

A medical orderly was cleaning the wound on Kit's temple. 'That'll stitch up nicely. Looks a lot worse than it is.'

'Bollocks,' said Drongo. 'That's what he told me.'

The Regia Nautica man was sitting on a nearby bunk, listening but unable to understand, a blanket round his shoulders, drawing on a Woodbine given him by the orderly. Drongo sniffed the tobacco smoke and looked at the orderly. 'Any chance of a fag?'

The orderly shook his head. 'Not wise, Sarge. Be patient. We'll get you back soon enough. I'll check with the skipper, see how long we're going to be.'

Watching him go Drongo muttered: 'Silly sod. I suppose he's scared I might burn myself.'

Now the Regia Nautica man stooped forward off his bunk, countering the violent pitching of the Whaleback with a seaman's skill, and held his Woodbine out butt first. Drongo nodded, and the Italian placed the cigarette with care between the Australian's swollen lips.

'Thanks, mate,' Drongo said.

'*Prego*,' said the Regia Nautica man.

# Six

In the kitchen of the Strawberry Hill mansion that lay in the fold of the downs conveniently close to Midhurst, Agnes Hobbes stood at the sink washing the breakfast things. When she leaned forward she could see the broad expanse of the drive through the open gateway of the kitchen garden. The postboy was late. Then she heard the rattle of gravel on mudguards and saw Harry Sharpe coasting towards the front door, swinging his leg over the crossbar of his scarlet bicycle, balancing on one pedal, a letter in his teeth. She dried her hands carefully on a tea-towel, not wanting to be seen to hurry, and went out into the hall.

The old man at the pine table looked up from his newspaper and watched her go, sipping his mug of tea. At his feet the Airedale had pricked its ears but only gave a token growl and lowered its head again, grey muzzle cradled on its paws.

The postboy's boots were scraping on the broad granite steps. The old man heard the big oak door swing back and voices, low and indistinct. He was seized by sudden dread. He stood up, the legs of his chair scraping on the flagstones, his newspaper falling to the floor. He banged down the mug of tea and spilled it, a brown stream running across the table and dripping off the edge. With a grunt the dog got up and licked the sticky pool.

In the hall Agnes closed the door carefully and turned, the letter in her hand. She knew what was in the old man's mind and said: 'It's all right sir. It's from Mister Kit.'

'I'll read it in the study,' said the old man. He took the letter. His hand was shaking. 'I'm afraid I spilled my tea.'

'I'll make another pot.'

'Where's my wife?'

'I collected her breakfast tray. She was in her dressing room. I haven't heard her come down.'

The old man was at the door of his study when he heard his wife on the stairs.

'What is it, Arthur? Anything for me?'

'News from Kit. Shall we read it together?'

'Later. I can never make head or tail of Christopher's schoolboy scrawl.' A cigarette was poised between her fingers. She lifted it to her mouth, inhaled, inclined her head and blew out the smoke, her lips just touching. 'Tell Agnes I'll take coffee in the conservatory.' She glanced at him quickly because he had not moved, just stood there staring, with the letter resting in his hand. 'For Heaven's sake, you worry about the boy too much. A letter means he's perfectly all right. Don't fret so.' She turned and went through the door to the sitting room. He heard her heels click-clacking across the parquet floor towards the conservatory.

By the time Agnes brought his tea he had learned that mostly Italians faced the squadron now; that there had been a certain amount of early chaos but new brooms had been promised to start the sweeping clean; that Kit was billeted in an old *palazzo*, which sounded rather grand. Provisions were meagre and nasty bugs abounded. And all-pervading dust. Poor boy. It sounded rather grim and far away, distant battles in the back-of-beyond, a wretched island that rang a bell. Surely a great-uncle in the diplomatic service had died there long ago, typhoid or was it cholera? The price of Empire, a cost uncounted. He turned a page. 'All very conscious of what the chaps achieved in the summer of 1940 . . . shows what the British can do when left to their own devices . . . everyone here convinced we will prevail. You and Mother should not worry.'

Curtis put down the letter. He felt a tingling in his eyes, a tightness in his throat. He picked up the fresh mug of tea and cupped its warmth in his hands, although the day was already hot, the study windows thrown open by Agnes to admit a cool draught, which rustled the chrysanthemum-patterned linen curtains.

'You and Mother mustn't worry.' Curtis imagined his wife in the conservatory, seated easily in one of the high-backed wicker chairs with her coffee, whatever magazine had taken her fancy, her supply of Balkan Sobranies, and soon a glass that she would fill quietly as the day wore on, not to soften any obvious anxiety but to dull the ache of a loss she would not accept, although the evidence from France seemed indisputable. As the advancing Wehrmacht troops had poured through the streets of Nancy little more than a year ago Maurice Maierscheldt had put a bullet in his wife's brain, then shot himself, rather than face the camps, leaving only their daughter, Hannah, to escape.

Diana Curtis would not have it. She would shake her head like an obstinate child. 'I would know if Karoline had left this world. I would know.' And still she resisted any suggestion that Hannah, known to be in England, should be found, because – to Curtis it seemed plain – she did not wish to be confronted with anything that might destroy her fierce belief that Karoline Maierscheldt had survived. Yet he reproached himself for failing to seek out the girl, who had almost been, to him, a daughter, and so close to Kit as children in those pre-war years; the girl who, but for the war, might have been more to Kit than a childhood friend and might be still. The girl who had inherited so much, the great enterprise created by her father, and yet was quite alone.

He took up the letter again, read of the wounded pilot Buster Brown in Hampstead, his fleeting glimpse of a girl like Hannah who might or might not have a flat in Holly Hill. This page, the second, was creased and grimed with dirt, as though trodden underfoot. The third was written in a different ink.

> This epistle interrupted by a scramble, I'm afraid. Seems a thousand years have passed since I wrote what went before. Much has happened, much I cannot tell you. Plenty of action and whatever the press might say the Italians are giving a good account of themselves. Had a most extraordinary encounter with one chap I must tell you about some day, the tightest of tight squeaks from which I was jolly lucky to escape unscathed. And blow me if I didn't have to jump for it a few days later. Big raid by the Regia Nautica on Grand Harbour. Very daring, in the Italian style, but unluckily for them we knew they were coming. Scrambled at dawn and strafed some of the attacking craft, then got bounced ourselves by a flock of rather useful Macchi 200s. Plopped safely down and got picked up by the RAF rescue boys, a bit bedraggled but otherwise okay. One of our fellows got somewhat singed but we knocked down three of the opposition, so honours more than even. They got me back in the air pretty quickly and I've done a fair number of sorties since but nothing so dramatic, the Italians no doubt licking their wounds.
>
> Thanks to the lull, some of us have been granted a few

days' leave so this is being written at the rest camp at St Paul's Bay. Oddly enough Ossie Wolf is here as well, recovering from a nasty dose of the Malta Dog.

It seems we're to be continually thrown together although we're as different as chalk and cheese. Whatever our differences, though, I suppose the end-result is much the same. I fear I'm becoming somewhat hardened by it all. I'm not entirely comfortable with that thought but I suppose I must accept it; the end justifies the means, etc. But still I wonder, does it?

In the conservatory Diana Curtis looked up from her magazine, her thin legs crossed, her right foot flexing. In the harsh light the old man realised with a shock that she was no longer youthful for her years. She had always seemed untouched by time, ageless, so that people they knew would joke about making pacts with Satan and she would smile a small, pleased smile, as though she had. Often she had been mistaken for his daughter. But now her face was lined and yellow, her body shrunk in her elegant, good clothes. It was like looking at a stranger. And yet he knew she had always been a stranger to him, unknown, distant. He did not understand her, never had.

Her remoteness had attracted him. He had thought at first he might reach her, a decent enough fellow able to offer security, warmth and a certain status in what passed for society in West Sussex; in trade, of course, so not quite there, but a big enough business to command respect. She took all that, took him, because it was what she had been born to, then lost, but always remained in some other place, where he was not welcome and could not go.

He had thought it might change when the child came, but it might have been another's child, except when the Maierscheldts were there and she made a show of fondness, smiling at Karoline in that way of hers, that rare and dazzling smile of joy, as if to say: 'See what a fine mother I am, how I can love.'

He held out Kit's letter. She made an impatient gesture. 'So what does he say, for Heaven's sake?'

'If you like, I'll read it to you.' He moved towards a chair.

'Oh, spare me your mumblings. I'm not in the mood. I assume he's in the pink as usual, that you've been fussing away for absolutely nothing.'

'Reading between the lines it's clear he's having a pretty ghastly time.'

'How exactly?'

'His plane was damaged and he had to bale out. Some sort of dust-up with the Italians.'

'Really? I thought they were meant to be utterly hopeless.'

'Naturally he makes light of it.' Curtis read from the letter. '"I plopped safely down and got picked up by the RAF rescue boys, a bit bedraggled but otherwise okay."'

'It sounds to me,' said Diana Curtis, 'as though he's having the time of his life. After all, it's what you brought him up to and now he's got his heart's desire. I refuse to worry for him, not a jot. You see, I know he'll be all right so I simply dismiss it from my mind.'

'I don't believe we should be so careless about such things.'

'Tempting Fate, you mean? Arthur, I trust to my instinct. How else do I know that Karoline is alive and well? That one day very soon . . .' She stood up, brushing at her skirt. 'I promised Marjorie Price nine holes before lunch.'

'I'll leave the letter on the table, then.'

'Surely you gave me the gist?'

'Hardly.'

'Well, put it there, then, if you must. Perhaps I'll glance at it later.' She paused at the door. In the shadow her beauty had returned. He looked at her with the same sick longing he had known so long ago, that day at the Pulborough point-to-point, where she won the ladies' challenge though scarcely more than a girl, mounted on the finest thoroughbred in the field. It had been only months before her father's death, before the great estate had been parcelled up to cover the running debts of unwise business ventures, before she was brought home from the *école internationale* in Thun, before she and Karoline were lost to each other until, years later, they found themselves again, but married, with very different lives.

'We have been . . . all right together, haven't we?' he said.

'What an extraordinary thing to say,' she said. 'Don't wait lunch for me. I may treat Marjorie in the clubhouse.'

He wondered if that entailed food. 'Why don't I get Barlow to take you over?'

'And have the man kicking his heels for hours when he could be making himself useful here? Sometimes, Arthur, you talk such rot. I'll give the Lea-Francis a run, on what little petrol they grudge us these days.'

He followed her into the hall, watched her pull on her kid driving gloves and shoulder her golf bag. She was strong and physically assured, in a way that he had never been: a sickly boy, indifferent at games, a trier but never interested, not like Kit.

'Go on,' she said. 'Back to your womb of a kitchen, with that damned dog of yours. No doubt Mrs Hobbes will rustle up something plain and tasty. Mince and mash and lots of gravy. Wouldn't that be nice?'

Diana Curtis drove too fast but well and, anyway, with the detestable war, there was little on the roads so she had the lanes that lay beneath Linch Down largely to herself, foot hard on the throttle of the little Hyper, the whistle of the supercharger cutting in and out with the rise and fall of the revs. She missed Ted Ruddock's tractor by a matter of feet, as it backed out of a field entrance. It was amusing to be recognised, glance in the rear-view mirror and see him struggling to suppress his curses.

At the golf club she kissed Marjorie Price on the lips and gave her the slightest touch of tongue. The woman did not react, neither pulling back nor returning the tiny intimacy. Just a stolid English bag, Diana supposed, without a shred of tenderness. She had not known her long, initially attracted by her greenish eyes and auburn hair, aware that her boorish husband Tim was charging round the Western Desert in a tank. She did not appear in the least anxious about that, and this Diana found attractive too. But, really, it was all too tiresome, tiptoeing through the county set alert for hints and clues; just little games, of course, amusements, not to be taken seriously, not taken too far at all because, for her, that side of things, taken to its logical conclusion, was not an option.

Now, in the changing room, she decided she would not seek out Marjorie Price again. And, anyway, she played golf far too well to be a friend. But of course it might seem very different after some brisk match-play on the links, limbs aching and face flushed, savouring that first consoling gin and tonic and wondering about her slightly sweating partner marking up her card, that lock of russet hair curling across her forehead. Could there, would there be someone else? For the present, even to think it seemed like a betrayal.

The odious Basil Yates was on the practice range, a ball of tweed, sucking at his briar. 'And how's that boy of yours, Diana? Any news?'

'No, none at all.'

'You must be very proud.'

'Must I? Why? He's doing no more than a thousand others.'

'Ah but to be a pilot now. That's something, surely?'

'Better than being in tanks, you mean? Marjorie, you must tell Tim.'

'Look here, my dear—'

'And what of Rupert? I hear he's something in Whitehall.'

'That's right.'

'You must be very proud.'

She lost to her opponent, her stroke-play wild and uncontrolled, not helped, she knew, by her growing taste for an early-morning bracer. Once she would have cared. Now it didn't seem to matter. She drove as wildly home, her golf bag slipping from the passenger seat and knocking the Hyper out of gear as she came into the sharp left-hander just the other side of Cocking; came in very fast in neutral, the thin tyres squealing, the back wheels drifting out, but caught and held in a long, exhilarating slide, the gear lever banged into third and power applied by just the correct amount.

The house was quiet. The smell of baking drifted from the kitchen. Diana realised she had not eaten. She was not hungry now. Snores came from the study, deep and rhythmic, man and dog slumbering together, two of a kind, happy to doze away the day, twitching and dreaming of nothing they would remember. She poured herself a good amount of Gilbey's with a splash of tonic. Her head was already swimming, her vision slightly blurred. She thought about Marjorie Price, just a provincial pudding but damnably good at golf. A pleasant little kiss, though, when they parted, with just a hint of interest.

She picked up the letter from her son and scanned it idly, sipping from her glass. The usual mannered reticence, the careful understatement they were taught at school, night-fighting a good frolic, plopping safely into the sea, one of the fellows somewhat singed. The language of facetious children confronted by situations and emotions beyond their powers of thought and speech. Useful slang to conceal the horrors and the fear. She knew she should feel compassion for him, ache for his safe return, but he was too like his father, the father who had shaped him, laid out for him the same narrow family path to Marlborough and Trinity where, said to be reading history, he appeared to spend rather more time rowing, on the rugger field or out at Kidlington with the university air squadron. He was too like Arthur for her to love, to hold for him little more than a mild affection, more often irritation at his boisterous clumsiness, the way he seemed to fill the house, his puppy-like eagerness to do the proper thing, his readiness to be led, to stand in awe of others, easily influenced by what they said and did, not think things through himself; most of all at his wearisome flying chat, the ridiculous jargon and numbing technicalities, assuming everyone must share his passion. He was, she concluded, entirely unoriginal and mundane. A very English Englishman.

She ran her eyes down the grubby pages, looking for something that might interest her. Significant how occasionally a sentence broke off to accommodate 'dear Farve', making it plain whom he thought he was addressing. She could hardly complain, of course. She had given him so little of herself. 'You and Mother mustn't worry about me.' She felt momentary unease, then recalled her words to Arthur: 'I refuse to worry for him, not a jot. I know he'll be all right so I simply dismiss it from my mind.' Yes, that was what she thought, that was what she knew: he simply wasn't the type not to come back and make a nuisance of himself, just as she knew that Karoline was with her still, living and breathing, somewhere, at this very moment. She could feel her thoughts, her presence, the fact of her existence, whatever others told her.

She gave a dismissive laugh at the mention in the letter of the woman Garencières and her snub-nosed child who had no English. It was so like Christopher to be led by a widow with her eye to the main chance, eager to exploit a fortuitous connection. She seemed to have the hapless Arthur wound round her little finger too: he had involved the mutts at the London office in helping to find her a place to live, and even, through his journalist chums, had arranged an interview with some Free French broadcasters looking for an office girl. No wonder he hadn't had the gall to read the paragraph aloud. He knew she disapproved. Men were such giddy fools.

Then the name jumped from the page: Maierscheldt. For a moment she could not breathe. Her hand was across her mouth, the alcohol rising in her throat, sour and sharp. No, it was not to do with Karoline but Hannah, that pallid girl who stooped to hide her breasts, less French than English, who rarely offered a word of the remotest interest but had some small facility for art, designs for her *maître-verrier* papa, pre-eminent in Nancy, his factory famous for products of glass, saccharine but pleasing, and commercial. Hannah, with her milk-and-water smile, secure in England. Why her? Why *her*? But still, the girl might know the truth of it, dispel the detestable rumours and conjecture that filtered out of France, suggesting that the ox-like Maurice had somehow ended the life of the woman he adored. Preposterous, of course, though possibly he, the Jew, might have chosen to go that way, faced with deportation. True to his roots, he had his moods and was prone to be impulsive in the middle-European fashion. But surely Karoline, who had never adopted her husband's faith, had no reason to fear, with her noble head, her white-blonde hair and violet eyes, the very picture of an Aryan *Mädchen* and such a contrast, she always thought, to the dark-browed Maurice, who was so very Semitic and intense, always smarting about injustices or affronts to what he called his people, as though he had no country, was not French.

For years she had dismissed his outbursts as tiresome paranoia though now it appeared they might have had some substance. But surely, even gripped by despair and fear, he could not have committed such an act. It was beyond belief, unthinkable. To end it for himself, yes, that she could comprehend; a faint-hearted creature, like many of his kind, quick with tales of persecution past, soft and complaining, used-up somehow beneath his blustering persona as a man of industry, dulled and fearful. But to destroy the woman who was his life? No, he lacked the will, the steadiness to kill. Against himself, perhaps, in desperation, he had found the firmness of resolve but she knew, she absolutely knew, that Karoline lived, and if she lived then life might yet be full of promise and fulfilment. And so she ran her finger lightly across the page. 'She's apparently got a flat in Hampstead . . . Holly Hill . . .' And she was filled with a confusion of hope and apprehension about what, if she made her way to Holly Hill, she might discover.

# Seven

Kit Curtis came up level with the priest on the steepest part of Pennellu Hill. The *kappillan* was moving slowly, pausing every few yards to catch his breath, wipe his brow with a square of white linen and look back at the vista of St Paul's Bay far below where ranks of tiny waves lapped the hot sand. His black cassock was blacker still with sweat, the hem encrusted with dust. On the nearby crest of Mellieha Ridge rose the dome and belfries of the town's baroque parish church, the roseate stone luminous in the fierce sunlight.

As Kit drew close the priest leaned against a low stone wall, blew out his cheeks and smiled. Behind him a field of standing crops dropped away to the wide green St Niklaw valley. 'It is my misfortune, my son, that Teresa Camilleri lives at the foot of Pennellu Hill and not the top. She is a woman of great piety and devotion, but unhappily infirm, who requests my presence and my blessing. Often. So very often. Pennellu is my little Compostela.' He sighed, raised his eyes and added: 'For which, of course, I offer thanks.'

'It's certainly quite a climb,' said Kit. He shaded his eyes and looked down the broad valley. A small green lizard climbed out of a gap between the grey stones of the wall and spread itself in the sun near his hand. 'I hear there are caves down there. Remains of ancient temples and Christian tombs.'

'You know something of our history, then?'

'A little.'

'Now we make new history. Together.'

'I suppose we do.'

The priest took in Kit's crumpled service cap, the flight-lieutenant rings on the shoulder straps of his short-sleeved khaki shirt, the pilot's wings press-studded to the thin material above the breast pocket. 'You are at the rest camp of the Royal Air Force?'

'Yes. Just for a couple of days.'

'I see you have been touched by battle.' The priest raised his hand to his own cheek, touching it tenderly as though it also bore a livid pink U-shaped scar.

'Oh, it's nothing to speak of.'

'Do you put your trust in God, my son?'

'I put my trust in many things,' said Kit, uncertainly.

'You are a doubter, then?'

'These days, Father, I'm afraid I tend to trust more tangible things. My comrades, in the air and on the ground, the machine I fly, the experience I've gained, my ability to survive somehow, whatever happens.'

'Your ability to survive is hardly tangible my son.'

'No, that's true.'

'Surely, then, that might be the hand of God?'

'Many of my friends have not survived. Is that also the hand of God?'

'Perhaps. I do not know your friends or what was planned for them.' The priest stood away from the wall and brushed himself down, looking up the hill towards the church silhouetted against the sky. There was a scratching sound as the lizard, startled, scrabbled back into the gap between the stones. 'You will visit the Sanctuary of Our Lady?'

'Of course.'

'Two hundred years ago this island was visited by a ruinous drought. Hundreds gathered at the Sanctuary to pray for divine intervention and while they prayed to Our Lady it began to rain.'

'Ah. The hand of God.'

The priest smiled gently. 'I simply recount what history tells us.'

'History again,' said Kit.

They began to ascend the hill together, Kit suppressing his urge to march ahead, shortening his stride to match that of the slow-paced priest, who scuffed his worn black shoes in the dust, leaning forward against the incline, panting. The road bent back upon itself near the summit and close to the verge was gathered a jumble of buildings, old-looking and deep in shadow: a farmhouse of some kind and, attached, a barn or shed.

'This place is called *ir Razzett tax-Xjaten*,' said the priest, 'the Devil's farmhouse. Legend claims it was built in three nights by demons.' He chuckled. 'Laughable superstition, of course.'

'Of course,' said Kit.

The church, with its twin belfry towers from which the great bells hung, plain to see, was set back against the rim of the hill, fronted by a *piazza* busy with people coming down from the cool, narrow lanes of the town that rose higher still; lanes flanked by stark white dwellings, undecorated, not picturesque; the people homely and plain, stocky of build and dark-complexioned, crossing themselves as they passed into the half-light of the church. There was an impression of marble and gold, of echoing space, of murmured responses to thin-voiced incantations, of faces brown and lined, rosary beads passing between bent fingers; at the font more fingers dipping into holy water, then touching lips and foreheads, swift familiar movements made without conscious thought; small children peering round, wiping noses on the backs of hands, fidgeting and impatient for the adults' devotions to be done, yet nervous and quietened by the mystery of it all, understanding nothing except that this was what their elders did and therefore must have meaning.

Entering the church the *kappillan* sank down on one knee and genuflected. Kit removed his cap and held it awkwardly in front of him. People began to approach the priest, gathering round him, talking softly, their expressions anxious, but nodding at Kit with hesitant smiles. The priest seemed popular, a source of wisdom and advice. Kit moved away from the little group and sat in a pew near the door, the faintest stirring of air cool on the nape of his neck and across his shoulders. The murmurings of the devout rose and fell, rhythmic and predictable, like the tiny waves that lapped the hot sand of the distant bay.

It was all wonderful nonsense, he thought, but moving nonetheless to see the belief and trust reflected in so many shining, credulous eyes. He envied the people of Mellieha their solace and their faith, not so different, he supposed, from the folk who worshipped in the chilly confines of St Mary Magdalene and St Denys in the grounds of Midhurst Castle, the church where as a child he had shivered and wondered and tried to make sense of it all. Finally, he had concluded that there was no sense to it whatsoever and had dared God to destroy him for his few small sins.

But what lengths the pious would go to to affirm their belief: the richness and elaboration of the Sanctuary of Our Lady of Mellieha, with its colour and gilding, its florid decoration and whiff of incense, so different from the reality of life outside its walls, comfortless and hard. Here was ornament, grandiose and foreign, carved figures, brightly coloured, vulgar to a nominally Protestant eye, plush hangings, glass, and tablets of fine marble.

Curiously he scanned the closest, running his eye down the lines of impenetrable Maltese script.

*Talba lill-Madonna*
*Tal-Mellieha*
*O Vergni Marija*
*Gewwa L-ghar Imqaddes Tal-Mellieha*
*Int Gejt Meqjuma Minn Missirijietna*

The priest had detached himself from his group of supplicants. 'This is the prayer of the faithful, my son, when they begged Our Lady to bring solace. The prayer of which I spoke. Is it possible, do you suppose, to see some purpose in the impulse that led you to this spot?'

'I'm afraid I can't see what particular meaning it might have for me,' said Kit. 'Surely it's just a simple supplication, something of its time and place?'

'We find the prayer has a broader application. It has stood us in good stead through many trials.' He began to translate:

'*Our Blessed Virgin Mary*
*Our forefathers venerated you in the sacred cave of Mellieha*
*From the first dawn of Christianity.*
*As they always put their trust in you*
*You always delivered them.*
*Today we likewise plead with you*
*To cast upon us a merciful glance*
*And to cure us of all ills of soul and body.*
*This we ask through Christ our Lord.*'

A merciful glance.

Instantly Kit was back in the cockpit of his Hurricane well north of Gozo at 16,000 feet, ammunition gone, canopy fully open and admitting the oil-and-petrol smell of the hard-used Merlin mingled with the faintest whiff of sea, his goggles up, oxygen mask unclipped, the warmth of the sun on his face, a beautiful day for flying, but waiting to hear the rattle of the Macchi pilot's guns that would end it all and send him down. Then, twenty yards away, the Italian pulling alongside slowly and looking across, a small man, wiry, like Nuvolari, *il Diavolo Mantovano*, nodding, grinning, waving a leather-gloved hand and firing his guns to show what he could have done but did not care to, then plunging away to the brown-grey coast of Sicily. A merciful glance . . .

Or that damned bale-out, caught napping chasing the Regia Nautica after the Grand Harbour show, falling clear from his stricken machine and driving boot-first deep into the foam-flecked waves and bursting to the surface, aware his life depended on the thin rubber of a Mae West life-jacket and whether his position had been reported by the others. The coldness creeping into his limbs and knowing he was alone now, a very small object in a very big sea; swimming because it was that or the unthinkable, and then, on a rising wave, seeing the *motobarca armata* and realising that, after all, he might not die; at least, not yet. A merciful glance?

And what of the Luftwaffe *Gruppen*, those well-drilled crews in superior machines, who had commanded the skies and bombed and strafed at will, softening up the island, wearing down its resolve until invasion was thought to be a matter of weeks or days away, victory seemingly assured, but suddenly sent to fight fresh battles on another, colder front. The defenders of this tiny place had been given a chance to recoup and reinforce, to plan for their inevitable return, hardened, stronger, more resolute still. A breather, as the saying went. Another merciful glance?

No, it was all too fanciful, fatuous mumbo-jumbo and, anyway, so glib, so neat, claiming to read the so-called Almighty's mind, discern his sympathies, which side he might favour. In God we trust? How did he choose? Finally, surely, it came down to the law of good and evil, and that only man could decide. Anything else was akin to soothsayers in Rome seeking divine guidance in the guts of chickens.

Kit looked at the little priest beside him, soft hands clasped over his belly, gently smiling, complacent and secure in his belief.

'I've been responsible for the deaths of many men, Father.'

'What is your name, my son?'

'Curtis.'

'I will pray for you, my son.'

'Would you say I'm an instrument of God?'

'That is between you and God.'

So swift and assured, those responses, Kit thought, passing the buck to God, or back to himself. 'Can such acts be justified in the eyes of God,' he said, 'even if you are compelled to defend yourself against attack?' He was speaking lightly, teasingly almost, as though only mildly curious.

The priest cleared his throat. 'You speak, I suppose, of the commandment that thou shalt not kill.'

'It seems pretty unequivocal.'

'In your English Bible, yes,' said the priest. 'But in the original Hebrew and Greek the commandment was "Thou shalt not murder". To take life in self-defence in time of war cannot be a sin.'

'But don't the Wehrmacht go into battle with *Gott Ist Mitt Unes* on their belt buckles?' persisted Kit.

'It is what is in their minds that counts,' said the priest, 'not on their belt buckles. They invade, destroy and murder in the name of power, ambition and greed. They hold themselves above others, the master race. They may delude themselves in their pride that God is with them.'

'Perhaps their real sin is to choose deluded leaders,' said Kit, 'or rather, allow deluded leaders to choose them, leaders who warp their judgement by twisting their traditions and beliefs to suit their own ambitions.'

The *kappillan* nodded thoughtfully. 'Yes, that is well observed.'

Kit looked up at the marble tablet inscribed with the prayer to Our Lady of Mellieha. 'You are a rational and educated man, Father. Do you really believe that it was God's merciful glance that made it rain, that he controls the weather, any more than he controls what is happening to us now, where people like me are driven to fight and kill, entirely against our natures?' Suddenly he was irritable and confused. 'A week or so ago I saw the so-called enemy, seven men with names and families, men whose lives I ended, whose futures I had taken. I doubt those men considered themselves the master race but their country has chosen to follow a prophet who preaches patriotism and calls for it to be expressed through war. They, and millions of others, answered that call, no doubt with *Credo in Dio* on their lips and in their minds, but for these men there was no merciful glance.'

'Perhaps, my son, because of their delusions, of following the wrong path.'

'Father,' said Kit, 'this is man-made nonsense and not to be seen in terms of black and white, nothing like as simple as you seem to think.'

The *kappillan* was disturbed by the sharpness of Kit's tone. 'I understand your discomfort, my son.'

'Do you? I doubt it. We have a way, in the air force, of talking about attacking the machine not the man. Very convenient. Some of us even mark the number of kills on the sides of our planes, our personal scores, like sportsmen, insignia, you understand, not pictures of men. That might be more honest, except our fuselages would not provide enough space because bombers have many crew. All a game, you see, a particularly nasty game we tend to deny even to ourselves. So we act, don't dwell too much on what we are required to do. Press on, as the British say.'

'I can offer only the comfort of Our Lord,' said the *kappillan*. He sounded sympathetic, as though he sensed an inner sorrow.

'You misunderstand,' said Kit, quickly. 'I realise this is the way it has to be. The awful thing is I wanted it. I dreamed of such things. At first I saw everything through a child's eyes, as a crusade, a passage of arms, an opportunity to prove myself and on the side of the righteous too. They say you should be careful about what you wish for, in case your wish is granted. Well, it was, and now I am bloodied and hardened and different, coarsened, I suppose, not the naïve young fellow I was two years ago when this mess started. And when I looked down on those seven dead men who had fallen to my bullets, do you know what I felt?'

The *kappillan* shook his head slowly.

'Very little,' said Kit. 'Indifference almost. A dull acceptance that this was what was required and what it had come to. That here was a business entirely down to man, in which no amount of merciful glances from some imagined deity could make the slightest difference. Good must prevail over evil, I'm convinced of that, but along the way a lot of innocent or misguided people are going to die. It's a pity but there it is. It has to be done, and it's being done by chaps like me.' He was frowning and staring at the floor where ants were busy about a triangular aperture in the tiles, one column filing into the nest with small burdens of struggling tiny insects, particles of leaves and scraps of food, another winding under the pews, casting about for more.

The *kappillan* folded his arms and looked at Kit with his head on one one side, speculatively, his eyes keen. 'You are angry, my son. But I cannot accept that you are indifferent to these things, as you maintain. A nature such as yours cannot sustain so bleak a concept. You have depth, compassion and a great awareness. Whether you subscribe to our belief, well, that is for you alone to decide. I would say you alone and God, but I know you cannot accept that, as you are. But I implore you to be honest with yourself and face up to your emotions. Don't allow yourself to be brutalised by what you and your comrades must endure. And don't close every door to understanding.' The priest stood back. 'Like it or not, my son, you will remain in my prayers. And I will ask Our Lady of Mellieha to cast you a merciful glance, whether or not you accept that such an invocation can in any way change your destiny. Or, indeed, change the weather.' Again the priest gave his good-humoured chuckle.

A thoroughly decent type, decided Kit, not riddled with cant but likeable and accepting. He could understand why the people of Mellieha came to him, a stable and unflustered source of hope and comfort, listening patiently to their anxieties and concerns as their world was pounded, stone by stone, to dust around them.

Kit stood up, dizzy for a moment, steadying himself against the back of the next pew. Its wooden legs scraped across the tiled floor, rasping and unpleasant, like broken chalk on a blackboard, setting his teeth on edge. The stitched wound on his temple was throbbing and the old fracture in his humerus seemed to have been disturbed by ditching in the drink, twinges of pain coming and going as he moved the shoulder, as though a nerve was being pinched. God's teeth, this wasn't the idea at all, going down the pan just when he wanted to get back to the squadron, restored and ready for action.

The long walk round the bay to Mellieha Ridge had seemed

an excellent idea, a toughening up, a preparation, a start to shrugging off soft ways. He had been wary of the comforts offered by the rest camp, conscious that he was enjoying them far too much. But now he felt distinctly ropy and it was a long walk back as well. He caught himself wondering if the priest could arrange some kind of lift, a *karrozzin* perhaps, one of those open-sided four-wheel cabs drawn by a gaunt little North African *barb*, or volunteer a donkey cart and driver, or even find him a bicycle to borrow, on which to spin down Pennellu Hill, away from the Sanctuary, realm of the immaterial, of mystic beliefs, and halfway down, on the twisting corner, the Devil's farmhouse with its darker fancies. Anything to convey him back to the world of here and absolutely now, where practical men toiled together to keep a clutch of battered aircraft in the air, leaving them no time to ponder the finer points of being.

It occurred to him, and he permitted himself the faintest of ironic smiles, that perhaps Our Lady of Mellieha might come up with something in the way of transport; spare him a merciful glance for his aching head and shoulder, his sore feet. But he did not get a sign. Instead he found himself following the *kappillan* out of the church and into the sun. The light was intense and blinding, fiercely white, and with it there was a savage burning through the soles of his shoes from the baked paving stones.

They passed across the front of the church and descended a flight of steps that led down to the hill-road. Around them the sound of birdsong rang back from the stone-block walls and balustrades. A thin-necked cat sat neatly in the sun, licking its paws, close to a scattering of feathers and fragments of bone.

Halfway down the *kappillan* halted and indicated a plain arched doorway set into the rock. They passed through and at first the interior was profoundly dark but then, as his eyes adjusted, Kit saw a pale, level tunnel stretching away, deep beneath the church above them, quite wide, perhaps twenty feet across, the floor even and well made, firm underfoot. Faint light filtered down at points along its length, where twisting narrow stairways led down from the surface, and at intervals, on the tunnel walls, oil-lamps burned, throwing shadows across the curving roof. Small chambers had been dug out, providing space, in most, for one or two simple beds, a table on which stood cups, plates and cutlery, ready for a meal, deal chairs, a metal washstand and water jug, in some a cot and, suspended from hooks or perched on shelves, unlit lamps primed for use. And common to all, on the facing wall, a crucifix.

'You see,' said the *kappillan*, 'even here Providence provides an answer. They tell me that more bombs have descended on our island than in your London Blitz. We are, they say, the most bombed place on earth. And yet in shelters like these our people can remain secure.'

Kit touched the walls. The rock felt soft and friable. He could scratch a line with his fingernail.

'Maltese limestone,' said the *kappillan*. 'On the surface it is as hard as iron, baked by the sun, but at these depths it is quite easily worked.'

They moved further along the tunnel. They could hear voices, muffled, calling to each other from different locations. Diggers were busy with long-shafted hammers and chisels, fashioning new chambers in a dull oil-light glow. Two of the men shouted greetings to the *kappillan* as he passed.

'*Kif inti*, Dun Vincenz?' So, thought Kit, Vincenz, the priest had a name.

'*Tajjeb, grazzi*, Louis,' said the priest. And then in English: 'Our good friend here is a British pilot. He fights in the air, you fight underground. Brave men all.'

'No bravery here, Dun Vincenz,' said the digger Louis. 'This is the safest job in Malta, eh, Enrico?'

'And the worst paid,' said his companion. 'Sixty cents a day to break our backs.'

'*Skuzani*, Dun Vincenz,' said Louis. '*Ahjar weggha minn demgha*.' He grinned at Kit. 'Better an ache than a tear.'

'Dun Vincenz, *tista tghidli x'hin hu*?' said Enrico, sourly. 'What is the time?'

'Almost noon.'

'Hah! It might as well be midnight for us mice.'

'Cease your squeaking, mouse,' said Louis, and turned back to his work.

The tunnel stretched away in front of the pilot and the priest, the *kappillan* leading, holding high a borrowed lamp. 'Nearly four thousand shelter here, the whole of our town, and a thousand more come in from other, smaller places. The little caves are used for long attacks, by families, the old and very young.' They were passing other diggers sweating at their task. 'A dozen such fellows labour here, and every day the women clean, to conquer another enemy. We can hide from bombs but not from ourselves and what we carry. When full the atmosphere is foul and pestilential. Our people are already weak from malnutrition and fall an easy prey to the ancient maledictions, scabies, lice, bedbugs, fleas, typhoid, tuberculosis.'

They came upon a padlocked gate set in an iron barrier as broad and tall as the tunnel. 'Even our treasures are sick,' said the *kappillan*. 'Ħere are stored the finest works of art from our museums – paintings, sculpture, books, artefacts of every kind. But they begin to rot, thanks to the dampness and lack of air. Soon they will have to be moved again, to Rabat.'

Outside, passing from the cool dampness of the shelter to the soaring midday heat, Kit's shirt was instantly soaked with sweat, as wet as if a prankster had doused him with a pail of water. He wiped the moisture from his eyes and saw, parked on the hill-road at the foot of the steps, its engine ticking over, chassis lurching to the revolutions of the prop-shaft, a small anonymous truck, the kind that plied the harboursides, collecting fruit and vegetables from Gozo and, before the war, wines shipped from Sicily, fortified Marsala, golden Moscato and, most popular of all, *il vino della casa*, farmers' home-made brew, strong and cheap; a memory now.

'In the Sanctuary old Anton Brincat perceived that you were weary,' said the *kappillan*. 'He offers his services in thanks for yours.'

'Now that,' said Kit, 'is what I call a merciful glance.'

'Sometimes,' said the *kappillan*, 'even Our Lady needs a helping hand.'

But at times, on that brief but alarming drive, Kit thought the lift was not such a mercy after all, as the leathery Brincat, with wild hair and a big moustache, took his eyes off the road and hands off the wheel for long, long moments, apparently oblivious to fast-approaching bends and wandering goats, chatting with gusto and animation, every word lost in the blare of the engine. Dust swept into the cab through the open windscreen, propped up with a chunk of wood, and when at last they reached the rest camp at St Paul's Bay, Kit wondered if, after all, Our Lady of Mellieha had spared him a merciful glance. The brakes were little more than a memory so Brincat thrust the clutch pedal to the floor, engaged second gear and turned off the ignition, locking the transmission. The truck slewed to a halt in a cloud of dirt and flying stones. Brincat jumped down from the driver's seat with the nimbleness of a younger man and ran eagerly round to the other side where his passenger, white with dust, was climbing out and banging his service cap against his knee.

With some difficulty Kit took his leave. It was a prolonged farewell. Kit promised he would return to Mellieha soon. He promised, without fail, that he would visit the Brincat dwelling for a pot of English tea and *kwarezimal* almond cakes, baked in his honour by Mrs Brincat. He promised, meanwhile, to kill many Germans and Italians. It was also entirely possible, Kit reflected, ears ringing from the ride, that he had promised to marry Brincat's spinster daughter.

Now, as Anton Brincat pumped the hand of the man who might just be his future son-in-law, Kit noticed a trio of officers studying him from the front of the requisitioned villa. He recognised Ossie Wolf, untypically gaunt from his attack of the Dog, always small but looking smaller still, a Mississippi mudlark – Tom Sawyer, perhaps, or Huckleberry Finn. By contrast his companions were well groomed and smartly uniformed, suggesting they were new to Malta. They seemed familiar, and as he detached himself from Brincat and went towards them he knew them.

'Good grief,' said Douglas Brewster to Buster Brown, as Kit got closer. 'Is that apparition Curtis?'

'Hello, sir.' Kit held out his hand and, after a moment's hesitation, the squadron leader took it. 'Scruff order on the Malta station, I'm afraid, not helped by my chauffeur insisting we took a breath of air.' He took off his cap and shook the dust from his hair.

On the road the churning engine of the truck finally caught and the vehicle moved away. Brincat leaned far out of the driver's door, resting his left hand lightly on the steering-wheel, which vibrated alarmingly as the wheels bounced across the rutted surface, waving a V-for-victory sign with his right and shouting his farewells. The words 'Eyeties', 'Jerries' and '*kwarezimal*' could be discerned above the blatter from the holed exhaust.

'Good God, man,' said Brewster. 'You look like the Ghost of Christmas Past.'

'Or Mr Bun the Baker,' said Buster Brown. 'I'd say it's time for another cleansing dip in the briny.'

Kit grinned. 'Buster, you old reprobate. Welcome to Malta. You heard about my brolly-hop, then?'

'Bounced by an Eyetie, old boy? You're losing your touch.'

'They're no chumps,' cut in Ossie Wolf, 'whatever you've been told. This guy's no rookie and they dumped him in the drink real good, as well as putting one of my best fliers on a boat back home. Get yourself a set of wings, brother, and try it for yourself.'

'No chance of that, I'm afraid,' said Buster heavily, 'stuck at Control in Lascaris.'

'None of that, Brown,' said Brewster. 'These cocky little fighter boys are two a penny. Controllers who've been through the mill are gold-dust.'

'Yeah,' said Ossie Wolf, relenting, conscious of the ravaged figure by his side. 'I guess you're right at that.'

Kit took a shower while the others walked round the villa to the shaded terrace overlooking the Mediterranean. Far to the right the settlement of Bugibba straggled along a low and rocky promontory stretching out to Qwara Point. To the left rose the higher ground of Mistra Bay and, just off shore, the sea broke blue and green and white around the tiny islands of St Paul. On one, the larger, a statue of the Apostle rose above the cliffs where seabirds circled, marking the spot where tradition held he had come ashore from his shipwrecked merchant galley, nearly two thousand years ago, on a missionary journey to Rome.

A magnum of Lanson '21 champagne was standing on a silver tray with four glasses when Kit came down, freshly shaved with his hair slicked back. 'To toast old times,' said Buster. 'Remember? Our favourite tipple at the good old Crillon before the balloon went up. I lugged this all the way from Blighty in a ruddy Sunderland in your honour.'

'France seems a world away,' said Kit.

'It's a world that's gone,' said Buster. 'Still, we gave the Hun a damned good run for his money, despite the best efforts of our gallant allies.'

'And taught the buggers a hard lesson when they had the brass neck to venture into our own skies,' said Brewster. Fresh from the fall of France, with the remnants of the squadron he had led from the Franco-German border in '39 to the final foothold in Brittany in June '40, and almost engulfed by the pace of Blitzkrieg, he had quickly been given command of a front-line squadron with a reputation for success in the air and a different kind of success on the ground. Through the late summer of 1940 he had battled with his young pilots quite as hard as he had fought the Luftwaffe. 'Cocky little fighter boys.' The phrase was apt. They had slept little, drunk a good deal, driven fast cars on black-market petrol, untaxed and uninsured, and had scoffed at the fuming constabulary. Most weekends, when not in London, their billets had resembled nightclubs. But they had died, too, and Brewster did not like his men to die for lack of discipline. So he changed it all, including the motley garb that had evolved with the pressure of combat and a looser hand that had once been in command: old school ties used as belts, suede chukka boots, cricket jerseys, Turnbull & Asser shirts, brilliant pyjamas under tunics on early-morning scrambles. Soon the score went up and the rate of casualties came down and, like his pilots in France, Kit, Ossie Wolf, Buster Brown and so many others, some who survived but more who had vanished, names and faces all but forgotten in the rush of history, these rag-tag pilots came to know that he was right and they were wrong, came to realise, as the screw was turned, thread by thread, by a determined foe, that the carefree days had gone and the time had come for the professional, not the amateur with flair, courage and youthful failings.

To Kit, Brewster had always seemed old, or older, a man among boys, leading by example, uncompromising, hard on weakness, difficult to please, himself a steady pilot, nothing more, a source of irritation this, falling shy of his own high standards. Yet still he flew and fought and somehow came through it all, sortie after sortie, his hair grey round his ears, although he was barely thirty. No squadron he commanded desired another leader.

'Well,' said Buster, 'how long are we going to sit here looking at that bally Lanson?'

Kit wound out the cork with a dull pop and filled the glasses. He passed them round and raised his in a toast. 'To Malta, a tiny dog with a lion's soul.'

'Hey,' said Ossie Wolf, 'that's very Shakespeare.'

Brewster took a cautious sip and sniffed. 'Can't get on with these blasted liver salts. Orderly, fetch me a beer.'

Kit ran the champagne round his mouth, savouring the scent and effervescence between his teeth. 'When are you taking command of the squadron, sir?'

'Yesterday,' said Brewster. 'Penrose has done a more than decent job so they're giving him a spell back home, then another shepherding assignment bringing out fresh machines.'

'Spitfires, sir?' said Ossie.

'Don't keep bending my ear about damned Spitfires, Wolf,' growled Brewster. 'I know your views. You aired them not an hour ago. Rely on me, I'll get you chaps the hardware you need but it may take time. In Whitehall things grind exceeding slow, but Portal's on our side, and others who know the score. Believe me, no one doubts the task we face and we're long overdue a return match with the Jerries. Thank God for Russia, I say. Whatever you fellows may think, the Regia Aeronautica's no match for the Luftwaffe boys. And when they return I want to be ready to hit them hard, not just sit on our backsides trying to dodge the bombs. As for Spits, it's a matter of priorities. Meanwhile it's down to us to do our best with the tools we've got.' The orderly poured a chilled Cisk lager into a tumbler and Brewster put his mitt round it, feeling the coldness approvingly. 'So,' he said, 'you've been a bit off-colour, Wolf.'

'You could say that, I guess,' said Ossie. 'I've lost about thirty pounds in a week.'

Brewster took a big gulp of beer. 'But can you fart with impunity?'

'Come again, sir?'

'Pass wind, man, without making an unholy mess of yourself?'

'Just about, sir.'

'I'll take that as a yes, which means you're fit to fly, whatever the medicos say. If you're wrong you can clean up the kite yourself. And you, Kit, are you ready to down your bucket and spade and get back to business?'

'This is hardly a holiday, sir,' said Kit. 'Just a few days' break.'

'I see no reason for my flight commanders to loll about by the sea, admiring the scenery and knocking back Frog fizz, when there's work to be done.' Brewster finished his lager and released a barely smothered belch.

'Flight commanders, sir?' said Kit.

'Why else do you think I came to see you?' roared Brewster. 'To chew the fat about old times? It's new times that concern me and the sooner we all get stuck in the better. I want you chaps back at Takali pronto. We won't win the war dabbling our tootsies in the sea. Report to me at oh-six-hundred, booted and spurred and ready for the fray.'

'We make a sorry trio,' said Buster, when Brewster had bustled off to his waiting car. 'Half cooked, half drowned and half the weight.'

'Still alive and kicking,' said Ossie.

'Oh, yes, the gang's all here, but only just,' said Buster. 'When did we three mutts last get together?

'On the piss, I guess,' said Ossie, 'in London.'

Kit topped up their champagne. 'What was the name of that ghastly club in Tenison Court?'

'Blue Diamond,' said Ossie.

'Dreadful dive,' said Buster. 'Only there thanks to that prize chump who was hung up on one of the tarts.'

'Frazer Cole,' said Kit, 'and his idiotic schoolboy crush.'

'Old Rita sure cooked his hash, all right,' said Ossie. '"Meet my fiancée," the poor sap said. And all she cared about was pouring liquor down his throat and cuddling up to that goddamned Greek.'

'Wasn't there some sort of trouble,' said Buster, 'after we shoved off?'

'Sure,' Ossie said. 'I punched that Demakis creep's lights out and old Drongo lent a hand. We sure raised hell that night. The cock-eyed bastard had it coming. They shut down his goddamned club soon after.'

'Thanks to you?' said Buster.

'Not exactly, no.'

'How is Drongo?' Buster said. 'I'm told McIndoe's Army's got a new recruit.'

'Yeah,' said Ossie. 'The poor mug's not too sunny. They've shipped him home. But he's not as bad as . . .' He hesitated.

'That's all right,' said Buster. 'Glad to hear it. Wouldn't wish it on anyone. The worst of it is missing the damned flying.'

'Yeah,' said Ossie. 'That must be tough.'

'It's these bloody hands, you see. I can hardly hold a fag, let alone a control column.'

Kit stepped in: 'Do you realise that if we hadn't met up in the damned Blue Diamond we wouldn't be here now? You sowed the seed, you blasted Yank. A fighter pilot's paradise, desert warfare, Kesselring's flying circus.'

'Quit whining. I promised you action. You're having a ball. Just wait until those yellow-nose boys hit town. Then you'll see some fun.'

'Talking of fun,' said Buster, 'is there much to be had round here?'

'What kind of fun?' said Ossie.

'You know, fun.'

'Uh-huh, I get you. What say, Kit? You know if there's a little tail on hand?'

Kit shook his head dismissively. 'I wouldn't know. Valletta's the place, I understand.'

'Boy,' said Ossie. 'Just thinking about that Rita chick's given me a hard. She was cute, no question. Funny how certain dames can hit the button.'

'I thought you were feeling groggy and knocked-up,' said Kit. He found the American's turn of phrase distasteful, crude, although he had felt the same, had known the same when he was thinking about Juliette Garencières. The difference was that he could not imagine admitting it to anyone.

'The CO said I'm fit for duty,' Ossie said, 'and the CO's always right.'

'Brewster doesn't change,' said Buster. 'Remember, Kit, how he hoicked you out of the sick bay after your prang at Revigncourt, the day of the Hun invasion?'

'If he hadn't,' said Kit, 'I'd probably have ended up in the bag for the duration.' He grinned, more comfortable with this conversation. 'The MO reckoned Brewster took the view that if your head was on you were fit for service. Doc Gilmour wanted to place me under observation, in case of complications. And there's the CO yelling: "The only complication I care about is the prospect of the bloody Panzers arriving on our doorstep." And passing me as walking wounded.'

'Like I say,' said Ossie, 'the CO's always right.'

'Rotten about Doc Gilmour,' Buster said, 'and all the other chaps. They'd been through too much to go down with the *Lancastria*.'

'That was the first time I got dumped in the drink,' said Kit, 'trying to keep those ruddy Dorniers off, strafing the poor devils in the sea.' He and Ossie exchanged a look. They had flown together that day, 17 June 1940, and seen the *Lancastria*, the old Cunarder pressed into wartime service, struck by bombs from Do 17s, going down by the head in fifteen minutes with thousands of defeated troops clinging to her hull and, trapped in her hold, men of their own squadron.

Ossie jerked his head at Kit. 'This character,' he said, 'decided it would be a great idea to let the poor bastards have his Mae West. An Me 110 got him while he was doing his burlesque act.'

Yes, thought Kit, he remembered now. The Hurricane staggering under a dozen hits, himself feeling dazed, his vision blurring. Tearing off his helmet and oxygen mask, raising himself into the slipstream and floating clear, waiting for the speed of his descent to slow before he pulled the D-ring. Moving his arms and legs, able to change his attitude in the air. Flying without an aeroplane. Falling. Ah, yes, blue man falling, like the Russian countess, Bébé Dubretskov's Tarot-reading mother, had predicted in that dingy little room in the rue de la Verrerie in Paris. Then his hand flying to the ripcord and landing close to the British destroyer whose crew leaned over the rail and screamed at him: 'Fucking RAF! Where have you bastards been? What the fuck have you been doing?' And him staring back dumbly, unable to explain. Now he had been bounced again, got away with it again. Was he on borrowed time? Or were the odds the same whenever you went up?

He had never spoken of the thoughts that came to him as he dropped towards the waters off St Nazaire that day. He didn't now. 'I see a blue man falling,' the countess had murmured, as the candlelight flickered on the few remaining relics of her sumptuous Russian past, and she had laid out, row by row, the antique Tarot cards bearing grotesque scenes. Why had it come to him then, as he fell, and why did he recall it now? It was as nonsensical as the so-called merciful glances of Our Lady of Mellieha.

He found himself going over in his mind a flood of recollections, each fleeting, a confusion of people and events, of flying, moments of joy and fear, faces, voices, laughter, death. Of Paris, and Hannah Maierscheldt, their childish fancies and small adventures, his fondness for her, his fears about her love for Bébé Dubretskov, so physically alike, the little Russian beautiful but cold and somehow dark, a mind of ice, unreachable until she drowned herself, surprising everyone who thought they knew her. A tragedy, of course, but free of her obsession, Hannah had at least been saved and made her way to England.

The orderly came out onto the terrace. 'Flight Lieutenant Curtis?'

'Yes?'

'A telegram, sir.'

'Don't tell me,' Buster said. 'You've been posted. A nice cushy billet with Their Airships in Whitehall.'

'It's my mother,' said Kit. 'She's dead.'

# Eight

The day was hot and oddly quiet, windless and oppressive, a time for routine tasks, essential and mundane, reluctantly undertaken: repairing blast pens with stone blocks salvaged from bombed buildings, constructing new ones, filling ammunition belts in the armourers' bays, tending the heavy ordnance and the Bofors anti-aircraft guns in their sandbag-walled emplacements, levelling the runways with a roller drawn by requisitioned oxen, laying the hanging dust with water-trucks. On the far side of the airfield the wind-sock dangled limp against its pole, and beyond the perimeter, on a slight incline, the six sails of a stone-towered grain mill stood motionless. A hundred feet above it two buzzards soared, broad-winged, moving their small heads, giving out their high-pitched mewing call.

On the ground an occasional Merlin would splutter into life, warmed up by ground-crews who ran the Hurricane engines slowly at 1,000 r.p.m., eyes fixed on temperature and pressures, testing hydraulics by lowering and raising flaps, opening up the throttles a little with two men on the tail, checking supercharger, propeller controls, magnetos, brakes, pneumatics. Yet even now, as hour followed hour, the men kept a wary watch on the sky, alert for the distant growl of an incoming raid, the jarring ring of the Dispersal phone, the rising howl of the hand-cranked siren.

Four pilots were on readiness, sweating in their flying gear, parachutes already in their cockpits. Ossie Wolf was working at his harmonica, 'Moonlight Serenade', one of the big-band numbers that had stuck in his mind, played over and over on the gramophone by the guys at the rest camp. He gave it plenty of tongued vibrato, cocking an eye at the others, who dozed, flicked through magazines or leaned back in their shabby chairs and stared at nothing. He fancied a little verbal sparring to break the tedium but could see there was nothing doing. Jesus, these guys were so goddamned phlegmatic, as though nothing could ruffle their calm, just waiting around like those big damned birds up there, kind of passive but ready to explode when the time was right and not before. He handled it a different way, hated squatting on his butt, preferred to create a little aggravation to get his juices going, to mask the boredom and fatigue.

He finished the Miller number with a little flourish but still failed to raise an eyebrow and shoved the instrument into the pocket of his flying suit. He went out of the Dispersal tent and looked around. Corporal Chalmers was on the wing of his machine, talking to the fitter, Tate, who was in the cockpit, sitting low and moving the control column so the fabric-covered elevators swung up and down, making a dull thumping noise. It struck Ossie that this was one hell of a primitive machine, insubstantial, just a lash-up, as the English said, a parcel of wood, fabric and metal tube. But deceptively robust, like a useful lightweight in a slugfest, able to soak up punishment, shrug it off and come back ready with the counterpunch.

'Hey, Chuffy, how you doing?'

'Spot on, sir. The stick's moving free. No hint of stiffness.'

'And the hood?'

'Wally's oiled it up and it's sliding grand.'

'That's swell.'

'There were some chuffing Malties after you,' said Chalmers.

'Malties? What goddamned Malties?'

'About an hour ago. We chased 'em off.'

'Why in hell did you do that?'

'Looked like a bunch of bandits. One even had a chuffing gun. We reckoned they were looking for a fight.'

'They always look like that, for Chrissake. Did they give a name?'

Chalmers looked surprised, as though it had not occurred to him that the Maltese might have names. He shook his head. 'Old bloke with a cap, another, younger like, and a nipper, a cheeky little sod I've seen around before somewhere.'

'Giorgio?' Ossie had spotted the kid when he'd checked back into his quarters in the *palazzo* in Mdina; not to speak to, just a nod and a grin because Brewster was making things hum and they all had stuff to do that he had dreamed up after his first inspections.

'Search me,' said Chalmers.

'A girl?'

'No girl.' The corporal's eyes had widened. Suddenly he looked knowing.

Ossie imagined he understood why an old bloke with a gun might be looking for the gaunt American who had yet to fly in combat after his attack of Malta Dog. Chuffing obvious, really, an ailing Yank with time on his hands chatting up local talent, leading on some bit of fluff whose family had cut up rough.

Chalmers was smiling slightly now. 'So what shall I say if the buggers pitch up again?' he said.

'Tell me, for Chrissake,' said Ossie. 'They're pals of mine.'

He knew it was old Farinacci and Giorgio, the kid. So who

was the third? Salvator Boero, maybe, that bastard with the wine-skin who had looked at Claudia in a certain way when she had brought them food; broken-nosed Boero, sticking close to the old man and trying to gain his favour, all the time with his eyes on the girl and maybe also the farm in the red-earthed valley near Tal-Bistra, because Giorgio was young and the old man had no other sons and much could happen in this lousy war.

Ossie headed back to Dispersal. Behind him Chalmers was saying something to Tate, who laughed. Ossie turned and hollered: 'Corporal, cut the crap. I want that stick to move like it's in a jar of goddamned honey.'

He hated Chalmers for thinking he could read the situation and hated Salvator Boero more, for the way he had looked at Claudia that day at Targa Gap when she had made her way towards them, advancing between the stunted vines, leaning against the weight of her bamboo basket, her small feet scuffing the russet soil, her hair curled and glossy black, bouncing as she walked. He knew he desired her, but not as he had desired the woman Rita in the lousy dive where he and Drongo had popped the Greek. He had looked at that young girl and she was a beginning, a fresh start, untouched. She had made him feel kind of old but also young, like ten years had dropped away and he was just a kid as well, awkward, speechless at her beauty and wanting very much for her to look his way and smile that smile and maybe spend a little time with him and walk quiet walks. Hell, after this thing was over he could be the one to work with Farinacci and Giorgio, Giorgio all growed up. Work with them and tend the land, grow the crops and rear the beasts; maybe rear some offspring of his own, snugged down in a square white house in the centre of a spread, with a dark-haired woman to watch him come back from the fields, the sun very high in the sky where he had flown an airplane in a war that was a memory now, a very long time ago.

Kit Curtis was asleep in his wicker chair. An opened letter lay near his outstretched feet. Ossie bent down, picked it up and placed it on the table by the telephone where Ellis, the duty corporal, sat and doodled noughts and crosses with a pencil on his pad. At the slight movement, Kit started awake. 'Christ, I was miles away. What's up?'

'Nothing, brother. Absolutely nothing. Looks like the Eyeties are lingering over their spaghetti.'

'Spaghetti,' said Astley-Cobb. 'Now, there's a thought. Did I tell you chaps about the time I spent in Pesaro on the Adriatic coast? *Spaghetti vongole.* Now there's a dish. Onion, garlic, olive oil, tomatoes, spaghetti with clams and topped with lemon. No wonder the bastards can't be bothered to fight a war.'

'Personally, Max,' said Brian Twigg, 'I prefer bully beef. Can't get enough of the stuff. Just on its own, straight out of the tin. None of this fancy foreign muck for me.'

'Christ, Twiggy,' said Astley-Cobb, 'are you serious?'

'What do you think, you fathead?' said Twigg.

Ossie passed Kit the opened letter. 'News from home?'

'It's about my mother. There's going to be an inquest. It's all a bit inconclusive. Sounds like an idiotic accident but I suppose they've got to be sure.'

'I was sorry to hear about it, Kit,' said Astley-Cobb. 'Didn't like to bring it up. Rotten business, particularly stuck out here.'

'If you are. Stuck out here, I mean,' said Twigg.

'Oh I'm stuck, all right,' said Kit. 'Out of the question to ask the CO for compassionate leave this far away. And, anyway, what's the point? An inquest could take ages. Brewster's hardly going to allow me to kick my heels back home until the funeral. Good grief, he begrudged me forty-eight hours at the blasted rest camp.'

'Hard on your father, though,' said Astley-Cobb.

Kit nodded. 'He's pretty cut up about it but he understands.'

'Duty and all,' said Ossie. It sounded glib and he hadn't meant it to come out that way but, still, it didn't really bother him any. It amused him to watch the Englishman flush and jump to the defence of the musty values of a country that called itself great but was growing small. He had a lot of time for the Brits but they didn't see the way the world was slipping away from them, that it would never be the same, particularly for guys like Curtis. To win this thing alone was a clear no-hoper. Sooner or later the States would be drawn in and they would win the war – and win the peace as well. Little England would be strictly small potatoes.

'Duty,' Kit was saying, his voice tight. 'Yes, that's right. My father believes in such things. Don't you?'

'Maybe I don't call it that,' said Ossie. 'Maybe I call it keeping an eye on the ball.'

'What exactly happened, Kit?' said Astley-Cobb, quickly. 'I've never quite understood.'

'No one does, exactly,' said Kit. 'It seems she fell under a train. God knows what she was doing. She hadn't told anyone she was going up to London, or why.'

'Christ,' said Astley-Cobb. 'What a terrible thing.'

'Yes,' said Kit. 'I suppose it is. But when you're surrounded by terrible things it seems like just one more death among so many.' He was rather relieved by his sense of detachment, of feeling so little emotion. It was more a vague embarrassment at the absurd circumstances of his mother's death: her pretensions and petty snobberies, her well-exercised prejudices and dislikes, her sense of superiority to those around her, her belief that one day she would rediscover a way of life she had lost as a girl, all brought to nothing under the grinding wheels of a train watched from the platform by a crowd of strangers.

Astley-Cobb was taken aback by Kit's apparent coolness. 'But still, your mother . . .'

'You have to understand,' said Kit, 'she had no real need of other people. Well, possibly just one. But her life took a particular turn and she couldn't get back. We were never close. I boarded, of course, then went up to Trinity. To her I was just a spotty youth mad about flying and apparently not much else. She took no real interest, let me go my own way. I'm afraid it suited me rather well.'

Astley-Cobb frowned. 'Was it an accident, do you think? From what you say . . .'

'Oh, an accident, certainly, yes. She was quite content in her own particular way. Entirely selfish, pleased herself in all things, led her own life. She had no reason to end it. It sounds damned hard,' he said, 'but my father's better off.' By now Kit was relishing his bluntness. He wondered if sorrow and regret might touch him later. It hadn't yet and days had passed. He had concluded, quite soon, that he owed his mother no favours. Now he saw no reason to soften his words, assume a regret he did not feel. He even thought for a moment that he might mention the drinking, to hint at how such a thing might have occurred but then relented: one twist of the knife too many, perhaps.

Suddenly he was aware of the duty corporal jumping up, his chair flying backwards, and coming to attention. Brewster had ducked in underneath the tent flap. He was wearing flying clothes. With the others, Kit was quickly on his feet. 'God's teeth!' cried Brewster. 'It's like a blasted dentist's waiting room in here. Don't you people ever get bored?'

Nobody said a word. They waited as the squadron leader threw down his helmet, goggles and oxygen mask on the corporal's table. 'All right, you fellows,' said Brewster. 'Now, listen to me well. I've heard a rumour, and correct me if I'm wrong,' this with the faintest wrinkling round the eyes that he always used to signal an attempt at badinage, 'that our job is to destroy the enemy wherever we find him. For the moment it seems he doesn't want to be found. Which means, at least to a simple soul like me, that we must go looking for him. I'm told that at Syracuse the Italians have assembled a rather tasty collection of seaplanes.' He waved a chart. 'I've marked our course. Wolf, have you still got the trots?'

'Excuse me?'

'The Dog, man, the Dog. Is it still biting?'

'I got the beast under control, sir.'

'Good enough. I understand you've got a reputation as a Malta hand. Here's your chance to prove it to me. I'll lead, you'll fly as my number two. Astley-Cobb and Twigg, you're three and four. Curtis, three chaps are on their way here now. You'll stay on readiness, as flight commander, to cover our backs.'

Kit knew Brewster well from France: he did not concern himself with personal feelings, what he saw as petty ambition, desire for glory, hunger for command, fear of being passed over. He ordered his men and machines without emotion, weighing the advantages and odds, as cool and clinical as if he was playing chess. Now all Kit said was 'Yes, sir.' He tried to sound keen but still he did not trust himself to look at the bright-eyed Ossie Wolf who had quickly spread out the chart on the table and was tracing with a finger the crayoned course along the east coast of Sicily; did not trust himself because he might betray the wave of disappointment that seemed to settle in his throat.

Ossie stood back from the chart. 'That's quite a distance, sir.'

'About a hundred miles,' said Brewster, 'and a hundred back. A doddle.'

'You bet,' said Ossie.

'Some of these Eyetie float-planes are air-sea rescue,' said Twigg. 'You know, sir, big red crosses on their wings. What are we meant to do about them?'

'Good grief, man, what do you think?' said Brewster. 'Their job is to pick up pilots we've shot down so they can live to fight another day. That doesn't please me and it shouldn't please you. We're here to knock the buggers flat, not see them helped back on their feet ready for another round. If you've got any qualms, shoot them down gently.' He turned to Ossie. 'I'm the new boy here. Haven't come up against the Italians before. What's the gen?'

'Oh, they're good, all right,' said Ossie. 'But if they've got a weakness it's that they love to fly. Lots of fancy moves, real precise, which makes things kind of predictable. So you just sit back, admire 'em as pilots, then hit the gun-button. Ain't that right, fellers?'

'For ordinary types like us,' said Astley-Cobb, 'it's not that simple.' He exchanged a sardonic glance with Kit. 'But as the CO says, it's obviously a doddle for an ace like you.'

Brewster laughed, a deep, pleased belly laugh. 'If you're as quick to spot a bogey as a line-shoot, Astley-Cobb, we're in for some fun.' He picked up the chart and folded it quickly. 'Okay, chaps. Get cracking. Take-off in fifteen minutes.'

As the others hurried away Brewster surprised Kit by taking him aside. 'Don't look so crestfallen, boy. I need a good man here to give us a hand if needed. If this little jaunt succeeds it will give us all a shot in the arm, taking the fight to the enemy, bouncing him in his own backyard. You and I go back a long way, Kit, so indulge me on this. I won't have many chances to get stuck in. There's a devil of a lot to get sorted and much of it on the ground. But you know the way I work. I can't expect chaps to do things I'm not prepared to do myself. Believe me, if we can pull this off it'll be the first of many and your turn will come.'

'Yes, sir,' said Kit, with feigned brightness. He saw, gathering outside the tent, three young pilots whose names he did not know and whose faces were only vaguely familiar from the mess. They shuffled nervously, waiting for Brewster to finish talking. Kit had seen such groups at prep school, waiting outside the headmaster's study, pale-faced and apprehensive.

'We flew out together on the Sunderland from Gib,' said Brewster. 'Not one of them's fired a shot in anger. The red-haired lad's logged barely fifteen hours on Hurricanes. Time to give them a taste of what's to come.'

'They're lucky blighters, sir,' said Kit. 'If they were up against the Jerries they wouldn't last five minutes.'

In the full heat of the day, placing his right foot in the stirrup-step below the fuselage of his machine, Ossie Wolf fought down a rising wave of nausea. It came and went. For hours and even days he would think he'd gotten this thing beat. Then, out of nowhere, the Dog would fix him in its jaws again and his guts would be shot to hell, every muscle aching from the puking. He knew they reckoned that once the Dog had you it never let you go, was always ready to drag you down. Well, to hell with that. He had stuff to do, stuff that allowed no lousy bunch of bugs to come between him and it, so for days he hadn't eaten. When he did, he threw up and the sweats came back, that goddamned clammy weakness that made it tough to get about, act normal and not alert the other guys, in particular the doc who'd ground him for another spell of kicking his heels in the damned *palazzo* with one eye on the john.

Not eating meant he didn't crap his pants because now there was nothing left to crap, only watery liquid he could just about control. It left him feeble and he had to put on quite an act but the choice was simple: if that was what it took to fly, until he'd got this thing licked, then that was what it took. At least the Dog had chased away the lousy dreams.

Ossie could see that Chuffy Chalmers was keen to be pals, that he knew he'd riled him some about old Farinacci. The corporal let the American pull himself up onto the wing of his Hurricane, step into the cockpit and slide down onto the bucket seat. Then he clambered up himself, leaned in, guided the straps of the parachute over Ossie's shoulders and helped to snap the securing pins of the Sutton harness. As Ossie pulled on his helmet it felt a size too big, as though his skull had shrunk. He held his oxygen mask across his face and switched on the supply, breathing the pure air deep into his lungs. Now he was clear-headed, aware of every sense, trying to ignore his churning bowels, new energy pulsing through his veins. His mind was alive with thoughts of action, going over what he had seen on Brewster's chart: the marked north-easterly course to Syracuse that skirted the Cape of Passero, staying out to sea until the final turn to port that would sweep them in on the Italian seaplane base. It was set well back in a bay encircled by hills that offered great scope for anti-aircraft positions, the guns perched high allowing the barrels plenty of elevation. From their cockpits, Ossie reckoned, he and the guys would likely find themselves looking right down the goddamned muzzles, unless they snuck in fast and low and caught the Eyeties with their pants around their ankles.

He secured the clips of his oxygen mask and plugged in the R/T lead. He looked to his right. Brewster gave him a firm thumbs-up. On his left Max Astley-Cobb and Brian Twigg were ready too.

'Okay, Red Section,' said Brewster. 'Fire 'em up.'

Prime engine, switches on, thumbs-up to the ground-crew waiting for the sign. Now press the starter button. Jesus, always that moment of awe as a thousand horsepower was unleashed. The whole machine quivered, fat tyres pushing at the chocks. Almost as one the Merlins had fired up.

Control came on, a familiar voice. 'Control to Red Leader, Control to Red Leader. This is your friendly duty controller. Nothing to advise you of at present. Get off right away and good luck. Over.'

'Red Leader to Control,' said Brewster. 'Red Leader to Control. Thanks, Buster. Good to have you along for the ride. Out.'

Kit Curtis watched them climb away fast, four abreast, on power boost to 27,000 feet, heading north with the sun behind them. The new arrivals looked at each other but said nothing. They were imagining it was them, as it would be soon, looking for the enemy in a vast and cloudless sky.

Poor chumps, thought Kit. They'd had their glory-days, the early training, the excitement of going solo, the thrill of taking the controls of a fighter plane at last, the satisfaction of learning a new and difficult skill, feeling they were master of their machine in all its moods, the fun of leave, impressing the family with their hard-earned wings, showing off to the girls a little, or a lot; delighting in the role of dashing fighter boy. And now here they stood, on a plain of dust and suffocating heat, far from home, on the threshold of combat against a determined, experienced foe, battles that would be fought above this smudge of rock and dirt that called itself a stronghold or over a cold, impassive sea. At home proud parents would still be passing round the well-worn photographs of George and Jonathan, Paul and Roger, Colin and Pip in flying gear – 'Yes, that's his Hurricane, no, not a Spitfire yet' – hoping the boy would be all right, were sure he would be, oh, yes, of course, a natural talent for flying, the instructors said, which must count for something, surely. Now, in this bleak and barren place, confronted with the truth, Kit did not wonder that his three young men did not exchange a word.

* * *

Brewster said little on the outward leg to Syracuse, only an occasional response to Buster Brown's report of empty skies, no big or little jobs mustering for a raid. Their throttles had been eased, and boost reduced, to save on fuel, cruising at only 160 m.p.h. and watching the sea that wags had christened 'Mussolini's Lake' move slowly far below, so slowly that they seemed to hang suspended, motionless, with only their instruments to show that mile by mile they were drawing closer to their objective.

The great bulk of Sicily began to show on their port beam, obscured by a creamy haze. Soon they could pick up the wakes of many vessels criss-crossing the coastal waters, crews secure in their belief that here, so far from Malta, they were safe, could not be touched. Ossie ached to peel off in a power dive and teach them different.

'This is Red Leader. This is Red Leader,' said Brewster. 'ETA five minutes, chaps. Over.'

'Roger, Red Leader. Out.' Ossie glanced across the space between their machines and saw that Brewster was staring fixedly ahead, hunched forward over the controls in that way he had, bristling with aggression, like a panther poised to spring. The others had checked in too, quick and brief, guys who knew the game, tough and battle-hardened, a crackerjack team that was about to give the Eyetie float-plane boys one hell of a wake-up call.

Ahead and to the left of his Hurricane's long nose, coming into view and then obscured by the leading edge of the port wing as the machine rose and fell, pushing its way through the thin air, Ossie made out the sprawl of a significant conurbation with, on its outskirts, the deep excavation of a white-walled quarry. He remembered the chart; the quarry clearly marked, the Latomia del Paradiso. And, sure enough, there lay Syracuse with its narrow isthmus linking the modern city to the island of Ortygia where the ancient settlement, the Città Vecchia, crowded down to the Porto Grande and the Ionian Sea. Beyond this panorama, away to the north, arresting and formidable, rose the scarified black heights of Mount Etna, the volcano's summit high enough to snag a few white fleecy clouds.

The Hurricanes were rapidly shedding height, still ten miles out to sea. Ossie and the others knew that, equipped with radar, the Italians would already have scrambled a force of Macchi 200s and that would have been the end for them, this far from home. But the Regia had no radar, had instead to rely on observers on land or sea and, so far, there was no sign that they had been spotted.

Brewster turned the flight towards the target. Down to a thousand feet now, the sense of speed exhilarating after the illusory, painful crawl at altitude. 'Red Leader to Control. We're on the button. Preparing to attack.'

'Okay, Red Leader. What's your position?'

'About ten miles east of target.'

'Good show,' said Buster Brown. 'Advise when the party's over, so we know you've had your return ticket punched.'

'Okay, Control. Out.'

The coast was rushing towards them. To the left of the isthmus connecting the mainland with the Città Vecchia, where the cathedral stood serene in its fine square, the distinctive shape of a cavernous hangar rose up above a concrete apron that ran down to the water, very like the hangars at Cattewater Harbour where Ossie, Drongo and the rest had boarded the Plymouth tender, then scrambled on to the Sunderland bound for Gib. But no blunt-nosed Sunderlands here. Close to a pontoon, within dinghy reach, bobbed a low-winged monoplane on twin lateral floats with three big radial engines, a Cant Z-506, the Regia's reconnaissance workhorse, also known to carry bombs or, with big red crosses on its wings, to rescue Regia pilots in the drink. Two more were further out, men moving in the long, raised cockpits, preparing their machines for flight. A fourth was already buffeting towards the open sea, its propellers silver, throwing up sheets of spray, poised to throttle up and lift away.

'Look up-sun,' said Brewster. 'All clear? Good show. Twigg, you stay up and keep 'em peeled. Wolf and Astley-Cobb, you come with me. Going down.'

They went in line astern, three hundred yards apart, at fifty feet, Ossie's machine bucking in Brewster's slipstream until he lost sight of his leader, intent on identifying targets of his own. The Cant near the pontoon flashed through Ossie's sights. He pushed the gun-button, quick, sharp bursts, conserving ammunition, consciously saving rounds for the journey back when the skies around them would no longer be empty. The Cant flew into pieces, the tailplane severed and spiralling into the air, an engine sliced from the starboard wing and plunging down, smashing through a metal float.

Ossie loosed another burst, this time at the broad dark entrance of the hangar. A rolling ball of flame shot up, illuminating the interior where more Cants were hit and the figures of running men showed up against the blaze. Glancing in his mirror, he saw Astley-Cobb holding his machine in a flat, elegant curve so his fire traversed the far side of the concrete apron, worked across the hangar and struck a crane that shook and began to fall.

Ahead and to the left, Brewster was already beyond the harbour, apparently unscathed. Ossie pulled up into a climbing turn, over the modern city, laid out neatly, block by block, not unlike a Midwest burg. He was tracked by a torrent of flak, reaching for him from the tops of buildings and from positions in the parks and hills, lazily at first, then whipping past in a lethal blur. He'd been right about staring down those goddamned muzzles. Some of the stuff was coming at him sideways. And, for sure, there had to be more trouble on the way. He reckoned the Macchi boys would be tumbling into their cockpits round about now, just up the coast at Catania, shaking with frustration, waiting for their nine-hundred horsepower Fiats to kick in. Fast sons-of-bitches with 300-plus m.p.h. to play with and a ceiling of nearly 30,000 feet. And all of them sore as hell.

Brewster was on the R/T. 'Twigg, stop stooging about up there. Come down and give these flak positions something to think about.'

Ossie screwed round in a vertical turn and looked down on the seaplane base. Three Cants wallowed at their moorings, damaged or destroyed. Small boats scurried back and forth, picking up survivors. Black smoke and flame poured from the hangar and a large square admin block had been caught in a storm of fire. Ossie glimpsed papers floating from shattered windows. Cars and trucks were ablaze in the road outside.

Again, the roar of Brownings. Twigg was coming in, beyond the harbour mouth, levelling out from a dive at 330 m.p.h., his Hurricane shaking with the recoil of his guns. His bullets churned the sea around the taxiing Cant, which slowed, began to drift and burn, struck squarely in the cockpit. A single figure threw itself clear and began to swim. Twigg flashed across the harbour, guns still chattering, burned cordite streaking back across his wings, bullets raking the rooftops, raising clouds of dirt and debris in the hills where the flak positions were. Something detonated with a dull thud, setting a cypress grove alight. 'Boy,' shouted Ossie into the R/T. 'Nice going, Twiggs.'

He had formated on Brewster now, a mile or two south of the harbour, and Astley-Cobb was closing on them both.

'Red Two to Red Leader,' Ossie said. 'Another pass?'

'No,' said Brewster. 'We've made our point.'

He swung the flight onto the reciprocal course for home, the Merlins on full boost and at maximum rate of climb. Twigg was with them, easing smoothly into his position in the finger-four formation, and already their altimeters showed 15,000 feet. A long way below, and falling away behind, a pillar of oily smoke rose from the harbour of Syracuse, foul against the brilliance of the vivid landscape washed with sun, a mocking imitation of the sulphurous clouds that rolled skywards from the crater of distant Etna.

'Damage, chaps?' said Brewster.

'A little ventilation in my starboard wing,' said Astley-Cobb, 'and I think my left aileron took a hit.'

'Max, I'll check it out.' Ossie dropped back and down and studied Astley-Cobb's machine. The leading edge of the wing was riddled, sheets of fabric were missing from the port aileron, the bulge of the radiator air-duct beneath the fuselage had been pierced, holes gaped in the rudder and even the tailwheel had been shot away. The aircraft's attitude was wrong, not passing smoothly through the air but crabbing to the left, the wing-tip dropping, only rising up as Astley-Cobb struggled with the controls. 'Yeah, Max, you been peppered some. How's she feel?'

'As responsive as a dying duck.'

'Hold the stick hard to starboard,' Ossie said. 'That'll keep her level.'

'Thanks, Professor. What the blue blazes do you think I'm doing?' Astley-Cobb's voice was hoarse and strained.

Ossie knew what he was thinking, how he'd got to nurse his sick machine across a hundred miles of open sea with a pack of Macchis on the prowl. There was nothing more to say. A fighter plane held a single pilot. This was where training, experience and nerve kicked in, when the chips were down and you had plenty of time to think about what you might have coming, entirely alone. How would it be? Falling behind to fight, a little like a cornered beast surrounded by a pack of predators, nailing a few but finally going down because there were just too many? Struggling on and dropping behind the others, mile by mile, to be bounced out of the sun so fast you wouldn't know what hit you? Or sinking towards the waves, perhaps evading the bandits, unseen against the moving sea, but ditching and jumping clear, if you survived the impact, seeing the Hurricane go into a final watery dive, the tailplane swallowed, leaving you suspended by your life-jacket in a patch of oil, feeling your body start to numb and your mind wandering, wanting it to be over soon because not a soul on earth knew where you were or what might have become of you? Nothing to say to any of that, except try to shut it out and focus on the moment.

'Red Two?' said Brewster.

'Nothing,' said Ossie. 'Not a scratch.'

'Red Three?'

'Took a few rounds through the hood,' said Twigg. 'Bloody Perspex everywhere, including my ugly mug. Lucky I had my goggles down.' He whistled. 'Still, we didn't half spoil their spaghetti.'

'Don't talk about spaghetti, Twiggy,' cut in Astley-Cobb. 'It's just possible I might be eating it for the duration.'

'None of that,' rapped Brewster.

Even as he said it Buster Brown came on: 'Control to Red Leader, Control to Red Leader. There's a plot on the board, heading your way. Eight little jobs at angels-one-six. Vector one-one-zero.'

Adding the vector was a real neat touch, thought Ossie, old Buster slipping in the degrees magnetic needed to intercept the bogeys, about as subtle as a kick in the butt, urging attack and not defence, disregarding the odds of two to one, with Max's machine a heap of shit. Not that Buster knew Max was little more than flying-wounded. Not that they had a choice.

Sure enough Brewster, with a terse command, turned them sharply onto course one-one-zero, climbing hard. The sun, behind them, fell across their wings. Astley-Cobb was lagging behind. The others didn't slow. Now, height was everything – fifty feet could dictate whether you lived or died. There was nothing to be done for Astley-Cobb. His fate was down to him.

Ossie wriggled in his seat, settling himself and getting comfortable for the work ahead, checking his gunsights, the gun-button switch, the range and wing-span indicators, running his eyes across his instruments, then turning his attention to the sky, a systematic search, a methodical zigzag, high and low, left and right, and then again.

Finally he saw them. 'Red Leader, Red Leader, eight bandits to starboard, two o'clock high.' So the bastards had beaten them for height. And now they had been seen.

The Macchi 200s began to peel off, half rolling and swooping down in line astern as the Hurricanes prepared to meet them head-on, fanning out and wide apart, Astley-Cobb more than half a mile behind. Again Brewster's voice crackled over the R/T as they closed: 'Go!' On his word they hauled back on their sticks and rocketed over their attackers as they dived, then throttled back, turning sharply with a small but crucial height advantage gained.

At Takali Kit and his flight were on cockpit readiness. The starter trolleys were plugged in, the ground-crews poised. The order to scramble would come over the pilots' R/T. An urgent thumbs-up to the men on the ground, a quick stab on the starter button and the engines would burst into life, the Hurricanes rolling in moments. The flight could be in the air in less than thirty seconds, no etiquette observed, the single aim to be airborne without delay, only forming up as they climbed to operational altitude.

By now Kit knew his pilots' names. They had talked a little before Control had sent them to their cockpits: Ken Laughton, a sergeant, Canadian, twenty, his face pockmarked with acne, quick to laugh at his own bad jokes, his fingernails gnawed, but steady-looking with a steely eye that suggested youthful grit. And the pilot officers Luck and Spencer, Tommy and Tom, the Tom-Toms, as they told him with broad grins, together right through training; Luck and Spencer who made his heart sink as it always did at mention of any special bond.

With Laughton, Luck and Spencer he had not laughed and joked or shown excitement; shown anything at all. Dour and unblinking, he had run through the drill, making his expectations plain. He imagined they found him disappointing, humourless and distant. It had to be that way. He wanted no part of knowing, caring, being concerned, sharing their thoughts and fears. His job was to take them into battle and get them back so they could fight again, so everything that had gone before would not have been a futile waste of time.

What had Brewster told him, so long ago at Revigncourt on the Marne in '39, that time he tried a wheels-down landing in his damaged machine, selecting a perfect meadow that turned out to be a bog and ended belly-up? 'I can always replace aeroplanes, boy, but I don't want to lose my pilots.' At the time he thought it had been concern for him but now he understood. It hadn't been sentiment or solicitude, just that he didn't want to waste the years of patient training, the gradual shaping of a pilot, the process of delivering those rare individuals who blended brain and mettle, men who could fly a fighter plane, then bring it to battle, giving them the chance to hone their craft in combat, the only school where the final crucial lessons could be learned. He did not want the loss of Laughton, Luck and Spencer against his name, to be seen as a flight commander who had failed to secure the service a good return on its investment. Sweating in his cockpit, he cursed Brewster for assigning him the role of mother-hen, half hoping the call to scramble would not come, but as he thought this so it came.

On the dais of Fighter Ops, duty controller Buster Brown looked down on the twelve-foot-square plotting table showing the Sicilian coast and, in the centre of the blue-coloured sea, the small brown outlines of Malta, Comino and Gozo. A trio of women plotters was marking the course of Kit's flight as it took off from Takali, tracked like every other movement in the air, friend or foe, by the radar stations at Dingli, Tas Silq and Madliena. Fifty miles north of the Lascaris tunnel complex, which formed Malta's war headquarters deep beneath Valletta, Brewster and the enemy had engaged. The sounds of battle could be heard in the head-sets of the ops room staff.

'Max, break right, break right.'

'Bugger me.'

'Two sods below.'

'I see 'em, Twiggs.'

'Red Leader, bogey coming up behind you.'

Brewster, calmly: 'Okay, no panic, I'm watching him.'

'Max, watch that bastard right above.'

'Okay, Twiggy, I'm on to him.'

'Hey, I'm taking the guy with the big white stripe.'

'Look out, Ossie, you silly bastard. We nearly collided.'

The sound of gunfire, then Ossie, grim and satisfied: '*Adios*, you sonofabitch. How do you like them apples?'

Twigg, urgently: 'Max, break left, break left. For Christ's sake, break.'

Suddenly, almost a murmur from the lame-duck Astley-Cobb: 'I'm hit, I'm hit.'

'Okay, okay, Max, I'm looking out for you.'

'Mayday, mayday, mayday. I'm baling out, Twiggs, I'm baling.'

'Watch for the 'chute, Twigg, get a fix.'

'Roger, Red Leader.' A moment's pause. ''Chute's deployed.'

A startling whoop of triumph. Ossie Wolf, focused on other things: 'There goes number two. Jesus, look at that. Boy, did he go up!'

'Good shooting, Wolf.' Brewster, gruffly pleased.

'They're lighting out.'

'Looks that way. Red Leader to Control, Red Leader to Control. Bogeys disengaging. One man in the drink.'

'Control to Red Leader, we're picking up his bearings now, alerting the air-sea rescue boys at Kalafrana.'

'Good show, Control. Pilot uninjured, repeat uninjured.'

'Control to Red Leader. More hostiles heading your way, six plus north east of you at 15,000 feet. Blue flight scrambled, ETA five minutes.'

'Roger, Control. We certainly poked our stick into that particular hornet's nest.'

'That you did, Red Leader, that you did.'

The tension in the ops room grew as Blue Flight's wooden marker was moved across the big grid-referenced chart by a plotter's long-handled wooden paddle. Buster Brown, poised above the table, his deputy close by and liaison officers issuing orders on their phones, watched Red Flight crawl south mile by mile. They had beaten off the first attack. How many had they accounted for? Two for certain, but one down too, Max Astley-Cobb, a decent type and proven in a fight, not one you'd want to lose, but seemingly unhurt, treated to a ducking by the Macchis, though probably safe enough. Nonetheless he silently wished Godspeed to Kalafrana's air-sea rescue boys.

'Blue Leader to Control, Blue Leader to Control. We have Red Flight in sight, repeat we have Red Flight in sight.'

'Roger, Blue Leader. Six bogeys closing north-east of you at angels-one-five. You should see 'em soon.'

'Okay, Buster.'

'Red Leader calling, Red Leader calling. Welcome to the party, Blue Leader.'

'Red Leader, enemy aircraft at two o'clock above.'

'Roger, Twigg. Blue Leader, formate on me. Preparing to attack.'

'Hello, Red Leader, what's your ammo situation?'

'What ammo, Curtis? I won't tell the Eyeties if you won't. Formate on me, dammit.'

A long silence, then: 'Roger, Red Leader.'

Immediately, keen-eyed Kenny Laughton, breathless with excitement: 'They're turning away, Blue Leader, they're getting the hell out.'

'Roger, Blue Two. Well spotted.'

'They reckoned we were down to three,' said Twigg. 'Now they don't like the odds.'

'All right, Twigg, keep it down. Time for tea, I think. I reckon we've all earned a good strong cuppa.'

'Roger, Red Leader.'

'I'm afraid we dragged you out on a wild-goose chase, Blue Leader.'

'Not at all, Red Leader. Glad we frightened them off for you.'

The plotters in Lascaris heard a smothered chuckle. It was Buster Brown, perched high above them on his dais.

Then the noise of Brewster thunderously clearing his throat rang in their ears. 'Red Leader,' said Buster, grinning, 'fly zero-nine-zero for base.'

Brewster gathered himself. 'Roger, Control.'

For fifteen minutes the seven Hurricanes steered due east. Brewster was humming a Gilbert and Sullivan ditty that Kit was unable to place until he realised it resembled, very loosely, 'A Wand'ring Minstrel I'. The pilots exchanged grins. Some minstrel this, some tune, scored for eight machine-guns.

Ten miles out Brian Twigg came on the R/T. 'Red Leader, I have a problem. Oil temperature's off the clock and I've got smoke coming out of both sides of the engine. Must have picked up some damage after all.'

'How bad is it, Red Three?'

'Lots of vibration but I reckon I can make it to Takali if I pop down first.'

'Don't risk making a dead-stick landing, Twigg,' said Brewster. 'If in doubt, jump.'

'Twiggs, from here it looks real bad,' said Ossie Wolf. 'Don't be a mug. Get out now.'

'Oh, I think I'll give it a whirl,' said Twiggs. 'I'd hate to write off a kite if there's still a chance.'

'Roger, Red Three,' said Brewster, resigned. 'Save your height until you're close. But if she starts to falter, jump.'

Kit, cold with tension, instantly recalled that familiar voice, two years ago in France: 'I can always replace aeroplanes, boy, but I don't want to lose my pilots.' Odd to remember the same comment twice in a matter of hours. God knows, he thought, the man's consistent.

'Okay,' said Twigg. 'Here goes.' He sounded composed, unruffled, although the smoke from the engine was darker now, streaming back across the tailplane, curling and twisting in the slipstream, marking his position for the crews of the fire-tenders and ambulances, alerted and expectant, a thousand feet below.

They were over Takali now and Twigg had begun his approach,

clearly light on power, a flicker of flame in the gouts of smoke, the Hurricane reluctant to turn, threatening to stall. Nine hundred feet, eight hundred, five. And then the engine stopped. A dead-stick landing, then. Too low to bale, Twigg tried gliding in, propeller windmilling, rapidly shedding height, still a half-mile from the runway, sideslipping in a series of S-turns, wheels-up so when he struck he would not somersault, ready to put it down just anyhow, knowing he had lost the gamble, knowing the machine could not survive a heavy landing. Wondering if he would.

The others, circling, watched in silence. The Hurricane's nose began to drop. It picked up a little speed, but not enough. All options gone, and no more room to play with, Twigg pulled hard back on the stick and let her wallow in, dropping forty, thirty, twenty feet. Did he, in those final moments, imagine how it might have been, baling with height to spare, hearing his 'chute crack open and, swinging from his harness, watch his burning Hurricane head out to sea, passing over the cliffs of Dingli, bound for nowhere, while he came down with a jarring bump and soothed his bruises with a glass or two of Cisk that evening in the mess?

It was to end in a very different way. First the tailplane struck the ground, and snapped off. The fighter was thrown forward onto its nose, the propeller ripping up great showers of soil. Then it rose and, for a moment, seemed to hang suspended in mid-air, the wooden blades of the propeller shattered, the engine bay not smoking now, instead a mass of flames, before the fuel tank, fixed between the engine and the cockpit, ruptured and released two hundred gallons of aviation fuel that instantly ignited with a hungry roar. Brian Twigg and Hurricane cartwheeled into glowing fragments.

When the others landed safely there was little conversation, but the details of the raid, carefully logged by Spy Threlfall, were well received. Brewster debriefed first, flushed from the action.

Then, with a muttered, 'Good show, chaps, drinks on me tonight,' he hurried off, suppressing his ebullience in deference to the losses. Half a dozen floatplanes and a brace of fighters; he knew he had made his mark. Soon the island would be buzzing with the news, just the shot in the arm he had intended.

Ossie had added to his score, a Cant confirmed, another probable in the hangar and both the Macchis in the dogfight over the Ionian Sea. Only now did it come to him that, for the duration of the flight, he had beaten his bowels as well. Nothing like a kill or two to put lead in your pencil.

He was talking to Kenny Laughton, laconic, North American chat, easy and informal, disregarding rank.

'You got sharp eyes, kid,' Ossie said. 'You a country boy?'

'Nestor Falls, Ontario.'

'Ontario, huh? Good hunting in those parts.'

'My old man owns a lodge. Whitetail deer, moose, bear, grouse, duck, all kinds of stuff. Been shooting since I was big enough to handle a twelve-gauge piece.'

'Any good in the air? Shooting, I mean.'

'Search me. All any of us was allowed to do was fire our darned guns into the river Severn. But they reckon I've got potential.'

'Potential, shit. You got to get up to speed real quick, kid, or you're gonna buy the farm. Maybe we'll have ourselves a little test flight some time, see if you can blow my ass away.'

Kit joined them and the tone changed. 'Well done, Sergeant. What did you think of your first op?'

'Exciting, sir. Except . . .'

'Yes, well, that's the way it goes.' Kit glanced at Ossie. 'This is the man who can teach us all a thing or two. Three confirmed and a probable, I understand.'

'Uh-huh,' said Ossie. 'And Max and Twiggs got a floatplane each.'

Laughton saw the talk was not for him. 'Well, thank you, sir,' he said to Ossie.

'Sure thing, kid. We'll see if you can nail my ass real soon. Americans gotta stick together.'

They watched the sergeant pilot go. 'So how did Brewster fare?' said Kit.

Ossie looked wry. 'That old bird couldn't hit a barn-door with a Big Bertha howitzer. But he drew the Eyeties' fire real good. Lucky for him their aim was even worse than his.'

'They can't have been so bad,' said Kit. 'They got a bead on Max and Twigg, all right.'

'Yeah, I guess,' said Ossie. 'Jesus, why didn't Twiggy bale when he had the chance? The stupid bastard. He should have known better.'

'He thought he did,' said Kit. 'What news of Max?'

'Nothing. The air-sea rescue boys have drawn a blank. How long can you last out there? I reckon he's a goner. Hey, aren't those children yours?'

Luck and Spencer were climbing on board the truck to take them to their quarters at Mdina. Luck was shaking, holding his right hand with the left to hide the tremors. His eyes looked wildly about, unable to fix on anything for more than a fleeting moment. When he opened his mouth to speak, no words came. Instead he licked his lips, wiped them and stared at the drool on his fingers.

Kit went over, studiedly casual. 'You chaps okay?'

'Yes, sir.' Spencer was fumbling with a cigarette.

Kit flicked his lighter. 'Well, you're blooded now. Always a touch alarming, your first op. You'll soon get used to it.' In the little time they both had left, he thought.

'Yes, sir. Any news of Max?'

'Don't call him Max,' snapped Kit, with a flash of irritation.

'You didn't know him. Anyway, the answer's no. He's probably bought it, along with Twigg.'

'I'm sorry, sir. I didn't mean—'

'They both had a good innings,' said Kit. 'Let's hope you can do as well.'

He looked at the two young men with sudden hatred. This was wrong, not how it was meant to be, two useless youngsters fresh from training with not a combat skill between them, alive and damned well kicking, and meanwhile Twigg and Astley-Cobb, among the squadron's very best, and excellent types, mature, with much to offer, dead.

He turned away. Half a dozen floatplanes and a brace of Macchis in return for what? More than thirty Eyetie lives in return for two. Fair trade, in Brewster's book? Well, put like that, he supposed so, yes, when totting up the score to see who was leading in the game. He considered the years ahead. How long would this thing go on? How big a score would it take to win? Deep down, where he knew it ought to count, his senses seemed dormant, numb, as though nothing could touch him now.

One week later Brewster called him to his office and told him he was going back to England . . .

# Nine

The city had been bathed in a brassy glare, hard on the eyes, that day when Diana Curtis had arrived at Waterloo on the midday service from Midhurst. She had hailed a taxi and directed the driver north. From Waterloo Bridge she saw a string of barges swinging downstream with the current, a sight so very normal, and yet beyond, where the river curved away to King's Reach, barrage balloons tugged at their cables in the sky beyond the Palace of Westminster. The taxi crossed the Strand and passed through Bloomsbury. The streets seemed drab and dirty in the harsh light, with great gaps where buildings had been bombed. There were many uniforms about and silly, perky notices displayed on ruined façades. 'Business as usual', 'Britain can take it', 'There'll always be an England'. Really?

Diana wondered briefly how it would be if Britain fell and German uniforms thronged the thoroughfares. She suspected not as bad as many people feared. Discipline, respect and pride. A sense of purpose, not this muddle-headed stumbling from one crisis to another. A new order that would preserve the best and stamp out the worst, suppress the undesirable elements that seemed to have surfaced between the wars. After all the fuss about invasion, and early humiliation, the French seemed quite content.

Perhaps it had been for nothing, all this sacrifice and sorrow. Perhaps Christopher and his comrades had fought for a cause already lost. And still she could not believe that Karoline Maierscheldt might have been removed to one of the fabled camps. Did they exist, or were they just propaganda, branding the enemy as beasts, like the stories of bayoneting babies in the Great War?

The taxi driver was garrulous, angling his head back over his left shoulder, talking out of the side of his mouth, voicing his tedious opinions about the progress of the war. His son was in the Navy, a petty officer on a North Sea corvette, and he was worried for him. Diana did not care to hear about people she did not know. She bore it for a minute or two, then slid the glass panel shut with an impatient sigh.

They passed through Camden Town, the people shabby with pale, vulgar faces, and began the gradual climb up Haverstock Hill to Hampstead where the prospect improved and in the high street sun-blinds stood out over the windows of the shops, quite Victorian, pleasant here, the houses elegant, a distant country scent drifting down from the nearby Heath. She ordered the driver to stop at the crossroads just by the Underground-station entrance and paid him off. She gave him the exact money. He had been familiar and did not deserve a tip.

Her heart was racing, as though she might be meeting Karoline instead of seeking out her daughter. She saw, across the road in Heath Street, a ladies' fashion shop, a suitable place to start her search. She had to smile. It was really quite amusing, this quest to solve a puzzle, a little adventure, not unlike the mystery novels with which she occasionally passed her time. But the two women in the shop frowned and shook their heads. They did not know of Hannah Maierscheldt. The name sounded foreign. Was she? They looked at Diana with suspicion and came to the window to watch her walk away and turn into Holly Hill.

Diana was vexed. She should have known that the graceless Hannah, with her penchant for dowdy, curious clothes, would not be known to the bitches at Gloria's Modes. She continued her climb up the pleasant rise and noticed, behind the chimneys of the Georgian mansions, the angular roofline of a large and ugly building. Ah, yes, the hospital. She remembered that Christopher's burned friend had been treated there. She must be close. She stopped and looked about her. It was uncanny. There was no one to be seen. She might have been the last person in the world alive. There was not a sound, not even the chirrup of a sparrow. Fixed in the sunlight she shivered, despite the heat, and felt suddenly fearful as though caught in a waking nightmare, knowing that something awful was approaching yet for an instant fixed to the spot. Then she resumed her search, with no clear purpose, unwilling as usual to ask for assistance.

She came across apartment buildings of various sorts but no one had heard of Hannah Maierscheldt. People were short with her, narrowing their eyes at the Germanic name, their minds full of nonsense from lurid posters about the enemy in our midst, walls having ears, careless talk costing lives. She was tired and wanted a drink, a stiff one. She remembered passing a public house. She retraced her steps and turned into the alley. Horrid smelly dive with an insolent oaf behind the bar. She took her gin and tonic and stood by the door while he studied her legs and rubbed his chin. She rapped the empty glass down on the nearest table and went out without a word. She wouldn't give him the pleasure of saying he couldn't help. She was further from the hospital now, closer to the Heath. Loosened by the alcohol she stopped the nearest passer-by: 'Is there a block of flats round here, do you happen to know?'

The old woman pointed up the hill. 'Only one. Up there. Oak Hill Mansions.'

Within a few minutes she had found it, a turn-of-the-century red-brick horror, apeing the appearance of a stately home. She pushed open the front door, rich with freshly polished brass. A uniformed concierge was propped up behind a desk reading the *Daily Mirror*. He threw it down and jumped to his feet. 'Miss Maierscheldt, yes. Third floor, Flat Two. Who shall I say?' He reached for the internal phone.

'You may not say,' said Diana curtly. 'I'm a family friend. I want it to be a surprise.'

'I'm sorry,' said the man, 'but I have clear instructions. Miss Maierscheldt insists. Not that there are many callers. Just the bank gents from time to time. Business, you understand. A lady like that, you would have thought . . .'

'I positively refuse to wait to be announced, as though I'm some person who's wandered in from the street,' said Diana. 'I'll go on up. Third floor, Flat Two, you say?'

The concierge, gulping, held back the door of the lift. 'I'll still have to warn her you're on the way. She's very particular about these things.'

'Warn her?' said Diana. 'What an extraordinary thing to say. As though she has anything to fear from me. Oh, close the door, man, for heaven's sake.'

She found herself shivering again as the lift jolted and began to rise. The small metal arrow on the indicator dial moved round to three. The lift halted with a clang, bouncing slightly, and she stepped out. A painted sign on the opposite wall pointed right to flats 1–4. Along the corridor the second door stood partly open. She heard a telephone receiver being replaced and the faint sound of a gramophone record, one of those throaty French voices warbling some nonsense about '*Paris sera toujours Paris*'. She walked towards the door, not hurrying, refusing to be ruffled although she felt that now she was being watched. She really would have it out with Hannah. It was too bad, to be treated in this off-hand manner. Heavens, what a way to welcome a visitor who had travelled miles, a family friend after all, forced to track her down like a fugitive because she hadn't had the common courtesy to get in touch when she landed in England. Not that she was concerned with Hannah's welfare. She was here for a different reason. But that was beside the point.

If only Karoline were here, she thought, to teach the girl some manners, this child always so confoundedly gauche, apt to sit in a corner like a housemaid, silent, thoughtful, but always watching with those weak blue eyes of hers as though she knew, as though she understood things that were naturally beyond her years. And here she was, demanding that visitors be announced as though she was anybody at all.

But, no, Diana thought, she must restrain herself. She did not want to create an instant rift. She did not care a jot for Hannah, never had, but the little dullard held the key to where her mother was, how she might be found, restored to those who loved her. So she must be patient.

She came to the door that stood ajar and saw it was number two. Slowly it swung back. A woman stood before her, so beautiful she lost her breath. Her clothes were plain, her hair unfashionably dressed, yet her face, despite a pair of hideous steel-rimmed spectacles, was the face of a Raphael Madonna, perfectly proportioned with dark-lashed eyes and gently curving mouth, androgynous, aloof. She gazed at Diana without a hint of recognition and Diana stared back, confounded. 'Hannah?' she said. But though she discerned that there was something of the Maierscheldt girl about this creature, she knew she was not Hannah. She did not, for the moment, care. The woman stood back from the door and Diana passed inside.

* * *

The Countess Anna Lvovitch Dubretskov, Bébé to a certain circle in Paris before France had fallen, had known this moment would come. A person would appear, someone from Hannah Maierscheldt's past, and everything she had schemed for would be at risk. She had no plan to deal with such a situation. Who could foresee the circumstances of such a thing, who the person might be or the nature of their interest? It called for improvisation, the solution tailored to the need. She knew she was good at that. Her instincts had already taken her far and brought rewards she was not prepared to lose. She did not know this woman who had called her Hannah, but in a doubting way. She had not replied, which, at least, had bought her time.

She watched her as she entered the flat. Her senses were sharp, her agile mind flicking through what might be done, what action she might be compelled to take. Her visitor was looking about her, curious and uncertain, taking in the *laideur* of the décor, the hideous English furniture, the absence of decent paintings on the walls, the ill-stocked bookshelves, the lack of any personal touch. 'So,' the woman said, letting the word hang in the air, ambiguous, hardly calling for an answer, as Bébé closed the door quietly.

'So,' repeated Bébé. She smiled and saw the woman soften, caught by the devastating smile, so full of warmth and promise, so loved by Hannah, Una and the rest. Bébé's instincts told her that she was being regarded with an interest not solely connected with what had brought this woman to her door.

'You were very difficult to find.'

'Perhaps I do not want to be found.'

'Why would that be?'

'I have my reasons.'

'Hannah,' the woman began, then paused. 'It is Hannah, isn't it?'

The question, so direct, took Bébé by surprise. *La putain*, she thought, she knows, she knows. She is playing games. She laughed. '*Dites-moi*, why are you here?'

'Just natural concern,' said the woman. 'After all, we have known you since you were a child.' Her tone was sardonic, teasing. She was looking at Bébé intently. 'Have we not?'

Bébé returned her gaze. 'You still have not told me why you are here.'

'You haven't the faintest idea who I am, have you?'

'Would you like some English tea?'

'Yes, that would be nice.'

'Well, sit down. Please.'

Bébé moved into the small kitchen and could be heard opening a cupboard and placing cups on saucers. A kettle began to bubble and wheeze. 'You know, of course,' called Bébé evenly, 'that I am not Hannah.' There. It was out. The confession lay between them. She waited to hear how the woman would react. That would suggest the course she had to take. Silence. Perhaps she had gone. That would be very bad. Bébé moved quickly to the kitchen door. But no, the woman was still there, sitting back in the drab armchair and lighting a cigarette, as though she meant to stay. For what purpose? *Quelle folie*. Did the imbecile not sense how the shadows closed round her, what peril she was in?

The woman looked up, eyes narrowed against the smoke. 'I know that these days camouflage is *à la mode*,' she said, gesturing with her hand to indicate the hair, the spectacles, the clothes. 'And for one who doesn't know you well, there's a resemblance, I suppose. But even so . . .'

'*Oui?*' said Bébé, from the door. 'Even so?'

'The girl was such a dowdy little mouse, while you, well . . .'

Bébé brought the tea. The woman took hers strong, no sugar. She sipped it thoughtfully, then replaced the cup and drew on her cigarette, blowing the smoke across her shoulder, picking the tobacco fragments from her lips. And finally said: 'My name is Curtis.'

So this was the mother of the stiff-necked Kit, thought Bébé, so tediously conventional, in the English way, earnest like a child of ten, eager to conform, to do the right thing, a hopeless virgin who, in all the years he and Hannah had found themselves together, had never tried to touch her once, Hannah had confessed. But brave, and in his element at war, and decent too, no doubt, but like all decent men, in her experience, deadly dull. 'I am familiar with that name,' said Bébé. 'Naturally Hannah spoke of you.' She did not mention that she knew her son, or that he had been the instrument of her meeting Hannah. She would not offer information unless she had to, or could see some tactical advantage.

'I see,' said Diana Curtis. She stubbed out her half-smoked cigarette. 'So, clearly, Hannah was known to you, and you have taken her place. I suppose you realise how bad this looks?'

'There is no need,' said Bébé, composed and speaking softly, with just the right amount of tremor in her voice. 'It is very simple. We met in Paris and Hannah became my dearest friend. We looked like sisters, everybody said, so much alike. It became a joke. And soon we were truly one, sharing everything.' She gave Diana Curtis a meaningful glance and saw a flash of recognition. 'Her father understood the danger to the family, as the Boches advanced. But he could not, would not leave the business he had spent his life creating.'

'And his wife?'

'She understood and chose to remain in Nancy too. At that time, you understand, it was hard to credit the stories going about. Even then they believed that, somehow, they would be safe. At least, it was a chance they were prepared to take. But

Hannah was given papers, and made to promise she would flee France. But she would not leave unless we, she and I, could go together. And that was quite impossible.'

'Why?'

Bébé gave a dismissive laugh. 'Papers for an *émigrée*? Without influence or money, all one's so-called friends running before the Boches, going south or crossing the Spanish border or sailing to America or to England? What would one have to do, with only a pretty face and body to secure the necessary documents in such a situation? Besides, I was not a Jew, my need was less urgent. So Hannah resolved to stay. I tried to change her mind but she was determined. She could be very strong that way. Somehow, she was convinced, we would make our way together. Why, perhaps even now, the Allies might prevail. But then the Boches reached Nancy and the Maierscheldts were about to be deported. And finally we learned that they were dead.'

Diana Curtis raised a hand to her mouth and drew in her breath. 'Dead? Surely in that chaos there must be room for doubt. How can you be so sure?'

'The police in Nancy reported this. Maierscheldt was popular there. The city was distraught.' Bébé saw that the woman seemed overcome, leaning forward, hands clasped, staring at the floor. Why was she so distressed? Had she and Maierscheldt had an understanding? Or the wife? Suddenly Bébé thought she understood. The initiative had shifted. Control was within her grasp. The solution would present itself as long as she continued to play her part.

'Even so, isn't there a chance that the reports were false, mistaken?'

'None. They were official.' Bébé felt an urge to laugh, as she always did when confronted by another's distress. She resumed quickly: 'From that moment it was as though Hannah no longer had the will to live. She felt she had abandoned them. Even our . . . love could not sustain her. One night she left the *appartement* we shared in the Rue du Faubourg St-Honoré and somewhere near the Pont des Arts she let the river take her.'

'I can't say I'm surprised,' said Diana Curtis, carelessly, as though she no longer had any interest in the conversation. 'She was always utterly self-absorbed.'

Bébé thought this remarkably hard and tactless, considering her current role as Hannah's bereaved companion. Here was a ruthless *gouine*, for all her airs, not to be trusted or, if it came to that, given the benefit of the doubt. 'She left a note,' said Bébé. 'She was very thorough. She even carried my own *carte d'identité* so that when she was found they would think it was me, as they did. Her final wish was that I should promise to use her papers to escape.' She smiled a small, sad smile, perfectly judged, and even managed to make her eyes well up, but the woman had recovered herself and remained untouched. 'The journey had its difficulties, as you may imagine. Many were trying to escape. My . . . Hannah's . . . papers were well scrutinised, the passport also. The little official at the English port looked at it for very long, so long I thought I was discovered, and then he said I should make the photographer return my money for taking such a bad picture. *C'était drôle, non*?'

'So here you are,' said Diana dully, apparently accepting Bébé's account.

'*Oui*,' said Bébé. 'I am here.' She shrugged. 'That is all there is to tell. I knew of the Curtis family, *bien sûr*, but why would I find you? What would be the point? More complications, and already I had enough.'

Diana Curtis was barely listening. Bébé was amazed that, for the moment, she did not seem to understand the implications of what she had been told: that the Maierscheldt business, big enough to survive a war, had naturally passed to her as Hannah, the only child, both parents tragically dead. But the woman was shrewd and in time would comprehend, and then what would she do? Inform the authorities? Demand some sort of price for silence? Probably that. Money or something else, something that would render her, Bébé, powerless to resist, *en extrémité*. Meanwhile, although she seemed the kind who would keep things to herself, what of her husband and the detestable Kit? She had noticed the woman smelled of drink. A careless word and all would be over. She remembered an old French phrase: '*finir par faire quelquechose*'. To end by doing something. 'Perhaps you would like,' she said, 'something stronger than tea.'

She returned to the kitchen and opened a bottle of Lussac Saint-Émilion. Diana Curtis drank the first glass in the usual English way, swallowing it quickly, impatient to feel its effect, untouched by its subtlety, indifferent to the Château Lyonnat label. In other circumstances Bébé would have begrudged the waste of a scarce vintage on a Philistine. Instead she poured her another.

'How did you find me?' she said. 'The bank did not give you information.'

'Bank?' Diana shook her head. 'What bank? No, it was pure coincidence. Too boring to tell.'

'You say it was natural concern for Hannah that brought you here,' said Bébé, 'but I see you really cared very little. Perhaps you cared for her mother more. I am sorry I could not give you hope.'

'I fail to see,' said Diana, coldly, 'what possible business that is of yours, a bloody little imposter.' She paused and took a mouthful of the light red wine. 'An interesting situation, wouldn't you say? Obviously you can't continue with this charade, so what's to be done, do you think?'

Bébé gave the tiniest of shrugs, submissive and demure, rotating her wine glass in her supple fingers. 'Perhaps it is already out of our hands.'

'No,' said Diana. 'It rests with me. Nobody even knows I'm here.'

'I am in your power, then.' Bébé laughed. 'What could I possibly do to make you my confidante?' She moved to Diana's side with the Lussac Saint-Émilion and carefully topped her glass. A bead of wine ran down the bottle neck. Bébé caught it with her finger and pressed it to her lips.

Two hours later the taxi halted outside the precinct of Waterloo. The driver turned his head, waiting for his passengers to move. The middle-aged woman was slumped against the good-looking girl in glasses and seemed to be asleep. The girl raised her eyebrows at him and shook the woman awake.

'Where is this?' the woman said.

The driver went round and opened the door. The woman stepped out unsteadily.

Bébé paid the driver and, with Diana hanging on her arm, slowly negotiated the concourse, checking the departure board for the Midhurst train. She knew the time and now she knew the platform. She was cross with herself. She had been too generous with the wine. Two bottles of Château Lyonnat. Not wasted, though, entirely, if all went well. The Curtis woman could barely walk. The man at the barrier smelled the drink as Diana held out her ticket. He looked at a porter and shook his head. Bébé hung back, allowing two or three passengers to pass through so she and Diana Curtis would not be connected later. The man took her platform ticket without a glance, his eyes fixed on Diana, who stood alone, unsteady on her feet.

The train had yet to arrive. The polished rails shone brightly above an expanse of rubbish, filth and grease. The platform began to fill. Lost in the crowd, unseen by the curious ticket collector, Bébé moved close to Diana. She was remembering how she had felt that night when she and Hannah had left the Rue du Faubourg St-Honoré and made their way, for what was to be their final walk, along the Quai des Tuileries arm in arm, the river very close and dark, rushing beneath the Pont des Arts. Hannah had been ecstatic. At last Bébé had agreed to apply for the necessary papers to start their life together in England. She had been reluctant to break cover, pursued as she was by hyenas who claimed she had removed the contents of an opulent flat on the Quai des Grands Augustins. Which was true, but Hannah had been indignant nonetheless, accepting in her infatuation Bébé's word that it was merely what a Philadelphian woman of means had promised her. Now the way was clear. Bébé, it seemed, would risk everything for love.

Bébé heard the deep rumble of the train approaching. Her mouth went dry, as it had that night on the embankment near the Pont des Arts, and her hands shook. Why this sense of trepidation? She reminded herself what a little thing it had been, the merest touch and Hannah had gone, her mouth open in a silent scream, Bébé's *carte d'identité* carefully placed to name her corpse. And Bébé, watching the surface of the river for signs of movement, had turned and walked quickly back to the empty *appartement* in the Rue du Faubourg St-Honoré where the necessary notes were ready, one from Hannah to her parents, at that time still alive in Nancy, a message from a dutiful daughter to let them know she was leaving soon for England and need no longer worry; a second, from the Countess Anna Lvovitch Dubretskov, to her mother, the Countess Sophia, in her mean rooms in the rue de la Verrerie, where poverty had brought her, saying she was concluding an existence that no longer gave her pleasure. Not exactly a lie, Bébé had smiled, and then she had gathered up the passport with the other documents and left for England.

The train was closer. The ground was shaking. Bébé was close to Diana Curtis now, but still careful that it should not seem they were together.

Diana turned her head. Her eyes were red and bleary. 'Oh, there you are. Come to see me off? God, my head.' She held a hand to her forehead. 'Of course I don't believe a word you've said. Why should I? Someone who steals her friend's identity? For all I know you could have killed her for it.' Her voice was rising. People were starting to take notice. Bébé moved a little away.

It was like being on a carousel, Diana thought, everything moving fast, round and round, the world a blur, leaving her senses to catch up. She heard voices near, was dimly aware of people staring. She knew she had to catch a train. Once she was on it she would be all right. She had to find a seat and sleep. Yes, sleep it off.

God, how much had she drunk? That devilish, delicious child, topping up her glass like that. She never could say no, finding herself in a darkened place and naked, caught in a maelstrom of desire. She had a remembrance of smooth pale limbs, of yielding, freed from inhibition by the heady wine, not caring any more, violent in her sudden passion, half believing it was Karoline she held so close, realising with a sob of disappointment that it was not, denying even now that Karoline was dead, but knowing, too, that Karoline could not have been like this, that all that mattered was the moment; this time of warmth, pleasure and surrender.

Afterwards she had talked, a torrent of reminiscence. She had no recollection. Heavens, what had she been saying? She knew she had spoken of Karoline, how she still believed she lived because she was not dead. She laughed. What sense was that? And yet she understood and that was all that counted.

Nausea overcame her. She brought up wine but managed to keep it in her mouth and gulped it down, the stench foul in her nostrils. Lord, to be sick in public. How had she come to this? She saw again the face of the girl, that wicked, lovely face, sublime but unconsoling, whatever she pretended. Even so dreadfully tight Diana hadn't been entirely taken in. She thought she recognised herself and therefore knew the workings of the cold, venal brain at work behind those dreaming eyes. Capable of anything, yes. She heard her own voice, startling and shrill, echoing as though she was shouting in a cathedral: 'For all I know you could have killed her.' But she was not in a house of God. Where was she?

Ah, yes, waiting for a train. What train? Was Karoline on the train? Was she here to meet her? Soon, perhaps, she might be and she would tell her that the lovely girl who pretended to be her daughter was not her daughter. 'For all I know you could have killed her.' Again that distant familiar voice, her voice, echoing round the cathedral. No, not a cathedral, a station, yes, where she awaited Karoline. Somewhere, in a corner of her mind, she was aware of something else, something to do with the Maierscheldts' business, something that had come to her only gradually. So big she hadn't seen it. Something that would enable her to control this arrogant, devious, delicious little bitch. Something to be remembered, stored away and savoured. A decision to be made, amusement to be had.

The platform was trembling beneath her feet. She swayed and stumbled against a man who cursed. 'For Christ's sake, woman, pull yourself together.'

The people were pressing very close. There was a sense of

expectation. She looked along the platform. A huge dark shape was sweeping towards her in a boiling cloud of smoke and embers. She was a child again, shrinking back as the monster advanced. The noise was unbearable. She wanted it to stop. She steeled herself to watch it pulling in. She seemed to know that when it stopped she might see Karoline again, stepping down and running lightly forward. The only one, the only one. Now life could begin. Begin afresh.

She felt a small, firm pressure in the middle of her back. She almost lost her balance, stepped forward a pace or two. The pressure was still there. Again, a step. Another. She tried to turn. Stepped back. There was nothing beneath her foot. She fell. She heard screaming. Her body struck the track, forcing the air from her lungs. Something had broken in her back, an agonising pain. She lay across the rails, her head lolling to the right. Some shred of consciousness returned. She opened her eyes.

'Where am I?' she murmured. 'Karoline, I'm here. Please help me. Help me, please.' The monster was upon her.

The crowd was pressing forward to the platform edge. There were cries of horror. The driver of the engine had leaped down from his cab and was on his knees trying to see beneath the wheels. The ticket collector had rushed forward too, with a gang of porters, pushing the people back.

Bébé passed quickly through the unmanned barrier, across the concourse and down the broad steps to Waterloo Road. Safer to find a taxi there. So easy, she thought, this removal of impediments. She admired her timing: watching for the moment, the locomotive fifty yards away, the slim arm slipped between the press of bodies, the knuckle forced against the spine and pushing, pushing, not to be resisted, suddenly feeling nothing, still pushing but against air. *Très facile*. A logical solution and the *garce stupide* had brought it on herself. *Mais ennuyeuse, oui*, definitely vexing because she had grown accustomed to her little flat, where she waited in limbo for this idiotic war to finish, whichever way it went; waited to gather together what capital might remain of the Maierscheldt inheritance and start life afresh.

Perhaps the Curtis woman had spoken the truth, had not confided in anyone about the purpose of her journey to London. Certainly she seemed a solitary type. But if she had followed the trail, so could another. In the morning Bébé resolved to make fresh plans.

# Ten

A week after Brewster had told him he was returning to England, Kit was driven to the airfield at Luqa, a few miles south-east of Takali, and boarded a twin-engined Hudson transport. It took off shortly after midnight. Pop Penrose sat beside him on the flight. 'The only consolation about being volunteered for another damned carrier fly-off,' said Penrose, 'is that you get a spell in Blighty. Still, at least I've got a number two who knows the form. Something of a feather in your cap that Brewster picked you, Curtis, though I don't suppose you see it quite like that.'

'What are we bringing out?'

'Hurricanes. Mostly tired old hacks, although I understand there'll be a few Mark 2s.'

'Good show.'

'Not necessarily. The last batch we saw hadn't been tropicalised. Blasted great air intakes on their bellies sucking up every bit of dust and filth. And they're faster in the air.'

'That's good, surely?'

'Have you tried leading a flight with the rest of the chaps struggling to keep up? Which means the latest kites go to the people who know least how to get the best out of them. Which means, in turn, they stand more chance of being pranged or written off. Vicious circle, or should I say flat spin?'

'No word of Spits?'

Penrose laughed shortly. 'Spits for the Malta station? You know the pecking order, boy. Good grief, it wouldn't surprise me if they dished out Sopwith Pups next.'

They landed at Gibraltar six and a half hours later. The contrast with Malta was startling, civilians complacent and well-fed, the military crisp and smart with much saluting and stamping of polished boots, people strolling along the streets, not looking at the sky, and business brisk in the cafés, pubs and shops. Buildings were intact, no piled rubble overhung with the sickly smell of death. As night came on so did the lights, shimmering in the sultry heat, an oasis of brilliance beyond the range of Axis raiders.

They had time for a meal before they resumed their journey. They chose a small restaurant recommended by friends of Penrose, close to the Rock with a view of Algeciras across the bay in Spain. The food and drink were good and plentiful. The two friends had come along. Both wore civilian suits. Something in intelligence, they said, describing in low voices how their German counterparts monitored every Allied movement, helped by the Spanish Fascists. They fed them phoney gen, they grinned, using anti-Franco double-agents. All very serious, though, they added quickly, with sabotage of military and naval facilities always on the cards. To Kit it sounded like enormous fun, a battle of wits *sans* bullets. One of the more appealing ways to fight a war.

Again it was dark when the Hudson lifted away from the jewel-like Rock and headed west, across the strait, out into the Atlantic wastes before changing course for England, a prudent distance from the coast. Four army officers had joined them, artillery men, immaculate, aloof, unimpressed by the tanned, gaunt airmen whose uniforms seemed too big.

'Malta, you say?' said a major with greying temples.

'That's right,' said Kit.

'Dickens of a shambles, so I'm told.'

'We do our best.'

'No doubt. Fortunate for you the Hun got sidetracked by the Ruskies. Gives you a chance to get yourselves sorted out.'

'Yes, that was a bit of luck.'

The major coloured at the mild response. 'It's vital, Malta,' he said sharply. 'The absolute key to the Med.'

'Yes, we know.'

'I certainly hope you do,' said the major, turning back to his companions.

Kit thought about the artillerymen at Takali, filthy with oil and white with dust, shrapnel and bullets keening past their ears but continuing calmly to feed their guns, empty shell cases flying from the breech, as they tracked an incoming raid. He imagined from his demeanour that the major had yet to see an artillery piece fired in anger. He pictured him in a Takali sangar, attempting to instruct the men on the strategic importance of the island while the bombs came down. It was a diverting image.

They made landfall at Land's End seven hours after take-off, with the light of dawn filtering across the Cornish pastures, impossibly lush and green; woodland, beasts in fields, spires of churches, teams of horses at the plough turning rich red earth, villages and towns, a little traffic on the roads, people stirring.

'My God,' said Kit. 'How beautiful.'

'Worth fighting for,' said Penrose.

They passed over Portreath at 3,000 feet and continued east. Devon, Somerset, Wiltshire, Berkshire. The skipper of the Hudson came back from the cockpit. 'ETA Hendon thirty minutes.'

Below Kit saw the Thames, a curling silver band, and Henley with its regatta course where he had stroked a lightweight crew in '37 but lost to Princeton. He looked across at Penrose and opened his mouth to speak. But Penrose was suddenly alert, head cocked, listening to the engine note, no longer smooth and constant but rising, falling, faltering. He looked past Kit at the starboard Pratt & Whitney, just forward of the window. 'I don't much like the sound of that.'

'See anything?' said Kit, quietly.

'Yes,' said Penrose. 'Black smoke.'

'I say,' said the artillery major, 'is something wrong?'

Penrose ignored him. He went forward and disappeared into the cockpit. Minutes later he was back. 'Jesus wept, these damned Yank engines. Ruddy thing's overheating, losing power. Thank God we're not over the Channel.'

'Absolutely typical,' the major said. 'I suppose this means we're going to be late for our briefing with Kirkman in Whitehall.'

They were close to Hendon now. Kit could feel the Hudson pulling to starboard, the pilot trying to counteract the swing with rudder trim. The healthy port engine roared as he applied full throttle. 'He's going to feather the dud,' said Penrose. Almost immediately the blades of the starboard propeller slowed, jerkily at first, became visible, and stopped. Instantly they felt the loss of power and their rate of descent increased. The Hudson was slewing to the left, sluggish, heavy, straining to maintain height to clear the airfield boundary. The second pilot appeared, trying to seem casual. 'Sorry about this spot of bother, chaps, but everything's under control. Should be a piece of cake.'

'Should be?' said the major but the second pilot had gone.

'We're on our approach,' said Kit. By flattening his cheek against the cool surface of the window he could see the Hendon runway three hundred feet below. The Hudson was shuddering with the effort of staying in the air. Kit noticed that the major was gripping the armrests of his seat, jaw clenched, staring straight ahead. They passed across a road and Kit could see their attitude was wrong, port wing too high, everything shaking now, vibrating with the stress, the port engine howling on maximum revs.

They sank towards the tarmac. One hundred feet now, seventy, fifty, almost there. But too far along the runway. 'He's going to have to put it down,' said Penrose. 'No chance of going round again at this height on one damned engine.' They felt a thump beneath them as the undercarriage was retracted. A belly landing, then. The Hudson began to porpoise as the pilot attempted to ease her down. Kit felt the pressure of his body on the seat fade, a lightness as though he was hanging in mid-air, rather like the time he had bungled a loop in a Tiger Moth and fallen off the top. So this was it. Nothing could save them now. It seemed a pity.

At forty feet the Hudson stalled, dived, then hit the ground.

# Eleven

There were two ways of looking at the attack on the seaplane base at Syracuse, Ossie soon discovered: a daring action splendid for morale, or a needless risk of scarce machines and men. After momentary hesitation the official line became needless risk. The attack was bad enough, Fighter Control in Valletta huffed, but to scramble a section including three sprog pilots to lend a hand compounded the offence. If the second group of Macchis had not declined to engage, the squadron might have had a thoroughgoing disaster on its hands.

Brewster had been summoned to the office of the Air Officer Commanding in the underground complex of Lascaris. Nobody knew what had been said but Brewster had emerged grim-faced and silent. It was rumoured that he had been threatened with an immediate posting unless he stayed firmly on the ground and concentrated on the job to which he had been assigned. Even before his admonishment, the loss of Twigg and Astley-Cobb, tough, experienced and difficult to replace, had effectively extinguished any short-term jubilation. No one was inclined to crow, even Ossie, who alone had added to his reputation, with three confirmeds and a probable, simply following Brewster's lead, not held responsible in any way.

The Fiat BR.20s and Savoia-Marchetti SM.79s of the Regia Aeronautica continued to come across at night, usually loosing their bombs at more than 20,000 feet, hopelessly optimistic, hoping to hit the airfields but more often flattening a farm, killing hapless families, vaporising grazing beasts. Ossie took his turn at night-flying, with the rest, downing a BR.20. Better that than listening to the bomb-loads whistling down, advancing across the dark terrain, unseen, explosions loud and growing louder until even the walls of the *palazzo* in Mdina, four feet thick, trembled with their impact. He also flew by day but operational trips were fewer now and often he led his section across the sea north of the island for hours without a sign of opposition. Even these exploratory sweeps, in the wake of Brewster's Syracuse adventure, required Control's approval, with po-faced warnings about overflying the Sicilian coast or succumbing to temptation and venturing inland to seek out strafing targets.

Frustrating, deeply so, but Ossie was compelled to acknowledge the need to conserve the island's power in the air, to understand Control's reluctance not to pay a price it could ill afford by losing men like Max and Twiggy, aware of reports of German victories on the Russian front that, if true, would more than likely enable Goering to divert significant *Geschwader*, fighter and bomber wings, to finish the job abandoned to the Italians months before.

In this time of sameness, torrid heat and boredom, with only short periods of action, Ossie had envied Kit his role as shepherd of a fly-off. Now that would be one hell of a test, barrelling down a pitching deck to navigate your way across 700 miles of open sea, dodging the Eyeties at Cagliari and Pantelleria, bringing your flock home on the button, safe, no foul-ups, more experience logged. And then he heard that Kit would not be coming back, for a while at least. Threlfall was among the first to get the news. Two flights were gathered in Dispersal, Ossie's section, Kenny Laughton, Luck and Spencer, kicking their heels on Readiness since dawn; and, relieving them, Duncan Reid, Ray Rimmer and two wide-eyed arrivals, greener even than Luck and Spencer.

'Just got some gen about Penrose and Curtis,' said the intelligence officer, in the offhand way the squadron dealt with injury and death, but less acceptable from those who did not fly. 'Apparently their Hudson lost an engine on approach at Hendon. Skipper tried to put it down. Not enough power. Stalled, went in.'

'Sonofabitch,' said Ossie.

'Two or three survived,' said Threlfall. 'Curtis was thrown clear and went back in to try to save the rest.'

'Penrose?'

'No. He bought it with the others. The thing went up before he could be cut free. Curtis was lucky to get out. Burned hands and face but otherwise not too bad. Keen to get back here, of course, but the medicos won't hear of it, until they decide if he's going to need some grafts.'

This was more than the pilots wanted to know. They moved away, except Ossie. 'Who's doing the fly-off, Spy?'

Threlfall laughed. 'Not you, Wolf. You're Malta's darling. We've even got a newshound here from *Picture Post*, eager to make you famous.'

'The hell with that.'

'The ministry boys are very keen. Anything to encourage your countrymen to jump down off the fence.'

'Bull.'

'Yes, very possibly. But, then, you Yanks are good at that. Play ball, old boy. They pressured Brewster to give it the green light. As things are he could hardly refuse. Do the poor chap a favour and don't make waves. He could do with a Brownie point or two.'

Ossie collected a pool bicycle and pedalled off along the white road to Mdina. A sirocco was blowing up from the south, with a hint of rain laced with fine sand from the Libyan desert, but bringing no relief, the temperature over ninety degrees, the gusts raising pillars of swirling dust that hung in the air like ghosts. He wondered how bad Kit's burns were. He'd seen some sights on McIndoe's wards, dropping in on Buster Brown midway through his treatment: the masks of faces, livid scars, noses being formed from flaps of flesh brought down from the forehead, stumps of hands; those cosmetic touches that seemed to make it worse, glass or plastic eyes and lousy wigs. Some reward for a minute in a burning plane. How long had Kit been fried? Just like the mug to go back into the wreck to try to get the others out. 'Not too bad' was what that wise guy Spy had said. But, hell, that was how it always went. 'Oh, he's okay. He's fine. He's on the mend. Can't keep a good chap down.' And then you heard he'd died or maybe, worse in Ossie's book, would never fly again.

Back at the *palazzo* he took a shower, put on a clean shirt and shorts, brushed off his service cap and set it over his eyes. Claudia Farinacci was waiting for him on the steps of the cathedral, small against the thirty-foot studded double doors. Giorgio was there, too, kicking a ball around the square. The girl ran towards Ossie and took his arm. Giorgio followed, trundling the ball across the paving.

'You have not been flying,' she said.

'No. Nothing doing.' They had embarked on their usual promenade, for all to see, a curious friendship but above reproach, crossing Archbishop Square and turning right into the shadowy length of Inguanez Street, narrow, with the shuttered balconies of its houses so close neighbours might shake hands. 'How can you tell?' said Ossie.

'When you have been flying you have a look about you.'

'A look?'

'As though you were still up there, as though up there you truly come alive.'

'You make me come alive,' he said, not catching himself in time, wincing at the inner phoney bastard so quick with a worn-out come-back. She was better than that and her liking for his talk just made it worse. 'You're a sweet kid,' he said, and ran after Giorgio twenty yards ahead, tackled him for the ball, won and booted it over the little crossroads where Villegaignon Street ran from right to left. The ball bounced down between the houses, striking steps and leaping high. Giorgio chased it, whooping, his odd, gruff voice reverberating round the eaves, lost to sight round a gentle curve close by the chapel of St Agatha.

Ossie walked back to the girl. She waited for him, solemn eyes fixed on his face, hands clasped across her narrow hips. She waited and he knew he must not touch her. A slip in time, ten lousy years, placed her beyond his reach. Also, four thousand miles between this speck of nowhere and St Louis, Missouri, different worlds. Also, things he had seen and done, still had to do. Also, the fact that any time now he might be a name and number on a headstone in the military cemetery in Valletta. He thought he would end it now, this nothing of a relationship, not physical, not intimate, just a kind of dream.

He came up to her but found he could not speak because he wanted to go on, and walk with her in just this way. It was what he needed, all she asked. That was enough. He had to talk of something else. 'We had some lousy news today,' he said. 'One of our guys was in a wreck in England. We flew together right through France and now out here. A stand-out pilot and now he nearly buys it in a crummy transport.' He was speaking quickly. He knew she wouldn't understand it all. It only mattered that she was there. Anger grew inside him. He cursed that cock-eyed English bastard for going back inside that burning plane; and Twiggy for sticking with his kite; and Max for disappearing; and all the others, faces crowding in, like figures in his goddamned dream. He realised, with a shock, that he could be touched, that the iron-man act had slipped, the pose that had started out as hick-from-the-sticks bravado but had grown to become the truth. He blamed it on the attack of Dog. Certainly he still felt like shit, except when he was flying and the buzz took over. Yeah, that had to be the reason, the goddamned Dog. Jesus, he was a spineless sap.

He turned to Claudia Farinacci to say he was going to end it there, standing in the cool half-light of Inguanez Street. It needed to be done. It was what a guy like him would do.

Far down the street, punting his ball towards them and letting it run back down the gentle slope, Giorgio was beckoning them to join him.

'Claudia,' Ossie started.

'I'm sorry about your friend,' she said. 'I will pray for him.'

'Uh-huh,' Ossie said, and paused. 'Oh, he'll be okay. He'll be just fine. What say we take in Howard Gardens? I'll treat you kids to sodas.'

# Twelve

Stretched out on a steamer chair on the terrace, watching the sun go down slowly beyond the sharply etched horizon, gold rays of light washing over the dreamy prospect of Linch Down, Kit thought life could be worse. But better . . .

He felt drained by the journey from Midhurst to the Middlesex Hospital where, in the nondescript two-storey building in the hospital grounds, he had been assessed by the specialists. The physical examinations of the Central Medical Establishment were notorious for their rigour, and flying careers, service careers of any kind, hung in the balance until the verdict was delivered.

He had been optimistic. A month after the Hudson crash his hands had begun to heal, the skin puckered into scabs but flexible, less shiny. His face was much the same, only a little worse now than when he had fallen asleep in the sun on one of those long, precious spells at Trebetherick, when he used to bicycle down from the big house Farve had built for them behind the town and fish for prawns and crabs in the rock pools of Mundy Cove. But his concern had grown as the medics ran through their routine checks: blood pressure, lungs, muscular control and strength, ears, nose, throat and eyes; particularly eyes, reading the wall chart with one eye closed, a moment of panic when a weeping lid threatened to blur the letters.

The manner of the staff was impersonal and brisk. Brief instructions, 'Grip my hands', 'Blow into that', 'Balance on one leg', 'Repeat the words you hear', 'Tell me what coloured number you see', 'Pee into this jar'. No clue to what conclusions they might have reached.

Finally, all tests done, he had joined the others, mostly aircrew, in the waiting room, scanning *Punch* cartoons and finding them unfunny. Then his name was called.

'Second-degree burns, hands, face, legs,' the president of the medical board had said, leafing through Kit's file, scanning the reports. 'No surgery required. No broken bones. Severe general bruising. Slight disturbance to the lower vertebrae but no suggestion of permanent mobility loss. Some contusions to the cranium. Everything healing well, no complications. Certainly good enough for me to pass you fit for non-operational single-engine aircraft.'

'Non-operational, sir?'

'Anti-aircraft co-operation, something of that sort. Then we'll see.'

'When, sir?'

'Three months. Then we'll board you again. Meanwhile, you'll have to make do with Masters and Lysanders, not quite what you're used to.' The air commodore smiled understandingly. 'It's an important job, you know. You'll find it has its moments.'

'But I'm absolutely fine, sir,' said Kit, desperately. 'I've already wangled some flying time on Spits.'

'Really. Where?'

'I can't tell you that, sir, strictly unofficial.'

The air commodore stroked his chin. 'Yes, I'm sure. Very well, Curtis, I'll review your case history with my colleagues. You're marginal, I'll give you that. If you're so keen to return to ops, well, I don't deny we need fellows like you. I'll see what can be done.'

'Thank you, sir,' said Kit. 'If it goes my way I'd like to return to Malta.'

'Not down to me, I'm afraid. You'll have to take that up with the powers-that-be. Incidentally, I gather you're in line for a gong.'

'A gong?'

'For going in to get the other fellows out.'

'I failed. That's hardly worth a gong.'

'Somebody seems to think it is. Very well, Curtis. You'll hear from us within a week.'

A week? Already the smell of autumn was hanging in the air. The mornings were fresh, and mist lingered in the hollows. Apples were falling in the orchard and, at the end of the drive, the leaves of the big old oaks were turning brown. How was it in Malta now? Good grief, a week to wait, and maybe even then the prospect of a non-op grade, three months of bumbling across the sky in a museum piece, on fixed routes and altitudes, helping the ack-ack types to train their gun-crews.

Farve came onto the terrace with a tray of drinks. 'This is quite like old times, my boy. Got used to having you around again. If only your mother could be here.' He sat down on a bench and added some tonic to his gin.

Kit poured the bottle of Harvey's ale into his glass. 'Cheers, Farve.'

'Good health, yes. So, cleared for flying, then? That's splendid news.'

'No doubt of that. But flying what?'

A silence fell between them. Kit thought about the mention of a medal, what pride it would arouse in this simple man who dreamed about deeds of arms and distant wars, of Sussex men who answered their country's call and crossed the seas for England's sake. Precious little glory in those frantic moments spent trying to pull Pop Penrose free, crushed against his seat half conscious, murmuring: 'Get me out, please, get me out.' Nothing worth a medal there, an instinctive act, unthinking, the obvious thing to do. Precious little glory anywhere. How would it be, he wondered, if Farve had seen the things he had seen?

For a moment he fiercely wanted to confront the credulous old romantic with the brutal, bloody truth. He recalled those bedtime tales of stirring adventures: Henty, Westerman and the rest, Jack smiting the shaven-headed Arab rascals, Tom driving his charger towards the Old Guard ranks, full of English pluck, Will springing at the Spanish galleon, brandishing his cutlass. That kind of nonsense had filled his head, and stayed there in the early days in France. He had looked for Jack, Tom and Will, and found them flying Hurricanes and Spitfires, Blenheims, Boulton Paul Defiants, spirited and eager for a scrap. Now most had gone, their places taken by a fresh supply of Jacks, Toms and Wills, no doubt bred on a similar diet of ripping-yarn heroics.

'Oh, I forgot,' said Farve. He went back inside the house and returned with a magazine. 'You ought to see this. Mentions Malta.' He held out a copy of *Picture Post*. The face on the cover was not scorched or marked by sores and lesions, like many of the faces at the CME. It was a good face, encircled by its leather flying helmet, bony and plain in the Midwest way, the face of a pioneer or frontiersman, strong and self-sufficient. The subject was looking right to left, chin raised, eyes focused on the distant sky, his mouth fixed in a half-smile. Kit wondered how the photographer had got Ossie Wolf to agree to such a gallant pose, so redolent of line-shoot. It said, in big white letters out of red across the bottom of the cover, 'The Few of Malta'. An inset caption read: 'An American ace who has joined the fight for freedom on Fortress Malta'.

Good grief, thought Kit, the clot will never live it down. 'I know this man,' he said. 'You do too. He came here briefly after France. Mother was incensed at the way he held his knife and fork. Can't imagine why he agreed to this. Not his style at all.' He turned to the inside feature: more photographs, Hurricanes in their blast pens being armed, pilots gathered round a chart spread out on a fighter's wing, a section taking off, a Bofors crew, Grand Harbour with bombs falling near the docks, civilians queuing outside a Valletta shelter, the statue of Victoria, untouched, surveying the ruined houses in Queen's Square. He wanted to be there, to feel the heat and taste the dust, to hear the sirens wail, the chonk-chonk-chonk of guns, the sweet song of Merlins, throttles wide, the far-off growl of an incoming raid.

A fighter pilot's paradise? He had thought it hell but, once away, he found he missed the tension, the imminence of action, the thrill of climbing on full-boost towards an intercept, the frenzy of a dogfight, half recalled, a blur of images and emotions, the elation and mild surprise at finding you were still alive. No existence, this, to be summed up in purple prose in *Picture Post*. It had simply become a job, to fly a fighter plane and kill the enemy, a daily task private and unseen, repeated and repeated, not understood except by fellows who also flew. And without this job, it was as though he had lost his purpose, was left with nothing.

He sipped his beer. It tasted sour. The mellow landscape seemed insipid, bland, beneath a rose-tinged sky, not fierce with the blaze of light that seared the surface of a smaller island fifteen hundred miles away, where great battles might be joined, even now, without him.

They heard the faintest squeal of brakes. The Rolls had collected their visitors from the station. Barlow was carrying their cases into the hallway. Louis Garencières ran forward, then hesitated, seeing Kit's raw face. He collected himself and took Kit's hand, shaking it gravely with a firm, but not too firm grasp, wary of the scars. '*Bonjour, Monsieur.*'

'*Bonjour*, Louis,' said Kit, smiling at the child's formality.

Juliette came in slowly, untying her headscarf, shaking loose her hair. He could see she had been preparing herself for this. At first she did not look at him, allowing Farve to fuss and peck her cheek. Ben, the dog, rushed in from the kitchen, slithered across the tiles and made them laugh.

And when Juliette laughed, finally she looked at Kit. 'Hello, Kit,' she said.

He had forgotten the timbre of her voice, melodious and warm.

She hadn't moved, the headscarf dangling from her hand. 'I'm sorry we could not come before. My work . . .'

'No matter. Now you're here. You look, well, as you always looked. Me, I'm a little different, I'm afraid.'

'I feared much worse,' she said. She came to him, took his hand and kissed him lightly on the lips.

Farve said: 'Come on, Louis, leave the case. Let's give old Ben a run.'

In the sitting room Kit enfolded Juliette in his arms, relishing her warmth, her sweet breath on his neck. He had not held a woman in this way since he had last held her, more than a year ago. He felt her breasts and belly firm against him. He had grown erect, but she only pressed more closely.

'I'm sorry about this blasted face,' he said. 'Horrid for you, I know. But I'm told that in a month or two . . .'

She touched his mouth with her hand. '*Non. Dit rien. Il n'y a pas besoin de cela.*'

They moved out to the terrace, slowly, hand in hand. Agnes Hobbes brought barley-water in a jug.

'It is very long,' said Juliette. 'Fifteen months since France.'

'Is it only fifteen months?' said Kit. 'It seems an age.'

'Bad times.'

'Not entirely bad. We met and here you are.'

'How shy you were, that day at Boulay, when you asked to billet your pilots in my barn.'

'We were on the run,' said Kit. 'It's better now. We beat them here and I reckon we've got their measure in the Med.' He passed her a glass of barley-water. 'Louis is growing tall.'

'He loves this place. After your mother died your father asked us down. You know he has talked of Louis living here?'

'Yes,' said Kit. 'A wonderful idea. And you?'

'No, I have work to do.'

'What is this job of yours?'

'I cannot say.'

'Something to do with radio, Free French broadcasts, Father said.'

'Something that led from that. I cannot tell you more.' She bit her lip. 'It was hateful, what happened to your mother.'

'Yes,' said Kit. Farve had given him the coroner's report. 'Excessive alcohol in the blood . . . seen to be confused . . . no suspicious circumstances . . . no suggestion of intent to take her life . . . verdict: accidental death.' He assumed a sad expression. He did not want her to think him cold, unfeeling. But with his mother's death the big house on the Down seemed quite reborn, undisturbed by tension, free of Diana's sullen moods, her unaccountable bursts of rage, her brooding discontent.

'You will fly again, of course,' said Juliette.

'Oh, yes.'

'How was it with you, where you were?'

'*Très dur*. Not just in the air but also in the way we lived, the heat, short rations, old machines and insufficient spares, disease.'

'And yet you are impatient to return.'

'It sounds insane, of course,' said Kit, 'but all pilots are a little mad.'

'This is your time, then, while the world is mad.'

'And after?'

'Our time, perhaps, if you think of me as I think of you.'

'Do you need to ask? I hold you in my head and heart.' He took her hand. 'I feared for you and Louis. I did not believe that you would leave France. You seemed unshakeable.'

'I was naïve,' said Juliette. 'The Boches are not inclined to be forgiving to one who billeted English airmen. Two villages away a mayor was shot for less. I had to think of Louis. You recall my brother was serving in the Ministre de la Guerre? He pulled some strings – I think that is your phrase – and got us to Bordeaux, where we found a neutral ship.'

'And your brother now?'

'*Je n'en sais trop rien*. It is possible he accommodates the situation. In Paris he is well placed. He was always more diplomat than soldier.' She shrugged. 'Meanwhile, I hear the Boulay house is used as a rest camp for Boches officers from Le Mans.'

'Who told you that?' said Kit.

Juliette flushed. 'Oh, I have contacts still.'

'Through this job of yours?'

'Perhaps. Please, Kit, do not pursue the point.'

'You also are impatient to return, I think.'

Juliette stood up and crossed to the edge of the terrace. Shadows were reaching across the landscape, like dark fingers. 'Tell me,' she said, 'tell me, Kit, do you hate?'

'I don't know. I have, for moments, but it seems to pass. I'm afraid these days I don't feel much at all.'

'I do,' said Juliette. 'I hate. You sense, I think, what I have become involved in. We see smuggled film, so-called reprisals, detestable, you would not believe. Really, Kit, beyond belief. Poland, Russia, yes, and France. The glorious Reich, its real face. Not those well-scrubbed farm-boys goose-stepping down the Champs Élysées on their best behaviour, for the world to see. From all the horror of those scenes I most remember one, a gallows in a public square in a Polish town, four men bundled up the steps, nearest the camera a prosperous man in an elegantly tailored suit, dragged from his office, perhaps, an architect, lawyer, doctor, well respected, tended by a grinning pig-faced *crétin* dropping the noose round his neck, and this man, whose hands were free, adjusting the noose to sit more comfortably, as he might adjust a collar. His face is calm, he does not protest, he goes to his death as submissively as a farmyard beast, stunned, I suppose, uncomprehending. I don't know why this moment stays with me. Perhaps because it shows the normal world upended, cancelled, where a man of culture and education can leave his home for his place of work and, within an hour, find himself facing a squalid death watched by his own townsfolk. One individual among millions. Men, women, children butchered to satisfy the ambitions of the Boches. Hitler and his gangsters have civilisation by the throat. Yes, I hate. And that is why, with Louis safe, I must go back and play my part.'

She turned and leaned against the stone balustrade. Tears were in her eyes. Kit went to her. 'I know you must do this,' he said, 'but, please, God, don't let yourself be caught.'

'How could I?' she said, smiling a little, wiping the wetness from her cheeks. 'We have agreed we will have our time together when the world is no longer mad and when, *peut-être*, pilots have also become more sane.'

Juliette Garencières stayed for two days more before she

returned to London. Kit had gone to her the second night and they had lain together in the darkness, listening to the country sounds drifting in through the open window. They had been at peace together, understanding that this was a beginning. They caressed but little more. It meant too much. It was a consummation to be saved.

At Midhurst station Kit stored a final image, of Juliette framed in the window of the carriage, smiling, waving, struggling with her tears. He stood with Farve and Louis on the platform, waving back. She called some final words they could not hear. And then the train moved round the curve and was lost to sight.

Back home the boy went to his room and closed the door. It was his way, had been in France, on learning of his father's death, killed in his tank by Panzers between Dinant and Sedan, when the Boches had broken through.

Kit found his father in his study, listening to Elgar on the gramophone. 'Ah, sit down, my boy. The Cello Concerto. Very fine.'

'Yes,' said Kit. 'A lament for a lost world, some say, composed a year after the Great War ended. It feels it, don't you think? Reflections on a war to end all wars. At least he died with that conviction, yet here we are again.' He studied the old man's face. The irony was lost on him, the expression tranquil and serene, head moving slightly to the rhythm of the music. 'Farve, I want to talk to you. Do you mind if we turn this off?' He lifted the needle from the record. 'It's a splendid thing,' he said, 'to take on Louis. The poor child's been through hell. But can I ask? Don't share those tales of empire, ancient battles, gallant deeds, trials of arms. Those tired old fables. These are not the times. Louis knows the real price of such things. He's lost his father and his country. His mother . . .' He paused. 'Farve, you can give him other things – a love of nature, beauty, art, good books, learning, fundamental decency and truth. Farve, you can give him hope.'

The old man raised his head. 'Yes, Kit, I think I understand.'

'Forgive me . . .'

'No, no, you're quite correct. These are not the times.' He went over to the bookshelves and found a volume. 'Yes, this comes to mind. Perhaps I should have paid it more attention. "No one is stupid enough to prefer war to peace; in peace sons bury their fathers and in war fathers bury their sons." Herodotus.' He closed the book. 'I'm a foolish fellow, Kit. Always have been. Noddle full of half-baked thoughts and dreams. Same with the firm. A hopeless head for business, your grandfather always said. Recruit a top head man and leave it all to him. Good advice I followed.' He restored the book to its place on the shelf. 'Thank Heavens you were always a level-headed little chap and took my fancies with a pinch of salt.'

Kit wondered if he had. But still he said: 'I loved your stories, Farve. It's just . . .'

His father held up his hand. 'No, no. Point taken. There's no more to be said. Let's hope, my boy, that you bury me, not t'other way about. That things will work out as they should. Now, let's get that lad downstairs, and introduce him to the doubtful delights of Agnes's English cooking.'

Within a week a letter arrived for Kit. The CME was pleased to confirm he was A1.B, the highest flying category, operational for fighters. And ten days later, as September died, came news of his posting: Malta, by way of Hendon and Gibraltar. He wondered if a Hudson was chalked up for the flight.

The evening before he left he found Louis in the garden, throwing a ball for Ben. 'There's something of yours I meant to return. You gave it to me in France, when we got kicked out.' He handed the boy a small cardboard box. Inside, wrapped in tissue, was a figure of Napoleon on Marengo. The leaden Emperor had once marched at the head of a toy Grande Armée in the attic of the grey-stone *maison du maître* in Boulay-sur-Sarthe.

Louis had presented him with the gift and said: 'You see, you must return. Otherwise the army will be without its leader.' Now he turned the figure in his hand. '*Merci*, but what use is he alone?'

Kit grinned, took the ball and threw it far for Ben. 'He may have lost his army, Louis, but he has not lost the war.'

# Part three

## November 1941–April 1942

## 'Spitchered'

# Thirteen

In the second week of November, a few days after HMS *Ark Royal* was sunk, Ossie Wolf was shot down. For the pilots the magnitude of the first event dulled the shock of the second, but both had seemed invincible. The carrier had been struck amidships by a single torpedo from a prowling U-boat, forty miles south-east of Gibraltar, shortly after a successful fly-off by Hurricanes bound for Malta. It did not sink immediately. The crew was given time. Only a single rating had died in the attack and more than fifteen hundred officers and crew were rescued as the great vessel was taken in tow. But progressive flooding could not be controlled and, thirteen hours after she was hit, she capsized to starboard and went down, twenty miles from safety. To the pilots of the fly-off, bringing in a fresh supply of fighters, it seemed beyond belief that such an ocean fortress, their home for weeks on the voyage from Greenock, was at the bottom of the sea. Yet very soon there was further cause for gloom.

'Have you heard chaps? Ossie Wolf has bought it.'

'You're joking. When was this?'

'Couple of hours ago. Bounced by one of those new jobs, a Macchi 202.'

'Christ almighty, are you sure?'

'Absolutely. Bloody great flamer. Hit the sea just off the Sicilian coast.'

'Sure there's no mistake?'

'Not likely. His wingman Kenny Laughton saw it all. That little sod's got eyes like a ruddy lynx.'

The news ran quickly round the island. *The Times of Malta* was compelled to report his disappearance as, little more than a month before, they had reproduced, front page, his image from *Picture Post*. The magazine had already rendered him mildly famous and the interest of the island's press had compounded his discomfort. But no photograph this time, and as before no name, simply a brief report, conscious of morale, just a single paragraph headed 'American pilot missing'.

Fresh from England, Kit Curtis was as disbelieving as the rest. He had expected losses, new faces in the mess, and there were new faces in the mess but most of the old ones were still there. The bar in the *palazzo* was as busy as a pub, more pilots than planes, they said, but thanks to fly-offs the balance was being redressed. Spirits were generally high as the temperatures cooled and the order came to switch from tropical kit of sand-coloured bush jackets, shirts and shorts to standard service dress of air-force blue. There was something reassuring about the change, the place assuming a familiar aspect, any air-force station, any time. Besides, the Regia Aeronautica was being well contained. Even the greenhorns were beginning to think they had their measure. Then Ossie Wolf went down.

He had seemed to fly with a shield around him, untouchable, and the shield extended to those who flew with him. He knew he could not be hit, this knowledge shared by the young pilots in his section and beyond. Even the way he handled his machine spoke of his self-belief, that he was better than anything the Fascist sons-of-bitches could throw his way. And now he was gone, along with the cover of *Picture Post* that had been pinned up in the mess and scrawled across with 'Champion, Takali Line Shooters Club'. And, in smaller letters, 'No contest'. His loss seemed to start a trend: people made mistakes, took off in coarse pitch or landed with the undercarriage up or overshot, cannoning through the ranked stone walls, usually paying with their lives. In battle they followed victims down, forgetting the rule to always look behind before pressing home an attack. Engines failed and 'chutes refused to open. It was as though the death of Ossie Wolf had ended the squadron's luck. And yet he wasn't dead . . .

Four miles east of Gela he had dived down on a lumbering Fiat BR.20 transport, on a course for Libya. The section stayed up high, at 15,000 feet, to watch the slaughter. He pulled out of the dive and came up dead astern and fired a four-second burst, no more, the bullets puncturing the Fiat's belly, advancing from the tail towards the nose. The Italian dropped into a vertical dive, port engine pouring a trail of orange flame.

To Ossie something in its attitude suggested the guy was faking, ready to level out over the sea and make for home. The BR.20 was known to be a tough old bastard. Maybe the four-second burst hadn't been enough. He half rolled and went down to finish the job. There was no need. The transport had fallen into a violent spin, fanning the fire that reached the fuel tank before it hit the sea. The BR.20 exploded with a flash. White-hot fragments spattered the plunging Hurricane. The controls began to kick and shudder and, as the fighter fell onto its back, Ossie heard Kenny Laughton shout: 'Christ, Red Leader, watch your tail.' He centred the stick, kicked the rudder right and left and somehow got the Hurricane stable, a thousand feet above the waves.

Burning debris from the BR.20 was falling all around him. A whole tail-section with its big white cross passed within twenty feet. He sensed that something big was closing fast. He looked up and to the right. A long-nosed fighter, jigsaw-patterned in mottled green and grey, was on him in a vertical, skidding turn, the leading edges of its wings alight with cannon and machine-gun fire. He felt the shells and bullets punching home. One pierced the armour-plating behind his seat, keening past his head to strike the inside of the windscreen, ricocheting round the cockpit and striking his left leg with the impact of a curveball pitched by Cy Young. His gaberdine flying suit was black and foul with oil and glycol, the fluid coursing back from the shattered engine as it struggled to maintain power before it finally cooked and died. Ossie checked the hood was fully back and locked. With the final vestige of control he rolled the Hurricane upside down and popped his belts. Moments later the fighter blew to pieces, a small and brilliant sun. The sky was full of fire, like the climax of a Fourth of July fireworks display. He waited a good long time, gripping the D-ring of his 'chute. There was so much stuff alight he reckoned it might ignite the goddamned canopy.

At little more than five hundred feet he pulled the ripcord hard and drifted down, spinning slowly, the outline of the 'chute lost against a confusion of falling debris, still alight, and wreckage striking the surface of the sea, raising great plumes of creamy spray. From above it was impossible to think that anything had survived. Certainly the pilot of the Macchi 202 believed so, delighted with his excellent new machine, heading back to base, impatient to land and report its first kill. And even lynx-eyed Kenny Laughton did not spot a tiny figure clinging to a severed wing not far from land.

Ossie doubted he'd last long. The sea was cold and he did not have the strength to pull himself onto the surface of the wing, part of the BR.20, burned and blackened, the aileron moving with the swell. But then he realised the wind was from the south, catching his Mae West and pushing him slowly landward. Within an hour he reckoned he was close enough to loose his hold and strike out for the shore. It was further than he thought and an undertow clawed him back, losing him a yard for every couple gained. Maybe he should have stuck with that goddamned wing. He stopped swimming, bobbing upright in the water, supported by the life-jacket. He could not see the wing, so no use going back. His shoes were heavy on his feet and he thought of kicking them away, but carefully eased them off, tied the laces and hung them round his neck.

He felt a twinge of cramp as he rolled onto his front. He forced himself to think of something else, anything to deny the spasm that threatened to knot his calf, close to where the Macchi 202's dead bullet had bruised the skin. In his mind he began a walk with Claudia Farinacci, starting at the cathedral in Mdina and taking the cool, dark turn into Inguanez Street where the balconies almost touched. It seemed to work and he started to paddle, conserving energy, hearing the thud of breakers now, picking up the scents of land. He gave himself a hundred strokes before a rest. Each time he craned his head to mark his progress, each time the strip of coast seemed just as far away, but then he began to feel a power in the sea, lifting him, impelling him towards the shore. Close in at last he let his legs sink down and felt his toes touch yielding sand. The sea grew shallow, swirling round his thighs, then below his knees. Unsteady on his feet he reeled towards a broad expanse of beach. Behind it lay deserted dunes topped with tufted grass.

He dropped into a hollow, sheltered from the wind, undid the buttons and buckled straps of his Mae West and shrugged it off. The filthy flying suit was next. His battledress jacket was reasonably untouched and he buttoned it to the neck. He pulled on his shoes and checked his Omega watch; still working. Four o'clock and growing dusk. Inland, not too far away, he heard the rumble of a truck, then another, then a third. Maybe a convoy, military stuff, shipping supplies along the Syracuse–Agrigento route. His clothes were drying on his back and he worked up a little extra heat by burrowing out a hole for the tell-tale flying kit. He pushed it in and smoothed the surface of the sand.

From the summit of the dunes he could see the potholed, well-used road and, beyond it, buildings; maybe the town of Gela or a nearby village. Immediately below, a pool had formed at the foot of a gentle slope. He scrambled down and tasted the water; brackish but okay. He cupped his hands and drank. He had no plan except to wait for dark, so he could move around, watching out for those skinny Eyetie dogs chained up in every goddamned yard. Maybe he could find some food, and extra clothes.

He was in a fix, no question. Hell, this wasn't France where once, cut off behind the German lines and on the run, he'd gambled on a friendly hand or two, and won. Here the bastards were at war, cheering on Il Duce, that hairless bag of piss and wind. No comfort there. Still, maybe he could grab an airplane, find a boat. He didn't dwell on it too much, or care to think about that spread of sea. He only knew that somehow he'd get back. There had to be a way and, if there was, it was a cinch he'd find it. He went back to his hollow and tried to sleep, pulling heaps of sand around his body to conserve his warmth.

When he woke the sky was purple-black and covered with a drift of glinting stars. As a kid they'd told him they were holes worn through to heaven, whose light was shining through. Staring up at infinite space he thought how crazy it was he couldn't see a way to cross a lousy little stretch of sea. He saw it was eight p.m. He reckoned the Eyeties would be busy tucking into pasta, swilling it down with wine. He brushed himself off, moved down the landward slope and crossed the road into a small straight lane. He passed some simple dwellings, moving as carefully as a man caught in a minefield, wary of every stone and stick.

The land was mostly fenced with wire. Somewhere he could

hear chickens and, inside a barn, cattle lowed, scraped their hoofs and coughed. From the houses dim light filtered out through cracks in shutters. People were talking, laughing. He smelt good cooking: hot oil, fried onions, garlic, meat, and breathed the aromas deep. Further down the lane, close by a farm, clothes hung from a line beneath a loggia. He crossed an open space, grimacing at the crunch of gravel underfoot, and unpegged a long-sleeved woollen sweater.

He got back to the lane as a dog began to bark. Someone cursed, a door banged open and light spilled out. He ducked along a track that ran beside a tall, thick hedge. Further on, beyond iron gates, he saw a substantial villa. Behind him the door to the farm had been slammed shut again. For a moment he relaxed. He pulled the baggy well-used sweater over his head.

Then he heard the muffled double-click of hammers on a shotgun.

A man of maybe eighteen, twenty, was standing feet away, the barrels of a twelve-gauge resting on the open ironwork of the gate, levelled at his chest. He wore a jacket and a buttoned shirt, a bent-peaked peasant's cap. He was not alarmed, he had the gun. He said something in a sing-song dialect, not Italian.

'*Sì*,' said Ossie, '*sì*.' The man said something else. '*Mi scusi*,' Ossie said. His Italian was running out. He made to move away.

'*Fermate*,' said the man, in Italian now. '*Venga qui*.'

Ossie knew the signs. This guy was the kind who would pull the trigger if he didn't play along. '*Sì*,' he said, '*capisco*.'

He walked in through the iron gate and felt the shotgun barrels nudge up against his spine, prodding him along an avenue of cedars towards a broad flight of steps. A fat man with a torch was waiting for them on a terrace that fronted a residence of some style. The fat man shone his torch in Ossie's eyes, then ran the beam across his uniform.

'*Inglesi*,' said the youthful peasant.

'American,' said Ossie, keen to score a point.

'Ah,' the fat man said. 'American. I have plenty friends in America. *Molti, molti.* Many times I am in New York, all over. Come.' He led the way indoors, to a heavily furnished room with tiled floor and a figure of the Virgin Mary in a niche. 'You are hungry, yes?' The fat man gave orders to the peasant, then grunted. 'He is just a *picciotto*, you understand, a little rough maybe, as is the way, but eager to gain respect. Honour and respect, *sì*, things are different here.'

'Uh-huh,' Ossie said.

'I am the mayor,' the fat man said. 'In Sicily the term means much.' His accent was Italian mixed with Brooklyn.

'Congratulations,' Ossie said.

Soon a stooped old woman came in with a tray of food, thinly sliced salami and tomatoes, a hunk of bread and a little jug of wine. She laid it on a table and gestured to Ossie to sit down. He ate the meal slowly, drank sparingly of the wine. 'So, when are you going to turn me in?' he said.

'Sicily is not Italy,' said the fat man. He was standing, thumbs hooked in his braces, belly straining at the waistband of his pants, eyes thoughtful behind his tinted spectacles. He had a frog-like mouth and worked his tongue across his lower lip. 'Tell me,' he said, 'how is it in Malta now?'

'Malta?' Ossie said.

The fat man laughed, his frog-mouth twisted. 'You are interested in a boat, perhaps? Difficult, of course, but not impossible, in return for certain . . . favours.'

'Favours?'

The fat man held up his hand. 'I am Don Stefano Carnelutti. My associates and I have no more reason to like the *Fascisti* than you. They have disturbed our island's balance, ruined our economy, tried to cast aside our age-old customs.'

The *picciotto* had come back in, was listening carefully, though unable to understand. His weapon, broken, rested easily in his arms.

'I'm with you now,' said Ossie.

Don Stefano was encouraged. 'All I ask is you convey a message to your commanders. That when the time comes we are ready.'

'What time?'

'America will join the war. Everybody knows this. Then all will be over very soon.' He took a piece of meat from Ossie's plate and thrust it into his own mouth. 'In Sicily we have a morality of our own, often misunderstood. At our heart we have the welfare of our people. We have our laws, and those laws are there to be obeyed. Only by discipline can a community prosper. Order and control are everything, are they not? Those, when the time comes, we can reimpose. We are strongly represented in your country, highly placed. This offer will be understood.' He chewed and chewed and swallowed. 'Naturally we will have other requirements and requests.'

'I'll bet,' said Ossie.

'So,' said the mayor, 'like you say, is it a deal?'

'And if I say no?'

The fat man glanced at the *picciotto*. 'You will not say no.'

'Uh-huh,' said Ossie, standing up. 'I think I get it. Well, I'll tell you . . .' He came close to the young *picciotto* and grinned. The youth grinned back. Ossie booted him between the legs and caught the flying shotgun as the boy fell forward, howling. He snapped the barrels shut. 'You must think we're nuts. Swap one bunch of gangsters for another? Let's go get your automobile. We're going on a little trip, up Syracuse way. I hear it's neat up there, although I've only seen it from the air.'

# Fourteen

The little Fiat CR.42 bi-plane burst across Takali at hedge-height, close to its top speed of 270 m.p.h. Despite its antique look it had won a reputation as a nimble fighter, robust and versatile, flown with *élan* by pilots of the Falco Squadriglie. It was well named, Falcon, manoeuvrable and quick to strike.

'Watch out, lads, another bloody strafing run.' Working parties ducked for cover. Airfield defences had been strengthened since Kit's return; perimeter and dispersal tracks had been laid, more aircraft pens constructed. With many of the surface buildings damaged or destroyed, the squadrons had begun to burrow underground, excavating caves from yielding limestone: administration centre, operations room, power station, fuel-store, even hangars. By now the Italian attacks had almost become routine, two or three bombing raids a night, each time men dying in the air or on the ground, the losses met with grim determination.

But on this crisp bright morning the Falco's purpose was not bellicose. An object fell, a bag with streamers, thrown from the cockpit. An armament officer rode out on a motor-bike but the package was no booby-trap. Instead a note: 'To the gentlemen of the Royal Air Force at Takali, from the gentlemen of the Regia Aeronautica, Sicily. We are pleased to inform you that the following personnel are safe and uninjured, but in captivity: Flight Lieutenant O. Wolf, Sub-Lieutenant J. K. Harper, Sub-Lieutenant P. D. Metcalf, Leading Airman W. Hudson.'

The word went round. 'Corporal Chalmers, heard the news?'

'Certainly have, sir. Chuffing marvellous. We knew the Eyeties couldn't get the little blighter. What odds he makes it back?'

'Hardly likely, I'm afraid,' said Kit. 'He's up against sixty miles of open sea.'

Kenny Laughton was watching his ground-crew work on his machine. 'Wow, that's great. He's in the bag, huh? How he ever got out of that darned inferno, sir, I'll never know.'

'How are the mods?'

'Hell, sir, what are we? Fighters or single-engined bombers? I mean, just look at this lousy lash-up.' Bomb-racks were being fixed below his Hurricane's wings to take eight forty-pounders. Long-range fuel tanks had been fitted too, extending the aircraft's range. Now a flight could stay in the air for three hours at a stretch, trying to intercept ships and low-flying Axis transports ferrying supplies to North Africa.

'Buck up,' said Kit. 'At least it means we can carry the fight to the enemy.' Inwardly, he had his doubts. He had tried it for himself with little success, droning south and west with Rimmer, Luck and Spencer, peering down from 4,000 feet until red blobs swam in their eyes, using the welcome cloud formations that were appearing in the early-winter sky. Others were more lucky, downing a Savoia 81, which proved that sometimes the tactic worked. But not for Kit, who completed three more fruitless search-and-finds, once close to the African coast, with nothing to show for a mission bristling with danger, the chance of ditching far from home or being bounced by Macchi 202s from Pantelleria, the new design as good, some said, as an Me 109. Command, it seemed, had growing doubts as well. Soon the emphasis would shift to strikes at land-based targets; Sicily at night.

Stood down, Kit hitched a lift to Valletta and met Buster Brown at the Vernon Club close to the Castille. They paid their entrance fee and sat with beers watching the couples dance, a pair of sad old codgers, Buster said, though word had got about that Lascaris's new controller had proved to have a way with women in the ops room, despite his scars. Kit asked him for the truth. 'Well,' said Buster, modestly, 'I must admit the Groupie's warned me I'm there to plot the fuckers, not t'other way round.' Was it bravado? Kit hoped not. The value of women's company, their nearness, voices, touch, women who could see the man within, was priceless, worth countless hours with well-intentioned therapists. Alongside Buster, Kit felt a fraud, with only a lingering shininess about his features, his hands well healed, and fully operational again. But Buster seemed to derive a certain comfort from knowing his companion had shared, if briefly, the wretchedness and doubt, unspoken, not admitted, of the badly burned.

The dancers passed before them, moving smoothly, bodies close. The small band played 'You Made Me Love You' and the dancers sang along, their unmarked faces smiling.

'Fancy a dance?' said Kit.

'What, you and me?' said Buster.

'No, you clot. That little blonde over there.'

'Don't think I'll risk it, old boy. Why don't you have a go?'

'I feel the same. Remember young Marlow in *She Stoops To Conquer*, when he was lost and wouldn't ask the way? "I am unwilling to lay myself under an obligation and stand the chance of an unmannerly answer."'

The band struck up a new number, 'I Don't Want To Set The World On Fire'. An army corporal had climbed onto the small stage, to cheers. He stood in front of the microphone, swaying to the music, his voice hoarse from alcohol and tobacco.

'Not my favourite ditty, in the circumstances,' Buster said. 'Why don't we take in a flick?'

'What's on?'

'You'll never guess,' said Buster.

They walked down Kingsway to the Capitol. They were in time for the eight o'clock performance. Soon the cinema was full of guffaws, but the film was not a comedy. Tyrone Power was the eponymous *Yank in the RAF.* Mild amusement dogged the story as it creaked along its painful course but Betty Grable, got up as a WAAF, was met with full-blooded hoots. Then the film was cut. A notice came up on the screen: 'All military personnel are to report to their respective stations immediately.'

'Sounds like a bit of a flap,' said Buster. 'Come on, I'll show you the ropes in Fighter Ops.'

As they left their tickets were marked, so they could come back another time. 'How long's this film showing for, old boy?' asked Buster.

'Ends on Sunday,' said the usher.

'Thanks,' said Buster. 'I'll be back Monday.'

Outside, the three red danger lights were visible on the Castille mast.

'Doesn't look too hot,' said Buster. 'Something nasty building up.' He led the way across Castille Square and down a long, dark flight of steps. 'Welcome to the hole,' he said. The hole, Lascaris, the maze of passageways and tunnels, deep below the bastions of Grand Harbour, where Malta's war was planned. They showed their passes to the guard and descended the cool, wide tunnel. As they walked they heard the moan of sirens.

'I hope the Capitol isn't hit,' said Buster. 'I've changed my mind. I want to go back and check out Grable's legs.'

'What ghastly rot that was,' said Kit.

'One thing's for sure. It's going to take more than some ruddy chorus-boy flying a cardboard fighter to get the Yanks to join in on this thing. Something's got to happen, something big.'

'Well,' said Kit, 'I can't imagine what that might be.'

They turned off the main passageway and climbed some stairs. 'Those Spits were genuine enough, though,' Buster mused. 'Sandy Johnstone's mob.'

'Poor old 602,' said Kit. 'Press-ganged into supporting the Hollywood glamour boys. Whitehall's wingless wonders have a lot to answer for.'

'Still,' said Buster, 'you've got to admit the propaganda circus offers a little light relief. Take *Picture Post*. Hilarious. Our own Yank, the bolshie little tick, looking like a soloist in the King's College choir at Christmas.'

'I doubt he feels like celebrating at the moment. Probably on his way to a prison camp right now.'

Buster opened a cupboard and took out of bottle of Johnnie Walker. The cork came out with a squeak. 'You can't help feeling sorry for them, can you?' he said.

'Not much he and the others can do,' said Kit, 'except sit tight and wait for a chance to make a break for it.'

'Not our chaps, you chump. The Eyeties.'

They heard, overhead, the distant thud of bombs.

# Fifteen

'My name is Capitano Bazzi,' said the Italian interrogation officer. 'I understand you are American.'

'Uh-huh,' said Ossie Wolf.

The Italian looked at his papers. 'A volunteer for the RAF. Courageous but misguided. I see you have provided name, rank and number. All very correct. But this information does not state your aircraft.'

'I did not give it.'

'A Hurricane, no doubt. A good machine but no match for our Macchi 202, as possibly you have discovered to your cost.' The Italian smiled. 'I believe you arrived here in some style. Chauffeur-driven in a Lancia Lambda.'

'Not a professional driver, you understand,' said Ossie. 'He kinda volunteered.'

'A *mafiosi* at the wrong end of a gun. Lucky for you we are sending you away. Don Stefano's vanity is great and his arm is long.'

'Sounds like you guys ought to rein him in.'

'Il Duce has his plans. We will prevail. The Mafia feeds on weakness and division. It is ancient and entrenched. To change such traditions inevitably takes time. But the people will come to understand our nation marches in step, as one.'

'The people might,' said Ossie, 'but Carnelutti and his cronies won't. They want America in the war, and stomping up your beaches. Then they'll stab you in the back.'

Capitano Bazzi shifted in his chair and frowned. 'Enough. Tomorrow, my friend, we fly you to Taranto. There you will be processed and taken to a camp. If you co-operate, you will find us not unreasonable. If not . . .'

'You'll be as tough on me as you are with Carnelutti.'

'A word of advice,' said Bazzi, standing up and beckoning to a guard. 'Empty defiance will get you nowhere. The fact remains that you surrendered yourself in a hopeless situation. That suggests you are a realist. My friend, you face a good many years under lock and key. Make it easier for yourself. Acknowledge that the time for fighting is over.'

'I'll quarrel with anyone who reckons he can whip me,' Ossie said.

'Tread carefully,' said Capitano Bazzi. 'For the moment you are in the hands of the Regia Aeronautica. But at any time I can arrange for you to be delivered into German hands. Their interrogation methods are said to be more rigorous.'

'Uh-huh,' said Ossie. 'So those sons-of-bitches are back in town?'

'*Buona fortuna*,' sighed Bazzi, wearily. 'I believe you are going to need it.'

Flanked by guards Ossie was marched away. The seaplane headquarters at Syracuse still bore signs of damage from the Brewster raid two months before. Bullet-holes had pierced the admin block where Ossie had been questioned, and further on, next to the main hangar's blackened walls, lay piles of wrecked machines. He could not resist. He looked at the nearest guard. 'This place looks kinda beat-up.'

'*Che?*'

Ossie pointed at the hangar and mimed a diving fighter. He did the noise of Brownings. The guard shrugged. '*Avete sigarette inglesi?*'

They reached a small hut with shuttered windows. The guard who wanted cigarettes unlocked the door and pushed it open with his boot. Three men were sitting at a wooden table, eating. They did not get up but looked at Ossie with suspicion. Their uniforms, dark blue, showed they were Fleet Air Arm men.

'Hi, fellers,' he said. The door slammed shut behind him, the key rattling in the lock. 'Boy, that food smells good.'

'And who exactly are you?' The nearest man had risen to his feet, bearded, tall.

'Well, who the hell are you?'

'I asked first.'

'Okay, brother. 5066609 Flight Lieutenant Wolf. That's all you're going to get.'

'A Yank. Unusual.'

'So's a beard.'

'Fleet Air Arm, chum. Allowed.'

From the table a second man cut in: 'Hang on, Jack. Wolf rings a bell. I say, you're not that American chap in *Picture Post*?'

'Yeah, yeah,' said Ossie. 'Well, at least it proves I'm not a plant.'

The three were the crew of a Fairey Albacore, striking shipping and shore-based targets from their base at Halfar: the pilot Harper, navigator Metcalf, Leading Airman Hudson. 'He's our TAG,' said Harper.

'TAG?' said Ossie.

'Telegrapher gunner. Versatile, our service.'

Hit by flak from an Italian merchantman they had managed to make landfall near Ragusa and baled out, hiding in the ruins of a Greek theatre at Palazzolo Acreide. 'It might have been a damned theatre,' said the bearded pilot, 'but we put on a piss-poor performance, I'm afraid. They picked us up before we'd gone a mile. Flying us to the mainland in the morning.'

'Taranto, I was told,' said Ossie.

'Yes, we heard that too. Take a pew. The grub's not bad.' Harper passed Ossie a piece of cake-like bread, thickly spread with onions, anchovies, tomatoes, and a slice of hard Sicilian cheese.

Ossie said: 'So what's your plan?'

'We tried to soften up the guard,' said Metcalf. 'Gave him all our fags to look the other way. He took the fags and beetled off to tell old Bazzi, who warned us to be good little boys. If not . . .'

'He'd turn you over to the Jerries?'

'Ah, you got the same.'

'It means those yellow-nosed bastards are back in the frame,' said Ossie, 'even if we haven't seen them yet. That's something the clowns in the Hole should know.'

'The Hole?'

'Lascaris,' Ossie said. 'Fighter Control.' He finished the bread and wiped his mouth. He checked the windows and found that the shutters were nailed closed.

'And two armed guards outside the only door,' said Harper. 'Anyway, what's the point? I was telling the chaps, even if we did succeed in breaking out, we'd still be marooned on this benighted island.'

'There is one chance,' said Ossie.

'Really? Don't keep us in suspense.'

'We go back the way we got here.'

'Come again?'

'In a goddamned airplane.'

'Well,' said Harper, 'you're the senior rank. Tell us what you've got in mind.'

They spent the night on horsehair mattresses on the floor,

with blankets tossed in through the door. It was difficult to sleep, no heating, shivering with cold, not talking much, each man considering how things might go for them tomorrow.

It started well enough. The guard came in with a jug of coffee, four tin cups and a bag of warm bread. 'This is some swell hotel,' said Ossie. 'Good thing we're shipping out. I could get fat.'

Outside it was raining. A tender was waiting by the slipway. As they scrambled in, escorted by the guards, Capitano Bazzi watched from his office window, then turned away.

In the bay the twin-float Cant Z506 seaplane moved gently at its mooring. The crew was smart in fresh-pressed uniforms and sported ready smiles. The first pilot introduced himself, like the captain of a commercial flight. He was stocky and looked tough, but friendly. '*Benvenuto, signori.*' He switched to decent English. 'I am Tenente Jano. For us, this is a happy flight. We go on leave. You see? Already we look our best for the *Bella Ragazze*. For you, it is not so happy. But we try to make your journey better.' He produced a bottle of Chianti. 'A present for my wife but I give it to you, to make the time pass well.'

Ossie took the bottle. 'Well, that's real thoughtful. A little early in the day, but later it'll do just the trick.' He saw that the second pilot and engineer had gone through to the cockpit. With the three Fleet Air Arm men he settled himself in a compartment next to the wireless operator's station, propped against the formers of the fuselage. A *Carabiniere* corporal pushed his way into the small space and sat down facing them. He was armed with a long-barrelled revolver, which he had removed from a leather holster at his waist. His face was drawn and tense.

Tenente Jano looked in through the doorway. 'Ginaldi is your guard. He has not flown before. He is nervous enough so do not provoke him.' He slapped the corporal on the back and went off laughing.

Soon they heard the triple Alfa Romeo radial engines fire up and the Cant began to move. Rain was coursing across the compartment's single porthole and the corporal leaned forward slightly from his seat, wiping away the condensation, watching the grey-green spray thrown up by the port float. As the aircraft plunged across the bay, thudding through the waves, he steadied himself by gripping the sides of his metal seat, the revolver resting in his lap, only letting go when the seaplane lifted clear and the vibration grew less fierce as the engines were throttled back. Again he stared out of the window as the panorama of Syracuse was revealed, wonder in his eyes. He jerked his head and grinned.

Ossie nodded, grinning back. He stood up and moved forward, pointing out of the window. '*Per favore, per favore?*' The corporal shrank back in his seat, cocked the revolver and shouted for Ossie to get back.

The wireless operator, at his table, glanced across his shoulder, breaking off from making his report. He waved at Ossie to sit down and patted a Beretta .34 lying on a sheaf of papers.

Harper scratched his beard. 'Twitchy types.'

'Hey, Luigi,' Ossie said. He held up the bottle of Chianti to the corporal, twisting an invisible corkscrew. The corporal shook his head. The wireless operator shouted: '*Aspettare un' secondo.*' He pulled open a drawer and threw across a metal corkscrew.

Ossie opened the wine and shared it with Harper and the others.

The Cant had settled comfortably to its cruising speed of 120 m.p.h., heading towards the Calabrian peninsula at 2,500 feet. Ossie knew the Z506 had an impressive range, more than seventeen hundred miles, but that was on full tanks. How much fuel had they pumped in for the shortish trip to Taranto? All he knew for certain was that each mile covered northwards meant a gallon less. Every moment counted.

It happened very quickly but not quite as they had planned. The Chianti was a bonus. Ossie shouted and pointed urgently through the porthole, as though the Cant was being attacked. The corporal half rose, alarmed, craning his neck to see. Ossie jumped forward and drove his fist into the man's left ear. The corporal grunted like a beast stunned in an abattoir, then sank to his knees, the revolver clattering to the floor. Ossie snatched it up and brought the barrel down on the man's skull.

The wireless operator had been quickly dealt with too. At Ossie's first shout Harper had called: 'Hey, *vino*.' The operator raised his head and Harper tossed him the uncorked Chianti, which flew through the air trailing a shower of crimson liquid. As the Italian instinctively raised his hands to catch it, Harper lunged, gripping the back of the man's neck and pressing his face against the surface of the desk, his other hand closing on the butt of the Beretta automatic.

The two men were quickly yoked together, back to back, wrists secured by their own belts. There was no need to gag them: any cries of warning were smothered by the roar of engines.

Ossie and Harper went forward to the cockpit to tackle the two pilots and the engineer. Ossie tapped Tenente Jano on the shoulder. The pilot turned in his seat. His mood was good. His mind was full of the forthcoming leave. He expected to see the wireless operator/gunner Sergente Galli with bottles of *acqua minerale*. Instead he found himself looking down the muzzle of the long-barrelled revolver. His eyes went wide. His hand flew down to a handgun in a recess by his seat. Ossie struck out with the barrel of the revolver. Jano gasped with pain and clutched his wrist, eyes closed, cursing, no longer in control of the yawing Cant. The second pilot pulled it back on course, sweating, darting looks at Harper, who moved the little Beretta back and forth, one moment levelled at his head, then at the forehead of the engineer.

'Okay,' said Ossie. 'We're going home.'

'Malta?' Jano groaned.

'Bingo,' said Ossie.

Jano's wrist had swollen with the force of Ossie's blow. 'You fools!' he said. 'Your comrades will make short work of us, unless you choose to fight. Tell me, does the Royal Air Force have a special medal for shooting down its own machines?'

'Let's put Metcalf on the radio to warn the chaps we're coming in,' said Harper.

'And give the Regia a chance to fix our position?' said Ossie. 'I'd rather be brought down by a Hurricane than a Macchi. No, we'll come in low, put her down fast and take our chances. If we're intercepted get one of your guys to waggle the machine-guns up and down. Our boys know that means friendly aircraft.'

'Waggle the machine-guns, eh?' said Harper. 'That's a relief. For a moment I thought we might be in trouble.'

Jano had resumed control, heading south-west with the Sicilian coast passing slowly on their right. Ossie's pistol was still inches from his head. Then, ahead, two fighters closed in fast, shot past, and screwed back in flashy vertical turns to pull abreast, flanking the droning Cant: Messerschmitt 109s, not yellow-nosed but camouflaged in shark-like mottled grey, both with a broad white band around the fuselage ahead of the tailplane branded with neat black Fascist swastikas.

Ossie crouched down behind Tenente Jano's seat, revolver angled upwards at the Italian's spine. 'Wave,' he said. 'Give the bastards a cheery smile.'

Jano looked across at the German pilot yards from his left wing and lifted his hand in a casual salute. Ossie raised himself a little. He wanted to be sure that Jano didn't pull any cute tricks. It was a risk but, hell, if he was seen he reckoned the German would assume he was a crewman. What else could he be? The

Me 109 pilot was nodding and pointing at his oxygen mask. 'He's trying to call you up on the R/T,' said Ossie. 'Can't work out why you don't respond. Stall the sonofabitch.'

Jano pointed backwards, gave a thumbs-down sign, raised his hands and shrugged, suggesting that the wireless equipment had failed. The German held station for a long, long time.

'What's the bugger doing now?' said Harper, standing well back from the bright light of the glazed cockpit.

'He's thinking,' said Ossie. 'He's asking himself why we're on this course. He may call up Control to check our flight plan. If he does, we're cooked. Give him another wave, Tenente, and take us down towards the coast, as though we're heading back to Syracuse. That might be enough to get him off our back.'

Jano gave the German a final salute, more formal this time, eased the control column gently forward and dropped towards the Sicilian coast in a gentle, descending turn. For a moment the Messerschmitts maintained their height. Was the leader, even now, radioing his suspicions back to base?

Then both fighters half rolled and dived. In seconds the men on board the Cant would learn their fate. The Messerschmitts passed within a hundred feet, heading north, waggling their wings.

'God's teeth,' said Harper. 'That's as close as I ever want to be to a brace of 109s.'

'One thing's for sure,' said Ossie. 'It confirms the Hun are back. And just as certain, those mothers plan to make things hum round here.' He prodded Jano with the big revolver. 'Nicely done, Tenente. Now drop back onto two-one-zero and let's put this baby down in time for chow. Can't promise you what you're used to, but you guys could do to lose a little fat.'

Jano smiled ruefully. 'Tell me, what about my men? Have they been harmed? You have their weapons here. That suggests to me you have rendered them *hors de combat*.'

'Oh, they're okay, a little sore. We got 'em trussed up good.'

The Italian pointed through the windscreen. 'See? Already we pick up Gozo. Soon we may suffer an attack. You have the strong advantage. I see no possibility of resistance. I request that you free Merosi and Ginaldi. If we go down, and their hands are bound, well, I would not wish that on any man.'

'I want your word they won't give us any trouble.'

'You have it.'

The outline of Malta was showing plainly now. Harper went back and freed the wireless operator and the corporal. They showed no sign of fight, grumbling as their circulation was restored, showing each other their bruises and abrasions. Metcalf covered them with the big revolver as Hudson pulled himself up into the dorsal turret with its Breda 12.7mm machine-gun. 'In position, Bill?' Harper shouted.

'Yup,' called Hudson. 'And it's quite an improvement on the old Applecore's Vickers K. Tempting to have a squirt.'

'Just waggle it, old chap,' said Harper, 'and pray to God the fighter boys remember what it means.'

In the cockpit Ossie said: 'Okay, Tenente. Keep us real low. We could be bounced at any time. When I say, "Down", you drop this baby like a goddamned stone, before the guys decide to fill us full of holes.'

'*Capisco*,' said Tenente Jano. His voice was dull. He understood his situation well: captivity or death. No leave with love's warm comforts and, later, games with the three *bambini* in the meadows behind the little farm and meals by candlelight underneath the loggia, hearing the village gossip, savouring a taste of life unchanging, far removed from war. No one at home to see his crisp, best uniform or receive the little presents stored in the seaplane's hold.

They were flying at less than a hundred feet, engines throttled back, passing through the air at barely 150 m.p.h. This was Ossie's plan. He knew this painful slowness rendered them easy prey. But he reasoned that their obvious vulnerability might make an attacker curious to investigate, hold back, even for a moment, and in such a moment a pilot might have time to see the machine-gun sign for friendly aircraft showing at the dorsal turret, see the big wings waggling up and down to signify surrender.

They were close to land now, apparently undetected. About five miles ahead lay Qawra Point, jutting out to sea from the western flank of Salina Bay. But then, as the coast emerged more clearly from a rolling bank of mist, the second pilot shouted. He had good eyes. With the sun behind them a Hurricane section was diving down from fifteen hundred feet.

Ossie yelled a warning: 'Hurrys at four o'clock.'

Instantly they heard the chatter of machine-guns from a single plane. Big holes appeared in the starboard wing. Bad enough, thought Ossie, but maybe Hudson's efforts in the dorsal turret had worked. Otherwise the storm of bullets might have pierced the fuselage, killing everyone inside. But this was no time to gamble. It could be that the Hurry pilot was a lousy shot.

'Put her down, Tenente! Put the bastard down!'

Jano sideslipped the big machine towards the mouth of Salina Bay. The Hurricanes were coming round again. At thirty feet he pulled back on the stick and eased the throttles. The Cant hit the water hard, at too steep an angle and crosswise to the waves, bouncing high, then falling back and striking the sea in an explosion of creamy spray. Ossie lost his grip on Jano's seat and fell across the throttles, his body forcing the triple levers forward. The engines screamed, the seaplane gaining speed, nose plunging deep and throwing up great quantities of water back across the wings. Then Jano gripped the back of Ossie's tunic, dragged him off, and heaved back on the levers. One by one the engines died.

Now it was very quiet, the aircraft pitching and rolling, the waves slapping against its sides. Soon, in the cockpit, they could smell sea air. Harper had opened the starboard hatch and scrambled across the riddled wing, waving the corporal's best white shirt. The Hurricanes circled, cockpit canopies fully back, the pilots curious but alert. From the squadron markings Ossie knew them: Kit Curtis, Kenny Laughton, Rimmer, Luck. Then three turned away, leaving only Curtis to patrol, probably calling up an RAF Whaleback rescue launch from Kalafrana Bay. They had a while to wait, as veils of rain swept across the bay and passed inland.

'Welcome to sunny Malta,' Ossie said.

'*Congratulazioni*,' said Tenente Jano. 'Now everything begins again for you. For us, it ends.'

'You did well, Tenente,' Ossie said. 'You did well to get us down.'

'I wished you a happy flight,' said Jano, drily. 'I did not mean this happy. Still, we live, and for that I suppose we must be grateful.'

'If you can think that way,' said Ossie, 'I guess you'll find it makes things easier.'

'*Siccome la casa brucia, riscaldiamoci*,' said Tenente Jano. 'Since the house is on fire, let us warm ourselves.'

A silence hung between them and, in that moment, Ossie thought of telling Tenente Jano he was sorry for setting the house on fire, but he stopped himself. Looking at this beaten man it was hard to see him as the enemy, but what if the guy had managed to grab his revolver in the cockpit and fought it out? Ossie was glad he had said nothing.

In little more than half an hour they were picked up by the launch. The Whaleback approached with caution, the crewmen in the aircraft-style turrets above the cabin swivelling their Vickers machine-guns back and forth. Ossie joined Harper on the wing. Closer now the launch crew recognised their uniforms. An LAC yelled: 'Blimey, we thought it was old Mussolini himself, throwing in the torch.'

The flight lieutenant in command was less fanciful: 'Actually, old boy, we reckoned the Eyeties were putting a fifth-columnist ashore. It seemed the only explanation. That, or the buggers had had enough, and wanted out.'

'No,' said Ossie, 'these particular buggers are okay.'

Soon, on the quayside of Grand Harbour, the captors and the captives stood together, waiting for their transport. The LAC produced a Box Brownie and snapped the little group. They leaned in, some bemused, but others smiling, even the Italians, like any bunch of fliers caught on camera.

A Navy 15 cwt truck came to run the Fleet Air Arm men back to Halfar.

'Well,' said Sub-Lieutenant Harper, 'thanks.'

'Sure,' said Ossie. 'So long, fellers.' He watched the truck move slowly along the quay until it was lost to sight round the harbour wall. Three guards from a Malta regiment had come to guard the Italians. They stood, smart and proud, not tall themselves but tall beside the Italians, bayonets fixed.

'*Arrivederci*,' said Tenente Jano. 'I realise I do not know your name.'

'Wolf,' said Ossie. 'Ossie Wolf.'

'American.'

'Yeah. St Louis.'

'I have a cousin in Kansas City. You know it?'

'Sure.'

'Flavio also flies. First officer on a Trans-World DC-1. We write. He thinks the States will join this war. His services will be needed. We worry we might face each other.'

'One less worry now,' said Ossie.

'Yes, that's true. That burning house again.'

'Well, *buona fortuna*.'

'Hey, *italiano*.'

'*Sì*. I learned it from one of your guys in Sicily.'

'It worked. Perhaps it will work for me.'

'As the English say, you're in the bag,' said Ossie. 'Take my advice, pal, stay there, see this thing out.'

'You did not.'

'That's different,' Ossie said. 'We're going to win.'

On an order the Maltese guards moved forward and marched the seaplane crew towards a Bedford transport.

Ossie was debriefed in Lascaris, questioned closely by a group of senior officers he did not know. They listened in silence to his story.

'Well,' said a wing commander, who chewed an empty pipe, 'it seems to have been a decent show all round, apart from being bounced by that Macchi 202. Pretty handy machine, or so we hear.'

'Handy enough,' said Ossie. He did not want to be offered excuses for losing concentration, making a dumb mistake and following that goddamned BR.20 down. 'But Macchis don't mean beans compared to Messerschmitts. The pair we saw, they looked like 109Fs to me, the latest type. Which means the boys are back in town.'

'Yes, Wolf, we know.'

'You know?'

'Our photo-reconnaissance chaps are on the ball. The Hun have been building up for weeks. They'll be over soon. It's only a matter of time. Then we're really going to see some fun.'

'No fun for our Hurrys to be fifty m.p.h. slower in level flight than a 109, sir, never mind faster in the climb and dive. And, please, don't tell me it's the man and not the machine. What we need is Spits, if we're to have a more than even chance.'

'Thank you, Wolf,' said the wing commander, coldly. 'I'm sure we all appreciate your advice.'

'More a request,' said Ossie, 'if you want to hold onto this goddamned island.'

'That's defeatist talk,' said the wing commander. 'I'll overlook it for the moment as you've been through a rather rough experience and, it has to be said, you handled it rather well. But may I say that I hope your attitude is not shared by the rest of your squadron? We need to know we can depend on you chaps in the months ahead.'

'Oh, you can depend on us chaps,' said Ossie. 'The question is, can we depend on our machines?'

The wing commander looked down at his pencilled notes, chewing hard on the stem of his pipe. 'I'd say we're done. Oh, yes, I'm to convey the Fleet Air Arm's thanks. Very appreciative of your efforts in getting their fellows back.' He paused. Another check. 'Yes, Wolf, there is just one thing more. Yesterday the Japanese attacked the American fleet, somewhere called Pearl Harbor. Your country's in the war.'

# Sixteen

Dawn. Red dawn. Not just red with sunrise, the universal weather sign that made those working on the land and sea study the sky with apprehension, but coloured in a different way, lent a deeper red from fires that burned in Valletta, Sliema, Mosta, towns unchanged for centuries, with familiar streets, squares and churches, homes, shops and schools, cool dark bars and small cafés where locals met to discuss the matters of the day, now wiped away, a memory, changed into a new and unknown landscape of piled masonry and shattered beams, at which men pulled with frantic hands having heard a cry somewhere deep below. So many dead, whole families, friends, familiar faces – but how much worse the toll without those caves and tunnels, a gift of God, so many said, to which the people could retreat?

Fires burned, too, at the airfields of Takali, Luqa, Halfar and the base at Kalafrana Bay, pounded by twenty, thirty raids a week, from stacked Ju 88s grumbling through the sky in waves, escorted by darting Me 109s. Life, to Kit, since the Germans had returned, was flying, fighting, eating, sleeping, little more. Often he did not have time, or inclination, to trudge back up the long, dusty road to his quarters at Mdina. The others were the same. It was simpler, much less trouble, to stay close to their machines. That way they knew the state of play, could be on hand to check the Hurricane they were to fly when another man brought it home, could judge when they might be scrambled next. Also, why waste time walking when they could grab more sleep on a makeshift bed, even if it meant an occasional befuddled dive for cover as the sirens went and the bombs came down?

Kit wrote home to his father:

> Constant action here, full-throttle climbs, never enough time to make the height we really need. We just have to do the best we can with the angels we've got and try and get up-sun. Massive formations coming over now, sometimes eighty at a time. We dive down on the bombers, they're the ones we're after, and get out quick before the 109s react. We got three Eyetie Savoias the other day, bang, bang, bang, without suffering a scratch. The Hun fighter boys just watched us. Sometimes they'll do that, stay up-top, apparently not prepared to mix it. Don't know why. Other times a *schwarm* (that's four) or *rotte* (two) will detach itself and come on down and then all hell breaks loose. Not much finesse, I'm afraid, just give a burst at anything that passes through your sights. As usual with these things, the moment comes when no one wants to play and then you break and land, watch the ground-crews refuel, rearm and generally check the kite, then try to remember what went on so our intelligence chap can write it up (jolly difficult, actually, often the whole thing's a blur), then grab a mug of tea and a bite to eat, if you feel like eating (I often don't), then find a chair and snatch forty winks, until some corporal bellows in your ear; 'Section scramble,' and so it starts again.

It's a bit like a continuous loop of film, except the details change.

We had a new man the other day, fresh from England. Poor chap, it must have been a dickens of a shock to see the way we exist out here. He was pretty pale, and in a bit of a funk at going up. He'd never fired a shot in anger back in Blighty. I told him not to worry, the usual platitudes, it'll come, stick to my tail, I'll see you through, that kind of thing. Anyway, he got back all right and our conversation, if you can call it that, ran along these lines: 'Crikey, sir, is it always like that?'

'Oh, pretty much. Get anything at all?'

'I don't know. It happened so fast.'

'Better luck next time, old chap. You'll soon get the hang of things.'

I'm afraid next time proved to be his last. He had to jump for it and landed in the sea south of the Dingli cliffs. He should have been okay but the water's cold at this time of year and the rescue boys drew a blank. He was nineteen, I believe, and came from Broadstairs.

Kit put down his pen. Hurricanes were passing over the perimeter of the airfield. Four had taken off forty-five minutes before. One, two . . . two. That made eight aircraft gone in half as many days. He was glad that Buster Brown wasn't there to see it. He remembered his visit a week before, for a few snatched moments in the *palazzo* at Mdina.

Buster had been unusually glum, and troubled by his burns. A graft on his left hand was weeping and there was a suggestion of infection. 'Maltese streptococci,' he had said. 'That's all I need.' He was tired, red-eyed and pessimistic. 'You know the island's running low on ammo, I suppose? Going to have to ration the stuff. The trouble is the convoys aren't getting through. The sun-dodgers are doing their best but there's only so much you can cram into one of those things.'

'Sun-dodgers?'

'Submarines.' Buster was inspecting his suppurating hand. 'I suppose you've heard about *Repulse* and *Prince of Wales*? Sunk by the bloody Japanese off the Malayan coast. No carrier support, no air cover. The Jap bombers had a field day. It makes you wonder who's running this war.'

'Come on, Buster. This isn't like you.'

'You forget, you hear things down at Lascaris. Like our elders and betters pondering about the ruddy Yanks. Nobody seems to have heard a peep. It's as though the Americans think they're only up against the Japanese.'

'Hardly. Didn't the Hun declare war on them four days after Pearl Harbor? Anyway, look at France and the Phoney War. It took us long enough to learn what it's all about.'

'Learn? You must be joking! Here we are, defending a patch of earth and rock we're told is vital to our presence in the Med, yet you chaps are still treated like poor relations, ropy kites, fobbed off with sprogs from training or types who haven't hacked it with their COs. And now, with the Jerries hitting the convoys hard, like the Eyeties never could, our fuel and spares aren't getting through and grub's scarce. If this goes on the bastards won't need to drop their bombs. They'll be able starve us out.'

'Oh, put a sock in it, Buster, for God's sake. Have another beer.'

Kit watched the two surviving Hurricanes taxiing in: Ossie Wolf and Kenny Laughton. What had Ossie said on Christmas Day, two months ago? The day had passed like any other, no squadron celebrations. Instead the pilots waited for the call, some strapped into cockpits, trolley-accumulators connected, ready to thumb engine starter buttons, others uneasy, pacing round Dispersal in heavy flying gear, unable to settle, to concentrate on books, or magazines, or a weeks-old newspaper, or an interminable game of draughts, occupied with considerations of a future gauged in hours, focussed on the task to come. Yet on that day it had not come, only a rumour that the Luftwaffe had announced no raids: a seasonal gesture. 'Santa Claus in jackboots,' Ossie said. 'Don't let let the sons-of-bitches fool you. They'll stop at nothing now.' As if to prove his point, on Boxing Day two Me 109s came in low over Marsaxlokk Bay and strafed a handful of *luzzu* fishing-boats with trolling lines out for late-season dolphin, filling the holds with a different, bloody catch.

Kit looked at his half-completed letter. He could not think of what to write that did not appear empty bravado, whistling in the dark, or that would escape erasure by the censor's pen – like the news that a convoy of three merchant ships *en route* to Valletta from Alexandria, laden with food, fuel, ammunition, medical supplies, had been attacked and two destroyed in Bomb Alley, the only route between Crete and the Benghazi promontory. That another attempt, this time a tanker and three merchantmen, with sixteen destroyers and four cruisers, had fought off a Regia Nautica task force, helped by other fighting ships putting out from Malta, but that Ju 88s had got through; that twenty miles from the Maltese coast a freighter had succumbed to bombs, and eight miles out, almost within sight of Zonqor Point, a tanker had gone down. And it had not been over yet. The surviving merchantmen, their superstructures twisted, blackened, had crawled across Grand Harbour towards the docks, cheered by the population, but then the Stukas and Ju 88s had sunk them at their moorings, with only a fraction of their cargoes safely on the quay.

He could have written, too, of the subject on every mind:

invasion. It seemed no false alarm this time, some ill-judged mission, very Italian, gallant, doomed. Instead, confided Buster, high-altitude photo-recon flights were coming back with pictures of Sicilian bases spread with ominous build-ups of enemy machines. So many that they raised the question: could this be to bomb, or something more? In Lascaris there was talk of gliders, airborne forces, barges. Preparations for invasion, clear and unmistakable, like France, like Greece, like Crete. Could it really happen here, in Malta? Could Malta be extinguished, freeing Axis shipping to supply, unhindered, Rommel in North Africa so he could drive eastwards into Egypt, barring the routes to Suez and the East? Hardly welcome news for home.

Again, Kit thought, he could have written of that mighty cock-up, the recent ill-starred attempt to deliver fresh machines, this time not clapped-out Hurricanes but brand new Spitfires, straight from the works at Castle Bromwich. The excitement at the news had been almost tangible. Spitfires at last, by God. The carrier, with thirty-one Mark Vs on board, had reached the fly-off point three hundred nautical miles east of Gibraltar. But then the Spitfires' ninety-gallon long-range tanks had been found to have a fault, a simple thing, an airlock, that should have been detected in pre-flight tests. Except there had been no pre-flight tests. Next the armourers found that the 20mm cannon were not set up, as none had been test-fired in England. Then the riggers discovered there were no spares: left behind in Gib. The carrier retraced its course, trailing recrimination in its wake.

And yet, despite all this, the setbacks, constant danger, day-to-day privations, Kit found in himself an unshakeable resolve, a refusal to bend, a deep belief that somehow they would come through, that this tiny island could be saved. He thought of the *kappillan* he had met near the crest of Mellieha Ridge. 'Now we make new history,' the priest had said. 'Together.'

Yes, these were times to make their mark on history, times to be recalled with quiet pride by those who fought, recounted by successive generations. Some lines of Shakespeare came to him, from *Henry the Fifth*, usually so familiar as to be unheard, but now, in this place and at this time, not so hackneyed that they failed to raise the pulse-rate, and the spirit: '. . . gentlemen in England now a-bed Shall think themselves accursed they were not here.' Kit was here. He knew this was his time, knew it was a pinnacle from which, if he survived, he would view the balance of his life. 'From this day to the ending of the world, But we in it shall be remember'd. We few, we happy few, we band of brothers.' He smiled. Or band of eagles? How had de Perignac had it? 'A band of eagles fears no foe'. That was apt. And there was another line, earlier in Shakespeare's text, that had once meant much to him, perhaps still did to the inner man who seemed to have lost his way: 'The fewer men, the greater share of honour'.

These thoughts sustained him through the next, tense battle over the South Comino Channel, north of Marfa Ridge. Later, when he landed, he heard that in the morning, anticipating dawn, before the day's first raids, with the sky fresh red from sunrise and the night's destruction, he and others would fly north-west to intercept and guide in a flight of fifteen Spitfires, this time fully ready for the fly-off from their carrier, and come to join the battle.

# Seventeen

Standing on the sandbagged parapet of the blast pen Kit Curtis and Ossie Wolf watched one of the fly-off Spitfires, engine stilled, being pushed backwards into its bay, pilot still in place, unclipping his harness and pushing his smoked goggles onto his forehead, eyes screwed up against the glare. There was something familiar about the man, even from that distance and bulked up in anonymous flying gear. The ground-crew was working fast, detaching the long-range tanks, then scrambling onto the hot engine cover with four-gallon cans of fuel. Underneath each wing the armourers were snapping open the half-turn fasteners of the gun and ammunition panels, making sure the guns were safe, and clicking home full boxes of .303 ammunition and 20mm cannon shells. They had fifteen minutes to complete their tasks. Soon the Spitfires would be engaged in their first action.

After a flight of 650 miles, the fifteen Mark Vs had swept in low across the island, the mellow thrum of engines sounding a note of hope. Kit had led a section to meet them out to sea. A brief exchange, cut off before their position could be traced. 'Red Host to Red Guest, Red Host to Red Guest, follow me. Over.'

'Red Guest to Red Host, lead on, Macduff. Out.'

The Hurricanes had circled as the Spitfires landed, alert for free-hunt Me 109s prowling for easy prey; tired pilots low on fuel, beginning to relax. Kit was low on fuel himself, already on reserve, and then the pressure warning light came on. The real thing, or false alarm, the instrument playing up? No time to risk a stall. He put down quickly and told his team: 'I want the damned thing sorted, problem traced, rearmed, refuelled and on the button. Get your fingers out. It's vital I get back up. The Jerries will be planning a welcoming party of their own.'

He watched the Spitfires land, beautiful in the air, elegant at rest, but endearingly ungainly as they waddled towards their blast pens, teetering on their narrow undercarriages, the pilots leaning from their cockpits to see round the long, elevated noses, guided by airmen on each wing and motor-cycle riders on sputtering BSAs. He had an urge to see a Spit up close. That was why he was on the parapet now, alongside Ossie, taking in the flowing lines of an aircraft built for purpose, no detail to be seen that did not serve a function, one of the world's best-performing, finest-looking fighters. Although he had logged more than eighty hours on Mark 1As, that seemed like another time and he felt an honest thrill to think that soon he would be at the controls, after the good-old, slow-old Hurry. The shiny new Mark V had the Hurricane beaten in every department, faster at 370 m.p.h. by 30 m.p.h. that powered it to its ceiling of 37,000 feet; better by a crucial 3,000 feet, as eager and responsive as any thoroughbred.

Each Spitfire was being handed over to an experienced Malta hand. Although he had led the welcoming flight Kit felt a pang of envy. This was Ossie's moment. Already the American had climbed up on the wing, ready to take over. The pilot was stretching, yawning, pulling off his helmet. He noticed Ossie, gave a nod, then looked again.

'Christ Almighty, it's Huckleberry Finn.'

'Goofy, you little sod.'

Ossie shouted down to Corporal Chalmers: 'Chuffy, this is Sergeant Gates. We flew in France together. This guy was the highest scorer in the squadron. I'm talking about mam'selles,' he added, 'but he also put away some Hun.'

'Sergeant bollocks,' said Gates. 'I've joined the toffs. Flying Officer Gates no less.'

'Brother,' said Ossie. 'Things must be getting desperate.'

'We knew that, chum. Otherwise why would they let you in?'

'It's good to see you, feller. How long is it?'

'June '40, the day the *Lancastria* went up at St Nazaire.'

'With our ground-crew guys on board. That was a lousy break.' Ossie patted the Spitfire's fuselage. 'How is it with this baby?'

'Everything you'd expect. How is it here?'

'Everything you'd expect.' Ossie studied the long barrels of the twin 20mm cannon, one projecting from each wing. 'I'm told these Hispano-Suizas pack quite a punch.'

'Explosive shells,' said Gates. 'Eight hundred and fifty rounds a minute. Make the Brownings look like pea-shooters. When you nail a Hun with this, the bugger knows he's hit.'

Kit was standing forward of the wing, and grinning up. 'Good to see you, Goofy.'

'Good grief, you too?' said Gates. 'Looks like the old firm's back in business.'

News came through on the operations phone that a plot was building up, a solid, glowing blob on radar screens at Madliena, moving south for the first of the daytime raids, normally as regular as a railway timetable, coming in at breakfast, lunch and dinner, but much earlier today, hoping to catch the new arrivals on the ground. Except the ground-crews had done their work. Twenty minutes after landing the Spitfires were in the air again. For once, the raiders faced more than a handful of time-worn Hurricanes panting to reach the safety of the sun. Kit, in his Hurricane, had not got off the ground. No faulty pressure warning light but something more, and difficult to trace, so he watched the battle from below, heard the rattle of gunfire, first at 27,000 feet, then lower as the combatants lost height, the sky criss-crossed with vapour-trails, each telling of a desperate fight.

The enemy *Staffel* was soon in disarray, gaps opening in the neat formations, as first one, then two, then three, then more machines fell away, tracked by curving trails of smoke and flame, crews tumbling clear through open hatches, small black somersaulting shapes, parachutes snapping open, drifting down, like wind-borne seeds.

A stricken Ju 88 skimmed the dome of Mosta church, in a shallow dive, and snagged the stony slopes of Bingemma Gap, a rolling, oily fireball marking where it struck. The German fighters had engaged. This was no day to stay up high, content to let the bombers drop their loads.

For most of the *Kampfflieger*, newly arrived from the Russian front, accustomed to minimal resistance from lightly armed Yak-1s, this was their first sight of a British Spitfire. For eight it was their last. One Messerschmitt came down in a vertical dive, no sign of damage, but its pilot disabled or dead, the Daimler-Benz's throttles wide, screaming, louder, louder, until it drove a twenty-foot hole in the shady glades of Attard's pride, the subtropical San Anton gardens. Another, a wing blown off, corkscrewed across Mtarfa, throwing the pilot clear before exploding, a lucky man until his parachute streamed and he hit the ground at 80 m.p.h.

Later, it emerged, four miles out from Delimara Point, two fishing-boats from Marsaxlokk had found three airmen clinging to a leaking dinghy. They were Germans, so they threw them back, remembering their fellow fishermen, machine-gunned by the Me 109s on Boxing Day.

Kit and the others on the ground understood that this first engagement for the Spitfires might be a turning point, the moment when the balance tipped, if only slightly, in their favour. Axis invasion plans required superiority in the air. The parallels were obvious. In a similar situation, Britain had been saved. Malta might be too.

It also seemed that way to Ossie Wolf, who claimed the Ju 88 that missed the Mosta dome, and to all the others, hot from battle, who landed unharmed. The island, always strong, took heart, particularly when it heard it had won a medal. 'To honour her brave people,' intoned the English king, 'I award the George Cross to the island fortress of Malta, to bear witness to a heroism and a devotion that will long be famous in history.' It did not have the timeless stamp of Shakespeare's prose, but it would do. Some even claimed they saw a glow of victory in the shadow of defeat.

But others, more prosaically, observed you could not eat a gong. Medals were very nice but food, and all the island's other needs, came in by sea and still only remnants of convoys were getting through. It was not enough, despite the Governor asking God for help. More Spitfires were the key but when, a few weeks later, the next batch came, this time the Germans were prepared. Nearly fifty British fighters landed, flown off the American carrier *Wasp*. The Luftwaffe hit them on the ground, destroying nine, damaging nearly thirty.

The balance had swung back. The glow of victory faded. The bombing raids intensified. In two months, March and April, Fliegerkorps II, the Luftwaffe's élite in Ju 88s, flew almost ten thousand sorties. One raid destroyed the general hospital, and damaged others, a deliberate act. Then a photo-reconnaissance pilot overflying Sicily returned with pictures of fifteen hundred glider strips at Gerbini airfield, suggesting imminent airborne assault. It seemed that God had paid no heed to Governor Dobbie. At a stroke the shadow of defeat seemed longer.

# Part four

## May–August 1942

## 'All hell'

# Eighteen

With the Airedale terrier bounding at his side Louis Garencières came down the woodland path, slashing at nettles with a whippy hazel stick, and crossed the little iron bridge that spanned the ha-ha. Boy and dog raced across the lawn, uncut and thick with daisies. The gate to the kitchen garden squeaked and Agnes Hobbes, bent low cutting broad-leafed spinach, smiled and stood up straight, easing her back and shoulders, the wicker basket full, scissors balanced in her hand. 'Mr Arthur's been after you.'

'*Ah, oui? J'arrive.*'

'Now, now, no French. You're in England now.'

'Okay.'

'And that won't do. Be off with you. Chicken for lunch, your favourite.'

Already Louis could smell it. His appetite was good. He was less scrawny than the child who had stepped off the boat from France, pale and weary. Now his hair was fair from the sun, face freckled, limbs tanned, indistinguishable from the other children in the village school, where he was doing well, popular with the girls who liked the way he spoke, and with the boys who liked his tales of Germans.

Arthur Curtis was in his study. The *Daily Express* was spread out on his desk. 'Louis, I want you to see this. Mrs Hobbes has brought it in. It has to do with Kit.' The boy came round the desk and stood beside the old man's chair. 'Air Knight of Malta Writes Home' ran the newspaper's headline over a report in column one. 'Battle of Britain Had Nothing On This'. Louis read it slowly, stumbling over a word or phrase, eyes bright. An unnamed pilot had given a vivid picture of the siege: the hardships, sacrifices, dangers faced by the island's population, the fighting services stationed there, the men at sea, the daily, desperate scrambles of the Spitfire squadrons, still outnumbered, but armed with a fighter that, at last, could do the job. The story rang with optimism and resolve. Could it be that, once again, the shadows of defeat had begun to lift in this seesaw battle for a far-off island, relishing its reputation as a thorn in Rommel's side?

'Did Monsieur Kit write this?' asked Louis.

'No, it was another man, but it tells you what it's like out there. It gives you a good idea.'

'The Spitfires shoot down many Boches.'

'Not just the Spitfires. The gunners on the ground got a hundred in a month. It seems we might be wearing the Germans down. How long can they sustain such losses?' Arthur Curtis folded the newspaper and handed it to the boy. 'On Monday take this to school. Your friends would like to see it. Perhaps Miss Simms will pin it to her noticeboard.' Curtis paused. 'You should feel proud.'

'Feel proud?' said Louis. '*Eh, bien*, perhaps. But Monsieur Kit is not my father.' He frowned. 'What would you say he is?'

'A special friend, perhaps,' said Curtis. He passed across an envelope, sent from London. 'There is something more.' Louis recognised his mother's writing. It was in English, brief, a single page:

My dearest Louis,

When you read this I will have gone away. I do not know when I will be back but you must know that I am very happy, and certain about what I have to do. When I return I promise we will have some joyful times. Be a good child and bring credit to me, and your country. All will turn out for the best, I am sure. You know I love you and think of you, *Adieu, adieu. Je t'embrasse tendrement.*

'Why has Maman gone away?' said Louis.

'She feels she has to. It isn't something we should enquire into very much. Many people find themselves doing such things these days. Just pray for her safe return, and pray for Kit as well.'

'I prayed the Germans would not come, that my father would be safe. God did not hear my prayers. They came, he died.'

'Who knows, Louis? It may be that God heard. You'll find there are certain things for which there seems no answer, until later . . .' Curtis stopped. He had thought of speaking of a greater goodness emerging from the war, a unity of purpose, of hopes for a new and better world rising from the ruins of the old. Did he believe it? He thought he did, although he was aware the words seemed trite and easy. But when he looked at the child's small, serious face he was caught by those blue, clear eyes with the steady gaze that had seen so much; too much. And he heard again Kit's words: 'Louis knows the real price. He knows.' He pushed back his chair. 'All we can do is hope, my boy. Hope and wait, and do what we can to help. But, still, a little prayer from time to time would not go amiss.'

At that moment Juliette Garencières was praying too, in the simple pew of a corrugated-iron chapel, near the hangars where they kept the aeroplanes that flew by night and returned without their passengers. Outside a cold wind gusted in from the North Sea over the flat fields of Cambridgeshire. She prayed for the safety of her mission, asked God to help her do her duty, retain her faith and firmness if she fell into the hands of the Gestapo. The months of training had led to this, kneeling in a draughty, crudely fashioned house of God, experiencing no real comfort but instead a sense of isolation, of being far from home, wherever home was now, cut off from those she loved and who loved her, who knew nothing of her work, might never know. A few hours of safety were left to her, and then it would be a very different matter, existing in a world familiar and yet changed, among one's people, where everyday life might seem the same and yet, beneath the surface, altered, danger in every word, glance and act. And yet this was her place. There was a rightness to it, right for those who had trained her, and absolutely right for her, so perfectly fitting the mould of what they looked for. She felt great satisfaction. So few were chosen. If there was any fear it was that she might forget her parachute drill and affect the drop. It was her weakest point; she had been the worst of her small group at Ringway. The others had found it *drôle*, her antipathy to heights. But even if she shook a little at the aircraft door, they were not to know. By now they had all been dropped in France. She was the last.

She thought about her son. He was strong. He had come through much. She need not worry. He was in good hands, although perhaps there was a risk he might grow up an Englishman. She smiled. Would that be so bad? She remembered Kit, on that last night, wanting him to weaken and forget his foolish notions about restraint, control and waiting – waiting for a time that might not come, but quietly accepting it because it seemed to mean so much to him and, from that, had understood she meant so much to him as well.

She left the chapel and went into the hangar. Men were busy round the big Whitley with its two engines, getting it ready for the night's work. They looked at her but not in the way that men normally look at women. They looked at her as though they wanted to tell her something, as though they were concerned she should be doing this, as though they wanted to tell her not to go.

In a small partitioned office Juliette found her co-ordinator, who sat behind her desk, methodically checking lists. She looked up but did not smile. For a moment her face wore the same expression as the men's. Perhaps it was always so, as she prepared to say goodbye, aware that the young women were here because of her, and others like her, knowing their lives hung on the thinnest thread, that the odds on survival could be counted in weeks or even days. But still the work went on, behind the enemy lines, whatever the risk and cost, sabotage, attacks, intelligence, preparing for the day when France, and Europe, might be freed.

When she spoke the co-ordinator was brisk and breezy, suggesting this was a matter of routine, a mission like any other. It had to be that way.

'All set Garencières?'

'All set.'

'A slight change of plan. Troops have been reported near your original landing site. Now you will be dropped north-east of Pontoise. As before, you will be met. They'll see you on your way to Paris.'

'Very well.'

'Oh, yes, you're going to have some company. A signaller. She wasn't due to go for a few days yet but Pontoise is most suitable so they've driven her up from Thame Park. It's quite a haul from Oxfordshire so she's been taking forty winks, but she's probably awake by now. Come on, I'll introduce you.'

The controller led the way to an empty billet, empty but for a slim figure stretched out on the furthest bed. A haze of cigarette smoke hung above the woman's head.

'Good,' said the controller. 'She is awake.'

The woman sat up, turned, slipped off the bed and came towards them. She had an elegant, attractive way of walking. With a start, Juliette saw that, despite a pair of ugly and unflattering spectacles and cruelly neglected hair, she was beautiful and surely would attract attention. She knew that recruits to SOE were scarce. It was not her place to question the organisation's judgement. 'My name is Juliette Garencières,' she said. She held out her hand.

The woman took it in a gentle grasp and smiled. 'My name is Hannah Maierscheldt.'

# Nineteen

For weeks the Malta spring had been like an English summer, one of those spells when the sun is high and shadows are short, when cracks open in the ground and dogs seek out the shade, when dust stirs at the hint of breeze and sweat breaks at the slightest effort. The air was thick with moisture and carried ripe smells: bougainvillaea, jasmine, wild thyme and fennel, mixed with the scent of Aleppo pine, hot limestone and the tang of sea. Then it changed, became unseasonably cool, as refreshing as a shower of rain, although it did not rain. Instead the island was buried in a low, grey haze. And through it more Spitfires came, another fly-off, arriving throughout the morning in successive flights, while those already there fought off Me 109s hunting the unwary on approach. The first batch had taxied in, unscathed, heading for the pens. It was a smooth routine by now. Whatever the rank of pilot who flew the aircraft in, he was replaced by a Malta man. Within ten minutes the ground-crews' work was done, the engines fired up, the dozen new defenders scrambled, one section led by Kit.

He lined up for his take-off, ran quickly through the drill. Elevator one division down, rudder fully starboard, mixture rich, propeller speed control full forward, fuel cock levers on, lower tank contents checked, flaps up, radiator shutter fully open.

Another smooth routine. To right and left were Goofy Gates and Tommy Luck. He gave the sign. They began to move, opening their throttles slowly to counter the Spitfire's usual swing to port, feet balancing the rudder pedals, abreast with wing-tips thirty feet apart so that they did not suck in the take-off dust. Now Kit's left foot was pressed hard down, as his left hand applied full throttle to take-off boost, to keep that long nose straight. He glanced at Gates and Luck, still there, perfectly matching his speed. Good show, no aborts. He felt a lightness, the slightest bounce and then the earth fell away. He pushed the undercarriage selector lever forward and the Spitfire shivered as the wheels thumped home.

'Little jobs north of you at angels three.'

'Roger, Buster. Out.' Kit touched the three-position gun switch; first position Brownings, second cannon, third, all hell let loose. They were climbing fast, already at 15,000 feet, north of Salina Bay. Six mottled 109s passed below and to the left. 'Okay, Blue Section, enemy aircraft at seven o'clock below.' He took a breath. 'Line astern, chaps. Going down.'

He relished the responsiveness of this wonderful machine. It fitted him like clothes. He felt invulnerable, so nimble he could outmanoeuvre any bullet. He was on the Germans now. They were holding tight formation, unaware. He had his gun-button on position three: all hell. He opened fire, a three-second burst at 150 yards.

The leading 109 was engulfed in a storm of incendiary, tracer, ball and armour-piercing shells and bullets, a lethal combination that ripped it into blazing pieces. Kit swept underneath, then swung up and right. Behind him and to the left there was a flash of flame. A black propeller with a yellow spinner was whirling through the air, detached. The sky was a confusion of tumbling, climbing, stalling, spinning fighters.

A 109 was almost on his tail. Kit looked into the mirror fixed above the Spitfire's windscreen. Tracer was curling past his tailplane. He changed position, as easily as sidestepping someone in the street. The 109 was trying to turn inside him. Kit throttled back, lost a little height and speed to fly an even tighter radius. He flicked his gun switch to position two, to see what cannon could do alone. The Messerschmitt was opposite now, wings vertical, and moving quickly right to left. Kit levelled out, raised the Spitfire's nose and watched the cannon bursts explode the big Benz engine, then run back through the cockpit and ignite the tank of fuel behind the pilot's seat.

Two 109s destroyed in barely sixty seconds. He had never felt so much at one with an aeroplane before. It was as though it had given him wings.

Back at Takali he found the others felt the same, much laughter, swooping hands to show successful kills and only a single Spitfire lost, the pilot safe, in exchange for three confirmeds, one probable. The opening score was on the board. And still the reinforcements continued to arrive, between and during raids, as successive waves of Ju 87s, Ju 88s and 109s poured in from Sicily, trying to destroy the Spitfires on the ground, but each time met by a formidable force of fighters; machines not only faster, nimbler, harder-hitting than anything the defenders had possessed before, but growing in numbers by the hour.

Halfway through the afternoon Kit saw Ossie Wolf, fresh from battle over Grand Harbour.

'Boy, have we been having fun. Goddamned Stukas were diving on a cruiser that made the run from Gib without an escort, loaded to the gunwales with ammo, food and a whole parcel of Spit technicians. The skipper laid a smokescreen and, boy, we blew those Ju 87s to hell before they could score a single hit.'

'Laughton was caught up in a circus over Naxxar,' said Kit.

'Just a mass of kites apparently. He reckons that one time he saw twelve Hun parachutes coming down together.'

'What did I tell you?' Ossie grinned. 'I said all it would take was Spits.'

Kit looked up. Six Ju 88s were passing overhead. They heard the whistle of falling bombs. No time to reach the nearest slit trench. They threw themselves face-down as the last in a stick of six 250-kilogram *Sprengbombe* detonated eighty feet away, riddling two Spitfires parked in pens. 'Perhaps not all,' said Kit. But Ossie didn't hear. Nobody could hear for another thirty minutes.

By nightfall Brewster, who had been flying too, gathered his pilots together at Dispersal. 'Anyone good at maths? Here are some numbers that might interest you. Sixty-one Spitfires landed from the carrier this morning. Despite the Hun's best efforts, at the end of a lively day we are left with no fewer than fifty battle-ready Spits, twelve more repairable, and twenty Hurricanes. We've never been in better shape. Tomorrow we can expect high jinks. The Hun's already nursing a bloody nose. This time let's knock him flat—' He broke off. 'What are you grinning at, Gates?'

'Nothing, sir. Nothing at all.'

'Think you've caught me in a line-shoot, eh? You should know, Gates, I never line-shoot.'

A gust of laughter greeted Brewster's biggest line-shoot.

Next day the Luftwaffe did not disappoint. At dawn came the day's first scramble, to strike at reconnaissance Ju 88s with fighter cover, probing the island's defences. Then, mid-morning, something big, twenty Stukas, ten Ju 88s with heavy fighter escort making for Valletta where the fast cruiser HMS *Welshman*, its vital cargo unshipped and stored, laid another smokescreen as she prepared to sail. In Lascaris the women plotters heard it all.

'Stukas at one o'clock below.'

'Okay. Attacking now.'

'Look out, chaps. Twenty plus 109s coming down at two o'clock above.'

'I see 'em, Kit.'

'Muck in, everybody.'

'Goofy, break right, break right.'

Gates, panting: 'Okay, okay.'

'This is Red Section Leader. Permission to join the party.'

'More than welcome.'

Ossie Wolf, laconic: 'Attacking. Red Section, help yourselves.'

'Wow. Look at that. What a ruddy flamer.'

'Wrap up, Kenny. Watch that bloody 109. Behind you. Break. Break left.'

'The bastard's overshot.'

'He nearly had you there.'

'Yeah. Okay.'

And so it went on, hour by hour, as the squadron's operations phone rang and rang again. 'Scramble. Big raid building up north of Gozo. Looks like forty-plus big jobs with hefty escort at angels twenty thousand. Climb to twenty-five thousand, south-east of Grand Harbour. I'll tell you when to come in. And watch your tails. There'll be a sweep of 109s trying to pick you off before you establish contact.'

'Roger, Control. Thanks. Out.'

Soon, another raid. Five Italian Cant Z1007s, covered by fifteen Macchi 202s and Reggiane Re 2001s. Soon, another: twenty Ju 87s and fourteen Ju 88s, escorted by thirty Me 109s. Numbers of interest, except no one had time to count, until the survivors of the Luftwaffe's final raid had grumbled north, leaving a trail of wreckage strewn across the island; dead men burning in their machines, or injured and taken to the shattered hospitals they had bombed, or clinging to life and flimsy dinghies as night came down far out to sea, listening for the drone of a Dornier Do 18 rescue plane that would only appear if their position had been fixed.

At the end of this second day Brewster had more numbers. Same audience, almost. Here and there a gap or two. Good pilots gone, more injured, some not to fly again. But Brewster's face showed grim satisfaction. Over two days, he announced, the Axis had lost no fewer than sixty-three machines, two hundred men, a fully trained élite that had learned its trade on battlefronts as far apart as Spain and Russia, Poland, France, England, Crete and North Africa, but whose war had been cut short by this so-called thorn in Rommel's side.

Less than two weeks later another sixteen Spitfires landed, the pilots all experienced men, canny and aggressive, volunteers, eager to see this fighter pilot's paradise for themselves, to join the struggle to save another, smaller island, where it seemed the Battle of Britain was being refought. Many who had missed the first were determined they would not miss the last.

# Twenty

After the vivid light outside, the long, sloping tunnel leading to the underground headquarters of Fighter Control seemed almost dark. The coolness, and suggestion of damp stone, Brewster found refreshing after Takali's shadeless tracts. A sentry directed him to the briefing room where he took his place among the other senior ranks and waited for the Air Officer Commanding. A group captain leaned forward from the row behind and tapped him on the shoulder. 'Still flying, Brewster?'

'Yes. From time to time.'

'Not strictly necessary, surely. We've got an embarrassment of riches now, in terms of pilots.'

'They need to know the old man's got it in him.'

'That's not in doubt. You're a useful man, Douglas. Be a pity to lose you now. Not that it's my concern.'

'That's right.'

A door banged open. They stood up for the AOC, who waved them down. 'Information, gentlemen, for your ears only. We have reason to believe that the threat of imminent invasion has passed. The principal reasons are these. We know that the losses Kesselring has suffered have been keenly felt, coming from his *Experten* force, key personnel, almost impossible to replace. The Luftwaffe did not expect such fierce opposition. Their recent attacks have cost them dear. Yet despite this setback we understand that the good Field Marshal has advised his High Command that Malta has been neutralised, if not vanquished, and the task completed. Therefore he has agreed to the transfer of bomber and fighter groups to other fronts, Russia, North Africa and Crete, where the need is judged greater. You might think this surprising. Apparently they believe they've got us bottled up, despite getting a hiding in the air. The prisoners of Malta, that's what they call us, and they mean to starve us out, deny us supplies of every kind, send our convoys to the bottom of the sea. Well, that's where they're wrong. We have the men, we have the machines to carry the fight to them. With the other services we will break this siege and loose their hold. They may think they've got us by the throat but there's many a move left to a canny fighter. It may also be,' concluded the AOC, 'that Kesselring has made as big a blunder as Goering in 1940, when he turned his attention from our airfields to our cities. Make no mistake, there's absolutely no doubt we face stringent times, everything in short supply, food rationing tighter still, but the population of this island is standing firm and shows no sign of weakening and we'll stand with them, shoulder to shoulder. We are winning, gentlemen, and victory will be ours. That is all.'

At Takali, Brewster called his flight commanders together. 'Tough times ahead, boys. Short on everything except action.' Put that way, it was hardly news. Later he joined them for a drink and muttered something vague about the invasion probably being off, thanks to some sort of tactical balls-up by Kesselring. He didn't mention the *Gruppen* being moved, in case it wasn't true. Nor did he repeat the Field Marshal's little joke about the prisoners of Malta. After all, what had the AOC said? 'For your ears only.' Although his pilots got the message well enough.

Despite Brewster's predictions there was a brief respite, as though the Generalfeldmarschall believed the assurances he had delivered in Berlin, and thought the task complete; the thorn removed. Brewster's interpretation was more blunt: the bugger was licking his wounds. Not that the raids had ceased, but for the moment the intensity was less, and the most hard-pressed pilots had a chance to look at something other than the cockpit of a Spitfire.

Ossie Wolf was one, despatched across the island to the rest camp, where he paced the sand and hurled stones at little piles of rock and played the latest Andrews Sisters number, 'Don't Sit Under The Apple Tree', on his Hohner harmonica at all hours of day and night, with Goofy Gates on lyrics.

The duo was not popular. 'For Christ's sake, you idiots, wrap up.'

'Ah, go chase yourself.' At which point they would resume, until Ossie invited a wing commander recovering from his second dose of Malta Dog to go chase himself, and the offending instrument was confiscated.

On the morning of his second day at St Paul's Bay Ossie was told that a boy was asking for him.

It was Giorgio Farinacci. He stood in the entrance hall running his man's cap through his hands and ran forward, with a broad smile, his teeth very white, when he saw Ossie come in from the terrace. '*Bongu, Sinjur Ossie. Kif inti?*'

'I've been in livelier joints.' The boy looked baffled. Ossie grinned. 'What brings you, kid?'

'I knew you were here.'

'I knew you knew. Giorgio knows everything that goes on in this doggoned island. How are the guys in Mdina?'

'They are good. They send their love.'

'Is that right? That's touching. Is that all? Is that why you've come?'

The boy laughed. 'Claudia also send her love.'

'Uh-huh.' Ossie nodded. He licked his lips. His mouth felt dry. He kept on nodding. 'Okay,' he said, 'okay.'

'She wants to see you,' Giorgio said.

'Sure. When I get back.'

'No, no, today.'

'Well, okay, I guess.'

'Mellieha church at six. You know it?' The boy raised his arm and pointed in the direction of Mellieha Ridge, although he was indoors.

'Yeah. A guy I know has been there.'

'Good,' said the boy. 'Very good. I tell her.'

'Okay,' said Ossie.

He had seen little of Claudia Farinacci over the past few weeks. He had been told she had waited for him outside the *palazzo* in Mdina, but he had not been in Mdina. He had been with the others, sleeping under canvas near the aircraft pens, or flattened into a slit-trench as the bombs came down or scrambled in his Spitfire for a spot of night-time action. He had gotten used to not seeing her, or thought he had. He told himself it was better that way. It was going nowhere, those quiet walks, the warmth of her hand in his, the skin quite rough from the work she did, the way she looked at him and asked about America. Always the same, and always Giorgio there, playing tricks with his goddamned ball, kicking it against the walls of the drowsing houses. The look of her was something like a miracle but that was all he really knew of her, that she was cute, and made him feel good in a way that couldn't be explained. But whatever it was he might be wanting, he knew it had to be more than a goddamned look.

He remembered the time he'd gone down to the farm in the red-earthed valley near Tal-Bistra and seen old Joseph Farinacci who'd wheeled out the hospitality, sure enough, but looked at him kind of odd, the way you looked at something in a trap. That broken-nosed bastard Salvator Boero had been there, working in the yard. He'd looked at him a different way, like he was sore, had something to say, but didn't. That was the day Claudia had murmured: 'I think you are my love.' He had been confused. Was there something more behind those dreamy eyes? Was she was just saying what she or someone else had thought he'd like to hear? And all those questions about the States. Where could that be leading? And then old Farinacci, acting like he'd got a big fat *fenek* in his sights. Were they playing him for a sap? Maybe they reckoned he was Claudia's ticket out of here. Yeah, maybe that was what this was all about. What the hell else could it be, a guy like him who'd led a life? It was like in France; characters who thought all Americans were millionaires.

The raids had been building up that day, with plenty of action above the bay. Ossie had taken the twisting path to the yellow shore and swum out to the bathing platform, tugging beer bottles behind him in a canvas bag. With Goofy he lay naked, drinking Cisk lager, wanting to be up there too. But he knew they would not let him near an airplane, even if he went back early. He was one of the lucky bastards, who had to serve his time relaxing. He stood up, tasting the sea-salt on his lips, dived in and began to swim towards the island of St Paul. Something was bobbing between the gentle waves. He struck out, curious. It was a human arm.

The girl was waiting for him on the steps of the Mellieha church. Ossie thought she was on her own but then he heard a football being kicked around the big square, out of sight. In the two belfry towers the bells were sounding out across the island. He wondered why. Maybe a service, or something special. Through an archway, where the hillside fell away, he could see the bay. It looked inviting but he knew the kind of thing that floated there.

Claudia Farinacci took his hand. Before, he would have felt a pulse of pleasure. Now he just felt her hand, its roughness. It felt like an old woman's. The square was hot and they went inside the church where she covered her head with a plain silk scarf. A small priest saw his uniform. 'My son, you are most welcome. There is much of interest. Tradition says that the apostles Luke and John preached here. And then there is the famous prayer, to Our Lady of Mellieha.'

Ossie was hardly listening. 'Right.'

The priest was not discouraged. He read the prayer off the wall. 'Our Blessed Virgin Mary, our forefathers venerated you in the sacred cave . . . always put their trust in you . . . you always delivered them . . . we plead with you . . . cast upon us a merciful glance . . . cure us of all ills of soul and body.' He beamed. 'It is wonderful, is it not?' He touched Ossie's arm. 'Is it possible you know of Flight Lieutenant Curtis?'

'Sure,' said Ossie. 'He told me about this place.' He made it sound like a nightclub.

'He is . . . in good spirits?'

'He's always in good spirits,' said Ossie. 'He's English.'

'My name is Father Vincent,' said the priest. 'Remember me to him.'

'Sure, Father.' Ossie walked across the aisle as though he was on his own and sat down near a pillar, partly hidden from the congregation.

Claudia joined him, a little space away. 'You are troubled,' she said.

'No. Well, yes.' He turned his head to look at her. 'I guess it's something I don't understand. You seem to like me but I don't see very much to like.'

'I think I care for you, quite strong.'

'You think?'

'I know.'

'You're too young to know.'

A sob ran through her. 'No, not too young.' She placed her small hand on her breast. 'You are here. But don't worry. I ask for nothing. I try to understand. How often can such feelings be both ways?' She tried to smile. 'My father warned me . . .'

'Warned you?'

'He likes you very much. He thinks you have some feeling for this land, and perhaps for me. But he is right. Soon you will go away.'

Go away, thought Ossie. Yeah, for sure he'd go away, one way or another. He chewed the inside of his lip. So old Farinacci had warned her. Here was no crummy plan, no playing him for a sap. Just a regular papa concerned about his kid and offering good advice. 'Don't fall for a fighter boy.' That was really it. He heard a very different woman's voice, Rita, in her low-cut dress with Frazer Cole, poor mug. He remembered how she had stirred him, in a way that Claudia Farinacci never could.

No question, he was drawn to chicks who knew the score. It cut out all the emotional crap. Nothing expected, just the same old ritual, same old outcome, no real disappointments because they'd known it would end this way. It always did. This deal with Claudia was different. She'd reached him in a way he'd never known before, made him wish he could unwind time. With her, he did not like the man he had become. With the others, it never crossed his mind. Sitting beside her in the church he knew he had to end it now. She was too good to spoil.

Outside a siren started up. The worshippers in the church rose, crossed themselves and hurried down the aisles towards the big main doors. The little priest was standing there, unflustered, reassuring, oddly calm. To Ossie he resembled the captain of a stricken ship, seeing passengers into lifeboats. A civilian protection officer in a steel helmet was calling out instructions in Maltese. He noticed Ossie with Claudia Farinacci. 'Come on, sir, just follow the others. The shelter's down the steps.' He removed his helmet and ran a hand across his scalp. 'Routine raid, we think. For us it's become a way of life.' He walked with them out of the now empty church. Across the square many people were hurrying towards them from the town, the old supported by the young, children running, pulling at each other as though it was all a game.

'Where's Giorgio?' Claudia said.

Ossie looked around. 'He'll be in the shelter.'

They pushed their way along the tunnel cut from solid rock. Already hundreds were sheltering there, and more were forcing their way in from behind. The air was rank with the smell of sweat. A few families enjoyed more space, occupying the small chambers they had cut out from the walls, but most were in the passages, sitting on the chairs they had brought or standing, impassive, patient, waiting, faces bathed in golden light from the oil lamps suspended on the walls. The sounds of battle filtered down the air-shafts as the moaning sirens died away: aero-engines, closer, louder, very loud, now the whistle of falling bombs, the crump of detonations that shook the ground, even at this depth, the chonk-chonk-chonk of anti-aircraft guns, regular, insistent, the sudden hum of Merlin engines that prompted a buzz of animated talk, a cheer or two when the people heard the rattle of the guns.

Claudia had slipped between the close-pressed bodies. Ossie could not see above the heads but heard the protests as she forced her way to the further reaches of the cave. Soon she was back. 'He is not there. Giorgio is not there.'

'He'll be all right,' said Ossie. 'That kid's no fool.'

'Oh, he is,' said Claudia. 'Very much a fool.' She pulled away from him and started for the entrance, towards the light. He seized her arm, and was startled at how thin it was, like holding bone. And in an instant, as he thought of bone, he recalled the dream that had come to him before he went down with Malta Dog. A tunnel, much like this, stained with slime and smelling of decay, domed, quite dark, with faceless figures crowding in, just shapes, so close he could not move. Somehow he had wondered, in his fever, if the faceless ones might be men he'd killed. He had not imagined they could be simple folk sheltering from bombs. He began to sweat but not from heat, for it was cool and even cold down there. He sweated from the memory of that dream, which suddenly seemed real, like everything was falling into place, particularly a rising apprehension that something might be approaching, something he did not want to see. And still he could not move for the press of people. He turned to create a little space, some breathing room, so he and Claudia could be together, because he suddenly understood, he finally accepted, that this was how it was, that her place was with him, that he must tell her so, that somehow everything would be all right, that whatever had happened in the past was junk. And as he turned to tell her this she loosed his hold.

She moved swiftly, small and nimble, and he had to force his way between resisting bodies calling for her to stop. She looked back but did not pause, slipping past the priest who stood, arms folded, lost in thought, or prayer, near the shelter's entrance. On the steps outside Claudia was calling for her brother, her anxious voice echoing round the deserted square. An aeroplane was passing overhead, quite high.

He recognised its engine noise: a Ju 88. He ran towards the tunnel entrance but as he ran the tunnel filled with light, growing in intensity, luminous and blinding, like in the dream.

He stumbled forward, putting his arm across his eyes, frozen at what might be about to come, and something like a wave engulfed him, threw him down. The sound came moments later. It seemed too loud to hear.

The three-hundred-pounder, jettisoned by a fleeing Junkers, had fallen in the square. He found her close to the entrance of the church. The blast had stripped her and she lay stretched out on her back, slender, and white with dust. She was unmarked, except for blood at her nose and ears. He could not stand to see her body and covered her with his tunic. Somewhere close the sirens were wailing the all-clear. He heard the voices of the people of Mellieha emerging from the shelter. The little priest was quickly there. He knelt beside her, his rosary beads dangling from his fingers, mumbling the last rites.

'You're too late, Father,' Ossie said. 'She's gone.'

The priest ignored him, continuing with his Latin chant. The people were moving across the square towards the town, not looking, pushing their curious children towards their homes. Except one child who waited uncertainly by the steps, a man in a steel helmet by his side. He started forward, but the big hand of the protection officer held him back. Ossie went across.

'Is it my sister?' Giorgio said.

'Yes,' said Ossie. 'I'm sorry, kid. It is.'

'She is . . . dead?'

Ossie didn't answer, just nodded. The boy already knew.

'I was with the Pullicinos,' Giorgio said, 'in their little room. Claudia came past looking for me. I don't think she heard me call.' He was only a step away from realising he'd been the unwitting cause of his sister's death.

Ossie said quickly: 'Just one of those lousy things, Giorgio. A damned Hun dumped a bomb after the all-clear had gone.' He did not want the boy to know the truth. 'It was quick. She wouldn't have felt a thing.' He caught himself at that. She'd felt so much and now she didn't feel a thing.

'Please, you get those devils,' Giorgio said. 'Please, you make them pay.' Tears left tracks down his dust-white cheeks.

'They'll pay,' said Ossie. It was softly spoken, but he felt a hatred greater than anything that had gone before. He also felt a hatred for himself, for what he had left unsaid to her. The girl had died not knowing he had come to understand his place was with her, and hers with him. Now that man was dead too, denied the chance to unwind time. He would go forward, remembering the small figure lying in the dust outside the church, remembering Giorgio's pleas: 'You get those devils, you make them pay.'

He walked across the square and waited by the road. The first truck stopped. 'Get me to Takali airfield.' Next day he added to his score, a Stuka over Dockyard Creek. He watched it burn, the two-man crew trapped in the cockpit, writhing, before it hit the sea near Ricalosi Point.

'For you,' he said, although he knew that Claudia Farinacci would not have wanted such a thing. He wanted it, though. He wanted it very much.

# Twenty-one

The young woman in unbecoming spectacles and shabby clothes arrived in Paris from Pontoise on the first train of the day. Her only luggage was the heavy suitcase that was also a wireless-set, with which she had been parachuted into France the previous night. It was a nuisance, particularly as she did not plan to use it and, if found in her possession, was a one-way ticket to a concentration camp. Unfortunately it had been dropped separately, securely packed with other equipment, so she was denied the chance to make sure it was damaged beyond repair before the shadowy men, who used only Christian names, had emerged from the woodland to sweep her and the other female agent by fast car from the landing place on the flat ground near Montgeroult to the safe-house in Pontoise.

The men had watched over them while they slept and, in the morning, had been amused by the way the two French women had wolfed their *croissants* and drunk much good coffee after so long in England.

At last Bébé had said goodbye to Juliette Garencières, bound for another destination. Then Raoul, the leader of the group, had seen her onto the Paris train at the Gare de Pontoise where, finally alone, she planned to leave the case beneath her seat in the third-class compartment. But a Wehrmacht corporal had taken an interest in her and studied her closely throughout the journey. He tried to engage her in conversation but spoke no French so, with a laugh, gave up. But as the train pulled into the Gare du Nord he jumped to his feet and said quickly: '*Kann ich Ihnen Behilfich sein, Mademoiselle?*' He seized the case and carried it onto the platform for her, puffing and shaking his head, a little pantomime to register surprise at its weight.

She thanked him coolly, careful not to meet his eye, and he let her go reluctantly, watching as she left the concourse and emerged onto the Rue de Dunkerque. She could see no taxis free so she crossed the road into the Boulevard de Denain, pausing for a moment to light a cigarette. She glanced back towards the station but the corporal was not there. She thought of putting down the case and walking off, but the pavements were thick with people and there were many German soldiers. If she was seen to abandon it, that would be the end. In the Place de Valencienne she flagged down a Renault cab and told the driver to take her to the place de l'Hôtel de Ville, far from the address at Clignancourt, given to her by Raoul.

'Where are you from, Mademoiselle?' the driver asked, looking at her over his shoulder.

'From?' said Bébé.

'Your *valise*. I see you visit Paris. And you do not travel light.'

Bébé did not welcome such conversation. Like the others, she had been warned in training not to offer personal details, even to a seemingly innocent enquirer, tempting though it was to practise her elaborate cover.

Her papers stated that she was Marie Robuchon, an *école primaire* teacher from Amiens, aged twenty-four, parents dead, no siblings. The school term had just ended and now she was in Paris to spend the summer months studying the artists of the Renaissance at the Louvre, for a new syllabus she was preparing for her pupils. All of this she could have told the driver and diverted herself by monitoring his reaction. Instead she instructed him to watch the road. He drove quickly, wishing to be rid of this insolent *jeune putain*. With a squeal of tyres on the hot *pavé* he swept into the broad reach of the Boulevard Strasbourg, going south, towards the river.

The city looked much the same, shops busy, the tables outside the cafés filled with what seemed to be the usual early-morning trade, couples strolling head to head, absorbed, through shadows of the plane trees on the pavements; above, the green leaves picking up the light, bright against the grey walls of the buildings. Green-grey, too, on the uniforms of the Reich, *feldgrau*, as the army of occupation moved about its business or, on leave, sought suitable diversion.

At the junction with the Rue de Rivoli, opposite the Hôtel de Ville, Bébé ordered the man to stop and paid him off, but did not move until he had sped off towards Saint Chapelle, unwilling to give even an inquisitive *chauffeur de taxi* a hint of her intention. Then she walked back a hundred yards or two and turned into the sunless length of the Rue de la Verrerie. Very soon she reached the familiar *appartement* block with its cracked plaster and peeling paint. She climbed the narrow stairs to the fourth floor, the suitcase banging against the wall, reached out and tapped her special tap on the thin wood of the door. She heard, from inside, something between a gasp and a cry. A key rattled in the lock and the door swung back. Her mother stood there, a hand across her mouth, trembling with shock as she stared with wild eyes at the daughter she had thought was dead.

The elegant hands of the Countess Sofia Pulcheria Dubretskov still shook as she passed hot chocolate to her daughter. The little cup was among the few pieces of Limoges porcelain remaining from her early days in Paris, when, compelled to earn a living after fleeing the Bolsheviks, she had used the mysteries of the Tarot card to build herself a reputation with society as a guide to the occult. But the fashion had quickly passed, and now she relied on a more modest clientele, *petit bourgeois* dolts whom once she would not have honoured with a word. Ironically it was a future entirely unforeseen and a way of life that her daughter, the Countess Anna Lvovitch Dubretskov, had quit to make her own way in a city rich with possibilities for those with sufficient beauty, an open mind and quick wits.

Bébé attempted to make little of the past two years. She told her mother almost nothing. She was suitably vague about Hannah Maierscheldt's death, simply said her friend had resolved to kill herself in despair over her parents' fate. When the body was identified as hers, thanks to Hannah having borrowed her coat, which happened to contain Bébé's *carte d'identité*, she had used her papers to escape to England. An easy matter, thanks to the extraordinary resemblance between them. Naturally she was sorry to have caused her mother anguish – and here the Countess quickly assumed a suitably sorrowful expression – but what else could she have done? She made it all sound very simple, but did not say that she had retained Hannah's name and with it the Maierscheldt inheritance. Nor did she explain her return to France, other than to say she felt her place was here, that sheltering in England had been wrong, that she had been unhappy there, that, after all, she was French-born and felt a need to share the woes of France first-hand.

The Countess, who knew her daughter well, looked doubtful. 'A patriotic streak. I must confess that love of country is a trait in you that passed me by. May I assume, then, that you do not continue masquerading as a Jewess? That would be most unwise, unless you have a liking for the yellow star. So, do tell me, who are you now? I'm curious, as you cannot be yourself.'

Bébé laughed but did not add to what she had said. And there was so much more she could have told: the Curtis woman's visit to her flat in London, the moment when it seemed that everything might be lost, until she learned her tastes and saw the answer. How, nonetheless, she had been forced to move, in case the woman's stiff-necked fighter-pilot son survived and uncovered clues that might connect her with his mother's death. Clearly it had been a dangerous circle, a ring of circumstance that might lead back to Paris in 1940, any part of which might take her to the gallows. Time, she believed, could put that right but meanwhile such great risks had made her yearn for France, where she could be swallowed up once more, French among the French, until Europe saw the end of war. It was then, when telephoning her bank to give her new address, that a careless remark by an official keen to make an impression suggested just such an opportunity and led, in time, to her reporting to a flat in Orchard Court off Baker Street where men and women were being recruited for very special, unnamed work that would require them to return to France with new identities. It was laughably appropriate to her needs.

'So,' said the Countess Sofia Pulcheria, 'the ghost of my daughter has returned. How long do you propose to haunt me?'

'Today only, until a certain time. Then I will die again.'

'You look as though you have already died,' said the Countess. 'Quite like an English bag of bones, and how long have your eyes been bad?'

'I wear spectacles so I won't be seen,' said Bébé, 'not to see.'

'Good,' said the Countess. 'I don't want you seen. Old Monsieur Girault still lives above. He knows you well.'

'Yes, and I know him, the *crétin* with his prying ways.'

'That is the policeman in him. He still has contacts in the Préfecture. One must be pragmatic, daughter. Girault has his uses. He is helpful to me. But I would not care to put his loyalty to the test. The police show great enthusiasm for complying with the orders of the Boches and a young woman rising from the grave with another name, whatever that name might be, would have them at my door *tout de suite*.'

That day, while the clients of the Countess came and went, Bébé lay in the bedroom that had once been hers, looking at the familiar photographs in silver frames: her mother in fancy dress at an Arkhangelskoye ball, pearls and rubies at her throat, serene, assured, confident that this glittering world would last for ever, the world to which Bébé had been born, then denied; and her father, the man she had never known, uniformed for the Imperial Hussars, hair cropped, heavily moustached, arrogance and impatience in his eyes – as, no doubt, there had been when he confronted the mob on the steps of the Winter Palace.

Now she listened to the flick-flick of Tarot cards and murmured conversation as the Countess plied her trade. She planned to cross the river to the Gare Montparnasse when it was dark, and board the 22.30 service to Bordeaux, a suitably good-sized city lying in Vichy territory and therefore safe. And if, somehow, the situation changed, the seaport offered many possibilities.

After the last client had left, the Countess prepared a simple meal of omelette, salad and watered wine. She came out from the kitchen, lifting a finger to her lips and pointing at the ceiling. Overhead they could hear Girault, moving about his rooms. 'I must confess I had grown used to being without a daughter,' she said. 'Particularly a daughter who trails danger behind her like a cloud.'

'What possible danger could there be for you, Maman?' said Bébé. 'Soon I will again be late and unlamented and your life can continue as before.'

Two hours later, with Girault listening to his gramophone,

Bébé slipped out of the apartment, the creaking of the stairs unheard above Arletty's 'Coeur De Parisienne'. She did not risk another taxi but followed a circuitous route to the Gare Montparnasse. The Bordeaux train was almost empty. She found herself a corner seat and slept soundly through the night.

For the Countess Sofia Pulcheria the day began as usual, with Girault's knock upon her door. 'Any tasty morsels, Countess?'

The Countess pointed at a notebook by a pack of Tarot cards. 'Nothing much to interest you, I think. Madame Regnier expressed a sympathy for the Jews. Your old comrades removed a family in her street to the velodrome at Drancy. Monsieur Bouilhet suggested that perhaps de Gaulle might not be regarded as a traitor but as a misguided patriot.'

'What? Well, that is worth reporting to the Abwehr.'

'And Mademoiselle Chantpie complained about the behaviour of the occupying troops and called them Fascist louts.'

'Well, she is quite charming, Sylvie Chantpie, so she must expect attention. However, on this occasion I am inclined to let it go. But may I suggest, my dear Countess, that you counsel her to act with more restraint? She trusts you as her spiritual guide.'

'As you wish, although she is a silly goose much influenced by the Left. Not surprising, perhaps, as her father was active in the Front Populaire.'

'Really?' said Monsieur Girault. He smiled. 'But still . . .' He liked a pretty turn of ankle.

The Countess went into the kitchen and prepared a jug of coffee. When she returned Girault was no longer smiling. There was a suitcase on the Tarot table. 'What is this? Explain.'

'Explain? Really, Monsieur, I find your tone offensive.'

'No time for fine manners, Countess. This is a serious matter. How did this come to be in your possession?'

'I have never seen it before. Where did you find it?'

'Hidden in the bedroom.'

'Hidden?'

'Behind the door at least.'

'You prowl about my apartment when my back is turned . . .'

'By no means, Countess. I was merely admiring your family photographs, those you showed me once before.'

'Well,' said the Countess, 'that may be, but why your agitation?'

'This,' said Girault, opening the suitcase. 'A wireless, Countess, and not for listening to Radio France.' He closed the lid. 'Someone was here last night. I heard them. Tell me who it was.'

'A person.'

'What person? The name.'

'It was my daughter.'

'Your daughter? She is dead.'

'No, she was here. I don't know how or why, but it is the truth.'

'Where is she now, this daughter?' Girault was openly scornful.

'I don't know.' The Countess thought of trying to explain, but where to start?

'This looks very bad for you,' Girault said. 'I will do my best to help. But the Abwehr will draw their own conclusions. It will not be in my hands. It is, of course, my duty . . .'

'Oh, spare me your nonsense, please. No one can doubt my loyalty. Let me speak to someone in authority so I can tell them what I know.'

Girault snorted. 'But you know nothing, apart from your ridiculous claim to have seen a daughter who killed herself two years ago. If that is what you intend to tell them, I suggest you think again.'

Later, in the office of the Abwehr on the Boulevard Raspail, the Countess was cross-examined by an elegantly suited German with perfect French. 'You really must be more forthcoming, Countess. I am extremely reluctant to deliver you into the hands of the Gestapo, who, as you are aware, employ more robust methods of interrogation, but I urge you to be co-operative.'

'This is too vexing. I cannot tell you what I do not know.'

'Come, Countess, there is this little matter of a clandestine wireless set. Such damning evidence cannot be brushed aside.'

'I insist, my daughter must have left it.'

'Conjuring up someone we know is dead is hardly information. Please, don't mention it again. Certainly Monsieur Girault confirms you had a visitor last night. It is a simple matter. All we require is the name the woman goes by and where she might be found.'

'I have helped you all I can. My clients . . .'

'Regnier, Bouilhet and Chantpie have all been questioned.' The man offered her a cigarette. 'All deny any knowledge of the wireless set discovered in your bedroom. Their protestations have the ring of truth to those who understand these things, although we may press other charges.' Suddenly he reached across and snatched the cigarette from her mouth. 'Tell me, Countess, does the phrase "safe-house" have any meaning for you?'

'No.'

'Today we raided two, one in Pontoise, another here at Clignancourt. A decent bag, I'm pleased to say, including a female agent newly arrived from England. But there was a second, a young woman, expected at the Clignancourt address. She did not arrive. This abandoned wireless set suggests she came to you. And left it as a memento of her visit, perhaps in panic, knowing we were on her trail.' The Abwehr man tore the cigarette in two and dropped the pieces in a wastebin. 'Give up this pretence. Make life easier on yourself. Yours is a safe-house also, is it not?'

He put his hand under her chin and raised her head. 'Countess, we are not naïve. We understand the game of double-agents. Such methods led us to the Pontoise cell. But now you are found out. Certainly I compliment you on your cover. For a time it convinced us all. But everything is over and you must tell us what you know. Otherwise things will go very badly for you, I'm afraid.'

Earlier that morning, as the Paris train had pulled into the Gare Bordeaux St Jean, Bébé had been shaken gently by an attentive guard. She stretched and yawned, removed her spectacles and shook out her hair. It was a relief to travel light again, without the detestable suitcase that was as lethal to its carrier as any bomb. She imagined her mother finding it, opening the lid. She laughed at the idea. But Maman was resourceful and quick-witted, a family trait. She knew she would find a way to make it disappear, no doubt with a few ripe Russian curses for her daughter who, as she had said, trailed danger behind her like a cloud.

Bébé descended from the carriage and left the station, bathed in golden light and breathing in the pleasantly breezy air of the Atlantic coast.

# Twenty-two

It was no good going into battle wearing shorts and a short-sleeved shirt. No man fancied being caught in fire, dressed for a summer's day. So pilots at advance readiness sweated in their cockpits in khaki battledress tunics, trousers, boots, helmets and Mae Wests, mouths dry and sticky, stomachs heaving, already weakened by dehydration and Malta Dog. It was no better for the ground-crews, pinned beneath an unwinking August sun on the crucible of Takali, where the metal of an aircraft wing was hot enough to burn the flesh.

In Mdina Kit had found an old umbrella and this he balanced on the canopy of his Spitfire as he waited for the signal to take off. Bathed in blue-black shade, he reread the letter from Juliette Garencières, forwarded by Farve, still in its small cream envelope with a London postmark. She sounded happy, and he believed he knew what work she might be about to do. There were rumours of such things, and some said women's lives should not be held so cheap for such a small return; that those recruited were young and green, impressionable and keen to please, with little understanding of what it meant to join an unequal struggle against the Boches, from inside a beaten France. Not Juliette, Kit thought. She knew the dangers, and accepted them, just as he did in the air. This was a quality they shared, a willingness to serve. Her note was brief:

*Mon chéri,*

I feel very close to you, but very far. You are always in my thoughts. Soon I will be starting a new phase of my life. I am very happy, but a little afraid. I take strength from knowing that you are strong. I do not know when I will be able to write another letter. It is always possible, I suppose, that this may be the last. If so, believe I love you. Also that I derive great comfort from the knowledge that Louis is safe and that his future is secure. Without that I could not do what I feel I am bound to do. In spite of all, I dream of how one day we might be together. It is wonderful, and sustains me,

*Je t'embrasse,*

Juliette

Holding the letter lightly in his hands Kit felt, for an instant, as though he touched her spirit. Somehow he was convinced that at that moment she, too, was safe, that it was beyond reason she should come to harm. He trusted his instincts. He breathed more easily, reassured.

Yet a world away, at an address on the rue de Saussaies in St Germain, innocuous from the street, already Juliette was alone. She lay on wooden planks above a bathtub full of ice. The cell was lit by a single ceiling lamp. A high, barred, open window admitted disturbing noises from the inner courtyard. On the wall, to which her wrists were manacled, she read scratched words: 'Marcel, arrived 2 June 1942', 'Don't talk', and 'Frankreich über Alles.' At that she smiled a little, and took a shred of comfort. She hoped she possessed such spirit. She wondered if the members of the captured Pontoise group were also here. She did not know that all but the man named Raoul were similarly chained . . .

Three days before, Kit had learned that soon he would be leaving Malta, not to lead a fly-off but for good. Brewster had called him to his office in the complex tunnelled beneath the Takali runways. 'Time to make room for new chaps, Kit. You've had far more than your fair share of fun. Expect your posting any time.'

'Honestly, sir, I'd prefer to stay.'

'Now why did I know you'd say that? Permission denied.'

'The squadron needs experienced hands . . .'

'It's got 'em, dozens of types as keen as you, fresh from England and better fed, full of vim and vigour and armed with nice new Spits. We've turned the corner, boy, I'm sure of that. The Hun may have raised his game but the odds have changed. He had his chance to put us on our knees three months ago, and missed it. We got our Spits in and the men to fly them, as we've shown the buggers to their cost. However, they still reckon they've got us beat, even if we're managing to kick their arses in the air. If they can stop our convoys getting through it's game, set, match. They've got a point. No fuel, no ammunition, no spares, no food. Nothing in the air, or on the sea. No Malta. Except . . .'

'Except?'

'The biggest convoy we've seen so far has just put out from Gib. Fourteen merchantmen protected by nearly sixty warships, including three carriers to give 'em air cover. Quite a party, and one we plan to join, as soon as they get close enough. A suitable finale for your tour of duty.'

Brewster jabbed his pipe-stem at his calendar. 'They're due

here at the latest five days from now, on the fifteenth of August.'

'The Feast of the Assumption,' said Kit. 'A priest told me it's the island's annual *festa*. Celebrates the Virgin Mary's passage into Heaven.'

'Well,' said Brewster, 'if the matelots can make it we'll have more to celebrate than a high-altitude flight by a virgin.'

Then the squadron heard that, on the second day at sea, cruising at thirteen knots with four hundred miles to cover, the convoy had lost the carrier HMS *Eagle*, struck by four torpedoes from a German submarine. In just eight minutes it had sunk. It seemed beyond belief, a vessel of nearly 30,000 tons to vanish in such a space of time. In calm and perfect weather, but perfect, too, for U-boats, nearly a thousand men were rescued, but a hundred and sixty died. And now the fleet was in range of Axis aircraft from Tunis, Sicily and Sardinia. The raids began, intense and lethal, the desperate actions seen only as markers on the plotters' table in Operations at Lascaris, where they tracked the convoy's course. Two days after setting out *Eagle* was followed to the depths by three merchantmen, a cruiser and eight destroyers. The markers were quietly removed as the force diminished.

But now at last Kit, sweating in his cockpit, heard the voice of Buster Brown: 'Get off right away, Blue Section, and make angels twenty-four on vector three-zero-zero.' Finally the convoy was within their reach. A thumbs-up to the ground-crew. A stab at the starter button. As the propeller began to turn, Juliette's letter was snatched away, turning and twisting in the air. Kit forced himself to take his time. He ran the engine slowly for thirty seconds, then warmed up to fast tick-over. Ahead was a long, straight route over open sea, little more than seventy miles, but the Merlin had to be on song. He completed the usual checks – temperatures, pressures and controls, cockpit hood locked open – then raised and dropped his hand.

They took off line abreast, Kit, Rimmer and Tommy Luck, and quickly gained their height, easing back to cruise at 150 m.p.h. to conserve their fuel. The Spitfires seemed suspended, blue above and blue below, their markings vivid in the sun.

Soon, on the horizon, the sky grew dirty black. Dense columns of oil smoke were rising, tree-like, from the sea, moving, growing and, at each base, outbursts of red and orange and a broader spread of white where debris from explosions churned the sea to foam. They could hear the sounds of war now, even above the thunder of their engines. Closer to, the convoy was revealed, toy ships on a flat and unconvincing sea, each stern trailing a thin white wake, straight for the dogged merchantmen but wildly eccentric twists and turns for the cruisers and destroyers. Some vessels were marked with broad white spreading patterns, opening up like flowers, as their hulls were straddled by sticks of bombs from Stukas. In the space between the ships the air was alive with little puffs of flak, and in places the surface of the waves was suddenly churned up, as though a giant child had thrown down a handful of monstrous pebbles.

Aircraft were being hit, some turning away and losing height, or spiralling down in flames. A cargo-ship, of perhaps seven thousand tons, exploded at the stern, and broke in two, its bow continuing to drive ahead and push below the surface. Fuel stacked on deck in four-gallon cans ignited and the sea became a wall of fire, spreading towards the tiny figures struggling in the water.

Kit picked out half a dozen Italian Savoia-Marchetti SM.79s, line astern, embarking on a bombing run. He went in first, coming in fast on the port beam of the leader, just below the dorsal gunner's eyeline. He closed to within two hundred yards and opened fire. The Spitfire shuddered from the recoil of the cannon. Its shells ripped through the wing-root of the target, where the fuel tank lay, and upwards into the cockpit where the crew was grouped. In that instant the mottled green-black Savoia was transformed from sturdy, pig-nosed monoplane of light alloy, steel and wood into a falling shower of fragments. The second Savoia banked violently away, its starboard engine feathered, and jettisoned its bombs. The others did the same.

Ray Rimmer shouted: 'They've had enough, the lily-livered sods.'

'Not yet,' said Kit. He gave the Savoia with the feathered engine two five-second bursts. Its wheels came down and it started a gentle dive towards the sea. Kit's thumb moved on the gun-button but faltered as parachutes appeared, first one, then two, then three. The bomber was still responding to the controls. The pilot was trying to put it down. Kit imagined him in his seat, juggling the throttles, scrubbing off the speed but wary of the stall, waiting for the moment when he pulled the stick hard back and let her drop the last few feet. The surface of the sea was smooth, his chances appeared good. Kit banked away, content to let him trust to luck. Except the Italian had forgotten his wheels were down. They touched, dug in and the Savoia scattered itself in pieces across a quarter-mile of placid swell. The others, light and quick without their bomb-loads, fled but Rimmer and Tommy Luck shared a third destroyed before they broke away.

The convoy had progressed a mile or two. Kit thought Brewster's numbers must be wrong. He had described a force of more than seventy ships. This numbered barely fifty. And dead-stopped in the water lay the single broken tanker, the *Ohio*, blackened, pierced with holes and, on its decks, the remains of aircraft, one a skeletal Stuka. Three destroyers circled but it seemed they faced a hopeless task. And, anyway, what plan could they have in mind? Already the tanker's central deck was virtually awash. Yet men were still on board, and guns in action, amidships and astern. They fought for what they carried in the holds, Kit knew:

10,000 tons of fuel oil and kerosene. A bomb exploded close by the bow, loosed by a diving Ju 88. As it levelled out, a Sea Hurricane attacked it from head-on. The Junkers dipped to avoid its fire and plunged into the sea. The fighter banked towards the carrier *Victorious*, its floating base. The small force of seaborne Hurricanes did not have the Spitfire's speed or punch, but so far they had been the convoy's only protection in the air, until it neared its destination and came within the reach of Malta squadrons.

Low on fuel and ammunition the Spitfires turned for home. Behind them the running battle raged. Another section passed them, heading for the convoy, led by Ossie Wolf. He gave no sign of recognition as they flashed past, intent on what lay ahead. Kit was not surprised. It had always been Wolf's purpose to kill more Hun. But now he was driven by a depth of loathing that consumed him, an obsession that seemed to occupy his every waking thought. The others kept away, impatient with his sullen moods, even the mild and tolerant Goofy Gates.

That night, as he tried to sleep, Kit saw again the stricken tanker with its vital cargo, not moving, effectively defenceless, a floating bomb. He did not imagine the *Ohio* could survive. And without that fuel the greater battle might be lost.

He read again the letter from Juliette Garencières. It had been rescued by his fitter, creased and grimed with dirt, no longer fresh. It looked as though it had been written a very long time ago. Written by someone he had once known, and greatly cared for, but whose image, previously so sharp, was suddenly indistinct, as though she was now in some other place where she could not be reached.

# Twenty-three

It was a while after Claudia Farinacci died that Ossie had taken a pool bicycle to go to Tal-Bistra. But the narrow lanes had been so badly potholed that he threw it down and walked. The sun was fierce on his back and he turned up his collar to stop his neck burning. The air was full of insects that rose from the verges as he passed. He heard the farm dogs barking half a mile away. He did not want to see the farm again, to enter Claudia's world, all that she had really known. It seemed impossible that she was dead. As he drew closer he half expected to see her suddenly appear, and run towards him. He had tried to write a note to Farinacci but had been unable to find the words. He guessed he would be hated, turning up like this. He wanted that. He wanted their hatred to match his own.

The dogs went crazy when he pushed open the sagging gate and walked into the yard. They charged against their chains, teeth bared. A small bird fluttered in a cage by the farmhouse door, singing an aimless melody. A bunch of chickens pecked the dirt and, against a square-blocked wall overhung with a great outcrop of cactus and bamboo, a few thin rabbits hopped about a wooden hutch. This was the life Claudia had been born to.

Farinacci's wife came out, wiping her hands on a piece of cloth.

She was like her daughter, but thicker-set in the Maltese way; still handsome, though, with wide-set eyes that hardened when she saw him. She was wearing a shapeless cotton shift, buttoned down the front, and her feet were bare. He had rarely heard her speak. Instead she had murmured greetings and listened to their talk, watchful, shy. But now she did not smile a welcome like before. She turned and went back indoors. He heard her voice, urgent, shrill, calling across the pasture that lay beyond the house, and Farinacci's answering shout. Across the lane, on the far side of a field of sun-browned grass that rose towards a rocky outcrop, a herd of goats was gathered in the shade of carob trees, munching at the dark green leaves and newly ripened pods. Nearby Salvator Boero leaned against a pale trunk, his shotgun slung across his shoulder.

Farinacci came across the yard. 'Yes, my friend?'

'I had to come.'

'For yourself, perhaps. For us there is nothing to be said.'

'I went to Mosta, for the funeral. It was well done.'

'I saw you there.'

'I cared for her, Farinacci.'

'Who would not?'

'Except for me she'd still be here.'

Farinacci shook his head. 'I sent her to Mellieha, to break with you. The same thing can be said. Except for me she'd still be here. It is God's will. It was her time. Nobody can be blamed. But her mother takes it hard. You must understand, she does not want to see you here. It is better that you go.'

'You sent Claudia to break with me?'

'Of course. She cared too much. But she was a child. You showed her another world. It confused her, made her dream. You see how we live. There was no place for her with a man like you. I let it go too far. Who would think a simple promenade could lead to such a thing? But she saw the sense of what I said. She was a dutiful daughter. And there were certain expectations.' Farinacci glanced across to the distant Salvator Boero. 'They grew up together. His father farms five miles away. Like goes with like, we Maltese say. It is the natural way of things.'

So that had been Claudia's future, mapped out by a peasant mind, like with like, the natural way, settling for this stinking patch of scrub and dirt and toil, and that bastard Boero, Claudia's body fattening in a cotton shift, ravaged by bearing Boero's kids, walking barefoot in the yard, tending the livestock with those small, rough hands and waiting for her old man to come in from the fields, heavy with the smell of goat.

Ossie did not tell Farinacci about the moment in the Mellieha shelter when he had finally understood his feelings for the girl, had felt that somehow everything might work out and be all right; that maybe he could unwind time at that, and be the guy Claudia thought he was, the guy he used to be. That maybe there was a way he could show her that this other world she dreamed of was no dream, but real, four thousand miles away, only a few days' journey to the west. To hell with 'like with like'. Except now she would never know. She had loosed his hold and he had lost her as she pushed out into that sun-white square.

Ossie left the farm, walking slowly, the valley echoing to the baying of the dogs. Standing in the shadow of the carob grove, Salvator Boero watched his every step. Ossie did not see him, thinking of something else unsaid, that day in the Mellieha church. Claudia had not told him she was going to break with him. 'I care for you, quite strong.' Had she been the dutiful daughter Farinacci thought? Or would she, hearing what Ossie had had to say, have known that what seemed impossible was not?

Next day, with Gates and Spencer, he had banked above Takali and headed out to what the locals were calling *Il-Konvoj ta'*

*Santa Marija*. By now the ships were close, and they knew how much depended on the cargoes. The last date by which the survivors could be expected was thought propitious. The Feast of the Assumption, 15 August. Was not the Virgin Mary the island's patron saint? God was with the operation. It could not, must not fail. Only pray, and Malta would be delivered.

Ossie gave no thought to prayer, but wished to encounter many Hun. Once, playing as a kid on a swampy patch of ground behind a derelict lumber mill, on the confluence of the Mississippi and Missouri, he had come across a timber rattlesnake, its jaws wide open, swallowing a young woodchuck whole, its coils sliding round the rodent's struggling body. His friends had fled but he found a rusty spade, and killed it. He freed the woodchuck from the severed head but it died quickly, injected with the rattler's venom. He had been filled with horror, and detestation of the thing, fury that he had been too late. Now it was the same. Cold hate. He reckoned he might be going mad. He guessed it looked that way to his comrades too. He could not bring himself to talk, in the usual way, or meet their eyes. He felt disturbed by the lust within him. The need to kill seemed almost a perversion, yet one he relished, consumed by the thought of wielding death. Alone he tried to reason with himself, stand back and see things clearly, but each time he saw Claudia Farinacci, stripped by the blast and stretched out on her back, slender, white with dust, unmarked, except for the crimson trickles from her nose and ears. Again, too late to save. But now, no mercy. That way he could stop the poison spreading.

Forty miles out to sea Goofy Gates said over his R/T: 'Spits approaching at ten o'clock, Red Leader.'

'Okay, Red Two.' Ossie had seen them thirty seconds sooner.

'Looks like Kit Curtis's little gang.'

'R/T silence, Goofs.'

They passed the other flight within a quarter-mile and Ossie thought of waggling his wings in recognition. It was the form, a brotherly gesture, but he felt fixed to the controls, part of the machine, and made no sign of seeing them. He wanted no distractions, glaring through his goggles at the darkening horizon where a predator's jaws were poised to swallow a convoy whole.

With battle joined, Red Section shot to pieces thirteen men, saw three more drown or drift into burning sea; two Cants, a Heinkel 111, a Stuka and a Messerschmitt 109. The Stuka and the Me 109 were Ossie Wolf's. He took his time. He out-flew each pilot and did not open fire at once but fixed himself on their tails, watching as they threw themselves about the sky, looking back to see if they had lost him but always seeing he was there. He knew that they began to hope that this ***verdammter schweinehund Englander*** was out of ammunition and playing games. He was, but not that sort of game. He took particular pleasure in watching his cannon chew apart the 109. The guy had reckoned himself a hot-shot. Ossie could tell by the way he handled his machine. He knew a thing or two, but not enough. As the canopy of the German's 'chute took fire Ossie murmured, but only for himself: '*Leck mich am Arsch.*' An obscenity for a dying man was an affront to every decent feeling. Ossie was aware that he had reached a new depth, or height. That there was no going back from this.

Below, a cruiser was sinking by the bow, with other vessels standing by to pick up the survivors, hundreds of bobbing heads lifting with the chop that had increased a little with a lively southerly breeze. Further out a merchantman exploded, struck by two torpedoes.

And yet the tanker *Ohio* was still afloat, and even under way, supported and driven forward mile by mile by two destroyers lashed alongside, with a big mine-sweeper made fast to the bow, its tow-line providing steerage. Ossie took a long, last look as she crept across the silver sea, the sky reddening in the west, the sun low on the horizon, turning the wispy clouds and vapour trails a pretty pink. Out of ammunition, Red Section turned away as a single Stuka howled down from 17,000 feet and released a thousand-pounder. It missed by a hundred yards but raised the hull from the water with its concussion. As the plume of spray blew clear the *Ohio* could still be seen, pushing slowly forward.

When Ossie landed, and jumped down from the wing, Kit Curtis caught him by the arm and told him that, from dawn next day, patrols of sixteen Spitfires would give the remnants of the convoy constant cover on the last stage of its passage. 'Poor devils,' said Kit. 'They've gone through hell. Christ, something like twenty boats have gone to the bottom. But if we can get our fingers out the rest are going to make it, including that ruddy tanker.'

'The spade is poised,' said Ossie. He could see that Curtis thought he was crazy as a loon.

# Twenty-four

Two days before the Feast of the Assumption the first few ships of the convoy had begun to reach Grand Harbour, moving slowly, their crews on deck, watched by the people of Valletta from the upper and lower terraces of the Barracas Gardens overlooking the ancient port. The Vallettans waved, and many cheered but they were solemn too, and thoughtful, confronted by the price the merchantmen had paid to resupply their island. The superstructures of the vessels were burned black, the bridges gutted, ironwork pierced by shrapnel, masts felled, funnels riddled, and around the gun positions thousands of empty shell-cases told of desperate battles. They struggled in, with failing engines, damaged steering and water in their holds. SS *Rochester Castle* came first, nearly forty feet below her water-line, with fuel and ammunition, mechanical spares and medical supplies. Then *Port Chalmers*, similarly laden. Then *Melbourne Star* with 1,300 tons of high-octane spirit, 700 tons of kerosene and 1,400 tons of high-explosive shells, this stowed in a ship where fires had raged.

But as the day of the *festa di Santa Maria* dawned, the *Ohio*, already hit six times, was still ten miles out to sea. Lashed to the destroyers *Penn* and *Bramham* she crawled towards the harbour at barely walking pace, guarded by patrols of Spitfires. And those who waited on the terraces of the Barracas understood that, without the tons of fuel the tanker carried, these fighters that Kesselring had let slip through might not be flying long.

Kit Curtis knew it was bizarre to savour such a time, to try to store each detail, each emotion of what promised to be his last big show in fighter pilot's paradise. Because for the pilot in him it had been a paradise, of a sort, with every skill and nerve tested to the limit, and beyond. But now he had shed his cold detachment – assumed, he guessed, to stop himself caring, being touched. It had been so ingrained he had believed it. But finally he felt he had come through, if not intact in body, whole in mind, aware. This war was concerned with more than killing and blunting the emotions so you could take a life without remorse. Mixed with the horror and the waste, the hollow beating of the patriot's drum, there was great goodness and nobility too.

He remembered the Italian pilot who had looked like Nuvolari and had chosen not to kill him, the *kappillan* who trusted Our Lady of Mellieha to cast upon the people her merciful glance, the Regia Nautica crewman who had pulled him on board the *motobarca armata* he had destroyed, the nurses in the burns wards who witnessed despair and pain, saw sights no person should ever see, and gave no sign of revulsion, but of love; and Juliette Garencières, anonymous, in daily peril under the enemy's nose, part of a secret army that disregarded odds, preparing for the time of liberation.

But still, this did not stop him wondering at each take-off if this would be his final patrol. The man in him wanted it to end: he did not want to die now, having come so far. The pilot in him wanted it to last for ever. Now, his was one of four flights circling the *Ohio*, a band of eagles, vigilant and poised to strike. At first it seemed the Axis might have made its final move in this protracted game of cat-and-mouse, in which the cat had found the mouse's teeth too sharp. Until the R/T crackled: 'Hello,

Mother Hen. Something building up over Sicily and moving south. A few big jobs with escort, at angels seventeen.'

'Okay, Buster,' said Brewster. His tone was joyful. He had not been prepared to miss this chance, airily asserting: 'I'm ungrounded. This operation calls for strategic nous.' And, much to Ossie Wolf's disgust, he had assumed command of Red Flight. Now he laid his plan. 'Red Section will engage. Blue Section cover us as we go in.'

'Roger, Red Leader,' said Kit.

'Due east of Gozo, Mother Hen,' reported Buster. 'Vector three-two-zero.'

'Okay, Control. On our way.'

The two flights climbed to 20,000 feet. Then Kenny Laughton shouted: 'Red Leader, bogeys at three o'clock, going across us and below.'

'Good show, Red Three. Right chaps. Tally-ho.'

Kit watched as Brewster's section dropped towards two dark-green Ju 88s shadowed by half a dozen Messerschmitt 109s. The Spitfires came out of the rising sun, with cannons spitting orange flame, and immediately one bomber rolled away, its port engine burning. Men tumbled from the forward hatch and spiralled down, their parachutes swept by a south-easterly wind towards Comino, the tiny island that lay a mile or so from Malta's northern shore. Bombs began to fall from the second Junkers, exploding in the sea.

'Now there's a pretty sight,' said Brewster.

Then Kit, urgent: 'Red Leader, 109s on top of you.'

Brewster, cool: 'Okay, Blue Leader. Breaking right. Come and join the party.'

'Blue Section, going down,' said Kit. He half rolled and dived, his windscreen full of big black crosses, firing several bursts at the nearest 109 but without enough deflection. He almost rammed it, passing close enough to see a fanciful decoration of a stinging bee painted on the nose. 'Christ,' he said aloud. Bullets were coming past him from the right. Something hit the armour-plating behind his seat with a shattering clang, like a blacksmith striking an anvil. Even now, yes, even now he could get the chop. He pulled back on the stick and applied hard rudder, flicking his machine into a spin from 13,000 feet.

'The bastard almost had you.' That was Ossie Wolf.

'Okay, I'm organised,' said Kit.

Then Goofy Gates: 'Shit, I'm hit.'

Kit looked up. Above and to the right a Spitfire was on its back and dropping into a vertical dive, the engine pouring smoke but no flames yet, streams of oil and glycol darkening the aircraft's pale blue belly. As the dive grew steeper, he knew, the engine would ignite and fire would lick along the nose to reach the fuel tank below the windscreen. That's where he reckoned R. J. Mitchell had got it wrong. Messerschmitt had placed his fighter's tank of fuel behind the pilot. The cockpit of a burning Spit diving at 450 m.p.h., with the fuel tank in the nose, was no place to be.

Ossie Wolf was yelling: 'Get outa there, feller. Now!'

Somehow Gates was trapped. 'Jesus Christ, the bloody thing won't—' Then suddenly he was clear, tumbling through the air, legs pulled up, arms clutched around his knees. He waited, canny, allowing the rate of his descent to slow, giving gravity a chance. At first he had been travelling at the same speed as his aircraft. To pull the ripcord then meant dislocated bones and ruptures. At little more than 100 m.p.h., the natural speed, you hardly felt a thing. Gates judged his moment well, was hardly jerked as he tugged the cord and the canopy filled and spread. Kit, circling, could see him checking his position, trying to drift inland. He stood a chance of coming down near Ahrax Point, not far from Mellieha. He waved. Kit saw he had lost a flying boot. The sky seemed clear. The wreckage of the Junkers was burning on the waterline near Ghajin Hadid. The second had disappeared across the South Comino Channel, leaving a trail of dense black smoke to mark its course, showing it was rapidly losing height. The 109s had broken away, their charges lost.

'Good bounce,' said Brewster. 'What news of Gates?'

'Okay, I guess,' said Ossie.

'Good show,' barked Brewster. 'Back on duty, boys.' He put his machine into a shallow dive, opened his throttle, pulled up into a tight loop and rolled neatly off the top.

'Red Leader, I'll see old Goofy down,' said Ossie Wolf.

'Okay, Red Two.' The others began to formate for the short flight back, keen to put on a little show of airmanship for the men of the Grey Funnel Line, despite the heat of battle. They had to show their mettle too.

The Messerschmitt came down from 20,000 feet. It loosed a burst at Wolf's machine and missed, a gesture of defiance and frustration, then screwed round in a vertical turn over St Paul's Island. Ahead, across Mellieha Bay, Gates's parachute was two hundred feet above the cliffs of Dahlet ix-Xilep. By impulse or design the German snapped off a burst as he closed at 380 m.p.h. The cannon shells ripped through the canopy, and it collapsed in shreds. For a moment Gates seemed to hang, suspended. Then he fell and struck the big rocks below the cliffs, his body moving as the waves came in.

Ossie Wolf was screaming into his R/T. Nobody could make out a word. Kit turned in his seat in time to see him moving fast over Mellieha Bay, but not fast enough to overhaul the 109 a mile or two ahead, outlined against the terraces of the Gozo *mesas.* Kit broke formation without thinking or considering.

'Where the hell are you, Blue Leader?' Brewster barked.

'Bogey north of us, Red Two chasing,' said Kit. 'Lending a hand.' Gates's 'chute was nowhere to be seen and, somehow, he sensed a connection with Ossie's wild pursuit.

'Red Two,' he called over the R/T. 'Red Two. Break off, break off.'

'Sonofabitch,' said Ossie. 'Lousy goddamned bastard sonofabitch. He took out Goofy. The stinking goddamned bastard.' But he throttled back a little, and within minutes Kit was on his wing-tip.

'The sonofabitch shot Goofy's brolly all to hell.'

'All right,' said Kit. 'All right. There's nothing you can do.'

They were passing over Regga Point, on Gozo's northern coast. The Messerschmitt had disappeared. Sicily looked very close.

'Head for the *Ohio*, Red Two,' said Kit. 'That's why we're here.'

No reply, for a long, long time. The American's canopy was open and he looked across at Kit. He had left his R/T on. His breath was rasping in his mask. But then, at last, he nodded and began a gentle bank to port.

A mile from Mgarr Harbour, where ferries left for Malta, they saw the dinghy. Three men waved, then stopped as they realised they were Spitfires.

'Those bastards from the Ju 88,' said Ossie.

'Lucky. They'll be picked up from there for certain.'

Ossie said nothing. Instead he pushed forward on the stick, dropped down to three hundred feet, then turned with Mgarr harbour on his right, picturesque and colourful with its bobbing *luzzu* fleet, and came in rather slow, to make sure he did not miss. His cannon shells raised little spurts of water, in two neat lines, as they rushed towards the dinghy. It vanished in a cloud of spray and blood. 'Not such lucky bastards,' he said.

# Twenty-five

It was already hot at eight a.m on the morning of the Feast of the Assumption. The sky was silvery blue, and very bright, glinting on the water between St Elmo and Ricalosi Points, where the sea grew flat and calm, as though a line had been drawn across, ruffled only by a scudding breeze. And yard by yard *Ohio*, yoked between its two destroyers, crept through the gateway to Grand Harbour.

On the Barracas the crowds were thousands deep, a brilliantly coloured cloud of waving flags and hats, and somewhere bands were playing, giving the scene a garden party air, 'Heart of Oak', 'Rule Britannia', 'God Save The King' and, from time to time, 'The Star Spangled Banner', to show that the men who had built *Ohio* in their Pennsylvania yard, and whose skill had endured the severest trial, had not been forgotten.

There had been music on *Ohio* too. Someone had found a scratched Glenn Miller number, 'Chattanooga Choo Choo', and relayed it over the Tannoy as the vessel inched its way towards its berth. Finally, at the dockside in shallow water and no longer supported by *Bramham* and *Penn*, the SS *Ohio* was allowed to settle on the bottom so she would not break up while her cargo was unloaded. She would never sail again. Nor would nine of the fourteen merchantmen that had set off from Gibraltar five days before, or four of the Royal Navy escort. But all but 30,000 tons of 85,000 tons shipped had been delivered. And so had Malta.

At Takali the mood was different. Kit brought in his Spitfire for a bad, hurried landing and half ran across to where Ossie Wolf's machine was being pushed back into its blast pen. The American was already out of his cockpit and giving instructions to Corporal Chalmers. It looked like calm routine, no sign of anything unusual. Ossie glanced up casually. Kit said: 'All right, Corporal, make yourself scarce.'

Chalmers looked at Ossie, who shrugged and nodded. 'Remember, Chuffy, I want you to check the trailing edges on all the fin and tailplane surfaces. The bitch is snatching in tight turns.'

Kit waited until Chalmers was out of earshot. Then: 'You bastard. You murdering bastard.'

'Oh, go to hell.' Ossie turned away.

Kit caught him by the arm. 'I'm going to have you grounded, you bloody butcher. Spy's going to get the whole damned story.'

Ossie pulled free. 'For Jesus' sake, you know what they did to Goofy. What the hell's the problem?' He was shaking his head from side to side, as though mystified by Kit's reaction. And he was almost smiling. 'You want to teach me how to fight this fucking war?'

'Those poor devils didn't have a chance.'

'Did Goofy? Wise up, brother. If that's how they want to play the game, well, that's fine with me.'

'You just don't do that sort of thing.'

'Oh, yeah? Says who? In my book that's three less lousy sons-of-bitches. What is it with you? You want those guys to get back in a goddamned Junkers to take up where they left off? The hell with that. We've got to rub out these bastards any way we can.'

'Not that way.' Kit was quieter now. 'Not that way.'

'I hear you're shipping out of here,' said Ossie. 'It's just as well.'

'What the hell's that meant to mean?'

'Maybe you haven't got the stomach for it any more. Maybe it's time that guys like you tore up your goddamned rules. This isn't fucking cricket.'

'Tell Brewster,' said Kit. 'He'll be most interested in what you've got to say.'

'So you're going to run to Brewster, huh? That figures.'

'Give me a reason not to. All right. I feel as badly about what happened to Goofy as you do but—'

'Go fuck yourself.' Ossie turned his back. 'Hey, Chuffy, haul your ass over here. You got work to do.'

When Spy Threlfall cycled over with his notebook he found Kit sitting alone in the shade of his aircraft's wing. He had stripped off his shirt and Threlfall saw the livid scars that stretched across his back. He had not realised the man had been so badly burned. He had done well to return to fighter ops. He noticed some of the grafts were weeping, but said nothing. It was not a pilot's way to risk being grounded. The same grim purpose had put Kit back at the controls. Anyway, he knew his posting had come through, that soon he would be back in England where something would be done.

He leaned his bicycle against the sandbags of the pen. 'A decent show I gather.'

'Not too bad. At least the tanker made it.'

'Bad luck about Goofy Gates.'

'Yes, rotten.'

'Damned Jerry shot him up.'

'I didn't see it. That's what they say.'

'They're filthy swine, but what can you expect? Thank God

we don't behave like that.' He transcribed Kit's bald account, then paused, head on one side, quizzical. 'Incidentally, some Malties farming on Marfa Ridge reported a dust-up of some sort near Mgarr harbour.'

'Dust-up?'

'It's all a bit vague. You and Wolf were up that way. Spot anything at all?'

Kit hesitated, then shook his head. 'Just an Me 109 with its tail between its legs.'

That evening Brewster organised some transport to Valletta for the pilots who had flown the *Ohio* patrol. As it pulled away a thin peasant with a broken nose jumped onto the running board, to hitch a lift, and Brewster passed him a cigarette. In the back the truck was full: Ray Rimmer, Kenny Laughton, the Tom-Toms Luck and Spencer, considered veterans now, and new men, their grinning faces red not brown, whose names were not familiar. Wedged in a corner, Ossie Wolf would not have been surprised to see others on the benches, moving to the motion of the Bedford: Drongo Palmer, Max Astley-Cobb, Vey Geary, Pop Penrose, Brian Twigg. And Goofy Gates, who'd hell-raised with the best. He thought about the sonofabitch who killed him, wondered what he was doing now, maybe aiming to raise a little hell as well in some Hun-loving dive in Syracuse. He wished he'd nailed the bastard but at least he'd got some back for Goofy. Yeah, and for Claudia too. He remembered the way the Junkers guys had held their arms across their faces, as though they could ward off cannon shells. They'd known they had it coming, and it came. He heard the haw-haw voice of that in-bred English mug who hadn't come along. 'You just don't do that sort of thing.' Well, he was glad he'd done it. He knew he was. He had to be . . .

Passing through Valletta, the streets were full of *festa* spirit, plenty of laughter, good-looking women, reeling drunks. Outside the Mayfair the truck shuddered to a stop. Brewster jumped down from the cab. 'Okay, scramble chaps, grub up.' He'd fixed a celebration, Cisk beer and jugs of *ambete*, the local wine they knew as Stuka juice, deadly when it hit the target, with bowls of pasta and a curious meat. Ossie moved it with his fork. 'What the hell is this stuff?'

'Rabbit,' said Kenny Laughton. 'Rabbit that miaows.'

Later, leaving Brewster in the bar, they straggled in groups to explore the Gut and size up the tarts that lined the walls or called out from the windows. 'Hey, you want nice time?' None did, not that kind. But it was good to feel a dryness of the mouth, a faster pulse, a stirring in the groin confronted by a girl with swinging breasts and sturdy legs who could be yours for a packet or two of Craven A.

Ossie had lost the others. His vision was fading in and out, as if his eyes were a camera lens, sharp-focussed, then blurred. He'd taken on a load. He could not hold his liquor now. The Dog did not approve. It growled inside him, ready to snap and take him down. He scanned the faces of the whores, looking for something to remind him of a small, pale, oval face framed by dark, thick hair. He saw only painted masks, moving close, tongues moving over pouting lips, saying words he could not understand.

Behind him he could hear another voice, some guy, some angry guy, hollering his name. He reached out to support himself against the wall, but found space. He stumbled into a cobbled alley. It was very dark. The walls were bricked and glistening with moisture, running down from gutters. He touched them as he passed, his trailing fingers leaving marks in slime. When he snatched them back they were stained with green and stinking of decay. Like that goddamned dream. No light this time, just blackness. He heard a movement. 'Is someone there? Is someone there?' He was a kid again, shaking in the dark. He could not move.

Then someone spun him round. Something hit him in the ribs, a kind of punch, but more. He stepped back and began to fall. His hands were pressing where the punch had landed, and they were sticky wet. 'Christ!' he cried out. 'Holy Christ!'

Somewhere, further down the alley, a blind was pulled in an upper room. Light spilled out and in its yellow wash he saw a man standing twenty feet away. It was Salvator Boero.

# Twenty-six

The small boy wearing a man's cap was lost in the labyrinth of corridors that led from ward to ward in the military hospital at Imtarfa. It had been much bombed and often the way was blocked by mounds of rubble, twisted metal beds and screens, burned bedding and broken glass. The staff were busy and paid him no attention. He was thirsty but did not want to show weakness. It had not been far to walk. Imtarfa was only a mile or so from Mdina, where he still helped the Royal Air Force men. But the day had been particularly hot, even for a Farinacci.

At last he was forced to stop and ask directions of a nurse. She ruffled his hair and smiled, and tried to take him by the hand as she led him to where the American was, but he tugged his fingers free, pretending he wanted to scratch his nose, so she would not be hurt. She was pretty and, another time, he would not have minded very much. But he did not want the American to see him come in hand in hand like a little child, or a boy who liked a girl.

'Visiting time,' the nurse said to Ossie Wolf.

'Hey,' said Ossie. 'How you doing, pard?'

'Well. How are you?' said Giorgio, taking off his cap as though he was in church.

'Still alive and kicking.'

'Good. You fly again?'

'Boy, you hit the mark. I don't know, kid.'

'What happened?'

'Some guy skewered me in Valletta. You know. Knife.' He mimed a stabbing, making a churking sound with his tongue.

'Why?'

'You're full of questions, kid. Who knows? Wrong time, wrong place. What's that you got?'

The boy gave Ossie a small brown envelope. 'This was my sister's. You should have it now.' Inside was a folded cover of *Picture Post*, the one with Ossie looking like a hero, full of bull, and a cutting from *The Times of Malta* reporting the taking of the twin-float Cant. On the grainy snapshot of the Italian prisoners with their captors, Claudia had marked Ossie's bullet head with a cross. That was all. That was all she had had of him.

'That's swell,' said Ossie. 'Thanks.'

The boy looked awkward. 'I leave now.'

'How is it at the farm?'

'I don't like it there, very much. My mother weeps. She looks at me and weeps. I think maybe I leave, go stay in Mdina.'

'You should help her, kid. She's lost her daughter. She doesn't want to lose her son.'

'You think?'

'Sure.' Ossie reached across and took something from the bedside locker drawer. 'Hey, I got something for you too.' He held out the Hohner harmonica. Giorgio took it, turning it over in his hands. 'Give it a go, kid,' said Ossie. 'I've kinda run out of puff.' He laid his head back on the pillow. 'I guess I was about your age when I learned to play one of those things.'

Giorgio saw there were dark patches under his eyes and his cheekbones stood out from his face. He wondered if he was going to die. 'How do I learn?' he said. 'Who will teach me?'

'Teach yourself,' said Ossie. 'It's like breathing. It'll come.' He paused. 'Your father. He's okay?'

'Yes, he's okay.'

'And Salvator Boero?'

'Daniel Falzon says he has crossed to Gozo. Nobody knows why.'

'When you see him,' Ossie said, 'tell him it's okay.'

Giorgio nodded. 'But I do not understand.'

'You don't have to, kid. Just tell him that.'

'I will.' The boy pulled on his cap. 'I go now.'

'Yeah.' Ossie held up the envelope with the cuttings. 'And thanks.'

'Thank you for this.' Giorgio raised the Hohner to his lips and blew, the reedy discord hanging in the air. He flushed and grinned. 'Like breathing, yes. A piece of cake.'

Ossie laughed. 'You got it, kid. A piece of cake.'

When Giorgio had gone the VAD nurse said: 'Sweet boy.' She saw the envelope on the locker. 'Did he bring you a little present?'

'Some stuff his sister had,' said Ossie. 'She was a particular friend of mine.'

'Was?'

'Died in a raid Mellieha way. And for Christ's sake,' he added quickly, 'don't say sorry.'

'All right,' said the nurse, 'but I am.'

The medical officer came in with X-rays. He held them up against the light. 'You see? A single penetration of the thoracic cavity. Something like a hunter's knife, long-bladed, used for gutting. Seems to have gone in up to the hilt. No turning, a clean blow in and out. A minor laceration of the lung and no damage to the liver. Odd business, even in that part of town. Have you got any enemies?'

'Yeah,' said Ossie. 'Two hundred million of them.'

Later, the nurse came back. 'You're popular today.'

'How's he doing, Nurse?' said Kit Curtis.

'He's a nightmare patient but he's going to survive. No permanent damage but he lost a lot of blood before they found him. We need to keep him under observation, naturally.'

'Rather you than me,' said Kit.

'Park yourself,' said Ossie.

'Thanks.'

'How are the guys?'

'We lost Tommy Spencer. A flamer. Caught a packet from a Heinkel rear gunner, just before the bugger hit the sea. Brave show, really, by the Hun, but rotten luck for Tommy, just when he was shaping up so well.'

'I haven't heard from Brewster yet, about those Hun sons-of-bitches in the dinghy.'

'You won't.'

'Why's that?'

'Actually, I came to the conclusion you'd got enough on your plate.'

'That was the conclusion you came to, actually, was it?'

'Yes.'

'Reckon I won't be flying again, that it?'

'No, not at all.' Kit paused. 'As I say, I imagine you've got enough on your plate. Besides, it's too late to do anything about it now.' He looked at his watch. 'Incidentally, Buster sends his regards. Reckons it was a jealous husband.'

'Is that right?'

'Seriously, have you got any idea who did this to you?'

'Sure.'

'Going to do anything about it?'

'Nope.' Ossie looked Kit straight in the eye. 'Seems there's quite a lot of stuff going unreported in this burg.'

'Seems that way,' said Kit.

'How's that posting going along?'

'That's partly why I came. We're off at midnight. Another ruddy Hudson.'

'Do your belt up tight.'

Kit said: 'I didn't know about the girl.'

'Who told you?'

'Her brother. He wanted to know what hospital you were in.'

'So you reckon that's why I did it, in South Comino? That and losing Goofy to that sonofabitch who laced his 'chute?'

'I'm just saying, I didn't know about the girl.' Kit stood up. 'I think this is about the time you invite me to go fuck myself.'

'About,' said Ossie. 'Say, let's meet up in London and get drunk together, look up that Blue Diamond joint, see if Rita's still peddling her tail.'

'Sounds delightful,' said Kit.

'Guess I'll be flying a goddamned desk by then,' said Ossie. In this he was proved wrong. 'But I reckon this lousy island's going to be okay.'

In this he was proved right. Two months later came the last big Blitz. After three thousand raids, the Axis assaults began to diminish. In Libya things were going badly for Rommel and the Afrika Korps. With the invasion plan for Malta back in Kesselring's desk drawer, the Luftwaffe was transferred to other pressure points.

On the Hudson transport bound for England Kit had found himself seated next to an army intelligence captain with a studious air. 'Been doing a spot of homework for the brass hats,' the captain said. 'Do you know? This is the longest siege in British history.'

Kit thought of the little *kappillan* mopping his brow with a square of white linen, that day on Pennellu Hill, looking back across the vista of St Paul's Bay far below. 'Now we make new history,' the priest had said. 'Together.'

'Yes,' said Kit to the intelligence captain. 'The longest siege. In Maltese history too.'

# EPILOGUE

*Saturday, 14 October 2006*

They came off the midday ferry, an elderly couple in a nondescript car. He had driven from the house at Boulay-sur-Sarthe with barely a pause, just a brief stop for petrol and a quick coffee. She had dozed fitfully on the journey to Calais and tried to sleep on the boat. But the lounge had been busy with children, people talking loudly into mobile phones and motor-cycle racing on the television set near the bar. Now, as the Rover 75 made its way through the suburbs of Dover, her eyelids finally closed and she began to breathe deeply.

He took his usual route out of town, past rows of red-brick Victorian villas with bed-and-breakfast signs in gravelled front gardens, selecting third gear as the old Folkestone road climbed between scrub-covered chalk slopes towards West Broughton. At the crest of the hill, beyond the roundabout, traffic flashed to right and left on the A20. He slowed, ready to join the rush and head west for Midhurst. But on impulse he changed his mind and went straight ahead, through the underpass, bearing left for Capel le Ferne, passing a brown sign to the Battle of Britain memorial and the Little Satmar Holiday Park.

The road ran past bland bungalows, pubs and garages. People busied themselves with weekend activities, cleaning cars, walking dogs, cradling pints at wooden tables in beer gardens. Washing hung from lines, moving slightly in a gentle southerly breeze, but still the sea-mist had not cleared and the mundane scene was bathed in fuzzy golden light.

When he reached the memorial he parked by a handful of cars and vans near the entrance and slipped out of his seat, closing the door with care. His wife still slept, her hands resting on her lap like broken birds. Already his mind had flown back sixty years. The consequences of war were still before him.

He passed through the gateway to the monument, walking easily, tall not stooped, his face oddly shiny beneath a crop of crisp white hair. He was obviously old but it was still possible to see him young.

He had been here before, had thought the monument suitably restrained. He found that since that visit they had added a replica Spitfire to the Hurricane close by the wooden visitor centre and that, three months ago, some royal had unveiled a marble panel bearing the names of all who had fought during that hot and close-run summer.

On the expanse of grass the shape of a huge propeller had been laid out in white and brown bricks and at the centre, like a spinner, sat the effigy of a pilot, helmet and goggles resting easily in his hands. His eyes were turned upwards towards the skies above the cliffs where vapour-trails still hung, white against deep blue. But today the trails tracked aircraft with a different purpose.

The old pilot stood in front of the stone pilot, a pilot ever young. Above him, screaming seagulls wheeled, mimicking the dogfights of long ago, when this same sky was a confusion of twisting, turning machines, the air thick with bullets and the imminence of death. He walked to the cliff edge and looked out towards the coast of France, obscured by a wall of mist. Below, a train hooted as it rumbled along the line at the foot of the mottled green and white cliffs, and somewhere out to sea he heard the engine-throb of Channel ferries.

On the black marble panels he recognised the names of many men he had known. Their faces were still vivid to him. Their voices and their laughter seemed to ring in his ears. His eyes ran down the columns . . .

A small voice said: 'We've just been looking at the Spitfires.' The old man looked down at a boy holding a football. 'Mum says I can't have a kick-about here,' said the boy.

'I think that's probably right.'

The boy's mother walked down one of the sloping grass banks and joined them. On the top of the bank her husband was reading text messages on his phone. 'Who you talking to, Darren?' she said. She looked at the old man warily. 'I hope he hasn't bothered you. He'll chat to anybody.' She flushed. 'Sorry. I didn't mean . . .'

'Don't worry,' said the old man, and turned to the boy. 'Actually, only one of those aeroplanes is a Spitfire. The other one's a Hurricane.'

'I don't know about Hurricanes.'

'A fine machine. People don't realise. There were many more Hurricanes than Spits in the Battle of Britain. Sturdy, could take a lot of punishment. Pilots were fond of the good old Hurry.'

'You sound as though you speak from experience,' said the woman.

Now the old man was embarrassed. 'Well, I did fly, yes, but it's all a long time ago.'

The woman said: 'See, Darren, you're talking to a fighter pilot.'

The boy looked at the old man doubtfully. 'Is your name on here?' He pointed at the marble panels.

'No, I missed this particular show. A silly injury.' He could see the boy was disappointed and added reluctantly: 'But I got involved in other things.'

'What other things?' The boy had begun to rotate the football in his hands.

'I fought in the Battle of France,' said the old man.

'Oh, Dunkirk,' said the woman.

'That was part of it.'

'Did you shoot down any Germans?' said the boy.

'I'm afraid I did.'

'Afraid?'

The husband had finished checking his text messages and half ran down the slope, snapping the phone shut, belly bouncing above his Levi's. 'What's going on here, then?' He lit a cigarette, puffing the smoke out of the side of his mouth. His head was shaved, reminding the old man of the camps they had come across on the advance into Germany.

'This gentleman was a pilot in the war,' said the woman.

'Really?' said the man. 'My grandpa was in the RAF. Malta.'

'I was in Malta,' said the old man.

'Really?' said the man again. 'Of course, Pop was just a corporal. Don't really know what he did. Spent most of his time digging trenches.'

'That sounds about right,' said the old man.

The woman said: 'We went to Malta on holiday last year. Bugibba. Do you know it? Very nice. Everything you need.'

'Dad and me went to the museum with the planes,' said the boy. 'They let me sit in the Spitfire because of my great-grandpa.'

'That must have been a thrill,' said the old man.

'It was all right,' said the boy. He paused. 'Your face looks funny.'

The mother put her hand to her mouth. 'Sorry.'

'That's all right,' said the old man. He grinned down at the boy, the burn tissue stretched tight. 'I got a trifle singed. Occupational hazard.'

They moved away, the woman looking back and giving him a tentative wave, still awkward, the man snapping open his phone again, the boy dropping the ball on to his toe and booting it towards the gate.

The old man walked round the curving path towards the statue. The sun was low in the sky now and the shadows long on the dewy grass. The carved face bore deep shadows too.

At the gate the old man turned for a final look at the outlines of the Hurricane and the Spitfire, wreathed in mist.

In the car his wife was no longer asleep. 'You should have woken me.' She smiled gently and touched his hand as he settled himself behind the steering-wheel. 'But perhaps it was better on your own.'

'I wasn't exactly on my own,' said the old man. 'There was a family there. Nice enough, but you wonder what it all means to them. They seem to know so little. But, then, why not?' He paused. 'Oh, yes, I paid my respects to the stone pilot.'

'I like the stone pilot,' said his wife. 'He is very fine.'

The old man said no more but as he drove away he knew that he had also been surrounded by an unseen host who had once scanned these same skies with eager eyes, just as the stone pilot did now, as past times receded into legend; the greatest legend born in the skies above this coast and lesser legends in which he had played a part; like France. Like Malta.

ACKNOWLEDGEMENTS

*Band of Eagles* was conceived in late 2004, as a sequel to *Blue Man Falling*, which dealt with the Battle of France and featured some of the same characters. Encouraged by the team at Headline Review, particularly my patient and perceptive editor Martin Fletcher, I began my research with a trip to Malta in May 2005 where I visited the sites of RAF bases at Takali, Luqa and Halfar as well as the cities, towns and villages mentioned in the text. Ray Polidano, director general of the Malta Aviation Museum, and author and historian Frederick Galea were particularly helpful at this time. In the case of some place names on the island I have adopted the Anglicised versions of their Maltese equivalents – for example Takali for Ta'Quali – because that is how the members of the Allied garrison knew them. I hope that Maltese readers will understand.

Seven source books stayed on my desk throughout the writing process that began in October 2005 and finished in June 2006: *Onward to Malta* by Wing Commander T. F. Neil, notable for its breezy and insouciant energy; *Malta: The Thorn In Rommel's Side* by Laddie Lucas; *Fortress Malta* by James Holland; *Malta Spitfire* by George Beurling and Leslie Roberts; *249 At Malta* by Brian Cull and Frederick Galea; *The Air Battle For Malta* by

James Douglas-Hamilton; and *Battle For Malta* by George Forty. Invaluable, too, were *Axis Aircraft of World War II* by David Mondey, and Crecy Publishing's facsimiles of wartime *Pilot's Notes* for the Hurricane and Spitfire, which helped me to find my way around the cockpits of both aircraft and, to some extent, understand how they were flown. I also owe a debt to *The Air Combat Paintings of Robert Taylor Volume IV* by Charles Walker and Robert Taylor, which included the artist's depiction of the oil tanker SS *Ohio* nearing the end of its desperate voyage to supply the defenders of Malta, which forms the climax of *Band of Eagles*.

Again I received great personal support from Squadron Leader Tom Rosser OBE, DFC who read the finished manuscript and whose technical knowledge, as a distinguished fighter pilot, was invaluable.

I also thank my wife Jan for supporting me while I travelled back in time, for more than a year, to complete what it is hoped is a suitable tribute to a critical period in the Second World War; a period that helped to ensure Rommel's defeat in North Africa and opened the way for the Allied invasion of Southern Europe.